PRAISE FOR *LOVIN*

"Incisive . . . razor-sharp . . . *Loving Day* is that rare melange: cerebral comedy with pathos. The vitality of our narrator deserves much of the credit for that. He has the neurotic bawdiness of Philip Roth's Alexander Portnoy; the keen, caustic eye of Bob Jones in Chester Himes's *If He Hollers Let Him Go;* the existential insight of Ellison's *Invisible Man.*"

—*The New York Times Book Review* (front-page review)

"Exceptional . . . To say that *Loving Day* is a book about race is like saying *Moby-Dick* is a book about whales. . . . [Johnson's] unrelenting examination of blackness, whiteness and everything in between is handled with ruthless candor and riotous humor. . . . Even when the novel's family strife and racial politics are at peak intensity, Johnson's comic timing is impeccable. . . . While it's tempting to call Johnson's novel timely or even prescient, he clearly longs for a time when it can be called historical. Sadly, we're not even close. Until we are able to have the kind of frank and open conversations about race that are commonplace in *Loving Day* but rare in the real world, the myth of a post-racial society will remain a comic book fantasy."

—*Los Angeles Times*

"A perfect new novel for Loving Day. . . . Johnson has no end of interesting things to say about straddling—or choosing not to straddle—America's binary, black-and-white race lines. . . . Surreal wonders lurk inside the book."

—*The Washington Post*

"A warm-hearted, gently humorous book about the ironies and conundrums of biracial identity . . . The book's title is a reference to the celebrations that take place each year on the anniversary of the Supreme Court's 1967 decision in *Loving v. Virginia*. . . . The climactic scene of this entertaining novel unfolds during a Loving Day festival marked by intolerance and a lack of understanding on all sides. Some see the Oreos and sunflowers of Mélange as a dangerous, idealistic cult; others view them as traitors to the more hidebound definitions of black and white. Johnson sees them merely as people. His book's greatest achievement is that the reader does, too."

—*The Washington Post Book Review*

"Giddy, biting Grand metaphors, unsparing social commentary, sharp characters, and sharper humor . . . propel the book. . . . Four years ago, Johnson published *Pym,* a showstopper that raised reader's expectations for future work. Inspired by Edgar Allan Poe's only novel, *Pym* reached such dizzying heights of incisive lunacy that its closest narrative analogue is *Dr. Strangelove. Loving Day* is an entirely different book with a wholly different aim: longer, less frenetic, its plot and characters more earthbound, its themes more human. It is, however, no less ferocious. . . . As it turns out, Johnson's readers have no need for lowered expectations. *Loving Day* is a welcome effort from a major talent."

—*The Boston Globe*

"A tenaciously observed, triumphantly entertaining father/daughter odyssey."

—*Elle*

"Satirical and moving . . . a smart examination of racial identity in America."

—*Entertainment Weekly*

"Mat Johnson's hilarious and touching new novel about family, identity and what it means to truly love other people . . . a lot of storylines for an author to juggle in one novel, but Johnson handles them all so gracefully, it's almost hard to believe. One of the chief weapons in his arsenal is humor—Johnson is one of the funniest writers in America, and even his brief descriptions of ancillary characters can be hilarious . . . He's a keen observer of human nature, and every relationship in *Loving Day* feels true. . . . Johnson gets at the heart of what it means to be a person—and he does so with more skill, generosity and, yes, love, than just about anyone else writing fiction today. 'Forgiveness comes later in life, after you've created enough disasters of your own,' Warren observes toward the end of the novel. The disasters make us who we are, and the results can sometimes be amazing—as amazing as this beautiful, triumphant miracle of a book."

—NPR

"Mat Johnson is best known for his excellent *Pym*, but now he will likely be best known for his novel *Loving Day*, a story of literal and figurative ghosts. . . . Lucid, poignant, sane—it's what we hope for in American fiction."

—*Flavorwire* (10 Must-Read Books for May)

"Impressive . . . [weaves] America's deepest problem into a yarn that is by turns provocative, heartrending and spit-take funny. . . . There's something jubilant, if not celebratory, about Johnson's book. . . . Enjoyable and poignant."

—*Houstonia*

"Hilarious, sometimes uncomfortable, always brilliant, *Loving Day* tackles identity, family, and finding that elusive place where you belong with such sly humor and so much heart. An awesome, viciously witty novel."

—Roxane Gay, author of *Bad Feminist* and *An Untamed State*

"Writers who are as smart as Mat Johnson are rarely as funny, and those who are as funny are rarely as smart. He is unique, and simply must be read. *Loving Day*—a tender, ribald, fast-moving novel about the strangeness of in-betweenness, the collision of fear and desire, and the impossibility of going back home—is the perfect place to begin."

—Teju Cole, author of *Open City*

"This is what happens when races mix: Mat Johnson. Not a soul or a post-soul is spared in his brilliant and hilarious satire of modern American tribalism."

—Danzy Senna, author of *Caucasia*

"*Loving Day* is wonderful satire, sharp and funny about so many contemporary themes and anxieties, including race, money, family, sex and love. Mat Johnson has a deep comic gift and his laughs always come with real thought and feeling."

—Sam Lipsyte, author of *The Ask* and *The Fun Parts*

"Genius! Mat Johnson is hands-down one of my favorite novelists writing today. He writes about the difficult stuff—the stuff that matters—in the most humorous and heart-wrenching way. *Loving Day*—a delicious romp of a tale about the mixed-race experience—is Johnson's triumph and a reader's great joy."

—Heidi W. Durrow, author of *The Girl Who Fell from the Sky*

"Since this is a book by Mat Johnson, one of the best American satirists since Mark Twain, I don't have to tell you it's as funny as it is smart. Instead, I'll just say it's the most poignant father/daughter story I've read in years. With great daring, and great care, *Loving Day* picks through the debris of the broke-down haunted house of our racial past to ask what treasures are worth salvaging for the next generation."

—Emily Raboteau, author of *Searching for Zion*

BY MAT JOHNSON

... Nonfiction ...

THE GREAT NEGRO PLOT: A TALE OF CONSPIRACY AND MURDER IN EIGHTEENTH-CENTURY NEW YORK

... Fiction ...

LOVING DAY

PYM

HUNTING IN HARLEM

DROP

... Graphic Novels ...

INCOGNEGRO

DARK RAIN: A NEW ORLEANS STORY

LOVING DAY

MAT JOHNSON

LOVING DAY

A NOVEL

SPIEGEL & GRAU NEW YORK

2016 Spiegel & Grau Trade Paperback Edition

Published in the United States by Spiegel & Grau, an imprint of Random House, a division of Penguin Random House LLC, New York.

Originally published in hardcover in the United States by Spiegel & Grau, an imprint of Random House, a division of Penguin Random House LLC, in 2015.

Library of Congress Cataloging-in-Publication Data
Johnson, Mat.
Loving day: a novel / Mat Johnson.
ISBN 978-0-8129-8366-1
ebook ISBN 978-0-6796-4552-8
Fathers and daughters—Fiction. I. Title
PS3560.O38167L68 2015
813'.54—dc23 2014036550

Printed in the United States of America on acid-free paper

randomhousebooks.com
spiegelandgrau.com

2 4 6 8 9 7 5 3 1

Book design by Liz Cosgrove

FOR PAULINE: A DOG

LOVING DAY

1

IN THE GHETTO THERE IS A MANSION, and it is my father's house. It sits on seven acres, surrounded by growling row homes, frozen in an architectural class war. Its expansive lawn is utterly useless, wild like it smokes its own grass and dreams of being a jungle. The street around it is even worse: littered with the disposables no one could bother to put in a can, the cars on their last American owner, the living dead roaming slow and steady to nowhere. And this damn house, which killed my father, is as big as it is old, decaying to gray pulp yet somehow still standing there, with its phallic white pillars and the intention of eternity. An eighteenth-century estate in the middle of the urban depression of Germantown. Before he died, my father bought the wreck at auction, planned on restoring it to its original state, just like he did for so many smaller houses in the neighborhood. Rescuing a slice of colonial history to sell it back to the city for a timeless American profit. His plan didn't include being old, getting sick, or me having to come back to this country, to this city, to pick up his pieces. This house is a job for a legion, not one person. It would kill one person. It did—my father. I am one person now. My father's house is on me. I see it from the back of the cab, up on its hill, rotting.

Donated by the Loudin family after the Depression, the mansion was used by the city as a museum until a fire that created repair costs beyond its means and interest. At one point in my life, decades before, I was a boy. As such, I knew this house. I used to ride the 23 trolley past its absurd presence and marvel at this artifact of rich white folks' attempt at dynasty. A physical memory of historic Germantown's pastoral roots, before the larger city of Philadelphia exploded past this location, propelled by the force of the industrial revolution. Most things from childhood get smaller with age, but Loudin Mansion towers, because now I have to take care of it. So I want to run. I sit passively in the taxi as I'm driven closer, but my thighs ache and my bowels are prepared to evacuate, and I want to open the door and run. I'll run. I'll run through North Philly if I have to, all the way downtown. Run along the highway back to the airport, then run away again from the whole damn country.

The white cabdriver makes no move to get out with me when he finally stops, just pops the trunk open with one button and with another relocks the doors after I open mine. That lock clicks hard. I'm on the street with my bags, and I can't get back inside. I'm not white, but I can feel the eyes of the few people outside on me, people who must think that I am, because I look white, and as such what the hell am I doing here? This disconnect in my racial projection is one of the things I hate. It goes in a subcategory I call "America," which has another subheading called "Philly." I hate that because I know I'm black. My mother was black—that counts, no matter how pale and Irish my father was. So I shall not be rebuked. I will not be rejected. I want to run but I refuse to be run off.

A kid walks by, about seventeen, not much younger than I was when I escaped this neighborhood. He looks up, and as I lift my bags I give him the appropriate local response, an expression that says I'm having a bad life in general and a headache right now. Welcome home. There are blocks around here where you can be attacked for looking another man in the eyes, and other blocks where you can be assaulted for not giving the respect of eye contact. I could never figure it, which blocks were which, until I realized these were just the excuses of sociopaths. The sociopaths, that's the real problem. The whole street demeanor is about pretending to be a sociopath as well, so that the real ones can't find you.

When I get to the porch, the front door opens. I can hear it creak before I see someone emerging from behind its paint-cracked surface. Sirleaf Day is carpeted in cloth. He's got a Kenyan dashiki, Sudanese mudcloth pants, and a little Ghanian kente hat. It's like Africa finally united, but just in his wardrobe. Last time I saw him, he dressed the same, but he only had one leather medallion. Now he has enough to be the most decorated general in the Afrocentric army. I give him a "Howyadoin," and the Philly salute, a hummingbird-like vibration of my forehead, the most defensive of nods. He gives me a hug. He hugs me like he knows I'm trying to get away.

"So you had your first divorce. That just means you a man now. Which kind was it? She stop loving you, or you stop loving her?"

"It wasn't like that," I tell him. Sirleaf grips me closer.

"Oh hell no. I hope it wasn't one of those where you both still love each other, but it's broke anyway. Those are the worst. My first, fourth marriages, they were like that. At least you didn't have any kids with her."

"Uncle Sirleaf, I really don't want to talk about—"

"Don't give me that 'uncle' mess. You're too old for that shit. And I'm way too young," he says, pushing me back for another look before pulling me in once more. "Your pop was waiting for you to come home, you know that? This house, it was going to be for you. You and your wife, your children. Bring you back to the community." Sirleaf's voice cracks with emotion. It makes me feel guilty for wanting to break free of his musky grasp. "And it did. You got to give that crazy honky that."

I look over Sirleaf's shoulder: there's a rusty Folgers Coffee can sitting on the porch, by the wall. It's there because my dad never smoked in a house. This can of ashes is full of cheap cigar butts, mixed with the cigarette butts of whoever visited. I know without looking inside it, because there was always a can like that on the porch of wherever my dad was living.

"He knew I wasn't coming back. He was just going to fix it up to sell it, like he always did." This gets him to release me, partially. He still holds my shoulders, pushes me back as far as he can to take a look at my face.

"Wasn't his fault you ran off, was it? My daddy left me when I was four and gave me nothing but my stunning Yoruba features. So stop bitching."

Sirleaf is a lawyer, a realtor, a griot, and a kook, and he's good at all of those things. My dad was his white friend, because they had the kook thing in common. For three decades, they would get together to sell a property or drink whiskey and get kooky together. My dad had his own realtor's license, but he wasn't good with most types of humans. Sirleaf is the people's man, knows everyone that matters in Germantown, from councilmen to people looking to buy their first homes. He speaks three languages: Street, Caucasian, and Brotherman.

Sirleaf's getting old and finally he looks it. Some people age, and some just dehydrate. Sirleaf looks like someone let the water out and the creases dried in its absence. I can't imagine how old my dad must have looked. They were the same age but my father was one of those pasty Irish people with no melanin to protect his skin from time. He could barely manage enough pigment for a mole.

"We should really have a funeral," I tell him. "Or a memorial or—"

"He ain't want one, and we're going to respect that. You know your pop—he wasn't one to spend good money on a bunch of bullshit. His legacy, it's this house, this property. And it's you. Now let's look at your inheritance."

With great flourish, Sirleaf turns back to open the front door. But it's stuck. The wood's swelled and it takes a lot to jar, a lot of effort to protect so little. Hell's lobby waits on the other side. If my father's soul is left in the physical world, it's in the tools he left behind. Sandpaper, ladders, and scaffolding. Plaster and tarps, rollers and paint tins. At the back of my nose I can smell the Old Spice and Prell even though he hadn't used either since I was eleven. I will be buried here too, I just know, and then I fight that thought with the words I have been thinking in the days leading up to this moment: paint and polish. Paint it, polish the wood floors, tidy up whatever basic visual problems might get in the way of a buyer's imagination. Build on whatever my father managed in the months since he'd taken ownership. Use all the tricks he taught me. That's what I thought, packing to come back Stateside; that's what I thought waiting for the plane. That's what I tell myself now. Paint and polish. I even say it out loud.

"There ain't no roof," Sirleaf says back to me. "Go on, take a look at that jawn. That shit's crazy. The wiring in here is, like, seventy years old. And exposed—I seen that old fuse box in the back pop sparks twice in the last hour. It's a miracle he didn't burn the place down running his power tools. I don't know how your pops lived up in this mess. Craig was one cheap bastard. No offense," and he wags his head at the shame of it.

I don't remind him about a childhood camped out in many a shelled home. My dad had been doing the same thing since my mother kicked him out, and that was twenty-seven years ago. I don't tell him about pissing in paint buckets and dumping it out the window.

"You sure you want to sleep here? I mean, what about Tosha's? They still in the house I sold them. Six bedrooms. Maybe you could stay there."

"I'll stop by, but I doubt her husband wants me under the same roof for an extended period."

"Up to you, but I'm out of here. This place creeps me out. You better see what you're dealing with on the second floor, before it gets dark. Power's iffy up there." He points to the stairs. I get the message that he wants me to go up. I also get the message that he's afraid to. That at least he understands the limits of his age. As he leaves, Sirleaf stares at his feet with every step, as if he's worried the old beams might give out on him.

"How soon can you get it listed?" I ask. He sighs. I've missed something.

"I told you. You can't sell this place the way it is, not without taking a huge loss. You can't sell it for the land; it's historic so it's hard to get permission to build on it. You going to have to pick up where your pop left off, and it's going to take a while to get it together. At least, the basics. You got shoes to fill, boy," he tells me. I just happen to look down when Sirleaf says it. His shoes have at least two-inch heels on them. He catches me staring and says, "I'm engaged to this new jawn: young sister. She likes me tall."

"Sirleaf, look: I just got divorced. My comic-book shop, I had to sell it. I owe my ex half of that, but I'm still living off the money. Whatever we got to do, whatever we can get, let's just get it soon, okay? I don't care if we take a loss, I just want out."

"Yeah. Sure. Right. You seeing the same house I'm seeing, are you not? I mean, take a look around," he implores me. I don't need to do that.

"My ex is a lawyer. A really, really, good one. And she'll sue the living shit out of me if I don't pay back the money I owe her. I'm already late on the payments. You read my emails, right? I need that cash, man."

"Your ex isn't an American citizen, so she can't sue you here. I'm telling you, Warren, it might seem like a big deal to get sued, but that ain't your major problem right now. You got other things to worry about," and he lifts a mudcloth-adorned arm and motions in a slow sweep around the whole damned building.

Sirleaf is right: there is no roof. There are walls. It has floors. Just no real top. In my book, that barely qualifies it as a house, makes it more of a massive cup. I brave the stairs, shining a flashlight above me as I pace the hall of the second story. In most parts of the ceiling, there's nothing but blue tarp separating the interior from the elements. There are a few charcoaled beams in those rooms where my father hadn't knocked the remains of the fire damage down. In the master bedroom, there's a green canvas tent, the old Coleman tent my dad used when he took me on trips to the Pine Barrens and the Appalachian Trail. Now its yellow plastic spikes are nailed directly into the blackened, fire-ravaged hardwood. Instead of camping out in the room of the house least damaged, as I would have done, as any normal person would have done, my father took up residence in a room that looks like a hollowed out piece of charcoal. There's a tarp on the floor to match the one glimpsed through the burnt shingles above, but besides that, the space is nearly unprotected to the heavens. It's the nineteenth of August, about 80 degrees outside and 90 in this room. The windows up here are covered with brown paper, taped to the glass, but the sun's heat gets in anyway. This is the place he grew sick in. Made the decision to not go to the doctor in. Then died in. Quietly, of pneumonia. I always assumed he would die on the streets of Germantown itself, loud. Knocked over the head for being the wrong race in the wrong neighborhood in the wrong century.

In the gloom, I drag everything—the foldout table and chair, the lamp connected to the car battery, the propane grill, the five-gallon jugs of water, and eventually the tent itself—one by one downstairs to the dining hall, the least damaged room in the whole house. My father managed new drywall in here, matched and replaced sections of the crown molding, and had gotten as far as laying out cans of primer for painting. With the sliding doors to the hall closed, the room almost seems habitable.

I try to narrow my mind to the pragmatic nature of my next steps. I am exhausted and jet-lagged and need to set up camp. Tomorrow, for spending money, I will go draw cartoons at a convention. And all this lets me ignore that I am deconstructing the scene of my father's death and then lying down in it.

I hear a sound and am awake, and it happens so fast that I don't know if I've dreamt it. I'm not married anymore, there's no Becks in the bed next to me to ask if she heard something too. No Becky, who knows what to do because she's so much smarter than me that I can resent that truth and depend on it at the same time. No Becks, because I never grew up or wanted what grown folks want and that's my fault and I can accept that. No Becky, with her sallow Welsh flesh glowing in the moonlight, an image I loved because its contrast made my own pale flesh seem sable in comparison. I sink into the despair at that, at the reminder of my failure to meet the needs of the one person I was legally sworn to love, and even though it's been almost thirteen months now I feel how alone I am. Then I hear the sound again and suddenly all I feel is fear once more. It could be the settling of the house, the symphony of old wood doing its opening-night performance. There are no sounds of cars outside to hide acoustics. Another sound. I think. I don't know. So I stop breathing. When I was a kid I would lie in bed at night till my fear of an exploding bladder was greater than my fear of the ghosts I was sure I'd see on my way to the can. I remain still in my bed for a minute more before my fear congeals into self-consciousness: I'm a grown man scared of the dark. I get up to take a piss.

My feet are so loud on the creaking planks that it reminds me that real objects make real sounds, not negotiable ones. Around me, there are shadows, and there may even be ghosts too, but I am old enough to refuse to see them. In the bathroom, my urine hits the water in the bowl, and I look out the window into the gray of the night, the mist hovering over the grass. And then I see him.

He's sitting on the tall grass. In the dark. All alone. His legs folded under him. Just sitting there. My stream runs its course, but I still stand there. I can't move. I look at him, bald, black, ageless, clothes without distinction in the gloom, in the middle of the massive lawn between this mansion and the street, and I become as frozen as he is. I don't move because I'm too scared to. Even though I don't know why. Even though he's not moving. He doesn't seem to be looking at me, or at least his head isn't facing my exact direction. It's facing the front door. I think he's a ghost. I know he's a ghost. He stays there. A minute passes and he stays there. Maybe not a ghost. Ghosts come in and out, dissipate, are insubstantial by nature. So it's a man. And when I move to pull away from the window, his head snaps and he stares up at me.

Shooting down to a squat, I stay low till my legs begin to hurt. There's no phone. I have no phone, not in this country. Not in this house. I cannot call anyone even if I wanted to. No Becks. My father is dead. I am alone. My breath, it's so loud, and I try opening my mouth wider just to get the sound to stop taunting me.

I am a big guy, six four, weigh 225 naked, and I decide to act like I am a big man and I shoot upright, head for the room my father's work materials are in, go to grab the biggest thing I can find. This turns out to be a long wooden spear, an extension for a foam paint roller. I hold it with two hands. I am an African warrior! Who looks like a Celtic one. I grip it so hard my hands become even more white, adrenaline having replaced my blood. And then I go to the window. And I want him to see me. I want him to see my size. My determination, my intent. My lance. I look out the window.

And he's gone.

And for a second I'm even more scared. I want to be relieved, but now I'm incapable of it. Rod in hand, I check the other windows. I see nothing. I go upstairs for a better view, but no change. Germantown Avenue, past the fence, is without life. I stare out for minutes. Then more. Occasionally a car drives past along the chipped cobblestones, but otherwise it's empty, too late to come home and too early to drive out, which puts the time around four A.M. I stand there, on the second floor, in the burnt-out room of my father's. He chose it because it has the best view of the lawn, I realize. And when, many minutes later, I grow more tired than scared, I head back downstairs to lie down.

Tomorrow, which is today, I will go sit at a table in a large crowded room and smile at strangers, drawing pictures of their heads on muscle-bound bodies covered in leotards, and they will pay me cash. It is so absurd I laugh a little in my head, and I need that to get into my tent again, slide myself into the sleeping bag. Fear *that,* I remind myself. Fear social failure, you're better at it. I saw a crackhead, in the night, in Germantown. This hardly qualifies as a supernatural experience. I chuckle a bit, and go to zip up the tent, and then I see a person standing by my door.

She's a woman. She's not looking at me; she's looking up the stairs. My breath gets heavy again, but she keeps looking up there, not over at me. And she's a ghost. Not the dead kind. She's clothed in a dirty gown, the lingerie of a drug-addled seductress. She's a white woman, gaunt cheeks like bones around the dark hollows of her eye sockets. If she looks at me I will pee myself, I will shit myself on this very floor, and I will scream too. I don't care what she wants, I just don't want her to turn her head and look at me. She coughs. It keeps going, phlegm rising from behind her toenails with each convulsion till it gets to the back of her throat and jumps to her hand. It echoes through the house. It is more here than I am. There's a splatter and then she's gone.

When I hear the front door click behind her, I pull myself frantically from my bag and out of my tent and grab my spear and head for her. I am rage. I am anger. All the fear has been recycled. But I am caution, too, and when I reach the door I think there might be a pack of them out on the porch, the monsters, the rags falling from the skin, prepared to ambush me. So I let go of the handle.

I. Am back. In Philly.

Landing in an airport doesn't count. Sitting in a taxi can be done anywhere. This, this feeling, this, is *Philly*.

They want something from me. They must or they wouldn't be here. Do they think I'm white? Out of my element? Vulnerable? They want something and I have nothing. I am a man who has nothing, all this time meandering through life yet all I have is wounds. I have no treasure, and I never want to know what they'd take from me instead.

There is a tattered curtain over the entryway's left window and I pull it aside and the glass revealed is hand blown and old and distorted. But I see movement.

And I see them. I see the figures. A man and a woman. Staring at the house. Standing on the lawn. Walking. Walking backward. Staring at the house, walking backward. Away from me. Until they reach the fence to the street and float up, and over.

I keep staring and waiting for more, but there's nothing there. I keep staring though, until my breathing calms down, but nothing happens out there. When I turn around, I look through the shadows at this home. I look at the buckling floors. I look at the cracks in all the walls, the evidence of a foundation crumbling beneath us. I smell the char of the fire, the sweet reek of mold, the insult of mouse urine. I see a million things that have to be fixed, restored, corrected, each one impossible and each task mandatory for me to escape again. I see Sisyphus's boulder, just with doors and beams. I can't take it so I look out the window once more, where nothing is coming to get me, because the neighborhood doesn't need to, because it knows I'm trapped and it has all the time in the world. Then I look back into the house.

And that's when I decide I'm going to burn the fucker down.

2

IF YOU'RE A professional illustrator, you can show up at a comic convention, rent a table, and then charge people cash to draw a picture of whatever they want. If you show up early, do this all day, you can make enough to last for a month, tax free. I am broke. So after barely sleeping, I get up. I get out of the tent. I don't look around. I stomp and bang so I can't get scared by any other noises from unknown sources. I gather my supplies and let them slap around too. I lock the door behind me. And I run away from Germantown before it can wake up and stop me.

I'm an inept comic-book artist. My work is too realistic, too sober. My superheroes look like grown men standing around with their underwear on the outside of their pants. Even as I draw, I'm embarrassed for them. There is a line between being a fan of something and actually being good at creating that thing. "A line" makes it sound like a narrow, slight thing, but the difference can be more like an untraversable wasteland of parched failure. At first, Becks took my lack of success as a comic-book artist as a sign that I was meant for a more sophisticated audience, the gallery instead of the newsstand. She liked that idea, that she'd be a successful solicitor and I her famous artist spouse. The reality of this never took hold, though. So she loaned me the money for a comic-book store instead, a gesture she clearly regretted almost immediately, for years telling people at parties "he sells comic books" as a passive punishment for not abandoning the whole venture and agreeing to become a stay-at-home dad.

Most of the illustration work I've gotten from comic publishers has been "fill-ins": some guy is supposed to draw a standard twenty-two-page comic but only shows up with eleven pages by the deadline, and they need someone to finish the job. Or to do a self-contained issue of a series that will appear between longer story arcs, put out by the publisher just to give the regular penciller time to catch up on his or her monthly due dates. After a while, I accepted that I will never achieve more than this. The closest I came was a 144-page hardcover published three years before. A real book, with me as the sole illustrator, not somebody else's backup. But this I only got because it was the story of a biracial detective who passes for white. The publisher wanted an authentic ambiguous Negro for political cover. With my days sitting in a comic-book store devoid of customers, and my nights with a wife disinterested in sex with me because of my own disinterest in procreation, I was free to commit the time needed for the project. So that worked out well. I still hated them, these anonymous people I was emailing in my pages to every day, for making this be my entrée into the larger comic world, but I took the job. My consolation was that finally the idea of race and identity, another aspect of my life that I'd failed to master, had actually paid dividends that weren't fruit of sorrow. I drew that thing like it might be the last image anyone would ever see of me.

The convention is underground, literally. It's at the back of Suburban Station, the commuter hub where I spent much of my childhood waiting for the R8 to take me back to Germantown. The place is gray, but only because of the plaster dust of the cracked walls. Low ceilings, no windows, the smell of mold dried dead, a hint of train sulfur. I walk through the paltry crowd with my portfolio of samples, my box of paper and pens, and immediately I fall deeper into depression. Hanging on the walls, from the ceilings, on pillars, are superhero pictures, fantasy figures I know too much about. It's a shameful place, this space, which reminds me that comic books are a shameful thing. Bright little pictures of tight bulging bodies. Visual masturbation for boys with manhood issues, and men with boyhood issues.

They are happy to see me. The guy running things, a skinny, red-bearded comic-store owner from the area, is named Travis, and he wears a badge that backs this up. It says TRAVIS! and he's taken time to make the exclamation point big enough to beat down the letters.

"You're here!" he says, recognizing me, and before I can wonder where I've met him before I see the event poster over his head and my face is one of the ones on it, which is a good sign because I'm a nobody and they didn't have to do that. Travis is so happy. He smiles the width of his wire-framed glasses. He looks like he just received an official letter that says he is not a juvenilia-obsessed dork. The letter is wrong. He twinkles on his sandal-clad toes as he pulls out my paperwork and I find myself feeling for him as he guides me to my seat. We walk to a table with a sign over it that says, presumptuously, TALENT. Behind the table are a bunch of middle-aged guys, which is just to say they're not young enough to be youthful but haven't yet achieved the dignity of the elderly. They're organized by company, and I recognize names of artists from the two big comic publishers, one of which is my own past employer. These are the heavy hitters, flown in from around the country to attract the crowd. I need to sit next to the heavy hitters. I need to sit next to them because when the punters show up there's going to be a line stretching back through the building to get an illustration from them, and there won't be enough time. I need to sit next to them because I have $1,103.86 in my bank account. My business strategy is: overflow. My greatest hope: lowered expectations. I see an empty seat by a guy who draws a Batman series—one of the bestselling titles this year. I've read his sales figures online: 150,000 copies sold a month, and that's with illegal downloads gutting two thirds of sales. Best part yet, I did a show with him in Cardiff just three years ago; we went to a group dinner with our shared editor. I get excited now because, if he remembers me, he might even send a few of his extra punters my way, and I start speeding up my walk, my portfolio and box banging at my side. And then I feel the hand on my shoulder.

"Oh no, we already have a place set up for you over here. We're organizing by theme this year. You're in the 'Urban' section," Travis tells me, and pulls me steadily to the corner of the convention room back by the exit. "Urban" is the nicest way to say "nigger." I try to tell him that my book took place in the rural South, and he says, "That's cool! You'll be on the 'Urban' panel too; it'll start in about an hour," and sits me at a long table with three other black guys.

There's a sign propped on the counter with my name and the cover of my book and my own face on it staring back at me. The folding chair is bent, slanted. I start to get angry. I have a race card in my mental pocket and I want to throw it down and scream "Blackjack!" but then I look at the other brothers looking at me, and they're not complaining. And if I complain, it will seem like I just don't want to sit next to them. And for a second I think, No, complain anyway. But the brothers are already set up, their art displayed and issues of their comic books stacked up for sale, so who am I?

"Who are you?" the man already sitting in the chair next to mine asks. He's around my age, with more gut to show for it. There's an eagle on his sweatshirt, its wings spread around his midriff as if it's trying to fly off before his belly explodes. The guy's tone isn't rude, but it isn't a casual entrée into small talk either. He really wants to know. He looks down at my seat as if some invisible, insubstantial Afro-entity had already laid claim to it, and really wants to know why I'm motioning to sit there? Why am I at the black table?

"I'm a local writer. Just back in town, you know, peddling my wares," I tell him, and then babble on a bit more, eventually getting to my name and the last book I worked on. The words don't really matter. What I'm really doing is letting my black voice come out, to compensate for my ambiguous appearance. Let the bass take over my tongue. Let the South of Mom's ancestry inform the rhythm of my words in a way few white men could pull off. It's conscious but not unnatural—I sometimes revert to this native tongue even when I have nothing to prove. Often when I've been drinking. I refer to my last graphic novel with the pronoun *jawn*. I finish what I'm saying with "Know what I'm saying?" He nods at me a little, slightly appeased, because he does know what I'm saying. What I'm saying is, *I'm black too*. What I'm saying is that he can relax around me, because I'm on his side. That he doesn't have to worry I'm going to make some random racist statement that will stab him when he's unguarded, or be offended when he makes some racist comment of his own. People aren't social, they're tribal. Race doesn't exist, but tribes are fucking real. What am I saying? *I'm on Team Blackie,* And I can see in the slight relaxing that he's willing to accept my self-definition, at least tentatively, pending further investigation.

I am a racial optical illusion. I am as visually duplicitous as the illustration of the young beauty that's also the illustration of the old hag. Whoever sees the beauty will always see the beauty, even if the image of the hag can be pointed out to exist in the same etching. Whoever sees the hag will be equally resolute. The people who see me as white always will, and will think it's madness that anyone else could come to any other conclusion, holding to this falsehood regardless of learning my true identity. The people who see me as black cannot imagine how a sane, intelligent person could be so blind not to understand this, despite my pale-skinned presence. The only influence I have over this perception, if any, is in the initial encounter. Here is my chance to be categorized as black, with an asterisk. The asterisk is my whole body.

I pull my book out of my bag, show it to him. It's about fighting racism, or racists, or whatever. I didn't write it, I wouldn't have, but I should get some extra Negro points for drawing it. It says, I'm not just black, I'm *conscious*. The guy looks over at it, but his eyes narrow in on the publisher's logo.

"So, you make a living selling your art to the big corporate machine, huh?" says brotherman.

"Well, you know, sometimes you got to fight from the inside," I tell him, and keep pulling out my materials. The fanboys are starting to come in now. I can see them queuing at the white guys' table across the room.

"Hey man, no judgment. If you got to suck the corporate teat, that's just what you got to do. Ain't no shame in that. That's a good gig. Not my way, but, you know, I just think it's important that we each do our thing."

The big white guys down at the other end, they've got the cash-money Caucasian customers all queued up. The place has just opened and they already have a little crowd growing to see them do their stuff. They're already making money. My new best friend and me, there's nobody in front of us. There's nobody threatening to come to our table either. As I watch the crowd build across the room, a white guy walks toward us, face buried in the latest Miracleman reprint. When he looks up and sees us staring at him, smells the desperation, he smiles sheepishly and then quickly walks away.

"So, you're publishing on your own. That's brave," I tell my neighbor as I watch our sole potential customer of the last five minutes waddle away. It's the truth. If I was going to risk further financial ruin it would be for something more than comic books. Installation art. Found-object sculpture. Or language poetry; that would be a rewarding way to fall into the pit of poverty. This guy, he looks vaguely familiar too. Not in a way that I know him. He just looks real Philly. His beard: perfectly straight-edged an inch above his jawline and dyed a deep black, its hair shooting long past his chin in a salute to Islam and anything else that scares white people. I want to get on an outbound plane back to Wales just looking at him. But I nod, smile, shake his hand, give it a snap, and listen respectfully as he tells me his name is Mandingo, which I assume means his mother really named him something like Maurice or Monty.

"Look at us, over here. Only brothers in the room," he tells me after fifteen minutes. I look up, pleasantly surprised I've been elevated to brother status. I've gotten two sketches done. Both doodles for free, done in autograph books, drawn slowly to keep these warm bodies in front of the table, to prove it's safe for paying customers to enter into our neighborhood. "You know that ain't a mistake. You know what that's about. It's all good, though. It's all good."

And that it is. Here I agree with Mandingo wholeheartedly. In failure, there was this mercy. No crowds means an early exit. The small blessing of obscurity.

"We've been color-coded," I tell him. The guys at the Caucasian table, I haven't seen them since their crowd obscured them in adoration. They're white guys and there are a lot of white guys here who want to appreciate them. Black, yellow, and brown ones too.

"That's right. You damn near white and it don't even matter. See, when you're doing work that threatens the preconceived notions of the white power system, they get real nervous. They get real scared. That's why my book would never fit into that world. They couldn't handle it."

"I'm sorry, what's your book about?" I ask. All his promotional material is facing out; I can't even see the cover of the glossies on the table for the glare. Mandingo looks a little hurt that I don't already know his oeuvre, but he nods it off.

"It's called *Aphrodite,*" I think I hear him say, and he reaches to get me one. "Aphrodite," I repeat, approvingly.

"No," he says, pointing to the cover. *"Afro-Dike-Y."* And there Afro-Dike-Y is in all her glossy glory.

"Why do you separate the *y* at the end?" is all I can think to ask, and because I really think people would get the reference even if it was connected, but then I notice that the little fabric she is wearing is actually shaped like a Y. Sort of a cross between a thong and a leotard. The fabric physics of the two-dimensional world. It's genius.

"It's ten dollars," Mandingo says, a bit nervously, as he stares at Issue 2 in my hands. I look back at him.

"Ten dollars?" I ask, in a tone that inadvertently reveals that ten dollars is a significant percentage of my current net worth. My dad left me a little money, but I won't get access to those accounts for weeks.

"Printing costs," he explains, as I give him his first sale of the day.

I'm going to burn my fucking house down. This thought relaxes me as panic rises. This thought worked last night, let me close my eyes despite the break-in. Everything's going to be okay. Because I'm going to burn my fucking house down and get rich. And I'm going to give Becks her money, with interest. I checked—it's insured for a fortune more than whatever I could clear after paying for all the repairs. I'll get the money and run to Costa Rica or Iceland and live off that shit forever. It's foolish and a desperate plan, but I accept that I am a foolish and desperate individual, so it's perfect. I'm going to find a way to burn the damned thing down that makes it look like an accident. You have to be a big man to admit total failure, and I'm just tall enough. Hey, let's face it, this life sucks. It is not going to get much better. I have no future to look forward to so I might as well indulge in the present. My path led into a briar patch barely worth detangling from, but that doesn't mean I have to walk the road my father paved for me either. I'm going to burn it down and move to maybe Tahiti or anyplace else I can live off the earnings till I die of something soft like diabetes from too much fresh fruit.

I get up and walk around the table, take a look, compliment Mandingo on anything I can see of merit in his art, but that isn't much. Mostly I smile and nod. I'm not trying to look down on his skills, but he's just not good. The pain is because I know I'm not either. And I'm older. Competence isn't enough. It would be great to be good at something. No, I would like to be great, to be great at something: public or personal, major or minor, I don't really care at this point. Mandingo stands up and helps spread out his pamphlet comics so that they can be witnessed in all their glory, and I see he has on some kind of wrestler's belt. I think this is for the special occasion, for this day. Some of the crowd are dressed even more flamboyantly. But even the most freakish who do dare to flutter closer to this dark corner can see the ineptitude and disperse again. An old Jewish guy comes to my table for a minute and picks up my graphic novel from the pile I've arranged. He looks at the cover, then he looks at me, then repeats this back-and-forth gesture for a while. "You're him," he says. It's not a question. He doesn't even open the book, he just holds it up to a teenage girl behind him, a granddaughter clearly, and says, "This is him." She nods, but demonstratively averts her eyes from mine the moment I look up at her.

This girl with her grandpa, she lingers in front of my table, she has my book. She looks, like, sixteen and wears a tight T-shirt and shorts that manage to do no more than cover the place where her tan legs meet her torso. Looking at her, I know I am an old man, because all I have the urge to do is wrap her in a blanket until I can get her to the Gap and buy her some clothes that fit. She holds my book in front of her like a shield.

"You know, I can sign that for you," I tell her. "If I ever go nuts, try to blow up the Statue of Liberty or something, that would make it worth something."

She doesn't laugh. She just puts on a smile too big for her face and then spins and stomps away from me. Off to the other end of the room, where her grandfather is watching the whole scene.

"Oh yeah, here we go. It's showtime now." Mandingo talks to himself, not me. He's got a fishing box full of art supplies, and he starts pulling them out. I look up and I see a whole pack of black guys moving in, high school age mostly, some older.

"My fan base has arrived," Mandingo says right before they do. Of course he has a fan base. The worse the artist, the better the marketing campaign. There's four of them, and Mandingo knows each by their first name. I hear them talking, and the intimacy of their knowledge of each other's lives is surprising. Turns out they follow one another on Twitter. They blow 140-character kisses at each other all day. These guys, they ask me a lot of questions. Polite, interested ones, and by the way they won't look me in the eye I can tell they looked me up before I got here. The usual questions come: when did you start, what's your favorite thing to draw, what book would you most like to be assigned to. Then this one lands:

"How come you ain't got more positive dark-skinned characters in your work?" one of them asks me. He asks it three times, too. The first time, I hear it, but it's barely audible, just above the din of the room, just low enough that I can ignore it, which I do. I can feel the dread building, but I swallow it for later consumption. About fifteen seconds later the question comes louder, but I keep staring down at the charcoal in my hands, drawing. This time, it's clear I'm ignoring the asker, that I'm not trying to play these race games, having reached my quota for the hour. Mandingo, for his part, offers to show the crew some of his new work, the pencils for his next issue of *Afro-Dike-Y*. Apparently, she is fighting a villain named Brickhouse, who from appearances seems to have been driven criminally insane by elephantiasis of the boobies. Some of the guys, distracted or flinching from confrontation, move closer to Mandingo's side of the table and *oooh*. But not this kid. He just asks the same damn thing all over again, so loud that even silence would be an answer to him.

I look up, and of course he is the lightest-skinned one here besides me. Of course he is. This defender of the darker masses. And what am I to say to him? I didn't write this work, I just drew it. They sent me a script, and I drew it. The characters, they all came with descriptions of how they looked, which were mostly based on images of famous people of the period, and I was given the images of those people as well. The guy who wrote it did this, not me. The guy who wrote it, go pick on him. The guy who wrote it, a guy I've never met or even talked to on the phone, he really might be color struck, but not me. You can get his email from his website. I'm sure he would love to hear from you.

I tell him this, and I am exhausted from it. I stay chipper though, smiling, and we are both relieved. If we were the type of people who enjoyed confrontation, we would have put down the comics years ago and started punching people in the face for real, instead of just looking at illustrated violence.

He buys a book, has me sign it to "Leon." Shakes my hand front and then sideways and ends it with a snap. With the final handshake test, I have proven I am black. I have returned to America to defend my Negro title triumphantly. Again I have used the timbre in my voice to show that I too speak the language, that I do not distance myself from him. I have temporarily compensated for my paler skin, my straightish hair, and the fact that my dad was a honky. I have passed the exam presented to me. Yay. Don't we all feel so much fucking better now? Weeha. Aren't we all just one big happy family? Woo.

They loiter. I laugh a little too hard at a joke, stuck in the gear of overcompensation, and then feel someone watching me. The teenage girl sits on the floor directly across the room from me, her back against the wall. My book is still in her hands, resting in the lap made by her folded legs, her Jew-fro like a chestnut cloud floating. The book is open, but she's staring at me. She appears as disgusted as I am by my inadequacies.

A good twenty minutes in, we've basically formed a Little Africa. Other black folks come in, some fans, some in the industry, and pool in our corner of the room. We talk about how so few white people will come to our corner of the convention, and joke until we convert our unease to laughter. We make reference to other legendary black superheroes, artists, writers, like they are our secret gods. There is a "we," and I am included. I revel in the conspiracy. When the mandatory light-skinned joke is made, dismissing a prominent illustrator for not being black enough, I laugh loudest. Aha, those light-skinned folks, with their moderately less stigmatized lives. I don't care because I haven't been around black Americans in a group in a while and missed the camaraderie. I miss my family. I want to belong in my family. I want acknowledgment of shared experience, worldview, ancestry. I have no more real family, I realize within the fragile bliss. My father's gone, Becks is gone, but in this moment it's less painful for me. I fit in and I don't fit in but it feels so good not to be thrown out. I see Caucasians in the room, looking over our way, puzzled and annoyed by the segregation. They stand in a pack of their own race, but their own race is invisible to them.

• • •

The group from around the table makes its way over to the conference room, and that means there is even a crowd worth facing. I sit with Mandingo and a few others as three dozen or so audience members space out in the chairs so the room seems less empty.

"What is it like as a black artist creating comics?" The first question goes. Serve, volley, pass the microphone. Mandingo answers it. I don't pay attention to what he says. I pay attention to what he says when he finishes, because he actually passes the microphone to me next to answer. And as Caucasoidal as I am, as racially ambiguous—again, again, because it never goes away—I still talk to them about my experiences as a black man in comics and the predominantly black crowd actually listens. No one stops me. No one stands up and yells "Fraud!" and challenges me to name the founding members of the Student Nonviolent Coordinating Committee. They just listen. The people sitting onstage with me accept my presence, so the crowd does too. My self-loathing at the glee I take from this is overshadowed by the joy itself. The usual questions follow: How do you break in to the field? What's your advice to an up-and-coming black artist? If you could work on any project, what would it be? I have answers prepared, prepackaged, marinated in whole milk in the fridge overnight. They love them. I am pithy. I am witty. As a child I worried about rejection, that my own community would gather together and cast me out like a bleached ugly duckling. My life's fight has been to prove I'm a swan. That has brought me to this moment. Now, surrounded by the superhero imagery of my youth, I flap my wings. Look at me y'all! Let me shake my tail feather. I'm a swan, yo!

We're hitting the zone known as Final Questions, when I hear a female voice ask, "But what is it like for you, as a *biracial* artist creating comic books?"

Mandigo looks out, brown hand grabbing the mike to answer, then stops. His mouth goes to say something, yet his jaw stutters free of sound. He looks confused. Then looks at me. I don't know how I look.

I'm pretty sure someone just called me out as a race traitor. The *b*-word, leaned on in the middle of the sentence, pushed like the last paste in the tube.

Squinting to see over the stage lights, I make out a standing woman, facing me, a looming triangle of shadow. I think it's that creepy teenager, but it's not. The questioner is in the back, on the left-hand side of the hall near the exit. When I shade the stage lights with my hand, I see she's dressed in flowing white wrinkled layers like a toga. She's a goddess. Or dressed up like one—she's got the crown of golden leaves on and everything. When the others on the stage next to me begin to whisper, I realize I still haven't said anything.

"Well, I don't think of myself as a 'biracial' artist," I say, laying my tongue on the *b,* pushing the word back to her. "I'm black, and I'm an artist. I'm a guy who draws pictures. I mean, that's the ultimate freedom, isn't it? To define oneself as a human being! Is 'Human Being' not a category? I draw my doodles inside the confines of boxes, but I refuse to let the preconceived boxes of others define me."

There's applause. I start to join in too, then decide that's bad form. And I don't really know what I've just said, as far as meaning. I have found that, in the African American oral tradition, if the words are enunciated eloquently enough, no one examines the meaning for definitive truth. So even the folks on the panel clap. There's a little murmur in the room, and people are looking back at this woman. They look at her, because she is pale but brown, but now she has told all of them she is *other*. She is the traitor of blackness. I wait for her shadow to get smaller, for her to be diminished by the crowd's disdain. But she just stands there.

Her stillness disquiets the audience. It grows silent, save for awkward shuffles. As she steps down the stadium stairs toward me, her sandals clap for her, and that's all the approval she needs. "But why do you call yourself a black artist, in this age? You're mixed, aren't you? I mean, clearly one of your parents was white, or you wouldn't look like that. Why do you find the need stick within the racial mold set by slavery?"

She looks like me. My tribe. Same skin color, same hair color, same eye color. I know one of her parents must be white as well. So she knows. My whole origin story. She could be my twin. I saw another lost fraternal twin once on Fifteenth and Walnut, in the summer, when I was sixteen. I only saw her for two seconds, maybe for four, before she turned off the sidewalk and into an air-conditioned boutique. A woman of my comparative height and general physiognomic presentation, a woman so instantly familiar I have thought of her for decades. I've thought of her and the idea that there could be someone walking around on this earth who was your mirror. That if you found them, if you connected with them, joined with them, you would never again feel alone. I believe this insanity as I believe that the rest of this auditorium can't see her the way I do: we all have different brains, her image only unlocks mine. The room looks at the stage, where I am frozen. They don't see the pale black man anymore, I'm sure. They look at me and now they see the fraud. The whole room. I can see Mandingo facing me with his body, with his jihadi beard, and I see myself through his eyes. And this is enough to bring my mind back into the reality of the moment again. To myself, not some attractive stranger. My hair is straight, my skin drained of melanin by three centuries of miscegenation with a final erasure courtesy of my father's Irish seed. In my head, I hear someone yell "Honky!" but just in my head. No one moves, except her. Until she's mere feet away, then she stops, puts her hands on her hips. Waiting. In the room, no one says anything. I want to say something to her, to talk to her, but the room is looking at me, changing me with their judgment, and I can't handle that so I speak to them instead.

"There's nothing 'mold-y' about being black," I say, and there's laughs. It's sparse, from the back of the room. Away from her. "And there is no such thing as 'biracial' in Black America. Race doesn't even exist," I tell her. I stand up, push the chair out with my calves. Not violently, but enough to make a screeching declaration. "There's black, and there's white. That's it. It doesn't matter if your sperm donor was a white man. That's the reality. Was Booker T. Washington not black?

Or Frederick Douglass?" There is some applause now, not overwhelming, but building. I hear a "That's right!" pop out of the audience anonymously, so I build on that. "Or Malcolm X's mother? His very own mother!" The crowd has decided it's safe to show appreciation, that by clapping they may obtain freedom from racial complication. "Or Bob Marley. Bob Marley!" I hit the last name hard, let it resonate in the room. They love me even more. I hear "Get up, stand up!" and I hop onstage a bit in response, and there's laughter. "Is there anyone here, anyone in this room, anyone in this world, who thinks that Bob Marley was any less of a black man?" I demand, and hold the reggae giant's legacy in front of me like a shield. No one challenges it. They're too busy clapping. But they stop looking at me. Now they look at her.

She doesn't care. She doesn't care at all, it's clear. She hears them, she must feel their gaze, but she doesn't flinch. She doesn't raise her voice to qualify. She doesn't laugh it off or use some other technique to deflect communal rejection. There is no bravery in her stance, because that would mean there was fear to overcome. She stands, just looking at me, undaunted, as if the crowd is mere mirage. It's an amazing performance. She is real. She is certain. And look at her: she is free. How the hell do you get free?

"Bob Marley!" Mandingo yells in a poor imitation of a Jamaican accent.

"Get up, stand up!" his crew sings as she turns and walks back up the aisle, and the rest of the room laughs, takes to its feet. I try to laugh along. Then she looks over her shoulder and laughs too. At me. She doesn't care.

Mandingo slaps my back and starts clapping. I'm smiling, nodding, but instead of feeling victorious I feel something of worth drain out of me with every step she takes away. The crowd joins the song, and the beat of the clapping takes up the rhythm section. Now everyone's happy. But I look at her. I keep looking at her. She is back in her seat, the only person in the room not standing. Staring back at me, hands on her lap. As rejected as I feared I would be, and perfectly composed, at peace with it.

When the panel is finally over, when the final clapping drifts off, I stand up and head straight for the lady. I have been rude, I know, and that hurts me, so I hustle into the filling aisle. She's almost faster than I am, has her big bag over her shoulder, moving to the exit. The straps of her white dress are made of yarn and I tap her shoulder around the fragile fabric.

"Miss, I'm sorry if I was too vehement. It's just important to me that people understand—"

"I'm from the Mélange Center, a mixed-race community organization. You know, I do outreach to mixed speakers all the time, but I have never—" She pauses, then gives a short chuckle. Up close, partially obscured behind the curtains of her hair, there are the faint traces of acne scars, there's the wrinkles around her neck, the imperfections of reality. But there's also a thickness, a fullness of body and personality. As I stare, she pulls back her hair and leans in to whisper in my ear.

"You're the worst sunflower I've ever seen. I feel so sorry for you," she says. There's so much disdain in her enunciation of the light little word, *sunflower,* that I look down to hide my grin at the odd imbalance.

"What the hell is a 'sunflower'?"

"It means you don't know who you are."

"Well, who are you?" She rolls her eyes, pulls back her hair on the other side, and it smells like cedar and oak leaves and a place you could lie and die content. I want to tell her, *you got nice pheromones*. I think, Why should I not just tell her this? She may be pleasantly surprised by the news, uplifted even.

"Someone who can't be bothered."

"Come on, I'll buy you lunch and I'll let you spend the time trying to convert me." Her response is a backhanded raised finger, pumping in the air as a parting farewell. It's an obscene display. Fist pumping high, middle finger pointing to the ceiling, bracelets and baubles jingling.

What makes you see a stranger, just that flash of image of their outer persona, and decide instantly that they can save you? I fall in love every day like this. I'm a functional moron.

Back at my foldout table, I now have a waiting queue. My performance has earned me an audience. I do a horrible job on the sketches, rushed, uneven lines, but they don't care. I do a horrible job because my hands are shaking and I feel nauseous, but I'm making cash money so I smile and try to ignore the sensation of falling because I know I am solidly sitting down. I look for the biracial militant walking around the room but don't see her. I am now certain that she could have rescued me. I don't know what from, but that could be part of the danger. I look for her again and tell myself if I see her I will apologize once more, but better. I will tell her I'm sorry and renounce my negritude and carry the biracial banner if she will absolve me. By *absolve,* I mean hold me. Just hold me. I haven't been held, not since Becks, not since the one when her things were already in the lorry. She will do this and then when she lets go I will be whole again. This makes sense in my head, the transcendent potential of me hugging the crazy lady. But I don't see her. Or I've already forgotten what she actually looks like. About an hour in though, I do look down my line and see that teenage girl is there again, with her copy of my book. When she finally gets to the front of the line, I have my Sharpie ready to giver her an autograph blessing.

"Saw you reading my stuff, you must have read the whole thing since you got here," I tell her. Good, non-flirtatious chatter. Her grandfather has his wrinkled hand tightly on her shoulder, forcing her forward. "Whom do I make it out to?" I ask her.

"No one. Do you remember Cindy Karp?" she asks me.

"Do you spell that with a *c* or a *k*? I never know," I tell her, and take her copy, looking for the title page.

"No. Do you remember, eighteen years ago, a girl named Cindy Karp? Did you ever date a girl by that name?" she asks me again, and yanks my pen right out of my hand before it hits the page. I don't know who she's talking about, but I no longer feel like I'm falling. I feel like I'm landing, on something hard. The crackhead in my father's foyer last night, staring up the stairs, flashes in my memory for no reason. Only when I look back up at the old man's face over the teenager's shoulder do things once again become lucid.

"Do you remember Cindy Karp. Who you slept with?" comes out of the young woman's mouth. I look at her, and I do remember Cindy, oh God I do, and it's like this girl is one of Cindy's classmates, not a year accumulated, frozen, waiting in Philly to damn me. But the girl's tone is not accusatory. It is scared. Desperation vibrates her vocal cords.

I grab the hand with the pen, and I look up at her. I look in her face, I really look in it. I do not see Cindy Karp, except in the little pimples around her hairline that all teens must have. I don't see Cindy Karp, but I am no expert, because I don't even remember what Cindy Karp looked like. What I do see, though, I recognize. I see my dad. I keep looking at her face. She lets me, connects her eyes with mine this time and lets me hold the gaze. And then I see my mom. I really see her, for the first time in twenty-four years. And then I start to cry. Just a little teary in the eye, it happens before I can put words to why. And I grip the girl's hand firmer. I see my mother, and her mother, Gramma Jones, and Aunt Katie. Faces I thought were gone from existence, they are right in front of me. Jumbled all together in this tan Jewish girl in dirty jean shorts ripped at the thighs. A whole collage of high-yellow matriarch is staring back at me like the aged photos at the bottom of my dresser drawer.

3

I HAD POISON in my cock and I had to get it out. From age eleven until about seventeen, I could feel it in there, threatening to burst my testicles, pulsing my vas deferens. I tried to take care of this on my own, to remove the compound manually, nightly draining the malignant fluid under my blanket in my bed. And this did provide relief, but only for a few minutes, maybe an hour.

And over time the procedure became less effective. After a month, I could no longer go to sleep without performing the exorcism at least twice. It wasn't long until mornings became the same way. And if I didn't, the consequences were horrific. Not only would urges plague my mind throughout the school day, but uncontrollable erections, brazen and adamantium, would haunt me as well. Not even the fear of social humiliation could deflate my phallus.

Returning home meant a race to the bedroom to release the mental succubi eight hours in the School District of Philadelphia provided. Once every ninety minutes, for the rest of the night, the act was repeated. But it was release without liberation. Self-pleasure was a meager panacea in lieu of the exorcism of true intercourse. I knew what I needed. A girl. Any girl; I didn't care about the specifics. Someone else to take my burden. I was desperate for the cure.

I didn't care who removed the poison. I didn't understand love or consequences. The only feelings I was concerned with emanated from my groin. I found a drunk girl at a house party in West Philly who was willing, after a twenty-minute introduction, to partner in intercourse in an upstairs study, but my strenuous masturbatory exercises left me numb to the real act, the latex condom I wore for her protection only making matters worse. Two weeks later, a casual encounter with a white girl at a hotel party downtown led to a week of phone conversations and then a meet up at a sweet sixteen at Society Hill Country Club. Intercourse was achieved, again drunkenly, in the laundry room, on a foldout table. One of the women working there, an older teen, maybe college-age, walked in on us and I leaped off, my shame hanging before me. The girl I'd found was amazed I'd disengaged so quickly, but in my fear and drunken stupor, my flaccid penis was no miracle.

The girl was Cindy, the last name was Jewish; that's all I retained of her. Of her face I remember a field of small pink pimples on her chin and along the line of her brown hair, the talcum smell of pancake makeup. I don't know when I found out she was fourteen, that she was just in eighth grade at a private elementary school. I was sixteen and in tenth grade, high school, and it was shameful and wrong. But I had been under this penile burden for years.

She said she was sick with a sore throat, home from school. I played hooky and came over. Her parents had money, a high-rise condo downtown, even if they only lived on the third floor. I don't remember any conversation when I arrived. There must have been one; there must have been a pause. What I do remember: a car caught fire on the street below, not far from her bedroom window. I watched the smoke build on the hood until you could see the building inferno blacken its paint. The windows, rolled up, burst from the heat mounting inside the car. There was no explosion, just casual ruin. The car parked in front of it was charred all the way to the driver's door. The car past that was still close enough that its wheels melted like in a Dalí painting. Even a parked car can be a disaster. From where we were, you couldn't even touch the windowpanes we looked through. So we must of talked.

But I just remember lying on the mattress on the floor of her room. She took my penis in her mouth and when she lifted her head back up a line of saliva as thick as glue connected us, and I realized she really did have a cold. And then I was on top of her, feeling nothing once more but pumping away to find the pleasure I knew eluded me. The chance of an orgasm was an act of faith, until her wetness suddenly surrounded me, and I could feel my objective within reach. It was as if I was wandering blindly up a hill then stumbled upon its blissful peak. I arrived at the greatest three seconds of my young existence. And there was elation, until I rolled over and saw that my increased pleasure was caused by the fact that the condom had broken and rolled back over my cock like a rubber wedding ring.

Past the fire trucks that now surrounded the building, I pushed forth into the traffic of Walnut Street, pumping my skateboard toward something I couldn't imagine. I had heard that there was a foam? That you could buy, that could kill sperm? But that was all I knew. No one else had heard of it though, at 7-Eleven or Wawa. I didn't calm down until an hour later, when I decided that if she did get pregnant, I would call up Trojan and get them to pay for the abortion. My groan, though, was silent. I did feel the release. I was unburdened.

In the days after, she began calling me. And we talked. And it was okay at first, even though we had nothing to talk about. But she kept calling, several times a night. I would come back to Germantown, walk into my father's latest renovation, and the phone would already be ringing and it would be her. After fifteen minutes of forced pleasantries, to get her off the line I told her I needed to get settled in, but if I didn't call her back by dinnertime she would call again. My father, annoyed, would get rid of her this time for me. If I didn't call her before I went to sleep, she would call late at night and I would pay the price for this piercing of my father's solitude. She wanted something, something besides sex. It scared me, how badly she desired this unknown thing from me. I was too young to realize it was just friendship. It ended as childishly as it started: she wanted to get together on a Saturday; I said I was staying home. An hour later, two of her girlfriends saw me on a bus heading downtown to Love Park with my skateboard. A crying call from her that night let me be single again by Sunday. The phone rang when I came in the door from school until Wednesday, but when I didn't answer it eventually I was rewarded with it going silent.

Sunday night, a week later, she called to tell me she was late. I didn't know the meaning of the euphemism. The calls started back up again from there, surging past their original frequency. Her narrative started with the conflict that she might be pregnant, and every phone call was to discuss the possible repercussions. After two weeks she told me that she had taken a pregnancy test and it was positive. This revelation brought me a mortal fear I had never conceived of and bought her several extra minutes on the phone. Now that the pregnancy was real, she told me she needed an abortion, that she needed $340.

Petrified that my father would find out, I offered to pay half, stopped eating lunches, and started pocketing the twenty dollars a week my dad gave me for food. Then she told me there was a complication, that she needed a special abortion. That the cost would triple. That her mother demanded I pay half before she authorized the procedure. I told her I would send it. I stopped eating regularly altogether. I lost weight. I did even worse in school. The stress cured my sexual desire, but I still couldn't sleep at night.

I could hear the phone ring even when it didn't. I would be upstairs in my room at night, and there would be a call and my dad would pick up, and I would stand at the door listening to the pause after his "Hello" knowing that my ruin was upon me. That he was being informed of my sins, of the fact that my life was wasted. Eventually he would begin to talk and the call would be revealed as something totally unrelated but I knew my demise had only been delayed.

She phoned three months in, wanted to know where the money was. She called less often now and when she called she was just mad and didn't try to keep me on the line like she used to. I had scrounged together 380 bucks doing some messenger work for Sirleaf Day, kept the cash in a shoe box that once held yellow and blue Air Jordans. But I had started to doubt, by this time. I had asked around at her school, had received the word that while the rumor was that she was pregnant, nobody noticed her actually getting bigger. Chubbier, baggier clothes, but not belly bigger. I decided I would offer her a check. If she told me I could make it out to her mother, I would send her the cash I saved. If she refused, told me to make the check out to her, then I would send her nothing.

When we finally talked, she said, "No, make the check out to me. That's what my mother wants." I said okay, and hung up. It really was okay. No mother wants the check made out to you. I didn't send it. I didn't spend it either. I was too chickenshit scared to. Her next call three weeks later began, "Where the fuck is the money?" It was the last sentence she said to me. In response I said, "I didn't send it. And I'm not going to send it either." And then there was nothing but silence.

So much silence. I could hear the radio on in the background, Hot Hits 98! WCAU FM. I knew she was still on the line. It was open audio territory, meant for me to step in and defend myself, to uphold my position. But I stayed mute. I was not going to say anything else. I was not going to call her a liar. I was going to let the silence hold, because I knew that if I could endure it, this silence, this final call, then she would disappear. Because I disappeared. Right there, I was holding the phone, but in my head, I was gone.

In the silence, I first understood you could do this fully, that you could just vanish. Or rather: I could do this. I could do this my whole life, and would, because the only thing it took was not being a good person. Now I knew: I wasn't a good person. I wasn't going to grow up to be strong. I was going to be a weak man who could do something horrible, unspeakable, shameful, and just vanish. Disappearing, like when my mom was in the hospital after her stroke and I stopped visiting because it hurt less not being there, seeing her there, unable to do more than witness. So I vanished. And then Mom was gone and I never had to go back anymore. After three minutes, three of the longest minutes of my life, three minutes of hearing ads for Krass Bros. menswear and Robbins Eighth and Walnut at her end of the phone, of hearing her breathing, hours in feeling but minutes counted on the red digital numbers of my father's alarm clock, she finally hung up. Cindy was gone. It was over. The conflict was erased, and now I had the money, and the only price was my delusion that I was worth loving. I spent the money on the next Air Jordans. All white and lizard skinned. And pizza, I think. And forties of Red Bull.

"You knew my daughter," Irv Karp says to me, eighteen years later. He's Jewish and I can hear in his question the Torah's sense of "to know."

"I barely knew her. I don't know her," I tell him, and I look frantically around the diner we're in, at the people in the other booths and tables, searching for Cindy's face staring at me. Preparing for the hate on that face. The anger from the last phone call undiminished.

That's how I'll recognize Cindy today: the accusation in her expression.

"You're right, you didn't really know her. And you never will. She's dead." He takes a sip of his coffee, then lets me carry the weight of the statement. I fumble my condolences but he still takes them. Outside, standing on the sidewalk, the girl smokes a cigarette. "She's dead. Seven years now. Stop apologizing, that part wasn't your fault.

"She had her demons. She fought them for a while. Sometimes she beat them. Mostly though, she followed them to hell. And seven years she's been gone. She was my angel, but I'm under no illusions that she was an angel to the world. A man's daughter is his heart. Just with feet, walking out in the world. A guy I went to grad school with, he said that. He turned out to be a gay, didn't matter: for him and his little girl it was the same way. You'll find that out now. This one, she takes after you anyway."

"You don't know me."

"But I know me. I know my wife, may she rest. And I knew my

daughter better than she did herself. And this one, she's not like my people. It was clear when she was little; it's clearer now. You get a seed, doesn't matter what kind of soil or light or water it gets, it's going to grow into what it is," Mr. Karp tells me. I want to know what this old white man means by "my people," but it's the way he says the word *seed* that hits me. She's looking through the window at us. At me. She holds one arm around her waist, the other leans its elbow on her hand as she bends the cigarette to her mouth, the way my mother used to do when she was thinking.

"Look at her. She's like three feet taller than me. She's like a giraffe. A cute one, I love her, but you get me. You wouldn't believe how much the girl eats. That hair: don't let it fool you. It's straightened now. But usually, it's like lamb's wool." He points up at my own hair, smiling. Then looks closer at my straight strands, and sobers. "Still my bubi's was the same way, so who knows which side that came from. But Tal's yours. She's very artistic. Not academic, this one. Always about the art, the dancing, the whole tortured artist thing. You'll get it. I been Googling you. Almost two years now, I been following you."

"So why today? Why didn't anybody tell me before? All this time, if you had my name, why not contact me?" I don't want to sound mad. I don't want him to get up from the table, for the girl outside, now on the cell phone, to fade away from me.

"My daughter." Irv Karp shrugs. "Promises were made. And I was particular about who I would let in my granddaughter's life, no offense. But I researched you, I saw who you became. And I saw on the Internet you'd be in town, at this little cartoon thing.

"This girl, I can't handle her anymore. And Tal's like you. She's your people."

This girl looks more like my mother's daughter than mine. She's even darker than I am. I'm proud: I knew I had more black in me than my own appearance implies. I'm jealous: that melanin should have been mine. The genes that gave me the palest of tans on her looks like a two-week Caribbean vacation. The African kink of her hair is chemically treated and combed straight enough to be European curly. She's been passing for white and not even knowing it.

"So, I'm a black. That's just fucking great. A black. That's just what I need right now."

"You're not 'a black.' You're black. It's a good thing, nowadays. You can be president." I grin for her. Her smile back is quick and fraudulent. She's trying to act composed and mature, and she's not old enough to know how to pull off the illusion like the rest of us.

"Jesus, I thought you would be Israeli or something. I hate rap music," she says, then looks off. "You know, I was the best dancer at Kadima, since like third grade. Guess that's explained."

"I can't dance, sorry."

"Maybe it skips a generation. God, school. He told you to tell me to go back to school, didn't he? He told you to tell me to get back in high school, finish up and go to a good college. That's why he's doing this to me, because it's easy to get into college for blacks. Don't they get scholarships or something? That's what this is about."

My daughter is a racist, I think. I adjust that to, My daughter is mildly racist. My daughter is casually racist, I settle on. She's casually racist. "You dropped out of high school?"

"I'm an artist too. I'm a dancer. I'm going to dance school anyway, so I just need my GED and an audition piece. Irv doesn't understand that. I'm going nuts in his apartment. You've met Irv; you have to see what he's like. I'm going to graduate, like, any minute. I'm almost eighteen. I want to get out of the house now. Tell him to let me go, and I'll leave you alone. You can go back to not being a dad." I want to protest this, but my mind doesn't have the words my mouth needs, so I choke on nothing for a bit till I raise my water glass.

"I'll take the year off, backpack in Europe, take some classes, just build my repertoire," she keeps going. "That's what matters. Ol' Irv doesn't understand that. I'm sure as hell not going back to Kadima Hebrew Academy. Look at you. Look at me. I don't even know if I'm even Jewish anymore."

"You're definitely still Jewish." Where is her old man? I ask myself, then realize this is the same question Irving Karp has been asking himself of me for seventeen years.

"Oh right. The whole Jewish Vagina Clause. I guess that fact hasn't changed." When she says "Jewish vagina" I think of her mother's literal one before I can catch myself. I'm so damn light, my blushing looks like the igniting of a funeral pyre. She sees this, and then her face goes red as well.

"I didn't know about you until a week ago, okay? Irv saw that you were coming to town, finally decided to tell me. I didn't know you were a black till today."

"Okay, look, it's not 'a black.' It's never 'a black,' okay? Just 'black.' Or African American."

"You don't look very African, but whatever." My newfound daughter rolls her eyes at me, twirls her straw. "God, I guess I'm going to have to start using hot sauce on all my food now."

"No, you don't. You can't possibly believe that," I say, kind of laughing, hoping she'll start laughing with me. She doesn't. "Hey, I didn't know you existed at all. But I'm glad, okay? I'm really glad," I tell her. I just say it. I don't say it because I mean it. But when I hear it out there I can tell it's true. Hey look, Becks, I'm finally a father. My own father's gone, Becks is so gone, but here is new family. Seventeen, but new to me.

"I saw your illustration, online. Some of it's okay." Tal shrugs. I want to tell her about her other grandfather, about my father, about how she just missed him, but don't. I want to tell her that my mother died when I was young, too, but it's morbid. Instead, I find myself saying, "You should go back to school. Your grandfather is right about that." It's a safe thing, an easy thing to latch onto, probably the only fatherly advice I'm qualified to give.

"I am so not going back to Kadima. I don't fit in there. I never fit in there. I never fit in anywhere. Especially not now."

"Then you'll go somewhere you do. It's important. I'll help you. Let me do that for you. For your future. Whatever you decide to do once you get your diploma, that's up to you. But you need to have the choices available to make—"

"You want to help me, want me to go back to school? Want us to be daughter and daddy? Fine. Just get me the hell out of here, and you got a deal. Take me back to Wales with you, that would be awesome. I could go to school there. Or just send me to boarding school. Send me someplace, like, Phillips Exeter. I have the grades. That's it, Exeter. Send me there. Irv will go for that."

"Exeter? That's, that's a lot of loot. And it's so *white,*" I catch myself saying.

"But I'm white," she says, and I look hurt. I must look hurt, because she leans over the table and adds, "I'm as *white* as you look." Then my new daughter pulls back again, twirling her hot-combed hair with a nail-bitten finger, my own snarl on the adjective mirrored.

4

"I CAN'T BELIEVE you're here. I didn't think you'd ever come back," Tosha tells me from across her kitchen table. She's got a table, a house, kids, her chosen husband. A whole established life. All new to me, and already old to her. She's done so well since she rejected me. "And you're a father, too! To a racist white girl."

"Not racist. I said 'casually racist.' She just . . . she just doesn't know better."

"Because you haven't been there to teach her. We never even met the wife, besides on Facebook, and now you're a single dad of a teenager just as fast."

"Biological. Biological father." And then I think of Tal's face and muster up all the nostalgia for yesterday and amend my statement. "Tal has a cleft chin. She got my mom's cleft chin. All this time there was someone walking around with a chin I loved, and I didn't even know it. She's my daughter. I got a girl. An almost grown, pre-woman, girl." This is the third rotation of this discussion. Apparently, we're going to keep cycling through this information until both of us firmly accept it. "And she's a white girl."

"She's not a white girl. She's black. You've got a duty. To let her know who she really is, who we are. What blackness means, not the pathology you see on TV. What it is to be an African American woman in this world. That's deep." Tosha shakes her head at it, or me.

The fact that I wasted a decade of my life being in love with Tosha doesn't seem to get in the way of our friendship now. This is largely because it's also been more than a decade since we've actually seen each other, as well as our mutual understanding that I never really had a chance with her anyway. There is a story of our never becoming lovers, a mythology that I have for us that is boring and false, filled with details that I use to try and convince myself otherwise. I met her the same time George did, at the Greek Picnic, the summer of my freshman year. I had seen her on occasion before this, biking around the neighborhood, once on the R8 train, once at the Value Village shopping for jeans; she was too beautiful to approach or forget. But that summer began our friendship, which over the following summers and Christmas breaks grew from casual to intimate, though all the while George's shadow hovered, as "I have a boyfriend at college" kept our relationship platonic. But because so many beautiful young women in my orbit had some placeholder boyfriend somewhere in the ether, Tosha's relationship wasn't something I took too seriously either. It was supposed to run its course, as was the norm.

After graduation, there was no formal announcement of their impending engagement. It was never mentioned to me, despite near daily interaction. It wasn't said until Tosha nervously invited me to be a groomsman, a role I was unable to fulfill, as I decided soon after the invitation to leave the country instead.

Tosha married George because she loved him more, or despite our connection she loved me only as a friend. It was either or both reasons, or one or the other. That is the story I eventually accepted.

But I have another scenario, still in my head. That scenario says that Tosha went with George because I am a pale fail of a Negro who would never be enough for a "Nubian Princess," a title which one of Tosha's T-shirts declared. This is a product of my paranoia and profound insecurity but also of that time a cousin of George's saw us at the movies and called him to warn that his girlfriend was "seeing some white boy," a moment laughed off when it was revealed it was just her castrato, high-yellow nerd. And from the time we left a club on South Street and she was called a "cracker lover" for walking next to me, and from the look of shame that stayed on her face as we continued to the car. And of all her light-skinned jokes, though not numerous, and usually focused at women "damn near white," and laughed off each time by me as I mentally catalogued. It was a product of the time I sprawled next to her on a park bench at Rittenhouse Square, studying our bare legs stretched out into the heat of July, noticing how pasty and inadequate my epidermis was lined up against her rich mahogany norm. I have never felt whiter than when next to her. I don't like feeling white. It makes me feel robbed. Of my heritage. Of my true self. Of my mother. So when I found out that Tosha was lost to me, I regrouped by enrolling in an illustration program in Swansea, Wales, where dear Lord I have never felt blacker.

Back, I'm glad I didn't try to stay and keep waiting for her, because Tosha still loves George. I like George enough, he's okay, and if I had to pick between the two of us, then or now, I would have picked him over me without hesitation. I see him in his white undershirt, serving scrambled eggs and cheese to their three kids, making them laugh, and yes, I would rather be him than me. He's a cop, detective grade, with a mortgage, and he knows where he belongs. I am a boy, still in my father's house. He puts cheese in the eggs. He puts sharp cheddar cheese in the eggs, and soy bacon bits, stirs it all together and calls it "Daddy Eggs." His kids, they love saying, "Daddy Eggs." They ask for more, comment on how much they've eaten, and who's all done, and they throw in that "Daddy Eggs" descriptor every time and it doesn't seem to be getting old for anyone.

"Why don't you just work on being a dad first, and then build up the expectations from there?" George offers, already on the dirty dishes. He's washing the damn dishes. He's not letting them sit in the sink till it overflows with shame.

All this sensationalistic talk about the long-lost mystery daughter, it's wonderful. I dreaded coming here to these two people and having to say that my marriage failed, that my life has failed, that I wasn't strong enough to do a basic thing like properly fulfill the one person on earth I was legally bound to love. I never gave Becks her family, and that's why I have none. Tosha and George are of my generation, my tract in life: their familial growth, in such contrast to the wilted state of my own, is a direct reminder of all my shortcomings. Not that they would ever gloat over this fact, to my face or elsewhere. It would be worse than that. There would be pity there. Someone would say something like, "You'll get it together," and I would smile and shrug and know that I wouldn't. I thought of not coming by at all—I hadn't seen either since before their wedding. But being in Germantown and not stopping by would be an insult. And now, who cares about something so mundane as another marriage turned to disaster when there is tabloid-level fodder like this being served for consumption? In comparison, talk of the ex-wife is mere canapé. I have a synopsis for that too now, a convenient story that offers everything but detail. It goes like this:

"It turns out when someone is brilliant and driven and hardworking, good things happen to them. Even in Britain. So Becks, she's got her practice going now, consulting, all that. She fronted me the money for the comic-book shop and I think she thought, I mean maybe I did too, that it would be a hit, that it would grow to a chain, maybe into an online juggernaut. But I'm not a businessman. I wasn't really driven, like she is. And also, you know, I'm a flake."

"You're an artist," Tosha offers generously.

"And Becks started to hate me for that. I think. Not for not being a success like her, but for not moving on. Having kids. She was getting older, the window was closing, she really wanted them. I just wasn't ready, you know? To double down on more responsibility. So I kinda pulled away. Then she tugged me back, couples therapy, all that. And then I got pissed and pulled away harder. Then she stopped tugging, and it was too late."

"That's horrible," she says to me, but she's looking at George, who must be listening but is pretending to keep on with his endless kitchen tasks. Tosha is more jarred by my divorce than I am. For me it's been happening for over a year, after four other years of misery.

"Becks is really very happy now. She's replaced me with another black American. A proper dark-skinned one with dreadlocks and everything."

This is true. Becks is *ecstatic*. Becks is *a new life*. Becks is *a great weight has been lifted*. Becks is so overjoyed, on her Facebook page she's become a Welsh greeting-card machine. If there is a greeting-card company in Wales, and they just need someone to write platitudes for a line of divorce congratulations, Becks has a good decade's worth of phrases for them. She now produces the happiest posts I have ever read in my life. The messages I get from her solicitor, those are straight venom and threats of financial apocalypse if I don't get her the money back, but on Facebook she still comes with lots of exclamation points. All that's missing is *Wish you were here!*

"What you need to do is relax, make sense of things. Your dad's passing, this girl, the crazy house."

"I got crackheads at that house."

"Everybody's got crackheads. Look, Germantown's changed—it's come back up. This is the hot new place to live, man. Prices are soaring. But this is still Germantown."

"That night was like . . . it was eerie. I thought they were ghosts. For a second I was like, 'This is some paranormal *ish* or something.'" I laugh this out, wait to see their reaction.

Tosha just wags her head.

"There are no ghosts," she says.

"How can you know that?"

"Because your black ass would already be packed up and leaving town again." I laugh at this too but she doesn't, and in the silence I get the feeling I might be being insulted, so I laugh harder till George spares me with his interruption.

"I'll make sure a squad car makes a regular drive-by, but don't let those crack fiends mess with your head," he says.

• • •

Tosha and George's children, these three great kids, they are everything my life is missing. I watch George with them, and I'm certain of this. He has purpose and joy, there is a slot in the universe he is fitting, without which there would be a black hole. I totally know, because I live in the black hole. Becks was right. Across the breakfast bar the kids yell out "Uncle Warren" at me and there is an authority in that title. I haven't earned even "uncle," and yet still it fills me. I never managed the duties of "son" particularly well, in regard to both my parents. At "husband" I was an even grander disappointment, and I stink of divorced man so bad that even I can smell it, as if every nose hair reeked of its own disappointment. I've been failing at "father" for years without even realizing I could claim the title.

"You got to make up the time." George leans over, puts a hand on my shoulder. Grips. "You have to educate her, man. Tosha's right on that one. That's your path to being her father, a chance to give her something. Make sure she gets back to school, and goes to college. You do that, you'll have started making an impact."

I make the mistake of asking George how much tuition costs. I don't know where their kids go to school, but I do know he has to send them to private. George is just a public servant, and that ain't paying but so much. Tosha is an administrator for the school district, but it doesn't matter. This is Germantown, and they are middle-class, and I know they're not letting their little angels loose in Lingelbach Elementary to eke out survival. Our childhood was all about Lingelbach Elementary. It was about finding a school to go to so you didn't have to go to Lingelbach Elementary. Seeing if you could use a mailing address in Mt. Airy, or getting your parents to send you to private. It was about staying inside in the hour and a half after those kids were released back into the community, lest their tsunami of juvenile chaos catch you in its wave. On some days you could hear their mob coming south on Pulaski at 3:30 P.M., watch the streets fill with the lumpen youth parade before disappearing again. Even my father, as oblivious as he was, would manage to keep in the back of the house during that procession. Tal would be too old for Lingelbach, but my father's mansion is zoned to Germantown High, the teenage equivalent. I had friends that went to Germantown, the ones that couldn't find their way out to a magnet program. My primary memory of Germantown was that they threw a math teacher off the roof. This story seems suspect now, maybe nothing more than an urban legend, but the fact that it has taken me thirty years to even question it is because Germantown High is the kind of school where a math teacher being thrown off a roof seems perfectly plausible. Still, when George breaks down how much he's paying for each child to go to their private Quaker school, for a second I imagine Tal Karp roaming the halls of Germantown High, books in hand. A pioneering young Jewess the likes of which those halls have not seen in sixty years.

"I can't pay that much." There's no sheepishness in my confession. It's not that I wouldn't do it; I just don't have the money. Maybe, maybe if my father's house sold, I could put that money down, but school starts this week. "Is Germantown High any better now?" I turn to ask Tosha directly. Her strongly negative response involves as much body language as syllables.

"Charter schools. That's what people are doing now. They're free, there's usually a theme. There's an Asian one in Chinatown and a black one, not too far from you, past Wayne Junction. Umoja. Guy I used to work with's the principal. I'll give you the brochure. That's what you need for her: real Afrocentric, positive. But not Germantown High." Tosha grimaces, her hand waving the idea out of the air like so much flatulence. "Don't let her first real experience with black folks be running from them."

"You need to clear your head, get out in the open air," George says. "You need to get back on your bike. I still got the Harley. Needs to be run and I don't have time. I poured a couple thousand into it since you sold it to me, but I'll give you a good deal on it. You want to impress your daughter, let her see her old man rolls in style."

"Buy the bike back, Warren. I'll show you where it is," Tosha tells me. When George briefly turns his back to Tosha, she mouths *Please!* and makes shooing motions with her hands.

"Look, they say being a father's just about showing up," George says when he turns back around. "It's true, too, the standards really are that low. You show up, you don't beat them, you love them, you pay for stuff. That's all there is to it." On this final phrase, George slaps my back. He slaps hard, not hard enough to hurt me but enough to say he could do it if he tried. He is a man. He is a father. He's licensed to carry a gun. It makes me love Tosha even more, because she saw all the way back then that he would become a man and I wouldn't. I used to want a time machine so I could go back and stop George from taking her from me. Now I want one to go back even further and make him my father too.

"George's fucking some white dude and he hasn't lived here in a year," Tosha tells me in the garage. It seems so improbable, illogical, that I just say *who?*, but she ignores me. "He just comes over for breakfast, tells the kids he's working the late shift. He tells me we're just separated, but he's leaving me. I know it, I fucking know he is."

"Who is?" I ask again, but it's such a stupid question she doesn't answer and I don't expect her to, so I follow with "Who with?" after an appropriate pause.

"I don't know but I'm going to prove it, too. I've got him under surveillance," Tosha tells me. I look at her, and I try not to smile, but there's a little hint there because I'm thinking she must be wrong. I'm not willing for her marriage to be in trouble. They have everything I am sure brings happiness. They have two beautiful kids, and one okay-looking one. They have a big house, a big solid six-bedroom house made of fieldstone and old wood and it looks sturdy enough to withstand a hurricane or tornado, even though none of those things happen in Philadelphia. George is a detective. George is a black detective. That's about as close as you can get to being a superhero. Tosha, her lips still full, her nose still broad and bold, is an African goddess sent to humble the racists who would mock any aspect of black femininity. She still stuns me, when I look over at her. Tosha's thick thighs can run half marathons and her red tongue can quote from *Hamlet* in the exact voice of Maya Angelou. If these two aren't happy, if they can't make it work with all the tools at their disposal, we are all doomed, and I refuse to accept that. I shake my head *no,* but she doesn't heed me.

"He's not supposed to see anyone, that was the agreement. Keep things clean. But when I call him at night? Not there. He says he's going to the gym when he isn't at the place he's renting. *For hours?* Yeah, right. I don't have, like, prosecutable evidence. But I know. It's over. He's just too much of a coward to make it official."

"You don't know," I tell her. She's filing her nails with an emery board she just plucked from her back pocket. The filing thing: I have seen her do this over the years when she is angry. First time I saw her do it, I thought she was sharpening them to scratch someone's eyes out. "You don't know. You're probably just in a rough patch. Relationships go up, they go down. It's just in a recess right now. Why would he be with anyone else? Especially another guy?"

"He swore it wasn't another woman, and it has to be someone. I tried to have sex with him, four months ago, tried to put my head down there. It smelled like hair conditioner. I did the research, Warren. That's what they do. That's what lying scumbag husbands do: they wash their cocks with perfumed conditioner so you can't smell the whore on them."

"That crackhead: she was actually in my house. She broke in my house last night," I shoot back at her. "Just in and out. Didn't take anything, but still." It's a horrible transition. It's supposed to be a horrible, noticeable transition. It's supposed to signal that I am not comfortable with the chosen topic, so let's leave it behind. I almost tell Tosha I'm planning on burning the place down just to shut her up, but I really am so keep that bit quiet.

Tosha, grinding with her emery board fiercely enough that I can see cuticle dust pouring down, ignores this response and answers whatever question I should have asked instead.

"Am I ugly now? Am I hideous? You used to say I was attractive. Am I still attractive? I'm a frumpy mom. Look at me. What happened to me?"

"You're still beautiful. Very beautiful," I tell her, and she is, but I can't look at her right now. Instead, I look at the motorcycle, parked on the side of the garage. It's still never been dropped. There's some slight grinding wear on the foot pegs, but that's it. It's just like when I sold it to him. Nothing has touched this bike but dust. George has done an amazing job of taking care of it. George has done a better job of taking care of the bike than he has his marriage. George has done a *far* better job of this than he has with his marriage.

"I'll talk to him," I tell her, and the fact that we both know I have nothing to offer George allows her to break the moment she created. Tosha puts the file down.

"Are we going to talk, then? About it? About what happened? Or is it just going to hang out there?"

"About what?" I shouldn't have come here. I should have just left. I should have saved more money. I should have stuck out my marriage. I shouldn't have come here.

"About what? Warren, you take off twelve years ago and don't write once? You don't respond to one letter? I had to get your address from Sirleaf—which you know took multiple attempts because you know how he is—and you never even bothered to write back to me? You were supposed to be a groomsman in our wedding"—Tosha says "wedding," and I hear her say "wedding," and even though I don't think of her that way anymore, the ghost of the me who did flashes in, then goes dark again—"but you just ran away! Like nearly five years of friendship didn't matter anymore! You missed my kids being born! We were close!"

"I'm sorry," I think to preface before I say, "I did friend you on Facebook." I did. And I looked at her pictures, and pictures of her kids, and her and George, a lot. I hit LIKE often too, which I feel right now should count for something, but I don't mention this. I got over it. I came back. I ain't staying but I came back.

Tosha glares at me. Then she sighs and says, "Yes you did. And so did your wife. And it was good to see the pictures she posted. Even though you never bothered to message me back. And I love you like a brother. And that's why I'm not going to smack the black off you for saying some stupid shit to me like 'I friended you on Facebook.'"

"Well thanks because I don't have a lot of black left and I really don't want to lose the rest through slapping."

"I need a friend right now," Tosha says, and then she's crying.

I'm trapped in a hug again, surprisingly. Every time I want to escape someone starts hugging me.

The bike is a gorgeous monument to nostalgia over practicality. Working the clutch is like trying to negotiate with a drunken bill collector. I was wrong: George ignored this bike as badly as he did his wife. Under twenty miles per hour, I'm riding down Germantown Avenue on the cobblestones and the motorcycle is shaking like it's scared of black people. Its roar bounces off the row houses, echoing accusingly back at me. The vibration feels like the bike's plea for me to slow down, to rethink the whole movement idea, but I don't. I'm late, supposed to be at my dad's place before Sirleaf comes through, but I'm looking down at the ground whenever I can because I have no idea where George's money went. He put a new, roar-enhancing muffler on the thing, but he attached it so poorly the main noise it's making implies it's about to fall. The tires are narrow and I'm trying to keep my front one out of the trolley grooves. I'm looking down on the ground right in front of me the whole time, which is dangerous but I have a scar on my right knee from getting my bicycle stuck in these tracks in fifth grade and I can't help myself. I know I'm late, but I can feel that scar on my knee now, the dead skin miraculously itching as it rubs on the inside of my jeans.

There's somebody at the front gate. It's not Sirleaf Day. It's a white woman. It's a white girl. My white girl. It's my black girl who looks like a white girl with a tan and a bad hair day.

"You shouldn't be out here, on your own. It's not safe," I tell her when I pull up. Tal pretends she doesn't hear me over the motor so I yell it again.

"It's okay, isn't it? I mean, now that it turns out I'm a black? I get a pass on 'the streets' now, right?" There are a lot of bags. Four big ones, a human-size duffel bag, and a portfolio case. There's a hamster cage, sitting right on the pavement. There's a hamster inside it, running along the sides manically as if some of the local rats might try to jump it.

"Tal, what's going on here?" I ask her, but I know.

"Irv kicked me out." She shrugs. "I told him I wasn't going back to Kadima. And about my GED plan. And he said if I didn't go back to school I couldn't stay there. So here I am." I keep staring at the hamster. But I don't say anything. I'm waiting till the right words come, but my tongue gets no offers. After a few seconds, Tal steps closer, puts her hand to my chin and aims my face back at her own. "I'm moving in. *Dad.*"

When she uses the *d*-word, with such palpable derision, my first thought is: I'm not old enough to be your father. The next thought is that not only am I old enough, but that I literally am her father. I look at her face. The neck, the cheekbones, the eyes, I recognize. Family. But the whole face, her face, I barely recognize it from the day before. This is a stranger. I feel some love there, or feel the need to want to love her, but I don't know this person. The clearest emotion I can identify is a sense of responsibility. I will meet that responsibility. Or try. I will try to make sure she graduates high school. Then after, when I burn the place down, I will use the money to take care of her. I will make sure she gets out of this town. Hell, we could run together. Someplace nice, with temperate weather and a low crime rate. And then I feel the Umoja flier Tosha printed for me scratching at the inside of my coat pocket and the impulse is given physical form.

"Here's the deal: you come with me, then you have to finish up at another school. You have to graduate, then you can do what you want."

"Fine. You get me in a school, you find somewhere I can still graduate on time, let me stay here, then we can make a deal."

"A school with black folks in it. Trust me, it's important. You need to know who you are. Who we are. I'm not going to have a daughter of mine who goes around saying things like 'the blacks' all the time. Agreed?"

Tal sighs, rolls her eyes a little, but says, "Fine," at the end of her performance.

"And no smoking. And you have to keep calling me 'Dad.' But in a non-sarcastic manner," I throw in, feeling momentarily sure of myself.

"I'll call you 'Pops,'" she says, and that feels okay. "'Cocoa Pops,'" she adds, and I get uncomfortable again.

Tal unpacks, and I try to make the house more livable. The painting equipment, the strewn tools, I pick them up, put them in the closet behind the stairs. In there, I find three poster-sized pencil sketches of Germantown. One of the long-vacant pool beside the Boys' Club. One of Chelten Station, from the perspective of the street, looking down to the tracks. The last, a façade of the Whosoever Gospel Mission. They're mine, or at least I created them.

They're the ones that didn't sell, the ones that weren't purchased out of mercy by Becks's coworkers at the gallery show she arranged. My father had them framed. He actually spent money on that. With his hammer and nails, I hang them in the living room.

As it gets dark, I wait for the crackheads to show back up. All the doors are checked, all the windows are locked, but crackheads have special piper powers and can probably flatten their skulls like mice and squeeze through the smallest cracks. Perhaps this is how they got their name. I have something to protect now, so I electric tape a steak knife to the paint roller stick.

"If you don't want people to say racist things, you probably shouldn't carry a spear," Tal offers, looking up from her phone to watch me pace around with the stick. Besides that, she doesn't seem to care much about her decrepit surroundings. After Tal does a little unpacking, she doesn't ask for a tour, or accept my offer of one. She doesn't ask why it's in a state of ruin. She doesn't ask why there's hardly any furniture. I try to explain to her too, start to tell her the story, but she walks around the room ignoring me, holding her cell in the air like it's some kind of ghost detector.

"There's almost no reception in here. I'm getting, like, one bar. It's true what they say about the ghetto," and then she pulls her empty suitcase over to that one corner, sits on it, and goes back to texting.

I have nothing to say to my daughter. I want to say, *I can't believe you're here* and *I can't believe you exist,* and *I want to know all about your life,* but it's impossible to hold a conversation when the person you want a response from is furiously typing away with just her thumbs. Instead I ask, "What do you want to eat for dinner?" and this gets her to pause, look up even.

"I don't eat red meat. I don't eat meat that's not organic, or at least kosher, and I don't eat produce that isn't locally grown. And I'm not eating anything that was frozen. I don't play 'reheated.'"

I've got nothing in the house. My father has a little fridge in the kitchen, sitting about two feet out from the wall, and it's a museum of beer and condiments. I look for take-out menus in the only full drawer in the pantry.

"The best I can do is halal." I hold the flier up. It says, *Still 2 Getha* in Arabic-styled letters.

"Not exactly the same team, but whatever."

When the food arrives, the bag has napkins and plastic forks, so now we have toilet paper and silverware. Tal takes her chicken cheesesteak hoagie out of the bag, unwraps the foil, which she flattens out beneath the food as a plate. I watch her. The lettuce and tomato she takes off, and then makes a separate pile for each. Then Tal removes the meat from the bread, scooping it out with her plastic fork until it sits in a gray ball. She rips bite-sized pieces from the roll, then lays them down one by one until they form a pyramid. When Tal catches me looking, I turn back to devouring my own serving. I haven't eaten a cheesesteak in a decade, and many a drunken doner kebab has failed to fill the void. Mine's gone before she's even done her preparations. So I watch her.

"I like to keep things organized," Tal says without looking up. She says it and the words are lifeless and congealed together as if they've been recited on many occasions.

"Your mother did that," I tell her as I remember. It is one of the only things I remember about her mom. I don't remember her face, but this bit I find within me. The time I went over there, I brought fried rice. I brought fried rice because I must have said I would bring her lunch, because she was sick, and it was the cheapest takeout I could find. And she took it on her plate, then separated the peas, then the carrots, then onions, till the rice was oily and naked. I'd never seen anyone else do that, and haven't since. Now I'm proud of myself. I have remembered something, something about my time with Cindy, that isn't horrible. But when I look at Tal, I see her staring back at me, her fork at her side, limp and hanging in her hand like she won't be using it.

There's anger there and I know Tal's going to curse me, for all I've done and haven't done. But she only says, "Irv. He was a nutritionist. Before he retired and became a drunk. It's not OCD; it's about portion control. He taught me." Tal pushes her foil plate away from her on the hardwood floor, sliding it carefully to nearly beyond her reach. Unfolding a napkin, she lays it over top like the sheet on a corpse. "And my mom."

"Do you remember her? Your mother?" I ask, and I regret it completely because I've been asked the same question, and it is one of the stupidest acts of small talk.

"Uh . . . yeah?"

"She was in her twenties then, right? She was in college?"

"She didn't go to college. That's why for Irv, it's, like, pathological for him. You take the Jewish 'go to college get a good education' thing, and then you multiply it times a thousand. It's like, if I don't go to college, I'm going to die. Too."

Tal looks as if she's about to start crying. And the combined threat of seeing a stranger cry and seeing my daughter cry for the first time is too much. I get up, find the flier for the Umoja Charter School in my jacket pocket, and stick it right under her face before the tears can come. She takes it, sighs, flips it open.

"Everyone in this is black. Why is everyone in this black? You said go to a school with some blacks, not all blacks."

"You ever looked at a flier that had all white people on it and said, 'Why is everyone white?' "

"Sorry," Tal says, and starts wrapping up the food that's remaining. It's a shutdown move, meaning the conversation is over, but I start cleaning up with her and pretend we are both still united in action.

"It's a black school," I tell her as we walk to the kitchen, greasy paper balled in hand. "An Afrocentric-themed school. It's not like white people can't go there though. You went to a Jewish school, now you can finish off at a black school. Makes sense. It will help you develop a black identity."

"I already have an identity, I didn't think I needed to get one in a new color." Tal hands me her food, she's only eaten half of it. I put it in the refrigerator, a machine so old it has a latch handle.

"Look, you're black. I know it comes as a bit of a shock, but trust me, it's pretty damn amazing. You've inherited a rich cultural tradition—think of it that way. But you're not white anymore. You never were. Sorry."

"Don't say 'sorry' for that." Tal's already down the hall. "It's not like I was great at being white either."

Tal, my daughter, who I keep telling myself is my daughter, takes my tent. I was going to offer it anyway. I gather what appears to be a clean towel and washcloth from one of my father's empty storage bins, and leave them on the floor outside the tent because the door is zippered. I can hear her moving around in there and I can see the light of her cell phone glowing. And I know she hears me, because the warped wooden floors in this place complain with every footfall.

I check all the doors one more time, make sure they're not just locked, but properly locked, look out each distorted window for a sign of the ghouls showing back up. But there's nothing. When I come creaking back to the tent, I expect Tal to say something, to ask a question, to make another comment. Nothing comes. Just the glow. The sounds of clicking digital machinations. I lie down on the wooden floor, another towel for my pillow.

"This is our first night together!" I say after ten minutes, with all the cheer I can muster. Tal doesn't respond. After a minute, after I've given up and closed my eyes, she finally says something back.

"It's like you think there's a race war, and you want me to choose sides."

"Not a war. Maybe . . . a cold war. And yes, there are sides," I tell her, because I'm tired. Because I think, just say the blunt thing now, and walk it back from there. "There's Team White, and there's Team Black, okay? You probably didn't even know you were on Team White before, most of Team White's members never do. They just think they're 'normal.' But if you're black, and you go with Team White, that makes you a sellout. A traitor. And plus, you'll never be accepted as a full member if they know the truth about you. It's all good though. Because there's Team Black where, okay, you may have to work sometimes to be accepted if you look like us, but you're membership is clearly stated. In the bylaws."

"Oh great. Well as long as I have a choice." I can't tell if she's being sarcastic because I can't see her and don't really know her that well anyway.

5

"WHAT DOES UMOJA even mean? Wasn't that, like, an R&B group or something?" When Tal first says this, I kick her under the table. This is the universal sign to "shut up," but she looks over at me surprised and hurt like I just kicked her and I realize: she's not kidding. She really thinks the school might have been named after an R&B group.

"'Umoja' is Swahili, a Bantu language from East Africa. It means 'For there to be an I, there must be a We.' Or, unity. You can learn about many of the African principles if you're in attendance here," Principal Kamau says, and there is no annoyance in his manner. We are lucky to have this meeting so quickly. Tosha called in a favor, and here we are, and if Tal screws this up I have no other options.

"They have a vegan salad bar in their lunchroom," I tell her, or remind her, because I mentioned it at least twice before we rode over. I want to add, *That means your food will come pre-divided,* but don't think she'll see the humor.

"I thought all the American blacks came from slaves on the west side," Tal says to him. But then she's looking at me. Because I'm the one now squeezing her hand under the table to tell her to shut the hell up. I bulge my eyes at her, smile wider.

"You were saying there's a tour my daughter could go on while we discuss specifics?" I ask the principal, and mercifully he calls in a student to take Tal out of the room before she can open her mouth again. The kid's Tal's age, tall, almost as light as she is, but the first thing I notice is the muscular arms poking out of his sleeveless dashiki. He smiles at me and nods with both hands clasped in front of him, as if I'm his sparring partner in a dojo. His locks are long and perfectly pulled to the back of his head, his neckline open, cowrie shells lining his leather choker chain. Clearly bright, confident, he looks to me like a young black warrior, a shining example of what the Umoja Charter School can accomplish. Tal must see something positive about him as well because almost immediately she jumps up with, "Okay, Dad, I'm out of here. Bye!" I catch myself reaching for her, scared of what will come from her mouth unbridled.

"I'm sure she will be fine. At Umoja, we teach our young men to be gentlemen, the future leaders of tomorrow."

"Sir, I'm sorry. I don't know what Tosha told you about Tal. This is all, y'know, new to her. To me. It's an odd circumstance. And Tal's only really known about her identity, her blackness, for a few—"

"Not uncommon at all, brother. Not. At. All. We get a lot of parents through here, they got these kids today, they're disconnected. Disconnected from the soul. All they know about being black is what they see in music videos. That's part of why we're here. To teach. To repair."

I like what I am hearing. There is a weight, so quickly laid upon me, that I feel magically lifting now. I imagine a life as he keeps talking. I see Tal and I rising together every morning, her donning her dashiki, me cooking her organic free-range eggs as she prepares for school. I see me giving her a ride to the door of this building, a converted Victorian mansion itself, and then returning to my father's to draw more pages to pay the bills before the great fire and the resulting windfall. At the end of the year, she will graduate and I will burn the house to the ground, using the insurance money for her college tuition. And then maybe I will follow her to whatever city she escapes to, far away from the charred ruins. Maybe to London. Forget Team Black, Team White, just join Team Not From Here again. She'll bring her friends over to our flat and I'll be the cheery but slightly aloof cool dad.

"We teach them African history—the real history, not the lies in most history books. In language we offer both Swahili and Igbo." His head is mahogany, round, shiny. While other people comb their hair, he must spend that same time rubbing his scalp with Muslim oils. "African philosophy, African mathematics, African food. The point is, we remove the toxins of Western decadence and replace it with purity. We make them whole."

This sounds basically fine. Why not? I've had a lot of European toxins in my life—weed vacations to Amsterdam, drunken club-hopping in Ibiza—and it hasn't worked out that well, has it? I would like to be whole, too. And I am currently trying to remove the European toxin of Becks, so I can sympathize. There is paperwork to do. There are transcripts to be sent over, but from the way Kamau is talking, it sounds like we have a completed agreement. I shake his hand, follow it through all its brotherman finger gyrations, and even though a part of me thinks he just gripped me like that to see if I was truly black, I don't care. A victory has been won. An education will be received. Blackness will be restored.

When I finally get out, Tal's not in the waiting room. I hear a rhythm beating, and I go to a window that overlooks the courtyard below. There's a drum circle, with adults at the center banging away hard enough to make the glass shake under my hands. The students have formed a ring around them and now take turns dancing the circumference one at a time before taking their place again.

I see my daughter instantly amid the class, her skin a blanched beacon, the lightest among them. There is an elegance in the movements of each kid's cakewalk, evidence that they have done this before, that this is a school ritual. I watch them dance in their uniform of dashikis and khaki pants, and then quickly excuse myself and head for the stairs to pull her out of there. I do this before Tal can mess this up. Before she can dance like a white girl and make a fool of herself on her first day of school.

By the time I get out to the yard, I've reconsidered. My thoughts about my own daughter's racial identity are prejudiced and false, even though I still believe them. I'm too proud to admit it by pulling her out of there, where other minds might be thinking the same thing, will know exactly why I extracted her. That I've created a white girl. So I just stand there, at the outer edge of the crowd, watching. Tal's talking to that boy, who hovers beside her. They both clap along to the beat as he leans in close enough to whisper in her ear. Seeing her respond to his smile, his flirtation, his perfectly groomed thin baby mustache, my newfound fatherly protectiveness is second to my relief that my daughter may have found motivation to attend the school.

Tal's turn comes last, and I expect her to demure, to shake her head "No" and let them finish, but she just thunders out the moment the girl next to her prances back. And, in the circle, Tal jumps. Her hands go high as she erupts out of the center, and like a sheet falling lightly on a bed she comes down into a split on the ground. Tal's legs divided on the asphalt; she is as long there as she is tall. A new fear rises, that she is acting like an uppity high-yellow show-off, but it quiets at the sight of Tal's joy at springing up and giving in to the momentum of her twirl. The drums go louder when she leaps, the crowd claps louder and hoots and there's a "Go on, girl!" at every peak. When Tal does her final split, back at her spot, the drums crescendo to the finish, where they are met and replaced by applause. I get another new father feeling: pride. But it's muted by an even larger realization. That is how my daughter looks when she really smiles.

"She shouldn't be jumping up," Principal Kamau says, walking beside me and handing me the application papers.

"I'm sorry," I tell him, a mix of regret and confusion.

"That was a good start, but she shouldn't be jumping up so much. We'll teach her. Jumping up, that's the European mind-set, you see?"

"Yeah? I've seen African dancers jumping before," I say, because I can't help myself, because that's my daughter. And I know I've seen African dancers jumping before.

"Sure, but not, not like *that.*" The principal shakes the bitter taste of the memory out. "See, the European mind-set, it's about distancing oneself from the planet, so their dancing is all about trying to jump away from it. It's arrogance, really. It says, 'I'm better than mother earth, I fly off of you because you're beneath me.' The African aesthetic is connected to the soil, see? So less of that flapping around like a pigeon. The dance moves down, to the source, because it has humility. It loves the mother earth."

"I totally love the mother earth. I only eat organic." Tal stands before us. She's with the boy. It only occurs to me now that she found the lightest-skinned guy out here to make her new friend.

"Don't worry, brother." Kamau slaps my back, ignoring her, nods a smile at her before heading inside. "You take care of the paperwork, we'll take care of the cure."

"A cure? What the hell is his problem? I'm not sick; I'm classically trained. Why are blacks so sensitive?" Tal is intentionally loud for everyone to hear. Kamau stops at the building's door. He looks at me. I'm responsible.

"What? I didn't say 'the blacks' this time. Oh, am I supposed to say 'African American' now?"

"There's no such thing as 'classical,'" I can hear myself snapping at her, loud enough for people to listen. "That's just the way white people say 'European.' It's subtle white supremacy. Don't use it anymore." I look over. My statement relieves some of Kamau's facial pressure. Still, the door slams a little when it closes.

"Oh hell no. I'm not going here. Dad. That guy is so crazy, he's racist against *jumping.*"

"That's not what he—look, you've been to the Jewish school, right? Your whole life. So are you going to tell me you can't do an eight-month stint learning about who else you are? Is that it?" I can hear my voice rising. The kids around us are now running through their recess, screaming louder, so I'm covered.

"Not going to happen," Tal repeats, leaning in and hitting the words harder so they find purchase.

Out front of the school, I can't even speak to her. I can't even look at her. Instead, I get the engine on the bike revving while Tal stands by playing with her phone. The boy she discovered, he's standing there too. I won't even look at him. Handing Tal her helmet, I scoot forward enough for her to climb behind me. Tal takes it, but puts it on the ground and just stands there, now talking to the boy. He gives her a note, his phone number I'm sure.

Lovely. I am fully prepared to just stare back, to wait her out until she realizes that I am the one driving in every sense of the word. But Tal's a teenager, and I remember teenagers are feral creatures, hormone-mad and erratic as wild colts, and after a good thirty seconds I cave and say, "You've made your point. Your complaint has been registered with the Ministry of Displeasure. Now, you're going to say goodbye and get on the bike so we can go home."

"You should try the biracial school," the boy says to me. He's nodding like this makes so much sense. He's smiling as if I know what he's talking about.

"Who are you?" I demand. It's easier being annoyed at him, this strange kid. Less morally complicated. He's got brass rings around the tips of his locks, and I've never seen that before but I instantly judge him for it. Clearly, he wants to sleep with my daughter.

Clearly, I am supposed to want to strike him for this. This is all very new but I'm pretty sure I have that part right.

"I'm Kimet," he says, like that is supposed to answer any of my questions. "There's another school. Another new charter school. It's themed for mixed kids. You guys could try there, too. They're enrolling."

"Listen to him, Pops. Mixed kids. I'm mixed, right? I qualify. You want me to do the whole race education thing, then let's try that one. If that doesn't work, we can move on to Chinatown or whatever.

Maybe I can pass for Korean. But I'm not going here. That man said I flap around like a pigeon."

"Tal, there are mixed kids here, and that doesn't mean anything. Mixed people are just a kind of black people anyway. You wouldn't be the only mixed kid here, I'm sure."

"I'm mixed," Kimet says.

"See?" I say, pointing at him, relieved.

"But if I could, I'd go there too," Young Mr. Kimet keeps going. I look at him. I try to muster the "look," the look that dads do when they want you to become silent or face some vague threat, but I have no training. When he starts talking again I interrupt him.

"Yeah? If it's so great, why don't *you* go there?"

"Because my dad won't let me. He's the principal here. My dad's Kamau." Tal finally gets on the bike, but tries to hand me a paper.

"Not unless you agree to take me by here first," she says, holding up the address. Atop it says, *Mélange Center*. I see these words and they're familiar and I assume it's from my distant past before I connect it to my recent one. Below it lists what street and such, but by the time I look at that all I see is the biracial militant and destiny or at least an opportunity to feign fate. I don't believe in fate, but I don't believe in ignoring fate when it disregards subtlety.

We ride to Mélange. Partly because Tal is insisting on it. And partly because I'm a lonely man who saw a person he keeps thinking about and wants to know why. Every time my motor idles, I yell to Tal all about "mixed" people. They are black people who hate being black, and the only reason they don't try to be white is that whites folks won't have them. That's one red light. They are color-struck brown-bag-clubbers, from the days when you had to be lighter than a brown bag to be admitted. That's at a stop sign. And African Americans have always been racially mixed, most of us are also of Native American and European ancestry. Even the name, African American instead of African, implies this. But that's not good enough for them. They just want to be special. They're self-hating Negroes, Oreos who will do anything to distance themselves from their race. That's while filling up the gas. Tal yells "Okay" every time I finish a sentence, yells even when the motor's off. She even repeats my words back to me, stripped of nuance or any attempt at understanding.

When we get to the address it seems like none of this might matter anyway. Her little phone says Wolcott Drive but the digits don't match up. It's an odd number and there are no odd numbers on this side of the street, just trees. We're by the park, Valley Green. "Nothing," I say and she just pinches my back and tells me to keep driving. I go up and down the street. I go on the other end of the road where there are a few stately homes, and show her they are on the even-numbered side, to prove my point. I'm disappointed, too, for my own reasons.

Maybe that woman was going to save me.

"The Umoja School won't be that bad," I say.

"Everyone kept staring at me," Tal says.

"It'll be a good learning experience," I say.

"They were all wondering, 'What the hell's the white girl doing here?' " Tal says.

"They'll get used to you. You'll get used to it. I have," I tell her. I haven't. Tal's silent. "Come on, let's go shopping, my treat. I'll buy you your dashiki."

"Oh my God, please. Please keep looking," Tal says, but I can hear that even she knows the truth, that there is nothing out here. And that's the truth; there's nothing out there. The Umoja School will be okay. She'll go. I'll make her go, or I'll kick her out. At least I'll threaten to, and since Irv already did, maybe she won't call my bluff. I give one more pass to show her it's hopeless, drive all the way down to where the street dead ends. Nothing here but fourteen hundred acres of part of the largest urban woods in America. I point to the trees, tell her if it were here, we'd see it, then kick the gear down from neutral when Tal says, "There!"

A sign. It's handmade, painted. It says, THE MÉLANGE CENTER FOR MULTIRACIAL LIFE. It looks like the worst hippie art project of 1972. But

Tal is already off the bike, climbing up the deer path through the woods.

I kill the motor, follow her. I call, but she doesn't stop. The path is steep, but Tal's shooting forward, using her lanky legs until she's over the lip and gone from me. There's a moment of panic, fear that I've already lost her. In the woods. But when I get to the top of the hill Tal's standing there, in front of a gate. It's metal, new, temporary, still has the fencing company tags along the side of it. Past it are mobile trailers, and the summer hum of belabored air-conditioning. I don't see anyone though, and before I can tell Tal this is clearly a mistake, that we should leave, she starts yelling. "Hello! Hello!" She keeps saying it. Tal is loud; she sounds scared. And she is, she's scared I'm going to send her to the Umoja School. But whatever's in her voice sets a couple of the trailer doors opening, and some brown people emerge and start walking toward us. And one white guy. He's an ogre. Seven feet tall, easy. And he has blond dreadlocks. Doesn't anyone comb their hair anymore? Damn near albino pale with his yellow hair matted together in thick rolls that shoot off loose and straight at the end like a dog's tail.

"Yo cuz, can we help you?" he asks and it's more of a demand than inquiry. The giant's close enough that we can see the pale blue of his eyes and read his T-shirt. It says *Malcolm&Garvey&Huey&George*. "This is a private area, my man. If you here to see someone, you best name—"

"Warren Duffy!" My name interrupts him. But I don't say it. It comes from a woman. She's tall, her sable mane tied up behind her head, the large glasses resting on her nose, her face's most prominent feature. I watch as she walks off one of the trailer's little porches, carrying rolls of rubber mats under one arm and a gaggle of hula hoops in the other. Look at that, her sandals, they still clap for her.

I smile, wave, yell out, "Hi, so good to see you again," but she just looks annoyed in my direction.

When she gets to the gate she says, "Look at that. The world's biggest sunflower has come to bloom."

6

RUSTY OLD TRAILERS, decomposing in the woods. There are different kinds of trailers—travel trailers with monotonous white ruffled siding, drab gray business ones the size of shipping containers, shiny aluminum ones shaped like suppositories. There's even a row of mobile homes that look like Victorian houses for oversized dolls, lined up side by side on the grass in imitation of a town house block. But that's it. Some moldy circus tents, but they just add to the feeling of bohemian impermanence. A good breeze and it's all gone.

"I assure you, we are very well funded, and have already begun building an endowment," the center's director tells me. As soon as we're introduced, she asks me to call her Roslyn, or Director Roslyn, but she doesn't give me her last name. "A literal building is the next step."

"But this is a public park, right?" It's totally a public park. It's owned by the City of Philadelphia.

"There's an ongoing litigation." She smiles calmly, the patience of a mother enjoying childlike naïveté.

It's hard to tell Roslyn's age because she's clearly fit and wrinkle-free, and conventionally attractive, but from the full white of her hair I know she's almost a generation older than me. She shows me her world and I look around this place thinking, Is it free? If not, can I afford it? But all I ask her is, "What's a 'sunflower'?"

"A 'sunflower'? Where did you hear that? That's a horrible word."

"It's a beautiful flower. You can eat it too."

"Yellow on the outside, brown on the inside. A slang term for a biracial person who denies their mixed nature, only recognizing their black identity." Roslyn turns her head to look over at me as we slowly walk down the wooded path, as if I'm the source of the etymology. "I don't allow use of that word here. The Mélange Center is about inclusion of all perspectives of the black and white, mixed-race experience. Our goal is to overcome the conflict of binary. To find the sacred balance."

"The sacred balance," I say back to her, to prove I'm listening.

"The sacred balance. An equilibrium that allows you to live a life that expresses all of who you are and hide none of it," she says, and she keeps talking. I look at her and offer an occasional "Yes" and smile, but mostly I watch my daughter across the lawn with that first biracial militant I encountered. She's taller than Tal. Much thicker. How can any grown straight man become infatuated with teens when there are women walking this earth? With cellulite and stretch marks because they're actually living?

"Oh. Sunita." The director follows my eyes. "Sun is a miracle, really, my little soul sister. But when you get called names your whole life, it's easy to revert to doing the same."

Sun. She's at the younger end of my generation, with a name like that. Creative, but predating the celebrity insane-name movement, which means her parents were also hippies and most likely young and idealistic when she was born. The Brits, they can tell your social station from asking you the weather, but in African America first names offer not only class and region, but year.

"That's fine. I'm sure Sun's just used to the word from being called it."

"Oh no, Sunita Habersham?" Roslyn asks, laughing. "Sun used to be the biggest Oreo on the compound."

There's a lecture. A spiel. I'm certainly not the first to hear it and by the time I do it's fairly glossy and filled with sentences like "We aim to help mixed children deal with the unique challenge of negotiating African and European hybridity." It's a beautiful sentence. I don't know what it actually means, or how you would do it, or what the end product would be either. "Now we're actively moving to the next stage. A cultural center, an artist retreat. And a school. For your daughter's age, it would be a GED diploma, by exam, but we offer teachers from the most competitive colleges and universities to give recommendations. We're building something that will last. A permanent oasis. When you consider that this whole enterprise started as an annual weekend event just three years ago, you get a sense of the trajectory."

"How'd you do it?"

"Nobody went home. On the last day of the retreat, nobody went home. And then more came. And here you are." Roslyn smiles again. The grin doesn't reach her eyes and it reminds me of the mask-like grins of the principals I submitted to from elementary through high school. Instinctively, I want to know if I'm going to be suspended.

We're by the Victorian cottages now, with their gabled roofs. There's more than a dozen in the row, with another row behind it. Beautiful little shotgun homes with intricate woodwork and little concrete block porches. But when you look under those porches, you can see the wheels. Roslyn notices me bend a little to look and says, "All of our teachers are well credentialed, and specifically trained in our method of multiracial balance. If you decide to enroll your daughter, I assure you, nobody will be absconding in the night with your tuition."

When I hear the word *tuition,* the rest barely registers. Whatever it is, I'm fairly certain it's beyond what I can afford. I have $532 in the bank, after buying back the bike and picking up some more furniture from Whosoever Gospel Mission. I will get funds from my father's cash accounts, but who knows when and how much will be left over. Even to live in the damn shell of a house he left me I've had to arrange for some roofers and get an electrician who doesn't care about codes. I'll be chilling when the house burns down, but even that payout could take another year. Knowing this, that this is beyond my reach, I blink and the school becomes suddenly desirable. It's an education out in the trees. It's small classes with teachers still fresh and not worn down by the friction of reality against their good intentions. It's probably the least threatening majority black place I could take Tal, and the only one where I wouldn't have to worry about her destroying everything by saying something offensive. They seem a little wacky, but all teachers are a little wacky. At least the ones I've dated. Crazy hippie school out in the woods. Naïvely earnest mulattoes starting a comfy commune. It's Mulattopia. Tal in tie-dye. It would be so adorable.

"How much is it, can you tell me? Monthly?"

She says a yearly number out loud that's so insanely high that I laugh because I think she's messing with me. She smiles again, her perfect teeth on display, and I know she's not. What kind of halfros have that kind of money? But she keeps going on, saying, "Fellowships and some financial aid are available. Although the forms are still being designed."

We continue our tour, but only because I'm too embarrassed to say, *Sorry, I'm one of those broke-ass Negroes you may have read about.* I get Tal as soon as I can break away politely. My teenage daughter's talking to Sunita Habersham, who after a half-hour to think about it still clearly doesn't care for me. But she does seem to have a real appreciation for what my X chromosome can create though, because she's holding Tal's hand like she's her aunt.

"We have to get going," I say into Tal's ear, give a little tug on her arm meant to move both of us toward the gate.

"What? We just got here. I actually like this place. I can take modern dance. And the boring coursework's only three hours a day, the rest is electives."

"We have to go."

"They offer an after-school Zumba class, Warren. We're not going anywhere."

"Tal, please. It's private," I whisper. "Look, I can't afford it. Sorry. We have to go now."

"Oh, so I have to go to the Umoja School?" Tal asks. Really loud. "I have to go to the *black* school, where I'll never be black enough? Where I'll never truly fit in?" Tal doesn't believe any of this. Or even if she does, she's instantly ingested their dogma so well she knows this is exactly how to push these people's buttons. Tal is a habitual button-pusher, clearly, and she's already worked out where their keypad is located. And they hear her, because Tal is nearly screaming now.

Sunita Habersham hasn't walked away. She looks over at me like I'm the asshole. I *am* the asshole, but there's no way Sun could know that. "Finally, I find a place where I can truly be myself and—" Tal keeps going. I try to yank on her arm a litter harder, drag her out. Instead, Sun's hand grabs my arm first.

"Your daughter hasn't finished her campus visit. What was the point in coming up here if you're going to leave halfway through?"

"Sorry, this was a mistake. And also sorry about the thing at the panel; I acted like an insecure jerk. But we have to go. I didn't know it was private. My error. I can't afford this right now. Honestly."

"If it's *really* a tuition thing, just join the center. Work for it. That's why I came to your silly panel in the first place: we need a part-timer in art. I mean, you know, if you don't think you're too black for us."

"See, work, *Pops*. That's what being a *dad* is all about. Working for your kids." Tal stops Sun's sniping to contribute.

"That's it? I teach some classes, and conceivably she can go here for free?"

"Not free, nothing's free. But I'll talk to Roslyn. And you'd have to take the Balance Test." And with that she finally lets go of my daughter, and leans into me.

"Because she really needs to be here," Sunita Habersham says, her voice hushed but firm. That smell: tea and a mouth of honey.

"Did she say something offensive?" I whisper back, but I don't get a verbal answer. Just raised eyebrows and that wide mouth silently pantomiming, *Oh yeah*.

"I can take a dance test. I have an audition routine I've been working on," Tal interjects.

"Not dance, honey: balance. The Balance Test. Everyone has to take it."

I stand on one foot, make a show of it. Balancing shakily, I put my arm out then bring my finger to my nose, giving a little chuckle. Sunita Habersham doesn't join me. I look at Tal as she turns to Sun and asks, "If he fails or otherwise makes an ass of himself, does that reduce my chance at admission?" and I laugh loudest and rustle Tal's hair like she's an adorable four-year-old and that shuts her up again.

The first question on the quiz is, *Was O. J. Simpson guilty?* That's all it says.

"What the hell kind of question is that?" I ask. Neither Sunita nor my daughter responds, so I stare back at the test. There are no boxes to fill in.

"Should I just put yes or no?" I ask, and at the other end of the dark little trailer room, Sunita says, "Just put your answer," not even looking up from whatever she's working on. Tal is writing away, so I get back to it. I write, *Probably, I don't know, but I do know white folks were a little too excited about a black man murdering a blond white woman.* I turn the page and the next question is *Name the most important musician of the twentieth century and explain your justification.*

"Is this some kind of pop-culture scorecard?" I ask. No response, once more. I see Sun write something again at her podium, and then I get paranoid that her notes are part of the test too, that I'm being tested on taking the test, so I keep going. I write *Bob Marley,* and a note about seeing his image across Africa more than paintings of White Jesus, and you see a lot of those in Africa. This proves very prescient because on the next page the question is *What race was Jesus?*

The thing keeps going. The next page features a picture of a black man and a white man running through the streets, the black man in front. The white guy behind him is a cop. I know this picture. It was used in an ad campaign against racism in Britain, I saw it across the tracks on a wall in Charing Cross station. It's a mental trap. The black guy in the front turns out to be an undercover detective. There's no way anyone can know that without being told. Next to *Describe Scene* I write:

They're both cops, but that is irrelevant. A picture of anyone who isn't wearing a suit running from a police officer would imply guilt, because businesspeople are the only criminals the law doesn't care about. Hence the question then becomes one of class. We assume middle- and upper-class people don't run from the law, because they defend themselves by manipulating the law. Like O. J. Simpson did.

This answer pleases me.

My daughter is turning pages before I am, but I am exasperated before her. The questions keep coming: *What do you eat New Year's Day? What card games do you know? What are your feelings about mayonnaise? What do you do with these?*—and a picture of dominoes. With every question, with every answer, I become more inclined to grab Tal's hand again and walk out, nearly overwhelmed by this impulse. I look up at Sunita Habersham, standing there in judgment. I'm used to having my blackness questioned, but never on paper, and never by an Oreo who would damn me for it. But my daughter is two desks over, just jotting away, unaware of this pretext or just uncaring.

By the final question, *Name your black friends [minimum three],* I answer, *Nat Turner, Warren G. Harding, and What T. Fuck?* and then get up to hand it in. All I get is a curt thank-you. Sunita won't even look up at me from her podium, and when I peek I see I was right; she's written notes on a page with my name on it. Next to her notes though, Sunita's reading a comic book. Sunita Habersham is reading *Mind MGMT,* which is a really good comic book, the sort you have to make the lifestyle choice of visiting specialty comic-book enclaves to find. The sound I make, the puff of air, is less a sigh than the reaction to a gut punch. I have no defenses against this combination of shared interest and physical attraction. I take −7 vulnerability points on all attractive female geek attacks.

Gone is my racial righteousness and in its vacuum I am so drawn to Sunita Habersham that I experience it through the lens of terror: that I will fail to connect with her on even the most platonic of levels, that this is a pivotal life challenge to which I will fail to rise. That the intuition I felt on the first day, that she can save me, was a premonition. When Sunita finally looks up, holding my gaze, I choose to believe this is a signal of mutual attraction.

"*Mind MGMT*. Do you like comic books?" I lead with.

"We met at a comic convention. What, did you think I was just there for you?" She shrugs, goes back to reading.

Mutual attraction is not equal attraction. No cartoon bluebirds sing around our heads or link our hands with ribbon, but I believe we silently share the knowledge that we are grown-ups who enjoy the same obscure hobby, are of close enough age, are of similar heights and fitness proportion, and that we both have faces several others have found pleasant. Also: I'm a big man. And Sun's a big woman. Tall, full, real. We share a sturdy similarity. Surely she must know we are both Kapha Doshas, in the ancient Hindu Ayurvedic tradition. And I can lift her. And she knows I can lift her—oh yeah, she knows—and not every man can do that. But I can because I match her. I want to lift her. I want to carry her and let whatever thing she's figured out about how to be black, white and not, carry through the strain in my arms. She knows. I know she does. I can feel it next to her. I can feel good next to her. I look down, as fast as I can past her breasts to her hands on the podium. A hell of a lot of bracelets clack above them but all that metal and not a thing on the only finger that means something.

"You're black identified," Sunita tells me. She's barely looked through my test.

"Really? I could have told you that, but it took me thirty minutes to fill the thing out. How did you—"

"The last question. Most white-identified mixed people actually try to list names. You expressed outrage at the question, a typical black-identified response. I already saw a few more answers, I doubt the rest will indicate different. Or you can wait here for the next ten minutes."

I want to wait. I want to wait and talk to her and tell her how silly this test is, this mixed-race posturing. I want to do it in a way that shows her how witty I am. I want her to be able to tell me why I'm wrong. I want her to be right, even though I am. I want to be on the same page in the same space and not feel alone but hinged to someone solid. Someone just like me, so I can know what it feels like to not be different. Someone just like me but happy. And eventually part of me wants that to lead to sex so I can complete the bonding. I step closer to the podium to hide when the erection starts to build. But Sunita doesn't notice, because she doesn't even bother looking at me.

"That's not some kind of sin here, is it? Did I fail or something?"

"No pass or fail. Not a judgment. It just tells us which realignment class to assign you. Almost everyone ends up in one class or the other." She looks up for a moment, offers a pharmacist's impersonal grin, then drops her head and expression as she looks down to my test again. "But I knew you were a sunflower when I met you. The male sunflowers always hit on me. Somehow they know they don't have a chance and need to prove their manhood by defeating reality."

"We're leaving," I tell Tal, and she gets off her phone long enough to stand and gather her things.

"Was my father being a dick? My father can be a dick. Please excuse his dickishness."

"Jesus, Tal, don't say 'dick.' She didn't mean 'dick,'" I tell Sunita, who actually winks and nods. Instantly, I feel less offended. Then I realize it's because she's agreeing with Tal.

Sunita Habersham's head bobs and I read that as, *You are a dick, a huge dick, isn't that funny?* but her mouth says: "She'll be in the opposite class. I'll talk to Roslyn; we can work this out. So come tomorrow, if you can make it. At eight A.M."

"We're going," I tell Tal again, and holding her arm we head to the door.

Riding back, I am so angry I say nothing. Tal, for her part, allows me the silence, or at least doesn't say anything loud enough for me to hear.

When we arrive at the mansion, Tal climbs off and says, "Warren? Between the two, you know where I stand. If that Thor-looking goliath at the gate can fit in at Mélange, I got no worries. I just want to get the diploma and go start my life, okay? Just help me. Just help me get the hell out."

With her helmet under her arm, Tal heads past the gate and up to my father's house like she owns it. She is beautiful, my big girl, her feet pointing off at ten and two, slapping straight down on the arch as she falls forward. I watch her walk all the way while I struggle to get the motorcycle's front wheel up the three steps of the walkway rather than try to unlock the rusty vehicle entrance. Tal, I realize, as I speed through seventeen years of parental epiphanies, is of her own making, not just proof that once I was young and reckless. She turns at the door again to add, "Jesus, hurry the fuck up," after she uses her own house key for the first time.

"She ran away!" Irv Karp yells out of his car window as he pulls up behind me. I recognize the voice more than I recognize him; first it's just a crazy man in a 1997 Buick LeSabre.

When he climbs out, he's sweating, his dress shirt's open, sleeves rolled up. In the outside light, his old flesh looks translucent and fading. "That little weasel ran away, came here. She didn't tell you that, did she? Did she?"

"I didn't know," I find myself yelling back to match his passion. The bike I give up on, lean it against the fence. Irv takes my hand when I hold it out to him, and I know then it's not me he's mad at this time.

"See this? This is what I've been dealing with. She just goes. I go to dialysis yesterday, I come back, I lay down. I wake up this morning and she's gone. Who does that? Is that how good people act? Who just leaves?" he asks and I shrug back at him even though the answer could be, *Me*.

"I would have thought she was running away to the street and who knows what, but she took that little rat pet thing and its cage. That's when I knew, she's coming here. To you. Did you know?"

"I didn't know," I tell him again.

"Of course you didn't know! That's the immaturity! That's what kids do! But now you know," he tells me, smiling at the absurdity of it. And then he breathes. He puts his hands on his khakied thighs, catches air some more. I offer to take him in for some water but he waves me off, stands straight again to continue. "How is she; is she good?"

"She's good. We found a school, someplace she can finish out her year." Moments earlier I was thinking about GED training instead, nights at a community college somewhere, but here this guy is and he wants a solid answer. I tell him how it's in Chestnut Hill and he really likes that because it's ritzy up there. I tell him it's surrounded by trees and adjoins Valley Green and he looks impressed, so I skip mood-killing details like the fact that it's actually in the park and composed of gypsy hovels. I hate the awkwardness of talking about race with white people, so skip the whole mulatto-themed bit altogether.

"Come in, let's talk this through, figure it out," I tell him, and I start pushing on the motorcycle again just to get it out of the way. There are a few seconds there when he's waiting behind me patiently as I struggle, but when I finally get it over the hump Irv doesn't move.

"Nah," he tells me, head wagging. "Nah, I'm going out to Philly Park, gonna bet on the puppies. Look, I'm leaving. She's okay, and she's going to go back to school? Good. She wants to torture her grandfather, just send emails to my niece to tell me she's okay? Fine. You keep her. You look out for her. I don't mean like forever or anything, don't get carried away, but for now, a couple of weeks at least."

"I can handle her, Irv. I can. We're bonding."

"Yeah. Let's just see. Seven years I've been struggling with this one. Let her think she's won. Let her think she got her own way. I need the rest. I need a day at the track and some good luck for once. I can't do this forever. You know I got the prostate cancer. I mean, I got it bad."

Irv just throws that last bit on to the end without pausing. I reply, "Okay," before I actually hear his last sentence. But it's not like I have anything else to say. He looks at my discomfort, laughs at it, waves it away with his big spotty hands as if it's cigarette smoke.

"Look at your face: it's like I told you that you got it. You don't even know me. Trust me, I'm no great loss to the universe. Plus, I'm getting the treatments, so who knows? But don't tell Tal. She doesn't know. The two of you, you should come to Shabbat at my place, next Friday. You should meet our family, get to know them so—" And Irv starts coughing like something is in him large and wet that wants to come out, but I hope it doesn't because I don't want to see it.

7

MÉLANGE CENTER, 7:55 A.M., cold even though it's still technically summer. What is a gathering of mulattoes even called? A murder? A motley? A mass? I ask these out loud as Tal and I stand gathered at the gate with the others, waiting for it to open. My daughter says, "A menagerie," and winks like we're conspiring.

"It's called *home.* Oh yeah, you betcha," an ebony-skinned woman says next to me in a thick white-girl accent that sounds like it was obtained in North Dakota.

There are mulattoes in America who look white and also socialize as white. White-looking mulattoes whose friends are mostly white, who consume the same music and television and books and films as most whites, whose political views are less than a shade apart from the whites as well. They ain't here. Those mulattoes whose white appearance matches up with the white world they inhabit, those mulattoes aren't coming to Mulattopia. The world already fits well enough for them.

Those mulattoes who look definitively African American and are fully at home within the African American community—they aren't here either. Those mulattoes who look clearly black and hang black and are in the full embrace of black culture—nope, they're not here, nowhere to be found. If they were they would denounce this lot of sellouts. I know they would. I can hear them from the place they have in my consciousness.

The people whose appearance matches the identity they project, they have a place in society that they fit into with minimal cramping. But here, standing next to us, is everyone else. The human equivalent of mismatched socks. The people whose racial appearance fails to mirror the ethnicity of their inner spirit.

They're going to let me teach three days a week, push my reduced payments off till Halloween, when I should have access to the rest of my dad's modest cashable accounts. I'm looking forward to a whole week of training with Tal, us sitting together making fun of the cultists in the back of the classroom, me and my teenage baby girl, bonding. But as soon as the blond Neanderthal comes to open the gate, Sunita appears right behind him, reading names off a list. And just like that my daughter and I are separated, broken off into two groups, and sent to sit in trailer homes at opposite ends of the encampment.

There are a dozen other people sitting around a circular table in the room for Balance Class B, and nobody knows each other yet so nobody is talking or making eye contact. But I am looking at them. And I am looking at some of the whitest-looking black people on the face of the planet. The only reason I know some of them are black is because they're in this room. I look at these people—a couple adults my age, the rest kids Tal's age and younger—and I come to the most blissful recognition. I am the darkest Negro in the room.

I am the darkest Negro in the room.

Finally. I—lighter than some white people walking around this world, always the palest of any black person, a man who can barely hold on to that mantle—am like an Asante chief in this room. The aspirational blackness of this group is clear in their aesthetic choices. The teenage boy to my left wears a do-rag, presumably so you do-not see the straight brown strands peeking out from around his ears. He has on the basketball jersey of a player most famous for being associated with the reality-TV star to whom he was briefly married. Next to him is a woman whose African braids must have been attached to her stringy mouse-brown hair with superglue. These people, they are not black like me. They are less black than me, and therefore I don't trust them. And I love it. Embattled groups have to police membership, for their own self-protection. But with policing comes power, and all power's usual intoxicants. Instantly, my own ethnic bona fides are shored up by the contrast to my present company. This, I realize, is a singular element of the Black Experience I've been previously denied. The guilty satisfaction of sitting in judgment over others for their insufficient blackness. I forgive everyone who has ever done this to me maliciously. How could anyone resist such a pleasurable self-righteous indulgence!

The blond Neanderthal comes into the classroom. I have a moment of panic that I'm going to have to take a week of lectures from Thor the Thunder Mulatto, but he sits down next to me. I can see his dreads close up and marvel at how a man who looks so white can have hair kinky enough to hold them. And then I almost chuckle when I can see that his thick strands are held together by some sort of product. Egg whites or wax, or more likely some organic paste that comes in a jar with a lot of little Africas or ankhs or marijuana leaves decorating its sides.

"One drop," he says when he catches me looking. I smile and look at him. And then he says it again, "One drop." And I know he's calling me out. Amazingly, all of my air vacates and is replaced with something the opposite of helium. Just like that. The familiarity of this next emotion's so complete that it takes only a moment to accomplish. Here I have sat in judgment, yet am no better. One drop of African blood, the legal definition of blackness in America. And really, look at me, am I much better? Does the wideness of my nose or my full lips somehow obscure the fact that I hold to this ridiculous fallacy as well? I am more ashamed for having forgotten this at the first opportunity. And when he says, "'One Drop,' like the Marley song. What do you go by?" holding his hand out for me to shake it, and I get that he's giving me his name. That he's actually telling me that he's willfully chosen to call himself this insult.

"Warren," I say. But can't resist asking, "You really like to be called One Drop?"

"They used to tease me with the name, when I was a young boy coming up. Now, I own it. And it can't hurt me since it ain't true. You feel me, Dubs?" he says, then offers me a fist bump, which is a nice way to accentuate that he understands the unspoken rule that any brother with a W anywhere in their name has the opportunity of choosing "Dubs" as a nickname. He has studied the culture well. I give a pound in appreciation.

"Don't be nervous, yo. First day jitters, but it ain't nothing. It goes quickly," One Drop tells me. He says it like he truly knows, like this isn't just conspiratorial bluster.

"You took one of these classes before?"

"Man, I've taken this jawn three times. My blackness runs too deep, yo," he says, putting a fist over his heart. "See, they make you take it till they whitewash you, yo. But the teacher, she's the best." And when Sunita Habersham walks in and authoritatively takes the front of the table, I turn to agree with him.

I stare at Sun, but she's the teacher, and she's lecturing, so it's perfectly appropriate. So she likes comics. So she's height-weight proportionate, in a manner I find voluptuous. Yes, she's displayed an unattainability that enhances her attractiveness to me. But still, rational thought here, what am I being attracted to? All those reasons are so petty, my desire doesn't accrue from their sum. I look at her neck. It's got all those lines running across. She's a little younger than me and blessed with more melanin, so those aren't wrinkles, its the skin of her neck being too long for the bones holding up her solid, monumental head. The size of it eludes perception because of the distracting oversized glasses masking a third of her face.

The enormous concave lenses shrink her eyes down to the size of a small child's. Her pupils are two little brown dots floating in empty aquariums. If Sunita Habersham wore contact lenses, they be as thick as Russel Wright plates. Sun could swim at the bottom of the ocean with contacts that solid. She is not attractive in pieces, but what human is? She is the most beautiful tall, half-black, female comic-book nerd in the world, of this I have no doubt. The whole is what matters. And she is whole and balanced. She must be or the blasphemy that she's preaching would shake her to the ground.

"Without accepting all of ourselves, we can never be ourself," Sunita declares. And then she repeats the sentence of import over again, slower, stopping to write on the board. I haven't been closely following her actual lecture, the entire line of discussion is too disturbing to take in big chunks. Fortunately, I don't really need to because Sun's done the same thing with all her key sentences and they're all written up there. *Love yourself for who you are, not who you wish you were.* Then there's *All of your history is within you.* My favorite is *You are half of nothing, for you are whole,* because ain't no one in this room half of anything. These people would kill to be half. Nobody in this room has had an ancestor who was "half" since Abraham Lincoln was president. Hell, the guy next to me is making do clinging to one drop and bragging about it. This mixed race stuff is heresy. It's the opposite of what I've been taught since a child: if you have any black in you, you're black—very simple, very American. It's worked fine since slavery but she treats the dogma like doggerel.

For two hours, I'm nodding my head and taking notes, mostly listing how to get Loudin done in six months, the order of what needs to be fixed, and estimates as to what each repair will cost. They don't have to be good repairs, just enough to get the appraisal higher for after the fire when the insurance pays out. When I reach an enormous, impossible sum, I look up, surprised. Sun sees this and she actually smiles, mistaking my revelation as a response to something in her lecture she is calling "tri-racial isolates."

Sun says, "We're writing our parental histories?" and I look at the others and they've got they're notebooks open and are jotting, so I ape them.

I start with my mom. Pauline Duffy, née Skaggs, who came from Chicago in the late sixties, running from an alcoholic father who only sobered up to preach on Sundays and to push a mop at the post office on weekday mornings. While he was drunk, he did some things too horrific to specify, to her, at night, and she had a hard time overcoming those memories, which is partly why my mom smoked a lot, which cut her time on earth to deal with said trauma. The name Skaggs came from his father, who showed up in Chicago running away from certain lynching in Acadia Parish, Louisiana, leaving behind the corpse of a drunken Cajun who overestimated his white privilege. I can't trace them all the way back to Africa, but I do know that his grandfather came from Haiti in the beginning of the nineteenth century—as to why he would chose to go from free Haiti to the Deep South before the end of U.S. slavery, I don't know. I do know that creoles can be hard-headed, so maybe that's reason enough. The rest of the family, my grandmother's side, came from Tennessee, where they worked for the same family they'd been enslaved by for another twenty years after the South lost its war. When my mom left my dad, money was tight. Bills went unpaid, and utilities routinely went out. Light's out. Water's out. Heat's out. When it was the water bill, we'd line buckets in the backyard to have rainwater to flush the toilets with. Sometimes it was the phone, which meant that when we got home my mom would spend all night talking to me, which was lovely. Sometimes it was the gas, which wasn't bad because we only used it to cook and that meant cereal for dinner. But usually it was the electric. We'd get back from work and school and it would be dark and stay dark. And my mom would get candles from the dresser drawer and ignite a cave of visibility for us. She was a skinny woman, skeletal in the shadows, but they were soft bones to me. Mornings there was no heat and too much cold, she would come downstairs and turn on the oven to take the chill out, leave its door open so you could see the hot air rippling as it escaped. And we would stay there at the counter, hands over the opening, Mom taking pauses to light her menthols on the burner. "Love keeps us warm," she said to me once, which was not literally true or particularly poetic but is lodged forever in my mind.

I tell this story to the group. I'm the first one to read out loud, too, and I volunteered. I stand up in front of the room and everything. And part of it is that just thinking about that time brought it back for me and I miss my mom. And I know that saying it out loud, sharing it, will amplify the feelings I just remembered. And it does. I can see the oval burns from the curling iron, on my mom's neck, and the smile that got so big you could see her missing teeth in the back. And I remember the lines of her gaunt face, how they raced down to her sharp cleft chin, how her neck was long and thin and she tried to wear high collars and shoulder pads to obscure that. I remember the smell of that horrible placenta treatment she used to put in her hair, sealed in a glass tube and broken with great care directly onto her roots. I remember the horror of visiting her in the hospital, skinnier every time. I remember that she told me to stop coming, that she didn't want me to see her like that. I remember, "I can't get out of this, but you can, so go." The relief of this reprieve would only be matched by the guilt of accepting it forever after. I tell them all this, telling far more than what I wrote down. There is a petty me in there that wants Sunita Habersham to know that I had been loved once. That I knew how to love once as well. But even that smallness is smothered under the details remembered. When I finish, I'm thinking that I actually like this Mulattopia, this campground of self-indulgence. That it isn't all bad, being forced to say: *This is me, this is me, this is me.*

"Okay, that was great. Do you want to continue?" Sunita Habersham asks me. She's wearing a Nehru collar today, on a knee-length, pale blue cotton shirt that's proudly wrinkled and wants everyone to know it doesn't go in for that ironing bullshit.

"That's all. Thank you. Thanks for listening," I tell her, and I go to sit down. But there is a hand on my shoulder, so I stop, look back at her.

"No, that's not all. You have two parents. They were an interracial couple. We are all here, because at some point, there was an interracial couple that conceived us. We all share that legacy. That's not something to be ashamed of. That's not even something to be proud of. It's just our reality, and we can't run from that and only claim one side. As long as we do, we'll be haunted by what we're denying. Your surname is Duffy," Sun tells me. And I think, Yes, yes it is. When I don't know what to say, Sun continues, "What about your father's side of the family?"

"They're Irish." I tell her. When this doesn't seem to satisfy her, I continue. "My dad just passed away. Very recently." This is a truth that's also meant to stop the conversation. Yet fails too.

"Where in Ireland are they from?" Sun asks, but it sounds like a demand.

"What?"

"How long have they been in America?"

"I don't know. When did they run out of potatoes?" I ask, utterly sincere.

"What were their occupations?" She keeps going.

"All I know about them is that they were really pasty," I tell her. Sun doesn't laugh. No one does, except One Drop, harder than the joke pushed him. Everyone just stares at him. Me too. He keeps going. I'm smiling, but I want him to stop. This is my family. This is my family, pasty but still mine. When he finally ends with, "Nice one, Holmes!" he holds a hand to slap and I do but I'd rather smack his face.

"Warren, you knew your father, correct? So give us something about him before you sit down. Something as detailed as your mother's anecdote."

The first thing I think of is that goddamn house. That rotting mansion. But I don't really think of that as my father, only as his European legacy, his aspiration for himself and for me if he really did imagine that I'd come back to inhabit it. So then I think about his car, and that's what I tell them. Craig Duffy drove a 1968 Volkswagen Beetle, black, that he bought in 1972 and never let die. I loved that car. It had such a distinctive lawn mower purr; when he'd pick me up from school I'd know he was coming from a block away. It used to break down all the time, but the thing had such simple mechanics. My dad would get used parts sent straight to the house, fix it out on the street, car radio blasting classical music in the middle of the hood to drown out the sounds of other cars blaring hip-hop as they drove by, which is hilarious now that it's not actively horrifying me.

I tell Sun that story, I tell the bleached tribe surrounding me, and feel the release. I usually don't like talking about my white side in public, in front of non-Caucasoids. I'm of the firm belief that, if I never bring up the fact that half my family is white, somehow the fact that I look white will be forgiven. But I look at these people, and among them there is nothing to apologize for. So I remember out loud the way the seats were so old that, where the cushions still remained, they'd oxidized into sand. I feel my dad again, even more than the first night back, and I want to sit down before the emotion it invokes overtakes me. But Sunita Habersham doesn't allow this. She sighs. Her breasts get bigger when she does but I barely notice it other than to notice it.

"That's good, but a car is a thing. Why do you think of that particular object in relation to your father, Warren?" Sun asks me. "It's just a car. What does that mean? To you?"

I know what I can give her about the silly little car, but I don't want to because I don't know if I can give it without losing something. But there's something there I want to lose and I don't trust myself to pull it out later. So I tell everyone in the room, including myself.

When my mom went into the hospital, I was eleven and they had been broken up for three years by then. My dad unexpectedly picked me up from school one day and that night I went to his house. Visits to my father were strictly every other weekend, so I knew something had changed, but there was no explanation. That night, we went to my mom's apartment, got more of my clothes and favorite toys. He had keys, somehow. At first, I thought this might be the beginning of a reconciliation, that I had them back together, that my mother would be joining us the next day. I wasn't actually that freaked out about it; they'd gone on a few dates after the separation, tried to see if they could get things started again, so this just seemed like another attempt. But the next night, she didn't arrive; my dad finally told me she was in the hospital. He made it sound like she was at a spa retreat. I wasn't worried; people stayed in the hospital on TV all the time, and usually they were smiling. That Saturday, we drove the Bug to Jefferson Hospital. Two months later, we drove the same little black car to her funeral. We drove that car to a boarding school in New Hampshire a week after the funeral, for me to have an interview and see if I liked it there. I was eleven. My mom had made him promise, with me in the hospital room, that he would make sure I got a good education. That this one thing, this one thing in his life, he couldn't be cheap on.

So there was this big fancy boarding school up in the granite state, like a six-hour drive first thing in the morning, but it was worth it. A campus of castle-like buildings surrounded by trees, right by a river. I liked it. It was like Narnia up there. When we left that night, my dad tried to make the trip back to Philly in one shot to avoid having to pay for a hotel room.

Thing is, we got hit with a rainstorm not long after passing into New York State. I mean, it was coming down hard, flooding, I could barely see to the next car. At points, we were creeping along so slow I watched the frogs jumping along the side of the road like they were planning an invasion. We didn't talk, we rarely did anyway, but at that moment we couldn't if we wanted to because the sound of water hitting the Bug's roof was so loud we would have had to scream. It was a horrible, horrible world out there, beating down on us. But I was protected inside that little can, with my dad at the wheel. Him staring forward, hands at twelve and two. I fell asleep a couple of times, the last time close to the end after the rain had stopped. We must have been in New Jersey by then. And I could hear my pop now. Craig Duffy was crying. Craig Duffy, freckles and mustache and bristles of brown stubble, was sniffing and crying, still staring ahead. He'd probably been crying all night, but I was laid out on the backseat and couldn't hear him.

We got back and we never spoke about boarding school again. I stayed with him, in Philly. I went to Greene Street Friends, walking distance right down Germantown Ave. My father raised me, every day of the year till I could run away on my own.

I tell this story, and now I'm crying. I'm crying about halfway in, but I don't stop because this is the moment. Come on out. Mostly I don't stop because I didn't cry when my father died and I know this is a shameful, shameful thing. So I cry for Craig Duffy now, and I deserve all the shame I feel for it. And even as I do I finally understand why he cried. Not just for my mother, not just for me, but for himself. Because he was scared he would fail me. And I know I don't just cry for Craig Duffy, even in this moment. I cry for myself as well. For the ways I have failed Tal, my daughter, and the ways I'm sure I will.

Sunita Habersham lets me sit down now.

But I see she's crying too. Just a little, but I catch the shine. And a small part of me, a part of me not crying, it sees her tears and thinks, Got her.

I leave class with a large, loosely defined assignment to do some research on my Irish heritage before the end of the week so I can complete the course, and a feeling of raw embarrassment at standing in front of a group of strangers and tearing up. There's a huge difference between "balling" and "bawling." Also, I leave with the need to get drunk or have a cigarette or find some other way to kill just enough of myself today that I can go on living. I want to go home. I want go home and come back for Tal after her student orientation session, but I have four hours to waste and I'm already too tired to drive back and forth twice. Strolling slowly and without much purpose, I come to the last trailer before the woods, where a group stands around waiting for something. I try to bum a loosey, but nobody smokes real analogue cigarettes anymore. Nobody smokes anywhere on earth. Humanity quit and abandoned me to negotiate the ghosts of my own nine-year addiction. I'm left, having exposed my habit to the crowd, standing awkwardly among them for another couple of minutes, straining at small talk until I see Tal literally skipping from the next building.

On Tal's ears are the biggest hollow gold bamboo earrings I have ever seen in my life. At least I hope they're hollow, because they nearly reach from her lobes to her shoulders, and with each hop their octagon shapes swing violently as if my daughter had attached gilded coat hangers to the sides of her head.

"Oh man, you got to see this. You got to. Come now. Come now or you'll miss it."

"What the hell is in your ears?"

"Class assignment. I'm on break till the student orientation. Come on, you got to see something, it is so cool. You got to see it now." Tal starts pulling on my hand and I grab hers tight and run with her for the chance to run with her.

We stop at an old RV lined up directly behind the trailer they have my art classroom set up in. Airstreams are supposed to be shiny silver and smooth and perfectly round like pods from a fifties alien-attack movie, but this one looks like the carcass of a mutant dung beetle. Its skin is dulled, oxidized, and covered with stickers, most of which are half-faded and peeling. Then I hear the moans inside. It's a woman. I look at Tal, who's giggling, and I think I must have this wrong. But I don't: there's a woman and she's moaning.

"Tal, no," I tell her and start to pull her away from this and sexuality in general, but Tal insists and pulls me again, this time to its door on the side and it's open.

In the dark small space inside, a women lies on a massage chair. Her head's captive to the hollow face cushion at the end of it. Over her stands a spider of a man, webbed veins lining his skinny arms. Literally webbed: there are blue lines inked between his bulbous blood vessels. He's shoving something into her back. When I hear the buzz I think it's some kind of spinal vibrator, but a moment reveals it as a tattooist's needle.

"You gotta see it," Tal tells me again, like this is not enough, then pulls me even closer, into the can with them, where the air reeks of burnt sage and rubbing alcohol.

"It's okay. I don't mind," comes from the lady getting her back split open. She's a heavy woman, and her exposed flesh looks as soft as a marshmallow. If you laid your head on that meat, you would be asleep before you sunk all your weight down.

"Check it, this is the biggest Sesa I've done yet. And I will be braggadocios: the dopest as well," the arachnid tells me.

"It better be because it hurts, Spider!" she yells back at him, letting the words and the pain out in mock whimpers.

"Tell her," Spider says to me, lifting a hand to beckon me even closer. "Tell her how amazing it looks. How original."

"Tons of people in the camp have this tattoo. It's like a biracial tramp stamp," Tal says to me. The lady getting written on just laughs harder, so hard Spider has to lift his needle up and nod at our good-natured appreciation of the spectacle of the fat on this lady's back rippling.

"Actually, it's the badge of mulatto pride. And everyone's is different. Look at this one, lovely right?"

I look at this lady's back. There is a big Star of David that goes from the tip of one shoulder blade to the other. Around it is a circle. If he drew it free hand he's a genius, because it looks like a perfect 360. Past the line of the circle, what looks like drops of water spin off of the shape.

"See? See how I incorporated her freckles into the rivets? None of them are covered up, instead they make it look as if the image is splashing off into her organic fiber. Really, you have to listen to the flesh for the art to work like this."

"You sound pretentious," the lady says, and she stops laughing. Her back stills.

"What is it?" I ask him. He's got a jeweler's visor on with a light attached and when he looks right at me all I can see above his nose is the glow.

"My greatest creation. First, I took the West African Adinkra symbol *Sesa Wo Suban,* which basically means 'Transform your character.'"

"Sounds like a diss." The guy's got no shirt on. The only thing covering his torso is nipple rings. Silver hoops, and a blue arachnid body painted right on the center of his chest like Spider-Man.

"Sure, it can be used as an insult, okay, but the meaning I like is that you have to change to become who you are. Perfect, right? So then, to further mulatto-tize it, I changed the classic Akan star to the star that corresponds with the wearer's European ethnic heritage, thereby bonding together their ethnic nature. In Doris's case, the Star of David. Which despite what it says about tattooing in the Torah, has been very popular around here."

"Leviticus 19:28 is very contentious," says Doris, and starts laughing again. She's high. There's no way she's not high.

"That's the one I'd get, Pops," Tal says, leaning in closer to get a better look at it.

"Not until you're eighteen. As your father I feel very strongly about Leviticus 19:28," I tell Tal. And I do, suddenly, though I'm not sure what Leviticus 19:28 says.

"Listen to your old man," Spider tells my daughter, then looks at me. "But Pops, you got to see them. Sixty-three different versions of this design walking around here. Linking us, you know? Spiritually. I once inked the entire *Leaves of Grass* on over a thousand people at Burning Man. One verse written on each person. That was dope. But the Sesa? It's, like, on another plane of consciousness. We're creating a people, man."

There's silence. There's no one talking because he was speaking to me, and I have nothing to say in response. Because I'm actually listening to him, and he terrifies me. The very idea, of creating a tribe where I would fully belong, of changing my definition to fit me instead of the other way around, terrifies me. It scares me because it's not crazy. It's attractive, logical even. It's just priced at abandoning my existing identity and entire worldview.

"G-d, you're pretentious," Doris breaks the pause, laughing.

8

THERE'S A FRIDAY NIGHT powwow the last workday before school starts, and all the grown mixies show up. They have a full bonfire burning and the faculty and staff stand around like a god might arise from the flames. Fresh tattoos shine on the oiled skin of the newly branded: I see six-pointed druid stars, Soviet-style red ones, two-dimensional Nordic sailor stars that look like shuriken, all encased by the Sesa's black swirls. There's even a Sesa with the star from *Star Trek*—presumably worn by Captain Kirk's lovechild. I recognize the intricately knotted Celtic pattern in several of the stars, and know if I got one, that would be it. And I also know I won't, though I think it does look good. I think things like: they are all connected, these people. I think these sorts of thoughts because I'm drunk. There are about seventy people here, and they're all shades from pink to dark ebony. Fat, thin, whatever. But they're all connected. Spider knew. How to draw a symbolic line between them, from calves to arms to shoulders to the meat on Doris's back. She walks by me and she's wearing a tank top and the skin back there is still red and painful but she looks so happy, as if the pain has been sensualized. And the fat of her midriff hangs out on the sides and again I am drunk and so don't deny its beauty. Doris knows. She knows that meat is her and she loves it and she loves everyone else here enough that she is willing to let them see all of who she is in this moment. I find that easy to envy. I want to live in a fantasy world too.

I get another drink, because they're free and my mouth has nothing else to do. I stand staring at the fire, wait for some sort of formal ceremony to begin, but it doesn't come. This is a school that doesn't feel like one even in the daytime, but as it gets dark its true nature unspools. It's less a school than a family reunion. I don't know these people, but I do, because they're like me. They don't look like me, they don't sound like me, but they know what it's like to be me. To be in the group while intangibly excluded from it. I know they know by how relieved they appear to be together. To be completely at home. Without question of identity or membership. I belong here, I catch myself thinking, and I'm too drunk to question or squash that joy. Spider comes over and, from my elation, my new admiration for his work pours.

"That's my thing. I haul my camper to all the festivals, tattoo conventions, you know, make my money. North April to July, south and out west till fall, hole up in Santa Fe the off months. Dude, I came to Mélange thinking I'd stay two weeks. And here I am, still. First time I've been still for a lunar cycle since 9/11. No lie."

"So you're one of the people who were here from the beginning?" I like Spider. He's a little guy, in height and weight, and I like little guys that don't immediately point out that I am a big guy. If he never mentions this, I could grow to love him. Surely I could.

"Yup. You know Marie Bella? The folk slash fusion singer? She's got a song that goes—" Spider sings a few bars I've never heard but I nod to get him to stop. "Well anyway, that's one of Roslyn's exes, she got bank; she funded it to start. A lot of her friends gave money. You wouldn't believe how many biracial cats get rich in the entertainment industry. It's like the family business for zebras."

"Yeah, but why squat in a park, in Philly?"

"We were already here." Spider shrugs. "Mutts take what we can get. I mean, it's a little crazy, right? This whole mulatto thing. But I say, enjoy it while it lasts, and keep a full tank of gas just in case."

I toast to him on that, and we both drink all the way down for good measure. A portion of his beer ends up on his T-shirt, but Spider doesn't seem to care. Without comment he takes it off and pitches it into the bonfire. It's a beautiful sight, the crackling flame, the way the glow reflects off his nipple rings.

I'm ready to leave, but my body isn't. I am allowed to drink one serving of alcohol every hour and still drive home. I can't mess up the ratio, not with the bike. Bad math is the single biggest killer of motorcycle riders. Based on my six drinks over the last two, I estimate I'll be drunk for four more hours, so I turn to head back to the art room. There's a pile of packing blankets in its closet, left over from the tables just brought in, and I plan to make a hobo cot with them. But then Roslyn walks by and squeezes my arm, pulls me around again.

"Don't go, sugar. Fun's about to begin." The words come in a hum of matriarchal authority strong enough to make my muscles stop and obey before I've even processed the words. I don't take it personally, the mothering is clearly for everyone, and as she releases me she's already hushing another attendee.

Roslyn stands before the fire and lifts her arms and we all fall silent and start forming a crowd around her. Immediately I am bored, and there's nothing to do with my hands but grab another beer. I drink that and think, You know what, I can get even drunker if I sleep behind my desk till dawn. Be fine and go back for a shower before Tal even wakes up. Then I remember the crackheads. Crackheads are a major responsibility. But there haven't been any more break-ins, and Tal has her cell anyway, so I grab another beer and lose count of how many I've drunk because it doesn't matter anymore.

Roslyn definitely gets her style from the black side of the family: the endless acknowledgments and appreciations. I get my introduction, which commends me for creating "the greatest biracial graphic novel of his generation," which could probably be qualified by "and the only," but I don't interrupt her, or bring up the fact that I just drew what some faceless dude instructed. I am tired. She keeps talking. I don't want a speech. I want a lullaby. I look at Roslyn, trying to think of a scenario where somehow, somehow it would be prudent of me to lay my head on her lap and take a nap as she kept humming.

"Congrats on completing your balance training. Sorry I made you cry."

Sunita Habersham is standing next to me.

"I made me cry," I tell her. I really did make myself. Not that I faked the tears, but I forced myself to feel the things I knew would bring them. I made a decision in the moment. I can do that without losing too much face because as guys go, I'm butch; tears are counterintuitive coming from a man like me. They make me interesting. And how upset can I be with losing control when I controlled the act?

"I cried, my first week. Everybody cries, everyone who gets it. Change hurts. You have to make the decision to undergo it, or it rips you apart. That's why Spider's tattoo is so cool. It's a reminder. To roll with it."

I want to make a joke about choosing change by marking yourself indelibly, but ask, "You get one?"

Sun hands me her wine cooler. I really look at it hard, because I didn't know they still made wine coolers. When she turns around, I think she's just going to walk away from me once again, but she lifts the white cotton of her shirttail and shows me the skin at the base of her spine. And there it is: a Sesa the size of my fist with an Anglo star right in the middle of it, beaming.

"Yeah. I went for the Kundalini chakra."

It's lovely. I say that out loud too, because the skirt she is wearing is long and heavy and the weight of the fabric has pulled it low, and my eyes are on her ink for a moment before the crack of her ass pulls them down. Everything there is so *plushable*. It's so plushable, it creates the word. Now the light of the bonfire flickers in that crack and makes it look deeper and living and I look away because it's wrong of me to even notice.

"I already had a tattoo there, since I was sixteen. It was Cutter from *ElfQuest*."

"Cutter the Wolfrider." I don't say this, I gasp it. She spins her head back, smiling at me.

"Nobody got the reference. They just thought it was a really shitty Hello Kitty. I was sixteen. My dad's girlfriend ratted me out when she saw it. Pissed him off, so it served its purpose. Spider did my Sesa over the top. Check out the woven design. It stands for the interconnectivity of—" what I will never know, because even if Sun finishes her sentence, I don't hear words. I just hear a pop and then the world goes mute and I'm on the ground because One Drop has gone Viking and punched me in my cheekbone.

I don't black out. I want to, want to just give the fuck up and fade to black and let someone else carry my body as my head fills with enough blood to completely reverse my center of gravity. But I keep my eyes open. And when hands come at me, I grab them, get back into a standing position. And I smile. I smile as big as I can without moving my jaw because I don't know yet that it isn't broken. I get that smile out though. I remember to do that, because it's the only way to fight the humiliation of getting dropped by a sucker punch, at least until you find out who's hit you.

I'm seated in the backseat of a minivan, its door slid open, and have already been given water and the repeated instruction not to go to sleep tonight in case of concussion. I can barely stay awake as it is. I don't even know why he did it, until Roslyn walks over with One Drop, their hands clasped together, and tells me that he has something to say to me.

"I'm sorry, bro. I shouldn't have punched you in your head." That's it. I wait for more to come, but he just buries his chin in his chest, not even meeting eyes with me. Roslyn looks up at the giant, and he sees this. He holds out his hand to me. I stare at it for a moment, realize everyone gathering is staring at me, so take it.

"Sorry I beat you down, Holmes. It's not you, it's me. I got issues. That was not copacetic. My bad. We cool now?" He reeks of Phillie Blunts and Pink lotion. And maybe the words work or maybe it's just that I want him to free me from the prison of his Icelandic death grip but I tell him, "We cool."

"You can be such an asshole," Sunita Habersham yells, and I know I can be, but she's talking to One Drop. Me, she's pulling away, across the parking lot to a station wagon, which is another thing I didn't know they made anymore.

Spider's laid out in the backseat with his legs hanging out the door. The whole cab smells like weed.

"I want, like, my own zonkey, man."

"A what?"

"Zonkey . . . half zebra, half donkey"—Spider's eyes are closed, even though his mouth is open—"like the most gangsta mulatto beast of all time . . ." but then he drifts off. I roll the windows down. The wind is loud as Sunita drives back down through Mt. Airy into Germantown and that's fine because aside from my directions nobody says anything, not until Spider wakes momentarily to offer "Woah. You live in the straight up hood, man. That's so cool," before rolling over, presumably drifting off into the zonkey dream from which we interrupted him.

In front of Loudin, nobody's out on the street, and the lights are off in the mansion, which means Tal had enough sense to go to sleep without me. When the car stops, Sun still doesn't say anything. Her hands are on the wheel, and the bracelets that line her arms jingle for seconds after she brakes. She looks ahead, as if she doesn't want the next thing to happen, whatever it is, that she'd rather the night keep going, even though it's been going badly for a while now. The tension of the moment seems to be making her angry.

My face is throbbing. I can count my heartbeat with the pulses of pain, and now that the adrenaline has worn off and taken most of the alcohol with it, my face hurts, and I think I deserve some understanding with the suffering.

"Are you sleeping with that WASPafarian nutjob?"

"Don't slut shame me. It's none of your business." Sun spins her head to stare me down and seems relieved to find a target for her anger. I whip my head right back at her, pointing at the side of it where the bastard hit me. I don't know what it looks like; I can't bring myself to look at it in the rearview mirror, but it feels like it has attained the size and texture of pumpkin. It must look bad, because Sun pauses a moment.

"Look, I'm real sorry about what happened. So yeah, we used to have a casual thing, is that what you needed to hear? It's really none of your business. Can you go to bed now or do you need to hear more? He's hung like a tree, does that help? Really, a big brown tree—in fact, it's actually the darkest part of his body. Is that good enough?"

"Great. I was punched by Thor Odin-Cock."

Sun's about to say something, but it trips over her getting the joke. "I just saw that, as drawn by Jack Kirby, in my head. *Stan Lee Presents: The Adventures of Thor Odin-Cock,*" she says then is lost in laughter and I go with her because I want the sound to keep coming. The sound, it takes a while to work out of our systems, and then finally it does. And there are sighs. And then quiet. Then Spider starts snoring in the back and we lose it again.

"Yeah. Not exactly a great shining moment in my life. It's been a long year up there. One Drop's not bad. Just damaged. Grew up on army bases, looking like he does with a mom everyone always thought was his nanny. All his siblings came out darker than him. A Dutch dad who's married four other black women since. How could he not be a little crazy? Mélange started as a retreat. You can't retreat unless there's something to run from."

"So what are you running from?" I ask her. Sunita thinks about it, and for a few seconds, it looks like she's going to tell me. That there's a story to tell, something shapely enough to be packaged into a synopsis.

"Guys who ask too many questions." And then all the humor is gone. Like it was never there. So I get out of the car.

On the street, I watch Sun pull around, prepared to drive back the other way. There's still no one out here, but I want to make sure she gets a least as far as my line of vision unmolested. She doesn't care that she's in the hood. She's comfortable. She's comfortable in the hood, she's comfortable in the woods. I'm jealous of that but it still makes me nervous, so I yell for her to roll up her windows till she's out of Germantown. When Sun's grille is pointed in the right direction, she stops her car on the other side of the street and yells back at me.

"You said your dad, he never threw out anything, right?"

"Right," I yell back. I'm waiting for her to give me my platitudes now. Something like, *And he never threw you out either.*

"So what the hell happened to it?" she asks. I don't know what she's talking about. I keep listening, waiting for her to make sense.

"Your dad's car? You said he never threw anything away."

When she drives off, I get the gate open, but it takes a minute because my hands are shaking. Instead of heading straight for the mansion, I follow the dirt path that goes alongside the property to the garage. Its windows are broken and boarded; dirt sticks to the surface of the doors as if they haven't been opened in decades; but I still can't believe I hadn't thought to do this before. There's a lock, a padlock. I have my father's keychain looped into my own. I take it out and try a few of the keys on it and start to consider the possibility that I'll have to kick the glass out of a windowpane to get in, but then a key fits and turns. I pull off the lock and the garage door opens out. I can feel the dust filling my nostrils but through it I can already smell my daddy's car. I can feel what it was like to ride on the cobblestones of Germantown Avenue with its spring suspension, what it was like when I fell asleep in there and he would pick me up and carry me to bed inside.

I get the garage door up all the way and there it is. The 1968 black Volkswagen Beetle. And there are the two crackheads, sitting inside. Their eyes ghostly and wide and frozen as they stare at me from its front seats.

My eyes are even wider.

• • •

I slam the garage door down hard, fast, quick, like the scream that shoots out of my mouth. I slam it down like the force will fuse it shut again, lock it and the vision away from me. I slam it so hard I fall backward to the ground, but I don't care about that because I can crawl away without taking my eyes off the door if they come for me. I get a good fifteen feet away, and the wood's still shaking. I should get up, but if I do I won't be able to stare as hard at that garage door and part of me is certain that's the only thing sealing the barrier. And then the wood stops. It's stopped shaking. And it's silent. And maybe this whole thing is a mistake, the vision a weird reflection of my own face. That when I stop breathing like this, it will return to normal. But the door springs up again before that can happen.

My dad's black Beetle flies toward me.

I roll over. I roll and roll. Everything is spinning. I can feel the air, the wind of it as it passes. The Beetle's still going. The Beetle shoots down the hill. That's my father's car. They're taking my father's goddamn car. I push to my knees and then to my feet to chase after it before they can get the gate open, before they take him away from me. But they don't stop at the gate. They're going to ram into it.

The gate's iron clasp is rusted shut. The thick chain lock sealing it just adds to the message of closure. The Beetle's got a good speed going by the time it gets to the entryway, aiming for the middle. I hear the crash, see broken glass powder out in the streetlight. The whole length of the fence surrounding the property shakes in response, angry at moving after a century of reliable immobility.

I stop running toward them, because I'm pretty sure I am now the owner of a his and her set of dead crackheads. I keep standing where I am. I keep waiting for the door to open. Now I just want to see them. I want to see their faces. I want them to see my face. I want them to know I'm standing now. I stare at those car doors. Just keep staring. Then I see a man standing fifty yards away, but over to my right, past the house on the other end of the lawn, who stares back at me.

I stand, his mirror, across the expanse of lawn. How he got all the way over there, I don't know, I have no idea, none. But I stare back at him. I insist to myself that I'm not scared anymore. I have my cell in my hand now, gripped hard enough to break the glass, and it has magical powers that transmit sounds and visions into space. I stand and I don't move because Tal is in the house, and I have something to stand for. I see the white woman. She also stands, twenty yards to his side. Just as still. Just as silent. If she was there before I don't know because she's just a dirty rumor in my peripheral vision. But he keeps standing there, staring at me. It's too dark to see his face, to see much of anything but his dark bare chest and pants. He's standing there, arms at his sides, chest out. So still. Standing there like he is waiting for me to state my intent. To tell him why I'm on his land. Tell him what kind of decent man disturbs the peace at this hour. Frozen in that inquiry.

"What the fuck?"

Tal's voice. I jump. I put my fists out at the sound of her voice, almost as startling as the car crashing. When I finally see her face, dimly through the screened door on the porch, both my fists are aimed in her direction.

"What the hell was that?" Tal asks.

"Do you see people?" I have to know. But she doesn't look at the lawn. She looks at me.

"You are so wasted," Tal responds, then shuts the window back on me. It thunders on impact and I hear it echo, off the rotting porch, down the hill, bouncing to the row houses across the street, then coming back again.

I look back at the guy. I look back at the woman. Both gone. Both nothing.

9

AT THE ENTRANCE, the Bug sits crumpled and indignant. One of my keys goes to the chain sealing the driveway's padlock, and I take the chains off so I can yank the twisted metal off its grille. I'm not even scared anymore. Just tired. If I wasn't, I would take Tal and we would leave this house right now. Run. That's what we should be doing. Running. This is what I really have to teach her. You can even run away from yourself—eventually, yourself catches up to you, but then you just run once more.

This house is going to burn because I refuse to be trapped inside its crumbling walls. I'm not going to wait years for this place to sell. I'm not going to rent it, and be haunted by tenant complaints every time something breaks, be indebted to it for life. I am not my past. I am not my hometown. I don't want any crackheads in my future. I'm not going to be stuck back in Philly for the rest of my life, back in Germantown, dragged down by everything I've worked so hard to be free from. More important: Tal is not either. It simply cannot happen. There will be fire.

After I call the cops I take the coffee can of dead matches and cigar butts off the porch, remove the cigar butts, then I walk to the side of the house and dump the remains there. I don't want to go near the garage because of the crackhead infestation, but I risk it and it's okay, no one's there. I dump the rest of the butts and matches inside the garage, in a corner, kick them around a bit for a more natural look. Evidence. When I get back in, I make coffee while we wait for the police.

The crackheads haven't stolen anything from me. No, they've given me the gift of a documented incident to later prove probable cause. Crackheads destroy things. First, their lives, obviously. And then their families. But they also destroy houses. They light fires and they have poor judgment; both things are required if you're going to be a crackhead. They make houses burn down. They're not as thorough as meth heads, who have the benefit of their exploding labs, but crackheads have left a respectable number of ruined buildings in their wake. *A crackhead did it* is a reasonable cause of destruction on any forensic report. A history of crackhead infestation is a legitimate explanation for loss of property. It's all so exciting I catch myself whistling.

"Are you still drunk?" Tal's wide awake, standing in the kitchen doorway, her hair hidden under the wrap of a pink scarf.

"What? What kind of thing is that to say to someone? To someone who's your father?" When Tal's quiet in response, and stands there till I feel my guilt starting to answer for her, I say, "I'm not drunk, okay? Anymore."

"You're not high, are you?"

"Jesus, Tal!"

"It's just, you were a mess last night. And now you're, like, entirely too upbeat for seven o'clock, Saturday morning. You're, like, serial-killer upbeat. It's freaking me out. Please stop."

"I'm just looking on the bright side. Of things." In response to that, Tal keeps staring at me. I go back to putting the milk away. Then drinking what I'd poured into a glass. Tal keeps watching, motionless, without comment.

"I need things. And I'm going to tell you what they are."

I put down the glass, say, "Okay. Hit me."

"I need quiet. At night. Late at night. After midnight."

"That's totally understandable. I do too."

"And no drinking. Not like never, but not like, on the regular. I mean, wine, that's okay, but no heavy stuff. Of any kind. I'm done with that. With how it was with my mom, even with Irv. Not doing that again."

"I don't drink often," I lie. "I usually don't get drunk," I clarify, which is closer to the truth.

"It just turns people into assholes."

"Glad you don't think I'm already an asshole," I tell Tal. Her response is just to continue staring at me, the process judgment visible in her eyes.

"Good," Tal says, and keeps standing there. I take another drink of milk. I don't know what else to say. I don't know what her life has been like. I know that I wish I had been in it, but I don't know where she was all that time, really. I know what it is like to lose a mom, but not to lose her mom, and not the way she did.

Tal steps forward, hand outstretched. We shake. And it's not enough; it shouldn't be enough. So I pull her in, wrap my arms around her. After a moment, her arms lift up and hold my back. I've never held my daughter this long before, and it's only a few seconds. The thought makes me grip tighter.

Before Tal can pull away, I say, "I'm going to have to go out, get some things this afternoon. But I'll be back to take you to dance practice, okay? I'll give you a ride to campus."

"Oh God, not on the bike. I can't sit for an hour after I get off that thing."

"Don't worry, I've got a car now."

"That car?" Tal says, and releases me to point out the window, where the Constables of the Police of the City of Philadelphia are hooking up their tow.

I don't call George. I call Tosha. I ask Tosha to talk to George, tell her that they're trying to impound my dad's car just because of an overdue inspection, a missing registration, and twenty-seven unpaid parking tickets dating back to 1982. Sirleaf Day's number leads to a recording of him saying "Hello?" followed by a three second pause. I fall for it, talk into the space, then hear the beep. The joke is old, but young compared to him. Into his voice mail I beg him to get over here before I'm stuck on a bench at the 14th Police District, staring at a linoleum floor. All I get in response is a beep, which is more than the dead expression I get trying to explain that my dad is deceased to the cops. The officers seem pretty intent on having me take "a trip" with them to "sort everything out" until George pulls up.

He's wearing a fedora and a raincoat. He's been a detective for four years and yet he's still playing at it. The awkward part about talking to George is that our friendship is based entirely on the fact that, despite my closeness with Tosha in those younger years, I never tried to seduce the girlfriend who became his wife. What George and I have is not even a real friendship, more of an established truce.

"Sins of the father," he says, and he laughs at me. It's the first smile he's broken since the uniformed guys pulled away. "Man, you got a $3,439 bill on a car that hasn't had legal tags for two years."

"Well, it runs. It did last night. Or rolled, at least."

"It won't again if you don't pay in ninety days."

"Yeah, well, we all got our problems." I try to shrug this one off. He laughs again. Harder this time, longer. Sighs at the end of it. "So Tosha told you."

"She told me. Sorry man."

"You are sorry, but not as sorry as my ass. My life is all kinds of fucked the hell up."

He slaps his hand on my back as we walk up the hill to the garage. It's a relatively weak tap, like he knows not to push me too far right now. "What else did she tell you? I mean, what specifically?" he asks.

"She said you moved out. That you come in the mornings so the kids don't know. She thinks you met someone else. She thinks," I start to say, and then I pause.

"You want me to help you? You got to help me. Just tell me what's going on so I can fix it."

"She thinks you might be fucking some white dude."

"'Some white dude?' She thinks I'm gay? What the hell?"

"Hey, I don't know what's—"

"You don't know because it's none of your business. Man, just show me what you got to show me."

I open the garage door. I bring him over to the corner to look at the cigarette ashes, but he's sighing, barely paying attention. I stand on the perimeter of my imaginary crime scene and point to them, like on cop shows. I give him my theory: that the crackheads moved in when my dad was gone. Maybe they were here when he was sick, but he couldn't do anything about it. "And they smoke too. By this old, wooden house. That's really dangerous, you know? I don't want there to be a fire," I tell him, and say it louder to break him out of his distraction. I try to sound as somber as possible on the *f*-word. *Fire.* Glorious fire. All-changing fire, destroyer of worlds, lifeblood of the phoenix, god of renewal. All that.

"Of course they smoke. They're crackheads. It's not like they're shoving rocks up their noses," and with that, George pulls his own cigarette out, pats himself for a lighter. He turns, barely even looks at the evidence I have so generously provided.

"That's some shit, that I'm gay. Man, I *wish* I was gay. I wish I got a pass like that. I'm the opposite of gay: I'm not happy. I've been unhappy for a lot of years now; she knows that. And I know—and trust me I know this—I got no no good reason to be unhappy. I got a beautiful wife, beautiful kids, beautiful house and all that, but I'm unhappy. That's the fucked up thing. If I was gay, I could point to that and say, 'Sorry, I fucked up. Turns out I'm gay,' and no one would be mad at me. Instead I'm unhappy with the perfect life and everybody hates me."

He's right about this: I hate him right now. That could have been me in his house. Those could have been my kids, even the ugly one. He took that. George is a good cop, because he can read minds. He turns to me and says, "Don't get no ideas. She ain't single."

I know she isn't single. I knew when I went to Wales, got drunk every night, then eventually married a woman who would give me her own well-earned "I'm not happy" speech. He gave his wife kids and yet fared no better. You start with "I love you" and then you build everything on those three words, but then it only takes those three other words to strip it all down. "I'm not happy," and then the misery goes from the speaker to the recipient. Speaking it wasn't the end to unhappiness, it was the transfer of it.

"Look, man. That's between you and her. I'm sorry this is happening, but you're right, it's none of my business. So . . . what do I do about the crackhead thing?"

"You move, nigga."

"That's not an option."

"You know how to leave town. Just do it again."

"I can't fucking move, George. I'm broke. I got to spend all the money getting this place good enough to sell. I got a seventeen-year-old girl in here to protect and this place is infested with crackheads. So now what?"

"Warren, you're on the border between Germantown and North Philly. You're dealing with the side effects of centuries of economic and social disenfranchisement. So yeah, there are drug addicts here. You know this. It's like complaining there are chipmunks in the woods. Don't get a gun. You'll miss and wound them and then they'll sue you and then you're really screwed. Just get a security system. Protect yourself, protect your daughter. Buy a Taser if you want—but don't get a gun unless you're willing to kill somebody, and trust me, you're not. Head to a security store. Matter of fact, have Tosha help you, because that woman knows all about that shit. I know she knows all about that shit. You can tell her I told you, that I know, that she knows, all about that shit."

"You know she loves you," I tell him. It seems like the right thing to do. Not for him, but for me, because he's starting to piss me off and Tosha is my true friend and I like the way he flinches when I say it. I know Tosha does, though. I'm sure no matter how bad he's done her over the years, she still does, and would take him back. I say it also because I want someone to say that to Becks every time I come up in a conversation. *I know he still loves you.* And I want it to hurt when she hears it, too.

"I know she loves me. And I love her. But saying that shit is easy and doing it, working on it year in and out, keeping it alive when it feels like it's slowly killing you, that's fucking hard. I'm tired, bro."

George sniffles that broad nose and walks off down the hill toward his car. He's bald, but shaves it so you can't tell, and there are enough brown men still doing that for style that he gets away with it. He puts his fedora back on, and between that and the raincoat he probably never has to pull the badge to prove he's a detective. Still, it doesn't look like a costume on him. It just looks like detectives must face some sorts of rainstorms they haven't told the rest of the world about. When George turns around to stop and look at me, he's got a dramatic strut going too. All he's missing is a synthesizer soundtrack and he'd be a living embodiment of the investigators we watched on prime-time television in our childhoods.

"*'Are you gay?'*" he repeats, yelling to me over his shoulder. And then he laughs again, pointing at me like he's caught the playful prank I was setting. "Man, I'd suck a thousand dicks if I could get away with that excuse."

With Tosha's credit card, I buy sixteen closed-circuit video cameras with night-vision and thermal detection, all of which feed wirelessly to an external hard drive connected to my laptop. I get the cheapest cameras I can because I want low-quality images. I want blurry faces and dark shapes. I don't want proof that any specific crackhead is haunting my house, I want proof of a general, unknowable infection, something to show the insurance company later without making some pathetic wretch's life even worse. I buy Digital Night Vision Binocular Goggles, 1x24 zoom, with head straps and a carrying case. I buy a M26c Taser gun with laser targeting, and a baseball bat—Triton Senior League model SL12T aluminum composite—the only sporting equipment in the store. Then I buy two more bats, one for each door in the house, another for upstairs.

"So he says I know surveillance? Damn right I know surveillance. Glad he knows I know surveillance," Tosha says a little too loud. She's been talking too loud since she picked me up, arriving a few minutes after George drove away. Tosha laughs and the sound is red, bitter, dry. It scares the clerk behind the counter and he motions to go help another customer, but she won't let him leave either.

"Can we get a GPS tracker? A little one. Real little. Hardly noticeable. Something like that." Tosha points to the one she likes. It's as small as a cigarette lighter. To me she says, "Oh I know all about George. I know all his secrets now."

"You still think he's screwing some dude?"

"Come on," she tells me, brushing off her earlier theory. "The only man that bastard loves is himself. This isn't about another man. It's even worse. It's a goddamn white woman." The white guy on the other side of the counter pretends he didn't hear that, keeps his expression passive and servile. We have truly arrived in a new age.

Already, the boxes of equipment are piled up as if we're in the early stages of invading a rogue state. Already, we have twice what I'd budgeted.

"Don't worry about it, just pay me back when you can. Unless they rob you blind first." Tosha is inspecting the GPS device, turning it in her hands. "This tracker's too big; I need a smaller one."

"They didn't take my car. They even left the keys in the glove compartment. I'm not really worried about theft, I'm worried about them getting in and getting near Tal. I don't need a tracker."

"It's not for you. It's for the white bitch."

I don't know if the "white bitch" is really white. I mean, even through the bookstore window I can see that the blond is bleached and she's got a tan that looks like it doesn't go away in the winter.

"I got to get back to the house. I got the roofers coming," I whisper to Tosha from the passenger seat. This gets her to drop the binoculars she's been staring through since we parked. They're not like the high-powered, professional scopes we were just looking at in the spy shop. These are pink, plastic, and have a purple strap that dangles loosely in front of Tosha's face as she peers through them. It almost makes what we're doing seem light, trivial, instead of wrong and creepy and probably illegal.

"Let me get this right, it's a whole big compound, with an education program and all, just for half-black people? In the park, with the bugs? What the hell is the point of that? All that just to run away from being black?"

"They're not trying to run away from blackness. Some of them are even learning to run to it. They're just mixed people trying to be themselves."

"They're not *mixed,*" she snaps back, the word wet and viral. "I'm black. You're black. African American, Bilalian, Negro, Colored folk, blackity-black, black. Those Oreos up there, they're black too, although I'm sure they'd cry if you told them. We're all mixed with something, no one is pure. Who cares about percentages?"

"Yeah, but it's not about genes, DNA. It's about being able to express all of who you are culturally. I mean, they would say that. That if you grew up connected to parents of two races, just saying, 'I'm black,' or whatever, negates part of who you are, culturally. As a person."

"They realize they're in America, right? You could dress in just kente and only eat fufu and you still wouldn't balance out the whiteness. We speak English. We wear European clothes. Really, all *that's* not enough white for them?"

"I'm telling you, they're not trying to be white."

"Because they can't. And they think they're better than black people."

"How is acknowledging that they're not just black acting superior?"

"They're trying to abandon the community. They're trying to cut black America loose, so they can live some post-racial fantasy. That shit is dangerous. It weakens us, as a people."

"They're just trying to be themselves."

"Okay, so you're mixed now? Then say it," she demands.

"I'm mixed."

"No." She looks over at me, studies. "Say you're not black."

"I am not . . ." going to say that. I can't. I even try for a second, and I can't. I can't bring myself. It's too damn scary. It's up is down and down is up and nothing is right. Just the thought of it. It brings the enormity of this whole line of reasoning to my mouth to clog there. "I could have used this, you know?" I do manage. "When I grew up. Having the world see me as what I was and not as what I wasn't. My daughter could use that," and that's enough to get Tosha to wag her head and raise the binoculars back to her eyes and focus outside the car once more.

"There she is. That fucking cracker whore," Tosha says, and there are two words I've never heard her say before. But I look at the woman in the bookstore window. She doesn't look like a whore, but I'm not sure what a whore is. I've met several sex workers in social settings—lovely people on average. When I think of the word *whore,* I think of a cancerous leach of human dignity, but that woman in there doesn't give off that vibe. She isn't even a seductress. She's dressed like any other young professional in work attire, a contradictory mix of attractive and uninviting. Her face, though, is really beautiful. She looks like someone you could see a movie with then fall in love with after the conversation it sparks.

"I don't understand how he could do this. I keep looking at this bitch—I've been here before, okay? I've seen them holding hands, kissing, this shit is real—and I don't know how that bastard could do this to me. Explain that to me."

I see the white girl and I think, George couldn't say no. That's what I think. He couldn't say "No" to coffee, then "No" to a beer, then "No" when their legs brushed under the table, then "No" to a kiss, then "No" to her bed, then "Yes" to never being with her again. And now his life is all fucked up. It seemed pretty simple. He didn't do it to Tosha. He didn't even do it to this white woman. He did it to himself. The clarity of other people's lives.

"I bet she has irritable bowel syndrome," I tell Tosha. "IBS: that's what they call it. I bet she has to shit every twenty minutes, and then when it comes out it's scorching stomach fluid and she sits on the toilet making sounds like a howler monkey."

"Do you think so?" Tosha pulls her binoculars back out of her purse, adjusts the lens. "How can you tell?" I'm about to tell her I was just joking, but then she says, "I can see it. IBS. I can totally see that now."

I look at Tosha. Her hair is straightened but matted, sealed together on the left side that she surely sleeps on. Tosha considers herself a proud black woman. Proud black women take excellent care of their hair. That's what they do. I want to go away. I want to go away and let her work this all out and then come back when it's all fixed and we can casually laugh about it from a distance. But I also want to be a man who doesn't go away. Not from his friends, family, self.

"I want you to go in there. I want you to go in there, and talk to that bitch, and when she's not looking, I want you to drop this GPS in her pocketbook. Got it?" She holds it up. It really is small. A third of a finger, small. Peter Parker *spider-tracers* tiny.

"That's a bad idea. Tosha, why do I even have to say something like this out loud?" Tosha doesn't respond because we both know the answer. I have to say this out loud because her husband couldn't keep his penis in its proper container. "I got a better idea. Let's call Sirleaf. Just invite him over for lunch, I'll come too. We can casually figure out what your rights are. He does divorces. He's done several of his own."

"Maybe. If I see him at the gym, maybe I'll ask," she says quickly, looking away, then turns to me and follows with the more focused "You married a white woman. Let's talk about that."

"What?"

"Yeah. What were you thinking?" Tosha asks me.

"I was just thinking, 'I'm marrying Becks. I'm moving on with my life.' "

" 'Moving on'? Don't you mean, running away?"

"No, just moving on." *Past you,* I don't say. "Trust me, I never felt blacker than on the streets of Swansea, Wales." *Or in my own bed with her,* I will not say either.

"I'm serious, wasn't that part of it? You fleeing to Europe and into the arms of a white woman? The abandonment of blackness. Abandoning black women. Did it have to do with your mom?"

"No! Look, people see mixed couples, they project their own issues onto them. Race traitors. Progressive heroes. Whatever. I saw people do this with my parents' marriage, and with mine. Me being with Becks had nothing to do with my mom, okay? It wasn't about abandoning black women." It was about Tosha abandoning me, but I can't say this. I can't say this and get out of the car with our friendship fully intact. It's old, it's over, it doesn't matter anymore. And Tosha already knows, I'm sure. She knows the "why" and she knows my hesitation.

"But when you flee, someone's getting left behind. The mixed thing, the white woman thing, they're both about leaving black people behind. That's the cost of your freedom."

"I'm never going to leave you behind," I assure her, although I already did once.

"Then we should start seeing each other. I'm basically single now." Her mode switched, Tosha looks through her binoculars again, target reacquired.

"Right." The me from a decade ago, he wanted so badly to hear those words. Where is he now? Can I forward his mail?

"No, listen: you and me, we should hook up." Tosha says this, but she's not even looking at me. She's looking through her binoculars again, and what she sees is the source of all her sorrows. It's amazing that someone can proposition you with no discernible desire. It's not till I decline that Tosha turns to look at me. "No, really, I'm fine with it. It would serve that fucker right. Just drop off the GPS in the white bitch's pocketbook first, then we can go do it before I pick up the kids from Girl Scouts."

"Jesus, don't do that. Don't try to bribe me with sex." I unbuckle the seat belt, put my hand on the door handle, then stop. "You don't need to track her. George's gone. You already know he's with her.

What can be gained by finding out where and when she walks down the street?"

"I'm not crazy, Warren. This isn't crazy. Crazy is letting your world be destroyed without fighting back," she tells me, pulling on a baseball cap. After she finds shades in the glove compartment, Tosha puts them on as she leaves the car to do the deed herself.

10

SPIDER IS GOING to teach history. He's talking lesson plans, target goals, lab days. I can't get over it. I keep waiting for the freaky little man to call an end to the joke and go back to his roving tattoo parlor, but he's serious.

"Oh no, man. I did the coursework for the PhD in history, but couldn't get into the whole, you know, dissertation thing. But I got a master's in gender studies, philosophy. One in French."

"Damn, dude! How old are you?" It's impossible to tell. He has the face of an early teen, but one that's been weathered by misfortune.

"Only took, like, ten years, give or take. I had a lot of early incarnations before I constructed my current form."

A kid comes in the room, about ten years old and round with fat he'd better pray burns off him with puberty. After waiting for Spider to sign a form, the boy says, "Thanks, Mr. Bezovski," and this is the first time I've heard Spider's last name; I'm certain he's got to be some kind of gypsy. We'll be team teaching together, all term, which is fine because it means I don't have to come up with my own lesson plans. I just have to get my students to draw. If I focus on arriving at the appropriate time, I'm pretty sure I can pull this off.

Spider's course packet sits on the desk. He's got his feet up there too, and he pushes the bound pages my way with a combination of bare ashy heel and flip-flop sole. There's a title on the front cover, "Tri-Racial Isolates."

"We doing chemistry?" I ask him.

"Tri: meaning three. Racial: meaning racial. Isolates: meaning isolated. *Tri-racial isolates*. It's the term for historic mixed-race communities in America. Whole communities where people were African and European and Indian too."

"Dude, that's every black American community."

"Yeah, but these mixed groups, they retained all of their cultural identities, because they were isolated. The same one-drop race rule of solely being black didn't apply. Places like this, they were all over the country."

"So I just have to get the groups to draw comic books about all this?" I open the packet, fan through the pages. Black-and-white photos head the section headings, each one with a different yet equally odd tribal name. "I'd probably be better at teaching them to draw muscle-bound freaks in capes, but hey, you're the boss."

"Oh man, I'm so not the boss. We're on Lenape land; I'd love to be teaching them about that. Or about the eighteenth-century German mystics that came to this forest after them. We're right here, standing on history, it's a shame not to bend down and dig in. But Roslyn commands and I am but a humble servant who depends on her generous health-insurance benefits."

The Brass Ankles was a tribe in South Carolina, formed in the eighteenth century that lasted all the way up into the modern era, in ethnic identification if not actual communal form. A mix of blacks and whites marrying into the Wassamasaw Tribe. Like many of the known tri-racial groups, such as the Jackson Whites of upstate New York, or the

Beaver Creek Indians, the group itself saw the classification it was legally under, "mulatto," as an invalid attempt by the white government to force them into the black/white binary caste system, and thereby further deny them their rights. This is what the first page says. It is a fascinating story, raising several interesting questions about the nature of identity and the history of our country, none of which will be answered because the group assigned to this project is in fourth grade. They'll be led by the chubby boy who'd stopped through Spider's class earlier, a young lad with the unfortunate name of Shields Steele. Actually, it was a heroic moniker, but ill fitting for a slump-shouldered boy who can't get through his introduction to the class without invading his naval cavity with his index finger.

Turns out Redbones are an actual group, and not just a word brothers yell out of car windows at light-skinned women. It's the name for a cluster of mixed-race Afro-Indian-Europeans living between the Sabine River in western Louisiana and East Texas. Unlike the Creoles, also from Louisiana, the Redbones are not exclusively French in their European ancestry, and reflect more of a mix of white cultures. The student group choosing to explore the Redbone experience is headed by a woman as tall as I am, yet clearly no more than fourteen years in age. Her voice is changing, clanging between high and low like a bicycle failing to shift gears. She screams, "Ho, Redbones, ho!" and her much smaller compatriots slap her outstretched hands. Spider explains to the girl, a miss Jackie McDuffy, that the word *Redbone* was also a slur, from the mistaken notion that the people were so light, you could see their blood flowing under their skin. "That's stupid. Blood is blue under the skin," Jackie informs Spider. Another child, the one who does the best job of standing even close to reaching Jackie's armpit, leans in pointing to Spider's face and yells, "You got served!"

I've just remembered I hate children. Only becoming a father to my own could have caused that amnesia. That fact is so clear now, no longer hidden in my mind. I told Becks this several times, every time she announced the alarm of her biological clock. And I just agreed to spend three hours a day, four days a week, with several of them. Before

I can digest this fully, I am hit in the face with the Melungeons. The ethnicity itself is no bother—one of the largest and vaguest clusters of mulattoes, stretching from Virginia out beyond into the Appalachians—but because of the complexity of this tribe it will be given to the oldest teens so that each may decipher an element of their story in comic-book form. Teenagers are difficult, and I have no desire to take more of them into my daily life, but even that is not what disturbs me. It's that leading their group is Kimet. The one who also led us here to Mélange. Kimet, Principal Kamau's child. He waves. He waits for recognition. He realizes when I just stand in front of the class staring at him and his silly brass dreadlocks, that I know who he is exactly. He's a spy. He's been sent to monitor the race traitors, to report back to his father. Or to the NAACP. Eventually, there'll be trials. That makes sense for only as long as it takes to think it, then my paranoia recedes. It's just a teenage boy again.

After class, I go to his desk as he's packing. "Kimet. How did you manage to—"

"My mom got custody," he says before I can finish even the first sentence of my inquiry. His response is preprepared and packaged tight enough to compel me to avoid his baggage. "I'm really excited about the class, sir. I really dig your work. I read the comic. The landscape pencils you did of Germantown Avenue are amazing. The depth of perspective with the telephone poles—I got to learn how to do that. I'm hyped to work with you."

He's an exemplary young man, this Kimet. Passionate. Well spoken. Great eye for detail. I'm so impressed with that I don't remember those pencils are not in print. Or online. Unless he attended a gallery show on King's Road in Swansea six years ago, the only place he could have seen those illustrations was in my father's house.

I was a boy that age once, and I know that 97.7 percent of their bodies are semen and the 2.8 percent is an incendiary device for spraying it. I don't trust teenage males, particularly around teenage females, but still Kimet's not the focus of my increasing anger.

I arrive at the tent while they're still dancing. Sunita Habersham flips through the air, hugging her torso, chin tucked, those legs up and kicking and then landing down again, her thighs shaking along the way. On the final twirl, Sun collapses to a kneel, holds the pose for three seconds, then looks up at Tal and walks away as if this is so simple. It turns out it is for Tal. My daughter does the same move, but her thin legs go even higher. Her turns even quicker, the final collapse even more of a contrast. Sun says, "Good, now faster," clicks the outdated iPod back to the beginning, walks across the parquet floor laid out over the grass. They line up shoulder to shoulder, staring at the long row of standing mirrors.

Through the speakers the recorded sound of Fela's band orders and Sunita Habersham leaps as demanded. Tal jumps in six beats after, the action repeating in a round, Sun opening the air so that Tal can jump right into it. They mirror. They are reflections, with the difference in age manifest as the variations in energy and experience. In both, there is grace. They look like mother and daughter, out there. There is a real connection. I want that connection. I'm jealous of Sunita, already.

Next to my daughter, it's obvious Sun is a woman, not a girl, which is the difference between a realization and possibility. She sees me staring before I can stop myself. She sees me looking back as I stand there, arms folded, all okay and not at all weird because that's my girl she's dancing with. Sunita smiles and even gives a polite wave before stopping the music with the clicker in her hand.

"Before you come home, we have to talk," I tell my daughter as I walk over to her, and Tal just nods, busy rubbing her neck down with a towel. She rubs her hairy armpits down next, which is disgusting and the smell of them hits me and the thought that maybe I'm supposed to remind her daily to take a shower.

"You're already talking, Pops."

"You had Kimet in our house? When I wasn't there? Without permission?"

"He stopped by," she says, not even bothering to be defensive. "We just hung out, watched Netflix. Is that a big deal to you?"

"Yes! You can't have boys over when I'm not there. You can't—"

"Get pregnant?" Tal says, finishing my sentence with something I would never say out loud. "Is that what you think your job is? To break the cycle, or something?"

"My job is to take care of you. To make sure you get to adulthood intact." And then, when she flinches at the last word, I add, "I mean unharmed. Prepared. Ready for the rest of your life."

My daughter answers with silence. She wipes her face now, then holds the towel there, so I can't see her.

"No more secrets."

"Fine. Whatever."

"I talked to Irv. He said you ran away. I know he didn't kick you out. And I don't care." Still nothing. Tal just rubs down her arms, drops the towel on the floor like a toddler, and starts untying her sneakers. I lightly steer her chin up with my fingers, face her directly. "I'm glad you came, but I don't want you lying to me. No more lies."

"Irv would say that, you know? Irv doesn't remember one day to the next what's happening. He's a drunk." Tal's shoving her clothes into her gym bag. Hard, like if she pushes them down far enough she can shut me up.

"He's your grandfather. And he loves you. He wants us to come to his house for Shabbat tomorrow, so we can all talk about it then."

"Fine. But then I'm going to need a new outfit. I need, 'go back to your grandfather's and show that dad who was absent for seventeen years is doing a decent job' new clothes. And that means I need some bread. Cash money, homeslice," Tal says humorlessly and puts out her hand. I just stare at it.

"Tal, nobody talks like that anymore. I don't know what those Oreos are telling you, but I'm pretty sure no one has ever really talked like that." It's meant to lighten the mood, but I see Tal drop her façade of indifference, look off blinking until she regroups herself.

"How am I supposed to know that?"

"You're not, honey. That's why I'm telling you." To end the moment, I pull out my wallet, put money into her hand. Tal walks off toward the parking lot counting it.

"Does she play any other instruments besides you?" Sunita asks.

"Her grandfather's Shabbat. She needs some clothes to look nice." And then immediately I think of all the luggage Tal has, still sitting partially unpacked, in my father's house.

"Whatever you say." Sun waves me off before walking toward the door of the tent.

"How do you do it?" I ask her. The vagueness of the question gets Sun to turn around.

"Do what?" she asks, clearly bracing herself for some pedestrian pickup line to follow.

"The mixed thing. Just, in general. Even saying I'm mixed, instead of black, makes me feel uncomfortable. Even thinking it, sometimes. I saw you stand in front of a whole room, a hostile room, of black folks, and declare you were mixed. How do you do that?"

"So you think there's, like, a big secret."

"If there was, would you tell me?" She laughs at that, and it's enough to get her to walk back over close enough to lean in and whisper to me.

"Okay, here's the secret. It's not really a secret, but I'll frame it to you as one. The same people who despise you for identifying as mixed? Those are the same people who, when you do identify as black, despise you for not being black enough. And there's nothing you can actually do to be black enough, for them. Because it's not really how you act that they despise. It's you. Your very existence." She leans back, raises her eyebrows in mock astonishment.

"That's the secret." I believe her. I don't know if those two types are the same person or if that's an oversimplification, but I don't care. I believe her, because I believe in her, because she believes in herself. That's the kind of confidence Tal needs. This is the kind of woman Tal needs in her life. Not just at school, but at home, actually in her life. A strong maternal figure, something I can never be for her.

"That's it. When you realize that, you realize you have nothing to lose," she tells me, and starts walking away again.

"Would you like to come with us? To Shabbat, with Tal and I? I could use the hand." She stops, turns, and is still smiling when she asks me, "You mean like a date?" I nod the positive. My head bounces. It says, devoid of cool, "Oh yes, yes, yup."

"Oh hell no. Not a good idea. I don't date students. Sorry." She's still smiling when she starts walking off again.

"I'm not your student anymore. Whiteness class is over. I'm fully bleached," I call after her. I want it to sound like a joke instead of a desperate, marinated whine.

"Still," Sun offers, but keeps walking.

"You know that's a bullshit excuse. That's like, 'I have a boyfriend in Canada.' Or, 'I have TB.'" To that, Sun looks over her shoulder at my body, my clothes. Then up at my eyes. Sun holds there.

"How about, 'I have a boyfriend, and while it's an open relationship, no.' Does that work? Or we could try, 'You're not unattractive, but you're also a mess and my life is complicated enough without someone else's mud?'" Sunita waits for a response this time. I have nothing. Those are pretty good reasons. I shrug, she nods; we're doing so well without words these days.

She gets me, I think, watching her ass as she walks off. And she really does get me, because then her head swings back over her turning shoulders enough to catch me; then she pulls down her shirt to cover her rear without even looking back.

I spend the ten-minute drive to Germantown feeling guilty about getting caught staring at Sunita Habersham's buttocks, pausing only to drop Tal off at the thrift store on Chelten Avenue. I used to come to this corner with my mom, when the Woolworth's was still open. On any Saturday, the streets were crowded with shoppers, the place was alive. This was when Allen's department store was still open. Before Asher's Chocolates closed its store and moved their factory away. When the Bell Telephone building actually had Bell Telephone inside. Before the industrial jobs left for overseas. Before the last monuments to a stable economy were eroded through numerous recessions. Before desegregation encouraged the flight of the black middle class. Before the crack epidemic raged through the weakened community like an opportunistic infection. That's over and it seems to be getting better—I can admit that: it's better than when I left. But I see it against the images of *before* and it's still devastating. What's left are the businesses that can stay afloat even after economic collapse. Now, it's a great place to buy overpriced sneakers. Or prepaid cell phones. It's a great place to search sidewalk kiosks for brand names printed on generic sweatshop clothes. There's African braiding if you have the money, the entire day, and a high pain threshold. "Go to Value Village. Rich people from Chestnut Hill donate clothes there. And be careful out here," I tell Tal as I pull up the Beetle to let her out. It's tuned up, its tickets paid off, headlights replaced and the dents pulled out. Everything is making a comeback.

"Germantown's not that bad. There's fancy parts of Germantown too. I know tons of rich kids who live here, in really nice houses, on really nice blocks. You act like it's some hellhole," she tells me, and I look around, and sure the street's basically clean, and it's mostly just a bunch of working people waiting for the bus, and she's right. But three miles up Germantown Avenue the white people have Chestnut Hill, and it's thriving, with microbrewers and Zagat-rated restaurants and a functional retail ecosystem and why can't we have it like that?

At the house, the security cams install easily because they're meant to go up quickly, discreetly, possibly before the owner comes home. I'm done with the hardware and finishing the install of the software by the time Tal walks in the door with bags and a look on her face as light as her load is heavy.

"Wow. There's like no white people at all at night on Chelten Avenue. I didn't see one!" she tells me as she closes the door.

"I hope you didn't feel uncomfortable." And I really mean that. Not as an apology, but because I hope I don't have a daughter who feels uncomfortable if there are no white people around.

"Why should I? I mean, I'm not, like, white anymore. It's very liberating. Totally." And she's off to the upstairs bathroom to change before I can question her line of thinking.

When she comes down the steps, Tal's wearing solid cork platform pumps tall enough that the top of her head threatens to brush the paint-chipped doorway she walks through. Her feet are held there, perpetually in sprinting position, by a band of what appears to be cheetah fur, if cheetahs were pink. No cheetah is pink. Then there's nothing but bare leg for a good eight inches going north, till a matching strip of print, presumably skinned from the same mutant feline, cuffs the bottom of her tight capri jeans. This feral pink fabric is on the collar of the jean jacket she's wearing too, and it's a good thing Tal's wearing a jacket because the T-shirt she's got on doesn't even bother to cover her navel. Above, Tal's hair is out. Out and screaming its inner Africa. Furious at years of bondage, and celebrating its nappy roots.

"I like your hair," I tell her, because there are about 413 things I can think to say, and that's the nicest one. Number two is: *What's the name of your twerk team?* I open up my mouth, but nothing more constructive occurs to me, so I just keep looking at Tal, slack-jawed.

"What about the rest? That thrift shop went out of business, apparently. It's a day care now. So I walked up Chelten and found this place called City Blue? Very urban. Very authentic. Don't you think?" Tal opens up her jacket and points to the label on the chest of her tattoo-pattern shirt. It says APPLE BOTTOMS.

"It's the name of the brand, Pops. Not a reference to my actual butt," she says. When that doesn't give her the desired response, Tal follows with, "It's a very popular black brand."

"You can't think I would actually approve of this. You're not going to your grandfather's like that."

"Yes, I am. I am so not worried about Irv and the whole Karp clan. If Irv can't accept my blackness, then that's his problem."

"No, you're not. Tal, those clothes have nothing to do with your ethnicity."

"I'm supposed to be 'transcending my assumed racial notions.' That's what the school you—*you*—sent me to, is telling me."

"Tal, there's no way they meant dress like that. Don't conflate ghetto culture with blackness."

Her mood, the smile, gone. She starts taking one of her hollow gold earrings out of her lobe and I think I've gotten through to her until it's thrown at me. It's a childish response. Possibly genetic, since I come back with:

"For the record, as your father I should let you know that dressing like a hoochie mamma is a bad life choice in general."

"Fuck you!" The other earring actually hits me. On my forehead. It feels like it cuts deep but it's only bleeding a little when I take my hand off it.

"You're right. That was harsh. Fuck me. I'm sorry." Sunita Habersham would know how to handle this. That's who Tal needs right now.

"That's right, eff you. I tried. You can't say I didn't try, okay? I'm trying."

"Try what? What's this about? Explain it to me, okay?" I pause for an answer. I wait for a few seconds, unsure if I should be breaking the silence.

"I knew," is all Tal finally tells me. I see her shoulders shake, think she's laughing, but then she lets out a wail and goes at it harder and I know she's crying. Tal's really crying; there is a sound long and hollow like it's being pulled out of her, ripping flesh as it goes. I reach out, pull her into me, but her arms are just limp under my own.

"I knew. I always did." Her voice cracks; her body shakes. I hold her firmer like I can stop this.

"Knew what?"

"I knew you were black. What I am. Nobody, like, had the decency to say something to my face, but I knew," Tal says after her breathing slows.

"So you knew. You kinda thought you knew, but now you really know. It's not too bad, right? It's no biggie. You're still you," I tell her, and I try to say it with joy. I'm hoping that if I say it laughing, if I laugh lightly at her reaction, then Tal'll start laughing too. But Tal just keeps crying. It's getting lighter though, her body still now. And then it gets quiet, but for the heaviness of her breathing. Until Tal says:

"I told all my friends that you were an Israeli soldier."

"Okay."

"Missing in action," she follows with, and then I do laugh for real. I can't help it. I hear myself and try to stop, but I can't. And then it's okay, because Tal joins me. And thus the dark spell is broken. "Just let it go," I tell her. I look down and she's got snot on me, my daughter, and snot all over her psychedelic cat print. But at least she's still laughing. Still with the tears, but mostly laughing now. Laughter I can deal with. Laughter I know.

"I knew," Tal says, quieter. She calms down. Calmer but the tears keep coming, as if something's broken in her and they're just pouring through the crack. "I knew," Tal says again, which makes no sense. Because my daughter doesn't know anything. Tal has no idea. Because I have no clue, and she has even less of one than me.

11

THERE'S SCREAMING AND whooping and noise itself breaking and then it starts again. The world has hit its wall, we all die in explosion and rage. I shoot up in my bed and see the broken plaster of the ceiling and know I'm in a crack den and the cops are outside and I don't know what to do and I've never even done cocaine and now they're going to shoot me. And then I realize I'm in my father's burnt-out room, on a mattress, and that my burglar alarm has caught something.

I own a Taser. I know I have a Taser, and I search around the side of the bed for it and there is nothing and they're coming for me, but then I find it. It's not night, it was just an afternoon nap, but the newspaper taped over the windows dims the light. I hold the Taser out to the dim. No one's there. The alarm is still whining. My head hurts from it and I remember Tal and push off my sleeping bag and jump to my feet and head downstairs.

Tal's tent door is open, Tal's not in it. Tal's gone. She's lost. No, she's at my laptop at the kitchen table, images from the cams up on screen, and she's screaming "Make it stop! Turn it off! What the fuck?!" back at me.

The control panel. It's on the wall. Tal points at it and yells, "Shut it down," like I need the suggestion. I open the plastic flap hiding the keypad and keep entering the code but it doesn't work and the whole thing is flashing with buttons on the side that say: DISABLE. ALERT POLICE. ALERT. FIRE DEPARTMENT. RESET. PANIC. I am panicked, so I hit the panic button. Strobe lights start flashing out of the alarms to the rhythm of the horrible sound. This is the worst nightclub ever. I make a panic sound too; it's kind of a moan, kind of a whine; it's a whole new tone in misery. Tal reaches past me and hits the code again and then DISABLE and everything stops.

We have silence. It's a gift that just arrived in the mail from someplace on the other side of the world. After a second, I hear Tal sigh and watch as her shoulders slump down with the weight of her exhaust. I can even hear the hum of the laptop now. When the footsteps hammer on the front porch, I can't confuse it for yet another sound effect of structural decay. Tal hears it too, starts for the door until I catch her arm. I wait for the doorbell to ring. We wait.

The doorbell doesn't ring.

There is pacing on the porch, a story told in slow thumps.

We wait for there to be a knock; there is no knock. We wait for someone to call out; no one says anything. Someone is on our porch. The footsteps are solid, hard. They are angry. Slow, boom, boom. Deliberate. They go from one side of the porch to the other.

It's dark in here but the sun is still shining on the other side of our walls. When the footsteps get closer to our window again, I can see movement through the blind cracks, past the distorted, blown glass. I see a dark hood float by and I look at Tal and she's seen it too, and that's when I remember the Taser in my left hand. I look at the computer again, at the camera feeds I have set up. There are none aiming at the porch. It is behind the lines. It is out there.

"Call the cops," Tal whispers to me.

"We. Are. Black," I remind her.

"Call that guy George, then," she says.

"No. Hell no." This guy is on the front porch right now, pacing back and forth in madness. The cops are for after. The cops are for notepads and "Can you describe the suspect?" and then once they leave nothing changes and you never see the cops again. Also, they are good at shooting unarmed black people. We are still black people by police standards. I power the Taser, and listen. The walking stops.

I get close enough to the window this time to look around. From the angle, I can see only empty porch. They're gone. It's okay, now. They're gone. Then the knocking comes. One bump. Then two. Not light. Not like a polite request. Hard thuds. Slamming their palms on the wood. I look at Tal. I can see her breathing, short heavy gasps as big as her eyes have grown. And then a third banging demand, shaking the door with its force.

There's no peephole to look through. There was no peephole needed in the eighteenth century, when this door was put here. If you wanted to stop by, you sent a letter. Servants would greet you in this foyer and take your calling card to the master. I have to open the whole damn door to find out who's on the other side. Tal, she gets it now, she feels it, she tries to stop me, puts her hand over my arm, but frantically I wag her away and she obeys me, and I don't start unlocking again till she's over by the kitchen, holding a knife forward like a beast is about to come charging. I turn the knob and slowly pull back the door. I have the Taser in my right hand, but no plans to use it.

They're there. Waiting on the far side of the door for me, silently.

I just fucking zap them.

There is a rational part of my brain and it says, Don't zap them, Warren. Ask questions first, find out who they are and why they're here, on your doorstep, lurking, banging. Find out their hopes and dreams. Offer them a glass of water. And that part of my brain has control of my left hand, which is holding the doorknob. The right hand fucking zaps the crackhead.

Two little twisty wires briefly connect me to the form of fear incarnate. And that right hand, it does a great job, aims for the stomach area to avoid giving it a heart attack and I hold the trigger for a good four seconds, which is much less than the twenty the instructions recommended but enough time for me to perform the even more recommended act of catching the body to avoid head injury and/or lawsuit.

I lay the crackhead on the ground. Its flesh is soft, not just because of the plush material of the jumpsuit. It's soft because it's a woman, I can see from the hips before the face. I got her. I got the intruder. I really got her. I turn her around to see her face.

"You killed my principal!" Tal says, over me.

I got Roslyn.

Tal drops the knife to the floor, and it bounces loudly in a way that I find judgmental and overly dramatic.

"I'm so, so sorry. I'm so sorry. I thought you were a crackhead," I tell my employer.

"Intensation," Roslyn utters, which is not even a word. Her eyes are shooting around, looking for pixies. Her gray hair screams out from under her hoodie. Tal squats down beside Roslyn, and the older woman's eyes actually manage to land on her for a few seconds before going off fairy-hunting again.

We are driving to the emergency room. It is twenty-seven minutes before sunset. We can drop her off in eleven minutes, then get on the Wissahickon entrance to the Roosevelt Boulevard to make it downtown on I-76 in sixteen minutes and still not break Talmudic law. The whole Karp family is supposed to be there. It's too late to cancel. They're already predisposed to hate me. For what I did. For what I didn't do, even though I didn't know Cindy Karp was telling the truth. This has to happen. We have to make it happen.

"We're not going to make it. Let me call Irv now," Tal tells me from the passenger side. She's not looking at me. She's looking at Roslyn, who's laid out in the back of the car on the sofa seat in a fetal position. More than five decades since her birth but she forms the pose as if she was born yesterday.

"We're going to Irv's Shabbat. That's not an option, you can't miss—you have to talk to him, clear things up. She's okay. You're okay, right?"

"Shabbat shalom," I hear behind me.

"Dear God, she's speaking in tongues."

"No, Pops. Miss Roslyn? I'm sorry, I know we're all in the middle of a little crisis here, but do you already have plans for dinner?"

I don't hear a response. I look through the mirror again and see Roslyn's eyes have closed. Her lips are moving, and I can just make out a slurred chant of *Nam-myoho-renge-kyo* so I know she hasn't passed out completely.

"She's fine," I tell Tal, who won't even look at me. As we sit at a red light, I reflect on the fact that I'm pretty sure I'm getting sued at the end of this. I'm pretty sure all this, the Tasing, this drive, it's all going to be used in a deposition of some kind. Sirleaf will confirm this, I'm sure. I can already see Roslyn on the stand, the blessed earth mother, and the whole of Mulattopia in the gallery staring at me. When the light goes green, I ask Roslyn again if she wants to go to the hospital.

"Like every cell . . . yodeling," she says. And then it goes quiet. Really quiet. Until the car behind me honks for me to move.

I haven't been to the emergency room at Germantown Hospital since I was five and stuck a cherry pit up my nose. I actually visited the hospital twice that day, for the same ailment—albiet for different cherry pits—due to the fact that I suffered from a combination of stupidity and poor fatherly supervision. My mother would never take me to Germantown Hospital, choosing instead to hire a cab to drive me to Chestnut Hill, where the hospital served a predominantly wealthy white clientele, and according to her reasoning, was therefore less likely to kill you. I pull up to the entrance, jump out of the car and open the back door. There's a wheelchair on the curb with G-TOWN spray-painted on the back of it like a scarlet letter. I pull it over, the wheels worse than a shopping cart, and I see Tal getting out too.

"What are you doing? We don't have time for you to take her in," I tell my daughter.

"We're not going to just leave her here."

"She's a grown woman," I explain, as Roslyn, almost as if in response to this, groans. At least, that's how she responds when I start pulling on her leg.

"No . . . Western . . . medicine," Roslyn manages. It takes a minute. She says all this without opening her eyes, channeling it from whatever dark pit to which her consciousness has been repelled.

"You've taken quite shock," I tell her. I try to make my voice as soothing as possible, while still yelling it at her. "It's probably for the best you get it looked at."

"No," Roslyn says again. At least that's what I think she says. It's hard to hear when the ambulance pulls in behind us with its lights on, and starts honking. When the driver gets out of the cab, there's some yelling too. By then Roslyn, eyes closed, has apparently drifted off again. I put my hand back on her leg and start to pull on it. She kicks me.

"Miss Director, we have a previous invitation to a Shabbat dinner at my grandfather's, would you like to come with us?" Tal asks, shoving herself next to me.

"Nam-myoho-renge-kyo. Nam-myoho-renge-kyo. Nam-myoho-renge-kyo," Roslyn keeps going, and we take that as a yes, throw the wheelchair in the trunk and peel out of there.

I am at Irv's doorstep with his granddaughter after being absent from her life for seventeen years. I have this other woman with me who's Irv's age and in a sweat suit and a wheelchair. I'm holding her back by one shoulder to keep her from falling over.

"Irv, this is Roslyn Kornbluth," Tal begins. She motions to Irv, then motions to Roslyn, who flutters her eyes in recognition. "Roslyn runs my school and Warren just almost killed her with one of those electrocution guns, so we thought it might be nice if she joined us for dinner. She's black and Jewish, so consider her a peace offering."

"Must look . . . a mess," Roslyn whispers, but not really to anyone, almost like she's talking to the strands of her curls.

"Nonsense, such a beautiful woman needs no embellishment." Irv smiles and bends over to her, and I get a whiff of his cologne, which is whiskey. Jovially, he picks up Roslyn's hand, and first I think he's going to check her pulse, but he kisses it.

"She's had a long day," I tell him.

And Irv just smiles and says, "I'm sure she has, I'm sure she has," and that's when I get that he thinks she's always in this wheelchair, this beat-up fraying thing, not just in it because I almost electrocuted her.

Inside, it's the same apartment. It's the same apartment I made Tal in. I remember it as soon as we get inside. The rest, the doorman, the lobby, all these prewar Walnut Street high-rises look identical to me but this apartment, this is it. The place I've been avoiding for eighteen years. My memories, my guilt, they were in here, waiting for me. The last time I was in this place, the less successful sperm from Tal's batch were seeping into my underwear. I'm pretty sure the apartment knows that, remembers my teenage trespass. There will be a sign, I know. Words forming on refrigerator magnets or something, something more than my heavy breathing. Ghosts are real; I can totally see that in this moment. And I really start wheezing, being in this place, being caught back here. We go in the kitchen and apparently there is a toilet handle at the back of my neck, and I can feel it now, I can feel it being pushed, and all the blood rushing from my brain, down, congealing in my jawbone, pulling my mouth slack and open. I know what's happening. I am fainting. I look at Tal. I look at her so beautiful and think, How bad can my sins be? I scream this in my head, *How bad can my sins be?* But my body isn't listening. I lean on the wheelchair to keep from falling over. I lean on Roslyn's shoulder. Roslyn says, "Ow!" with surprising clarity.

"Here, I'll take her," and Irv yanks Roslyn away, and is moving down the hall offering "We'll get you a nice seat at the table" before I can stop him. Somehow, I didn't imagine Roslyn coming to the table. I imagined we would just wheel her into a dark and calming room and drape a sheet over her head till it was time to leave. I start to feel dizzy again and Tal takes my hand.

"You can't lose your shit, okay? Warren? Pops?"

"No," I tell her. I can't. I straighten up. Tal grips my hand harder.

"No nervous breakdowns until after the kiddush."

The rest of the Karp family turns out to be just three people, which is a bit of a relief. I can handle three. That's just: this, that, and the other. This and that are an elderly couple who look like they're in their sixties or seventies, or white-people fifties. They are introduced as Dot and Art.

"Twins!" Dot says, and there is graveled triumph in this declaration. Victory that she's still alive to say it, again, and Art winces, dramatically. It is clearly a practiced overture, the signature opener of their repertoire. Still a crowd pleaser, even after years of being downgraded from the Broadway of youth to old age's community theater.

"And this is my daughter, Elissa," Dot tells me and I look to the side and there is Cindy Karp, twenty years older and back from the grave to haunt me. Same kind of eyes, same kind of hair, exactly the same kind of general disapproval I imagined on her face that last phone call. I know it's not her, just a cousin, a co-sharer of genetic memory, but I start to sway anyway. I remember to introduce myself. I am Warren Duffy. I'm a grown man now, but I was once the callow youth who owned the penis that once poked your angelic little Cindy, no doubt dooming her. This is my lovely daughter, you know her much better than I, but without her I would be unconscious at this moment. But all I say is my name, and my great joy at meeting them. They look down to the side of me. Smiles freezing. At Roslyn, who has been pushed up to a place setting at the table. They look at Roslyn's skull; her neck has quit its job. The head has lobbed forward, stopped only by her chin on her breastbone. All you can see of her is the curls of her hair: thick, mostly salt-and-some-pepper spirals rolling from her scalp and stopping just short of the table in front of her.

"This is my friend. Roslyn. She directs the learning center Tal is enrolled in," I tell them when they look back at me, wondering. "Roslyn?" I ask, leaning in closer to her, smiling enough for both of us. "Roslyn?" again, yet nothing but a light moan comes back to me.

"Is she . . . ?" Art drifts, waiting for me to complete his sentence. What he is asking I have no idea. Is she disabled? Is she my mom? Is she sick? Is she dead?

"Yes," I tell him, then give a sad look as further answer, and both he and his sister smile knowingly and suddenly all this is normal.

"I thought you'd be blacker," Dot tells me.

"Mom! No! You can't say things like that. Please forgive her," the daughter says to me. Elissa even reaches out her hand in front of me like she can shield me from her mother's lack of tact.

"No, it's okay. I totally expected to be blacker also. Every time I look in the mirror, it's a shock, trust me."

"You know I don't mean anything racist by it," Dot tells me, and I look deep within myself, but I don't know that at all. Still, I'm very willing to pretend, so nod accordingly. "It's just, I remember when Cindy said she got pregnant by a black guy, we were expecting a much darker baby, but Tal came out white. I just thought maybe she got confused: Cindy was a wild one."

"Oh my God, please kill me," Tal says, and with a thump her forehead hits the table as she hides her face like an ostrich. She looks like she's doing a Roslyn impression.

"Mother, cut it out, or I'm leaving. Just stop. Just stop now."

"My daughter thinks I'm a racist. Ever since I voted for McCain."

"You are not a racist. So stop acting like one."

"This is why I never had kids." Art laughs.

"You're gay. That's why you didn't have kids," Tal mumbles into the table, but we all hear it. Oh dear. Oh my. My daughter is a homophobe.

"Tal!" both mother and daughter yell together. This family, they yell. Now mother and daughter are united. They look at each other silently, and the look says, *The demon is back*. Art gets up, asks if anyone wants anything from the kitchen, and leaves. Then, no one talks.

Dot reaches for her drink, then finally mutters, "Not true. And mean." Elissa excuses herself to escape to the kitchen as well. On my side of the table, I'm the only one sitting upright to witness this disaster.

"My brother has always lived alone. Always has. That's the problem with being a single man of maturity. People cast aspersions. It's as if, despite all of the overcrowding on this planet, the environment and all that, somehow living the life of a bachelor is suspect, perverted. Now that's racist."

"Yes," Art says, returning with a glass of Irv's whiskey in hand, looking me straight in the eye. He winks at me.

"And because he chose to work in the theater. He's just creative," Dot adds.

"Sure," Art, rolling his eyes at someone, agrees with her.

"I mean: even his name is Art!" Dot says, and we all laugh too hard, because we are back on script again.

Horseradish is hot sauce for Eastern European Jews. These guys put it on everything, even apples. When the food comes, Tal lifts her head up, acts like nothing has ever happened, and thereby joins the rest of us. I turn to Roslyn.

"It's dinnertime," I tell her, just to not be rude, and a miracle takes place. Roslyn's head lifts. The hair pulls back, and that face pops back into play.

"Starved," she says, and we're back to single syllables, but this is still an improvement. The others look over at her, grin and nod, but keep talking, as if she only left to take a little nap, a little necessary self-indulgence, and now she's right as rain and not reaching all the way across the table to violently yank a chunk off the challah. Roslyn says no more after that, but it's okay because I don't talk either, and Tal barely does, even when asked direct questions. Seeing her interacting with them, I realize how honored I am. In my presence, she has been downright gregarious in comparison. Tal catches me staring at her, and her tongue sticks out in my direction. There are bits of bread on it that look like little brown slugs and I flinch in disgust. Tal looks at her reflection in her spoon, giggles. I smile with her. Irv looks over at her, me, grins too. His face is red. He is completely lit. In a second, he's up to get even more wine, but he leans over and whispers into my ear, "So what, I'm drunk. Tonight's the night I got to tell my granddaughter I'm dying."

...

I feel tipsy, decide to slow down. For my daughter. And so I can drive out of here. The door's closed to the study and I can see it from the table and Tal went in there with Irv and after ten minutes I know she knows he's battling cancer. I strain to listen for crying. The table is loud, though. Because they're all drinking, too. Just a few bottles of malbec, but enough to get things lubricated. I stare at the door, and I keep one of the bottles in front of me and when the family is distracted I pour back the rest of my glass.

"This school you have Tal at, the one for all black kids, what's that all about?" Dot asks. I don't really hear the sentence at first, it's background noise, something I have to go back and decipher once I realize it's aimed at me.

"It's a special program for biracial children."

"Black, kinda black, black-ish—you know what I'm talking about."

"Mother, please. I will leave. You're being a boor."

"No, you always say I treat you like a child—you love saying that—well don't treat me as one. We're all adults. We're all adults here. This is an adult conversation. We're all supposed to be 'post-racial' now, right? Everyone's saying we have to be 'post-racial.' It's segregation. I don't know why Tal couldn't just go to Kadima like Cindy and you did."

" 'A school for open Jews who want their children to have it all.' " It comes from Roslyn, who's looking up at Dot. Dot stares back, speechless. I can't tell what she's more surprised about: what Roslyn said, that she's not mentally impaired, or that she's even talking.

Roslyn looks fine now. Groggy, but fine. I have not killed her. So there's that.

"That's offensive," Dot says, and I agree with her. I would say I agree with her, but my mortification has moved me past verbal expression.

"That's the motto, Mom." Elissa smacks her own head. It's the first time I've ever seen a real person do that.

"Class of '74," Roslyn tells them. "I did all thirteen years at Kadima. Well, twelve really, I did my junior year abroad at Kibbutz Lotan, in the

Arava Valley. That's where the concept for the Mélange Center comes from: a holistic community of outreach, a society of ideals, a home for the wanderers. What I set out to do was give mixed-raced people that same vision my faith gave me." Roslyn keeps going. She is just starting, and she's already going. There's a speech coming; this is the preamble.

A text message that appears on my phone says, *Come to the door.*

I go to the door Irv closed. I try to open it again, do so as loudly as I can, but nothing follows. So I knock. Tal opens it. She's been crying. She knows. Past her, I see Irv sitting on the edge of a made bed, head in hands.

"Never mind. I'm fine."

"Are you sure? I'm here. I'm here for you. You know that, right?"

"I'm going to spend the weekend here," she says, staring off. Then, looking back at my eyes again. "I mean, I want to spend the weekend here. I need to. With Irv. Is that okay?" my daughter asks me, and of course it is.

When I come back to the table, the wheelchair is empty. Roslyn is standing. Roslyn is talking with Elissa; Dot leans in too. Art sits on a chair in front of them, legs folded, taking it in.

"We create our communities, our identities, but we do it by maintaining our heritage," and Roslyn makes it sound like something she has never said before, like she's just thinking it up on the fly. I wait, listen to the whole spiel one more time, just like I listened to it at the campfire days before. After a while, Roslyn pauses for air, and I lean in to tell her it's time to go.

Goodnight, Pops, my phone's display tells me. I look back at Irv's door, it's closed again. I want to text her that I love her. Because I do. But I haven't told her this truth to her face, and a text is no way to begin.

I take the wheelchair out to the car, then come back for Roslyn, who's still going. She ends with, "As Rabbi Hillel said, 'If I am not for myself, who will be for me? If I am not for others, what am I? And if not now, when?' "

The first contribution comes from Elissa. It's written out leaning the checkbook high against the wall, and with a look to her mother as soon as she puts it in Roslyn's hand in exchange for thank-yous. The older lady follows.

"I gave McCain and Romney less than this, combined. Am I absolved now?" Dot asks her daughter as she writes out her check as she presses it vertically on the armoire.

Roslyn looks at the donation amount and says, "I believe you are."

I drive Roslyn back to my house, where she says her car is parked. Down Kelly Drive, through the woods, windows open to wake me up. She plays with the radio, sings along to some oldies I've never heard before, turning it up loud enough that we don't have to talk. Around us, the trees of Fairmount Park, the snake of Lincoln Drive, as we go through the forest that brings us to Germantown. I want the night to be over. The whole night, from the alarm to this moment, all of it needs to be over.

It isn't until after I drive the Beetle up the hill toward the garage and turn off the engine, that Roslyn says anything to me. And that's after I go to open my car door but she doesn't, and I'm forced to ask her why.

"Where's your ride?" I ask, and she points to an old hatchback on the street. She didn't say anything when I drove past it. Still, she makes no move to get out.

"You want me to drive you back over there."

"No. I want you to give me the Taser."

"What?" I ask, but I know what. I start laughing. Roslyn laughs too. But then she stops, and waits for an answer, and I realize she's serious. And suddenly this isn't funny anymore.

"Come on, Warren. You were a bad boy; you have to face the punishment. Families have rules. I have my dignity to consider. It's going to hurt me to do it, but now I have to Tase you, then we're even. You have it on you, don't you?"

"Yeah, right. Listen, I'm so sorry about before. I thought you were a burglar."

"I'm not," Roslyn says. "And you shouldn't have done that; it was very naughty. Now hand it over."

The Taser's in my pocket. It has been all night. Roslyn knows this; she's looking right at it. Its bright yellow plastic handle is hanging out. She could just reach in and take it if she wanted. But she doesn't. She wants me to hand it to her. She wants me to go out back and pick my own switch for my whupping. But she's not my mother. I don't know who she is, really, beyond someone who wants something.

"Give it to me, Warren. If you want to continue at Mélange," Roslyn orders, and I, too exhausted to argue, give it to her.

Roslyn inspects it for a moment. She holds it out to the window, says "Pow," smiling. Her other hand goes to the rearview mirror, angling to herself. She holds it straight up beside her head, squinting into the reflection of her own action-hero pose. Then she turns it on.

"Yo! You got to be careful with that." I scoot away from her in my seat as if three inches will change anything.

"It's a beautiful thing, Warren, to actually feel a physical representation of power," Roslyn says. "In your hands," she adds, and then shoots me.

I wake up and it's still dark and I'm still buckled into the driver's seat and every cell in my body has been individually extracted, beaten with a ball-peen hammer, then set afire before being shoved back to its original form. I ache in spaces between crevices I could have gone a lifetime without feeling. I'm wet all over, from sweat mostly, but in some areas probably from urine. My testicles have retreated so far into my body cavity I very well might not ever see them again. I turn to the street. Her car is gone now. It isn't until this moment that I think, Wait, why did Roslyn come to my house in the first place?

I look over at the passenger seat to ask her. But Roslyn's gone. There's someone there though.

In her place, sitting next to me, is a crackhead dude. A naked one. In the seat, in the dark, in Germantown, at 2:37 in the morning, next to me, is a naked crackhead man.

The hair on his chest is thick and blacker than the brown of his skin and it runs from his nipples to his thighs. His cock is shriveled and deflated and lies in a crevice of dark wool. His chest shakes, the upward head snaps repeatedly back, violent shudders, and it's this that forces me to look at the face.

The mouth is open as he shakes his head. He's crying but the only sounds are gasps. There is no hole blacker than the space between his lips, and it grows wider. It swallows his words. It must. Because I hear nothing before losing consciousness once more.

12

WHEN I WAKE back up, I stay in the car, immediately start it up, and begin backing out again. It's daytime. It's possible I've just dreamt the vision. But I'm not going in the house. Not alone. Never alone. I don't even like being alone on the lawn.

Something happened in the car at my father's house after my boss electrocuted me, but I don't think about it. I drive the same car to the store, back, but don't think about it. Can't think about it. Won't let myself. Instead, I spend Saturday prepping the classroom for the rest of the term, go to sleep in my office studio that night and don't open my eyes until I'm sure the sun has retaken the sky once more.

I don't leave the art trailer. I don't use the lights. I don't want Roslyn to know I'm here, or any of her followers. I only go out to use the porta-potty after I've checked to make sure there's no one around. I pull the blinds closed so the dim light of my computer screen isn't visible to anyone wandering through the camp. I see the others, the rest of the resident staff, out there walking around. I go to the window and watch them pass. So many couples; with school out they stroll the grounds, holding hands. I hear their music, their laughter. Then late Sunday afternoon, I hear someone try to open up my door. I manage to kick the blankets I've been sleeping on under the lectern before the keys unlock it the whole way.

Spider's standing there.

"I knew he was in here. I knew it. I'm like fucking psychic. This is some telekinesis-level shit."

"What are you doing here?" Sunita Habersham, trailing behind him, thinks to ask me. I don't look at her. I'm tired of looking at her. I'm disgusted with my lusts and desires. Testing this theory, I steal a glance. Yes, Sunita Habersham's so beautiful. But so what? There have to be other attractive women of similar interest to me on the surface of this planet. There have to be other women with whom Tal could form a maternal bond. This reoccurring notion, this desperate belief that Sun is my sole avenue to secure romantic love, is obviously absurd.

"I'm squatting," I tell her, and give up all pretense. I pull the blankets back out from under the podium, put them back into the shape of a bed, lie down.

"You know, my couch folds out, if you need someplace," Spider says, but I'm fine. I like being alone. And that's what I tell him.

I look up again, because they're still here, making noise.

"Why are you here?" I reverse on them. "Why are you bothering me?"

"I'm going to need you to stop making sounds with your mouth hole, Warren," Sunita insists. It's a tone I've never heard her use before, both unusually firm and utterly informal. "I see the way you're looking at me. Let's establish something between us. Before we take this conversation any further."

"Okay," and behind that word comes a flood of anger. I wasn't even looking at her, for once. I wasn't even thinking about her.

"Good. Now listen: yes, we are really, really high right now."

"Totally high," Spider chimes in. "Yet not like, 'Danger, danger, Will Robinson' high."

"But still, very, very high," Sunita Habersham clarifies. "So I'm going to need you to talk slowly. And quieter. And I'm going to need you to not make any sudden movements."

"We want your snacks. We just need to get your snacks. I know you have them. Give us your snacks and nobody gets hurt. We'll share. Your snacks."

"I don't think he's hungry." Sun swings around, arms out like she can feel the wind ripple. Walks away yet again. This is how she's flirting with me, now I am certain. By showing me she doesn't even have to face me to get to me. Sun's wearing a Wonder Woman T-shirt that drapes so far down you can barely see her shorts. And underneath that, hiking boots. Heavy, worn gray, mud-covered hiking boots.

"Can we ask you something?" she asks. "Did you really Tase her?"

"Yeah, did you do it? Tase Roslyn? Tase her with a Taser?" Spider wants to know, but I can see from the way both look at me that they already do. Roslyn told them. So I give them my version. Tell them the circumstances of said electrifying and its retribution, and finish with "I'm pretty sure she shocked me for longer than I did her."

"Is that why you're hiding? She scare you that bad?" Sun wants to know. Spider's nodding at me slowly, still smiling, permitting me to say yes, to succumb to her patronizing conjecture.

"No. I saw a ghost," I say to shut them up. To let them know I'm crazy, that they're high, and to leave me alone. I even tell them what I saw, in detail. Not just Friday night, waking up in the car, but the time by the garage, and the first night I moved in there. Into their blank silence I add, "These crackheads, they've gotten into my head. They've got me seeing things. They got super crackhead powers."

"But Warren," Sun says. "You didn't say, 'I saw a crackhead.' You said, 'I saw a ghost.'"

"Okay, I've heard enough. Change the subject. I'm too stoned for this." Spider goes to my desk, grabs some Tastykakes and starts walking toward the door. "I don't mess with spirits. I draw the line at ghosts. Also, I'm against denigrating victims of substance abuse."

Sunita Habersham's not leaving. Even as Spider calls for her.

"Show me them. The ghosts," Sun whispers, as if one might hear us.

• • •

Sunita Habersham's got her window open, and her hand out. Her fingers are flat together, angled off her wrist and bent from her arm like the head of a swan. As I speed up, she tilts her hand forward, lets the weight of the wind push it up and back again. Slowly, Sun repeats, only pausing when I hit a light as we drive down Wissahickon Avenue.

"Spider says this street used to be a toll road. Two hundred years ago. Some old lady would sit on the side with a gun, make people pay to use it. That sounds like a great job."

"That's your dream career? Sitting on a road and shooting people who don't pay you?"

Sunita turns, looks at me, seems to realize for the first time that I'm really there. That I'm not some animated character from her THC haze. She sits up and shakes her head a bit like this will make her lucid.

"Yes. Yes, that would be my dream job. It's very simple, isn't it? No politics. No people, really. Just, *guardian*. Plus, you get to work outdoors. I wouldn't use a gun, though. I'd get something harmless, like your Taser." She picks it up from where Roslyn left it. I forgot it was even there, between the seats. Sun aims it out the windshield. She's turning it around to aim it at me.

"No." I knock her hand so it's pointing at the window again. Sun laughs at me. She puts the weapon down, but she's still laughing.

"Oh, come on. It couldn't have been that bad."

I stare straight ahead. "That old lady Tased me."

"Come on. I'm sure there was a larger, holistic reason. She doesn't just do things like that for no reason."

"She had a reason, she wanted revenge. She did that shit in cold blood."

"No. Roslyn's not like that. She's like our . . . Professor X. And we're her school of runaway mutants, training for the new world."

I let that stoner logic soak in. "How do you know she's not Magneto, taking those same runaways and warping them into The Brotherhood of Evil Mutants?"

"Come on, Warren, they didn't call themselves that, only the X-Men did. They called themselves just 'Brotherhood of Mutants.'"

"That's my point."

"You're just mad because Roslyn zapped you back. You ever wonder if the state of not being in pain, if that is the true deviation?" Sunita asks me. "That the pain is how life really feels, and moments of trauma, they just make it so you can't ignore the fact? That that's . . ." Sun pauses, and she's lost in the labyrinth of her own philosophy.

I pull onto Greene Street, past Manheim. I lived here with my mother until she passed. It hasn't changed much. The same two-story homes, now further along in their decay. All the little semidetached row houses huddling together, covered in all the paint that's failed to chip. Many of the solid wood pillars on the porches have been replaced with cheaper metal pylons. The streetlights have become stop signs because the city's broke, and there's another layer of trash, but basically it's as miserable as it's always been.

At my gate, I get out, undo the padlock then pull the twisted metal rails back. When I get back in the car, Sun says, "That's why you feel so alive in those moments of suffering?"

"You're stoned."

"I think we established that fact. Take me ghost hunting."

I should not be here. I've brought my crush to my house, at night, but I have no immediate plans for seduction. I have the desire, the pragmatic reasons too—they haven't gone away—yet still I lack adequate motivation to risk getting out of this car and going in that damned house. I don't even want to shut the engine off. I just wanted to be around her. Sunita Habersham. All this is because I must have wanted an excuse to be in her presence.

"Are we going to go in?"

"Look, you asked me where I saw the intruders. There. I saw them right there. Coming out of the garage. And right here, next to the car. We done, yo. We don't have to go inside."

Sun gets out of the car anyway. I don't. I think she's going to go look in the garage window, which is fine by me, but she comes to the driver's-side door. I roll the window down.

"You've got cameras out here. All over."

"Security."

"It looks like you're running a meth lab. Where do the recordings go?"

"I've got a hard drive set up with my laptop, in the house."

"Then we have to see what's on the tape." Sun skips off into the darkness toward the front porch. I don't even unlock my door. I look at the garage. For a second, I think I see movement in the window. I do see movement. It's the reflection of a bus's window as it pauses to let off a passenger on the street behind me.

Sun yells, "Come on, you can't just burn the whole place down because you had one crazy vision." And there it is, out loud. Exactly what I'm thinking. And that scares me. But Sun comes back to the car, reaches in for the handle then pulls my door open. Grabs my hand and pulls me out. She keeps holding my hand, even when I'm standing outside.

"Take me into your *House of Mystery*." And that was one of my favorite comics when I was a kid, but still, I don't want to go. "Look, my life is hard and boring too, just like everyone else's. Entertain me, Warren. You want to get me in your house, this is your chance," she says, and I believe her. And I remember how Sunita was, dancing in the air with my daughter, and how Tal talks about her. Like she needs her. So this time, I answer the call. Then we're walking into an empty mansion at night while holding hands.

"In third grade, I watched every season of *Scooby-Doo!* Finally, my paranormal investigative training is coming in handy. Knew I'd grow up to be Velma."

"Who in their right mind aspires to be dumpy Velma?" I ask her.

"I was pudgy, had thick glasses, wore a short bob cut. Velma isn't a mantle you attain. Velma is thrust upon you. I just embraced it, wore matching clothes. It wasn't called cosplay, then. It was just called, 'That Fat Girl Is a Loser.' "

As the computer boots up, I give Sunita Habersham a tour of my father's house. This is the old tent I make my daughter sleep in, it's conveniently located in the dining hall. This is the part of the ceiling that hangs down from water damage, despite repairs. That flash is from the fuse box outside. This is the dining-room table; it's made from a door. The chairs are empty buckets of primer paint. There's a couch over there: it's from the thrift shop. All the furniture is from thrift shops except the mattresses, which were new when I had them delivered. Tal won't use hers, which is upstairs, because she prefers the tent. Even though my father died in it.

"This place is huge. It's like an abandoned bus station. Don't you get lonely here? Just you and Tal?" Sun asks. "I mean, I think of these old houses as being small, built for small people. But these ceilings must be fourteen feet high. And the rooms are wide, too. Even bigger than they look from outside. You could fit a small army."

"The British Army, during the Battle of Germantown, actually. The upstairs, those rooms are smaller. I'm in the master bedroom and it's tiny. Let me show you," I say, and I genuinely mean that. Still, I hear how it sounds, even before I see Sun turn her head at my directness. Just the tiniest of reactions, but I see it, and I want to say, *That was not an attempt to get you up to my room so that I can have sex with you.* Why would I need to do that? People have sex in living rooms, and we're standing right next to one.

Then there's the sound.

It comes from upstairs.

Sun looks at me. "Did you hear that . . . ?" she begins, but answers her own question. "Yeah, let's go upstairs. Adventure time."

I shake my head. "No." I am perfectly fine not to go upstairs. I am perfectly fine never to go upstairs again in the history of all that is everything. In fact, I'm okay to seal off the entrance to the upstairs altogether, keep it like that from now till the moment it all goes up in char and red ember. But Sunita Habersham starts walking. She walks up. Why walk up? But she walks up. Toward it. We are supposed to be going in the opposite direction. It's time to run. I follow behind her.

"Hey, hey, remember that joke? About black people, that they'd run away in haunted-house scenarios? I think it was Eddie Murphy. Or maybe it was Paul Mooney, one or the—" I stop when Sun flings her arm back at me. We're at the top of the steps. The plaster from the ceiling hangs down into the hall in shreds. The walls, murals of water stains. Five doors. All closed. Each one hiding something. One's to the bathroom. One my room. Three, bedrooms I don't go in, I never go in them. There's been no reason to, there's no reason to now either. Sun stares, at the doors, then at me. She wants me to shut up so she can see which room the sound came from. So she can swing a door open and whoever's in there can be, I don't know, surprised. I don't want them to be surprised. I want them to be gone. No, I want us to be gone.

"Well, you know that joke? That black people would just leave at the first creepy sound? I've been thinking about that. Escaping? That's actually normative behavior. Staying, when you know there's a ghost, that's what makes no damned sense. So when you think about it, that's really the pretense of all ghost stories: white people are so confident of their omnipotence that they've lost their goddamn minds."

"Sunflower bullshit," is Sun's muttered response, but she's barely paying attention.

When the next sound hits, she grips me. My palm is mush and hers a solid object contracting.

It's coming from behind my bedroom door.

"Don't," I say, so light, just the idea of a word, but Sun hears it. She looks back at me, even. She keeps walking, but she looks back. Her face pulls away but her eyes are on me.

Sun looks away when her fingers reach the knob. She just turns it, no fanfare, no pause. It's so loud, the metal mechanism doing the same job it has for the last two hundred years. My room, it's how I left it so many days ago, when the alarm went off. The blankets still on the floor. The box spring and the mattress not much higher above it. The window's open. Did I leave the window open? I don't remember.

Sun walks on toward the open window. I come in behind her. I don't look around, because I don't want to look around. I just want to look at her. And it's so easy to just look at her. Sunita Habersham leans her head out the window, bends down to do so. Her shirt goes up, her shorts stay level, and the result is a view of her Sesa tattoo once more. The bottom of her back, that soft place.

I reach for her. Just to say, *Don't go any further*. To say, *Don't go out the window*. But I reach for her flesh. And then I'm holding her, by her hips, and the previous logic is eclipsed by the reality of the intimate position I've placed myself in. I don't know what's come over me.

I literally don't know what comes over me, I just see something dark floating right above my head and out the window, leaving behind only a physical chill I can feel even under my arms.

I hug Sun from behind. She thinks I am doing it because I desire her, which I do, but I hold her because I'm fucking scared.

I hug Sun's waist. She moans, or groans, I don't know which, but she definitely makes a sound before she closes the window. The breeze stops, and I feel warm again.

I saw a moving dark shape, and it felt cold, because of a window. Logic shifts back into position. Reality reseals all its tears. I got spooked. I got scared. By a shadow.

Sun turns around, looks at me, concerned.

"I was cold," I tell her. She grabs my arm, lightly. This action makes me keenly aware I have not released her midriff.

I kiss her as if this was always my intention. I tell myself that it was, that it always was, that the last five minutes have no meaning. I kiss her but I think about that shadow, which was probably caused by a car riding by outside, something I would have never even noticed before.

I don't believe in ghosts. I'm scared of being wrong, but I don't believe in them. Ghosts are what we want to see when our brains have no rational story. I want to tell Sunita Habersham this. Before I can, though, Sun says she has her own confession to make to me, and I grip her hard at her waist to tell her to give it to me.

"I really do have an open relationship, and a boyfriend. I don't want another one. We do this, it's just tonight, and then that's it. Just once. For fun."

"You're funny."

"No really, Warren. I'm serious." And there's no humor there. "This is what I told Jessie, and he didn't believe me. I didn't mean to hurt him, and I don't want to hurt you. So if you're willing, you have to understand that I'm serious."

"Who's Jessie?"

"'One Drop,'" she says, and my grip loosens.

The "boyfriend" doesn't bother me; I've loved a woman with one of those before. The whole "open relationship" part doesn't upset me either; it's just a concept, a dislocated notion. But I know what One Drop looks like. I see him, big, pale, that mockery of locks. I see him with Sunita Habersham. I'm not possessive. I don't consider myself possessive, but I can see him and her and don't see myself fitting into that image. As my hands lightly pull away, hers grasps them.

"Come on," Sunita Habersham says, pulling me even tighter, drawing me into her. "Let's pretend desire isn't the first stage of despair."

I lust. I know this. I lust all day and in ways that seem to transcend my otherwise limited imagination. I desire endlessly, and constantly encounter women that fill me with want. If I was bisexual, I'd have wasted away pining for all of humanity. My body is promiscuous in its hunger. But my heart has no such appetite. It wants only one. It understands only the equation of me plus her. Sunita Habersham touches the bare flesh behind my hip and my mind wants only Sunita Habersham, in that moment and every moment that will follow. There's no more Becks. I don't believe Sun, that she wants just one night. I don't because I can't imagine that to be true. When I kiss her neck, and she moans, I can't believe that it's just the physical act of having teeth lightly bite her flesh, the flicker of the tongue between the pain; I have faith the pleasure is solely because it's my mouth that does this. Already I have a vision of Sun, me, Tal, together going nuclear with family. I am a fool. Even Brer Rabbit gets stuck in the tar baby. I know this, even as I fall into her. There are few kisses. There are just my kisses, then her biting my lips back. Sunita Habersham kisses with her teeth. She turns from me, leans on the windowpane once more, signals me to take her from behind, and I get a flash that this is because she doesn't want to look at me but when I'm back inside her, my fear is gone. Minutes later, she pulls away, guides me toward the mattress. There she picks up my pillows, drops them on the floor, pulling me down to the floor with her to rest on them. There is less intimacy on the hardwood than on the bed, or less romance, but again I'm in her so it's a paltry symbol of detachment. Sun's lips are close enough to kiss once more, and I do, and she's too distracted to deflect me. Our lips meet in our second actual kiss, and stay there through long seconds of the rhythm.

All this and it's great and this is what I wanted but another part of me goes: so my genitals are entering Sunita Habersham's. That's it? This is the physical act I've obsessed over performing with her? This simple contact? Has anything truly changed between us? Because we both allowed our hidden skin to meet? This is just a literal expression of the attraction I already feel for this woman. Nothing more. Except it also feels fucking amazing.

Sun takes the pillow she's resting on and puts it over her face. She holds it there, with two hands. For the rest of the act. I can't see her. So she won't see me. And for a moment I get a glimmer of just how bad she's going to hurt me.

"Shazam!" Sunita Habersham screams, and throws the pillow across the room. She's so loud that I expect a thunderbolt to shoot down through the blackened ceiling and turn her into Mary Marvel. There's no lightning, but her body thunders, shaking for seconds afterward, and that's the only thing that keeps me from laughing. Then she rolls away like I'm not even there.

Sun falls asleep almost immediately. Or pretends to fall asleep. I lie on my side, staring, waiting for her to open her eyes, to talk to me or something, then fall asleep that way.

She said just that night, but it happens again in the morning. I wake up sore on the hard floor, fully engorged, and then we're at the dance once more. The second time is more of a digestif, sure, with only one position, the side by side spoon we woke up in, yet it's enough to remind me that the previous night not only happened but was seemingly deemed worth the inevitable trouble.

Sunita won't look at me, won't turn her head when my lips slide up her shoulder and neck, kiss until they run out of epidermal real estate. Instead, she thrusts her hips back into mine in several heavy jolts, finally shudders, then pulls suddenly off and away from me. No "Shazam" this time, but she's clearly finished.

I watch Sun stand up, her knees even less prepared for the change of posture than I am.

"Can I marry you?" I ask. "Like, right now? Let's run away to Costa Rica together. Tal too. Let's do this!" I know I shouldn't say this but I am so blissful in this moment that, though my testicles didn't, my mouth is ejaculating.

Sunita Habersham gathers her clothes from across the floor in response, holds them to her chest and starts heading out the door. Then she stops, looks back into the room, but not directly at me. "I was engaged once. He jumped in front of an Amtrak train. No note," Sun says, and then before I can respond she's gone, down the hall, into the bathroom.

She stays in there for an hour. Which is fine because it takes me that long to stop asking myself, What the fuck just happened?

When the bathroom door opens, I hear her walk back through the hall, then down the stairs. I don't believe she's leaving until I hear the front door close behind her.

There are no more sounds. Not in the house. I'm still on the floor. It's even harder than before. I get up when she honks my horn.

Sunita Habersham is waiting at the car when I get there.

"Do you want to talk about it?"

"About what?" Sun asks me, refusing to look my way.

I go to kiss her, right after I buckle. She leans her head away from me.

"We're just apes," Sunita Habersham tells me.

"We're just apes, sure," I mirror, then go in for the kiss once more. She meets me with her cheek.

"There are no monogamous apes. Humans are like bonobos—"

"Bonobos are famous for screwing everything. I get it. Fine."

"It's like a stress-relieving thing. It's not about ownership. You don't own me now. I like you, so that's why I'm saying this. Just know this doesn't end with us walking up the aisle."

"Don't worry. I'm still trying to pay off my last failed marriage."

"I'm saying this because openness is important. Honesty is important. I'm trying not to lie to you."

"Look, we went through this. I don't think just because we had sex, a few times, that I have some kind of exclusive rights to you," I tell her. This seems to work, because Sun finally buckles up, so I can start pulling out of the driveway. As I'm driving in reverse, contorted to peer through the back window, she pops a kiss on my cheek.

"Shazam!" she says again, mocking her own breathless tone, and starts giggling, putting a hand on my knee to brace herself. "I'm so embarrassed. I should have yelled, 'Kimota.'"

"Yeah. Miracleman is definitely cooler than Captain Marvel. But given that they're both rooted in the same intellectual property, I forgive you."

"It makes me really happy when you talk like that," she tells me, and squeezes my flesh in a way I take as a thank-you. And I look there where Sunita Habersham touches me, past the end of my shorts, and the skin of my thigh and her hand. Our skin. It's nearly the same color. It's the same flesh as my flesh, just in feminine. Which I've never seen before. The way it blends, the illusion it creates that both leg and fingers could be part of the same body, all this I've never seen before. I am naked and exposed, but not alone. Not paler or darker or any kind of other.

After dropping her off, I catch myself driving back to my father's house out of habit, then continue on past reemerging fear out of stubbornness. Once there, I immediately go to my laptop at the dining-room table, opening the security program. It's my first time scrolling through the CCTV archives, and it takes a minute to navigate the system. The camera aimed at the driveway is labeled CC9. I know it's named CC9, because I checked cameras 1 through 8 and that was the last one I installed, stuck right on the garage's rain gutter. But the feed doesn't have that angle, the footage doesn't make sense; it's all black. I go back through the other feeds, every one of them, 1 through 8. They all look good. It has to be CC9 messing up. I pull up a window again for CC9, this time a live feed. Really dark, but you can kind of see something, something there. To get a better look, I turn on the table lamp. And oddly, I can also see the image on the screen better, because it's also gotten brighter.

The closed-circuit camera I installed by the garage is now the house.

The camera is in the living room.

I didn't move it there.

I stand, and can see it. Sitting on the fireplace mantel. I look at my screen, and recognize the tent Tal sleeps in most nights.

13

IN 1958, EIGHTEEN-YEAR-OLD Mildred Jeter got knocked up by her boyfriend, Richard Loving, a family friend six years older than she, and they decided the best thing to do next was get married. They drove up from Central Point, Virginia, to Washington, D.C., because Richard was a white guy and Virginia had a law called the Racial Integrity Act of 1924 that said white people and black people couldn't get married. Soon after they got back, the police raided their home in the dark of night, hoping to catch them in the act of fucking, because that was illegal too—which is really ironic when you reflect that the God of Virginia is Thomas Jefferson. They were sentenced to a year in prison, but allowed to have that downgraded to probation as long as they agreed to leave the state and never come back. Six years later, sick of not being able to see their family and broke in D.C., they decided to sue the State of Virginia. It took three years for the Supreme Court to rule in their favor, but it did unanimously, and *Loving* v. *Virginia* became the case that decriminalized interracial marriage in America. Sixteen states still had antimiscegenation on the books when it passed. There's even an unofficial holiday for it in June, Loving Day, which the mixies at Mélange talk about like it's Mulatto Christmas.

Roslyn wants our class to do a special comic to be handed out at Mélange's Loving Day event. They're going to print a thousand copies. All the other mixed-race organizations in the area are coming, and not just the black/white ones either: the Asian/white, the Latino/everything, the all general mixed the hell up. It's going to be huge. Tosha IMs me while I'm doing the research for all this and I make the mistake of telling her what I'm doing when her message pops up on my screen.

They really need a holiday, to celebrate a white guy having jungle fever? That's all Virginia white guys live to do: get some strange.

That's really racist.

No, that's not, "really racist," Tosha insists.

The next message takes longer, as the English language struggles to convey her fury.

You could argue that it's prejudiced, but I'm not racist. Racism requires power to back it up, and I don't have a goddamn bit of that. George led a police tactics training course in Buchanan County, Virginia. All white, Irish. Do you know what the crime rate is down there? Do you know some of the names they used to call George, that summer?

I can imagine.

Not just "nigger" either. They were creative. And that was from the other cops. They thought it was funny. It's like 1861 down there. Those Paddy bastards are crazy.

You know my dad was Irish, right? I'm Irish.

You're fucking Irish? You're serious, aren't you? Since when are you Irish? Your black ass is not Irish. You're losing your mind over in Uncle Tom fairyland.

Nobody gets to define me but me, that's what I'm learning.

What kind of Kool-Aid do they have you drink? Is it gray?

This text comes with a smiley face emoticon. But I can hear past it to Tosha's tone. I know her well enough to insert her sneer of condescension.

Get it? Gray? Half white, half black? Or do they make Oreo flavor now?

You know, "Virginia is for lovers," I finally respond.

I wait a few seconds. The screen flashes *Composing* for a full minute, but only seven words finally come through when she sends.

I want to tell George we're dating.

Bad idea. Why would you do that?

I've been checking the GPS tracker. He denies it, but he keeps going over there. He's taking me for granted. At least imply we're thinking about hooking up.

Bad idea, I write again, then send, barely resisting all caps. *Did you contact Sirleaf about your rights?*

I'm not ready for that. I need this favor, Warren. He has to come home. Or not. This can't keep going on like this. I need a catalyst.

Bad idea, I send once more.

We already lying to the kids. This is a smaller lie. It could help things.

Again, I pause, but Tosha doesn't need me to continue the conversation.

It will free me, comes when I take too long to respond.

And then, *He was just here. I'm sorry. I kind of already did it.*

I slam the laptop shut, curse.

Tal looks over at me, sees my face. "What?" she asks.

"My friend. Is acting like a lunatic." I get up, head to the kitchen. There's no alcohol in the house because of my daughter, so I settle for putting a pot of coffee on instead.

"That wasn't Sunita, right? Everything's cool with her, right?"

"Yeah," I say. Though I don't catch the transition.

"I mean, I haven't even seen you guys talk lately. I thought you were into her?"

"We're just friends," I tell her, but at the moment even this sounds like a stretch.

"I'm not a baby. I'm not clueless. You think I'm like some little kid but—"

My phone thankfully rings before we can take the conversation further. Tosha's face flashes on the screen and then her voice is in my ear.

"I'm sorry. He was here and I know from the GPS that the bitch was at his apartment, and he had the nerve to deny it. I got mad. And, just to see the look on his face, I said you were coming over, later tonight. I'm sorry."

"I understand," is all I say, because Tal is interested now, trying to look at my screen.

"Thanks for getting my back."

"I got your back," I tell her. George might have my ass, but I have her back.

"Good. So let me get your back: that biracial thing is a bunch of brown-bag divisive bullshit and you know it. That shit is dangerous and it's brainwashing and you can't get sucked into that. Or let your daughter get sucked into it either. I know you're beige, but stay black."

"I will," I tell her, because I just want to escape.

"Loving versus the state of my ass," Tosha says before hanging up.

I'm standing in front of a statue of an Indian, big as two men. He kneels down, hand over his eyes to block the sun, staring through the trees, down at the white people jogging across the Wissahickon on Forbidden Drive.

"He's looking west," Spider tells the kids, all gathered around with their notepads and charcoals, looking up at him and the statue, trying to figure out which one to pay attention to. "He's supposed to be looking for the Lenape who once lived here, the ones pushed farther inland when the Europeans invaded."

"Look at the angles of his arms, legs. Try to capture the angles. Even if it's just stick figures, focus on the lines. Check out the lines on his headdress, all those straight feathers," I say, because I'm supposed to be team teaching, and I have to say something. I look up at his massive thighs, and I think of Sun's thighs shaking as she rose to get away from me that weekend. I think of the dimples of the cellulite that were so much more real and beautiful than this statue's spotless hard quadriceps. That really happened. Sunita Habersham does speak to me, passes me without saying anything, but it still really happened.

Shazam. Those little details, like that red fuzz ball of lint hanging from her hair, bouncing when I was behind her, they tell me that really happened.

"That warbonnet? Completely historically inaccurate. That's ceremonial headgear for the Plains Indians, like the Cheyenne. The Lenape wore a sort of turban."

The kids look up at Spider, then at me. I shrug. So the ones who did the headdress start tugging at their pictures with their erasers.

"She got in your head, didn't she?"

I don't know how well Spider knows Sun. I don't know if they're best friends, or lovers, or just two people who occasionally get high together.

"Dude, it's obvious. Since your ghost hunt, both you guys been walking around like you *did* see something."

"You guys ever hook up?" I just ask him. I would never ask anyone else this, but I ask Spider. He's too open not to reach in. To not would almost be rude.

"Oh no. I like my ladies tall. I mean real big. You know what I mean?" I have no idea what he means. Sun is at least five ten. "Statuesque," Spider adds, and one hand goes up, and one hand goes out, and it doesn't make a damn bit of sense. The guy's barely five feet, almost all women must be tall to him. But he winks and there really is no possible negative response to a wink, so I say, "A'ight, a'ight," which is a great Philly way of agreeing without saying anything.

"Well, you need any advice on the woman thing, hit me up," Spider tells me.

"Okay. Well, thanks," I say in a sincere yet apparently unconvincing way.

"No really, dude. I know women. I used to be one, in a past life."

"In a past life?" I look over at Spider to see his joking smile. It ain't there. This little guy, lined with muscles and little ball naps forming a beard across his jawbone, he's definitely a man. Specifically, a madman. He berates the class playfully and they hurry. All these little mixie pixies, up and up, through the trees to Mulattopia. He's so good with them, this carny. Spider even knows the kids' names. He calls out to them like Santa addressing his reindeer. I can reliably recall one name, Kimet's, and that's solely because he's dating my daughter. Still, I say his name when he walks by. He nods and smiles and is suitably nervous, befitting of a boy being investigated by a girl's father for signs of normative teenage heterosexual male behavior.

"Let me see your sketch." It comes out sounding like I'm a soldier demanding documents. The boy stops walking, reaches for his satchel. It's got a National Organization for Women patch on it. Just to throw me off.

"Kinda needed more time, if you could—" he tries to tell me, but I interrupt him with a grunt. Kimet stares at my face. I stare back. So he starts pulling out the sketch. The other kids are passing us now. Some stop, want to see, I shoo them on. Kimet holds his image to his chest until we're clear again.

"I don't think—" he protests, but I quickly get a hand on his paper and he releases it because he doesn't want it to tear. I start hiking again as I inspect it, and he follows.

It's good. Structurally, anatomically, the sketch is informed, skillfully rendered. Even the perspective he's chosen: from the side, completely imagined because we did not get a clear view of the statue from that vantage. And of course, our statue was kneeling, peering into the expanse, not leaning forward as he sat defecating on a large stone toilet, as Kimet depicts.

But the subject is not the wrong-hatted Lenape. It's me. He even has my jeans in a pile at the bottom of my hairy legs.

I look up at Kimet. Teenagers, they feel everything so distinctly, desire, hatred, and right now I hope, fear. My laughter bursts; I don't even mean to, it just erupts when I attempt to maintain severity. I find other people's fears so amusing; I might even enjoy the absurdities of my own if they weren't petrifying.

"I'm really glad you captured the cut muscularity of my ass."

"Shit" comes out of Kimet's mouth. It's not directed to or at me though, but to the small crowd up by the Mélange Center's front gate.

The door is closed, the metal mesh sealed up, which it never is this time of day. In front of it now loiters our entire art class, two police cars, Roslyn, and Principal Kamau of the Umoja School. Kimet's father.

"You forget you had to leave early?" I ask, but when I look over Kimet's already turned around, walking back down the trail again. I call to him, but he ignores me, and it takes a couple of quick hops to catch him.

"Sorry, I can't. I'm not going." He tries to pull away, but I have too much of a lock on his elbow for him to do it politely.

"You afraid of going to the dentist or something?"

"My mom sent me here, not him. He's not even supposed to be here. You know, the divorce."

Divorce. Yes, I'm familiar with the malady. I don't even think of mine, but of my parents'. That's the only reason I let him head around the perimeter, to wait in the woods at least for a little while.

Cop cars aren't that surprising in the park, they roll up and down the valley road most of the day, checking to see if the leaves are still there. The cops themselves are standing outside their vehicle. One with a phone to his ear, the other farther down the hill, smoking. Cops make me nervous even in casual mode. Kimet's dad, he makes me nervous too. Here I am in the buttermilk, having chosen this Europeanized blackness when I was offered the full, undiluted glory of Africana. *We still cool, right,* my expression says, and I attempt to cut off all awkwardness by approaching him directly as he stands next to Roslyn.

"What?" is all he says to me. Then he looks at my outstretched hand as if this is some curious custom the local vagrant population insists on. He takes it, limply, and lets it fall again with only the slightest of nods. I have not joined the Oreos, I want to tell him, but he doesn't recognize me. No, he does, I see a faint glimmer in his eyes. He just doesn't care. Somehow, the current status of my racial patriotism, while highly important to me, is of shockingly little concern to him at the moment. He stands with his arms folded and stares down Roslyn, while she types into her phone with her thumbs as if spell-casting. I wait for her to finish, but when she does, no conversation follows. Eye contact brings a flash of a grin my way, but it just says, *This is the face I'm supposed to make when I'm happy,* and then it's gone as soon as she turns away again.

"Let's go for the second leg of the nature hike," Spider yells over. I look at him, waving at me frantically, the students all huddled around him. But there's no second leg. That hike was a one-leg beast and we hopped it.

"Excuse me," one of the officers comes through, breaking the silence. He's got a roll of yellow tape in his hand. He walks past, heads to the sealed gate.

"Really, do you have to? Isn't that a bit dramatic?" Roslyn purrs, but apparently he lacks the necessary mommy issues to be swayed by her. And then it says POLICE LINE DO NOT CROSS as yellow tape decorates the entry.

"The cops are just doing the whole 'You're not supposed to be squatting on public property thing.' It's no biggie," Spider tells me. We cut back and walk single file around the side of the perimeter after feigning like we were walking north toward the creek again.

"What do you mean it's 'no biggie'? Why are they doing that?"

"Because we're not supposed to be squatting in a public park."

The kids trail behind us, Kimet, the oldest, picking up the rear. A few kids actually ask, "Are we there yet?" They just arrived on earth, so lack all consciousness of cliché.

"It's over there," Spider yells and keeps hopping forward, short enough to avoid all the low-hanging branches that I have to push through.

"What's over where?" I can see the fence through the brush. We're at the back of the camp.

"The VIP entrance," Spider tells me, then lifts up one end of a flap created by a cut in the mesh fence. I pull up the other end, make sure the kids don't get snagged on the edges while crawling inside. I count them off. We still have eleven, and I'm pretty sure they're the same kids we left with. The mixie pixies, they love this. They think it's a joke. They think it's an adventure. They laugh. I don't laugh.

"Come on, it's fun!" Spider insists. He actually is having fun. Kimet is the last one through, and he's out of earshot walking with the others back to the classroom when I say, "No, this is bullshit. So this place really could get evicted at any minute?"

"Roslyn's got good lawyers, though. Like, the best ones. They get a judge to get an injunction, it's a whole thing. Usually takes about four hours, tops."

"Usually? What do you mean, 'usually'?"

"Like a dozen times. Once a month since last year. First it was the neighbors fussing, but Roslyn finally won them over. Last couple times it's been that guy from the Umoja School. He keeps calling the cops, I'm pretty sure. You know the type. Black folks like him are used to having the power to say who's black and who's not. It really pisses them off that some people just opt out."

"It pisses him off now because his son is here. Kimet."

"Oh. That makes even more sense. Oh well. It's cool, though. The whole place is on wheels. If it hits the fan, we just roll." Spider giggles at the vision. I see it too, and the only response I make is the clenching of my jaw.

I look around at the buildings. I look around again at all the wheels. Even the fence is attached at its base to mere concrete blocks. I can see the grass beneath our feet and imagine this whole space empty again, with just those blades remaining. For a second, I am standing on a vacant lot. Gone are all the black-and-white harlequins.

For her crucial final precollege year, the launchpad to a life of more promise and less struggle, the sole paternal gift I'm not too damn late to offer, I have enrolled my daughter in a school that can literally disappear overnight.

I'm Googling "prestigious GED programs" on my phone before I even get home. I'm searching for "Philadelphia Magnet Schools Late Enrollment." I start thinking, if Mélange collapses maybe I can get Tal to stay with me and do over her senior year. Private school, even—I might be able to cash in on the house by then, possibly even sell it. I start hating myself for not plastering and painting before, not doing all I know how to do to repair this hermitage every moment of the day and faking what I don't. We've already compiled the list of prospective colleges, schools with decent dance programs in California, Rhode Island, and Washington State, the latter being my favorite as it's the farthest away. It seems an impossible goal, remote yet imminent when I think about how I have to pay for it.

Irv's car is in my driveway. I get the gate open, get back into my car then pull up slowly behind it like it might decide to suddenly lurch back and smash me. My headlights flash into its cab as I head up the hill. It's empty inside. The lights inside the house are dark, upstairs and down. There's someone lying on the porch. Not Irv. Not Tal, either. I can see Tal in the kitchen, through the window.

The fear comes back but I don't listen to it. I decide the fear itself is nothing of merit, a few little chemicals in my brain, dripping the wrong way. I walk right over and if I must I will walk right through.

"Tal's home," Sunita Habersham tells me, pulling herself up off her back and onto her elbows. "She looks exhausted, needs the quiet. She came by Mélange looking for you, but it was locked up. She gave me a ride here in her grandfather's car. I said I'd wait out here for you."

Sunita Habersham in the dimness of the one yellow lightbulb. Life can have a sepia tone.

"And why'd you want to see me?" I ask, because the time to ask her is now, before it gets weighted.

"It's Wednesday. I brought the new batch of comic books. My whole pull list."

"You came to show me your comic books. You don't talk to me for weeks, and now, comic books."

"I had to think, okay? And I decided I wanted to see more of you."

"You seemed finished when you left before." My aim was to be jovial. The actual sounds that I emit are nothing like that. No humor can be found there, by either one of us.

"I guess I wasn't finished with you yet." She shrugs, as if her own self was a mere acquaintance. "If that's not okay, I can go. I need a ride, though. You can still borrow my comics. Except for this . . . one." She flips through the comics, pulls out an issue of *Locke & Key*. "Haven't read this one."

I roll my eyes, but take her hand. Sun lets me. Soft, sweating palm. I pull toward the door.

"Not in the house."

"What? You just want to sit on the porch?"

"Tal's in there," Sun tells me. "It's too weird." The only thing I find weird is that statement.

We go, back to my dad's little Volkswagen Beetle. We don't read comics at first, optioning to begin our meeting with fondling instead. It's almost roomy, with the seats pushed all the way down.

As we progress toward fornication, I look at my father's house when the angle permits it, waiting to stop if a curtain moves. One never does. Even as our sounds starts building.

"Don't yell 'Shazam!' this time."

"Right, this time *you* yell a catchphrase when you come."

"Which one?"

"Surprise me!" We stop talking.

I don't come. And I don't want her too either. I go as slowly as I can. Because when she comes, Sunita Habersham will leave me again. So I don't let her. I break rhythm, keep pausing. I look out on the vacant lot of the lawn, the grass long and unkempt and dead from the winter's first frost. It's so bare. I focus on anything but the pleasure. But eventually the car windows are steamed and I can't see out anymore.

Afterwards, we do read comics, with the windows cracked. She only stays until the glass has gone transparent once more, and then, per her request, I drive her home.

The times Sun visits me following this one, she still won't go in the house. So in my driveway we meet. She shows up every Wednesday evening, for new comic-book release day. Sometimes she even comes

Thursdays as well, if we haven't read all the issues, sitting in the car postcoital the day before. Sun never mentions the "boyfriend" again. I don't ask about her "boyfriend." I ask her to come in the house, I ask her to have dinner with me and my daughter, but I stop doing that eventually since she keeps saying "No."

14

THE WOMAN WHO breaks into my house breaks into my dream. She sits at the end of the mattress, facing away, but I know it's her. I know the bones popping through the back of that wet paper flesh could only be hers. And she's crying. I hear her crying, want to tell her to stop. But if I do she'll turn around and look at me, and I'll remember her face and I don't want that memory.

I put all my energy into lifting one arm, nothing. I put all my energy into kicking one leg, get the same. She leans backward to look at me, like she will fall once more into the bed, and then we will all be doomed. Doesn't turn around, just leans back. Arches her spine, throws her head far enough that I see her nose and know her eyes will be next. I try to close mine, my eyelids do work, but I can't close my ears. I hear the whimpers. I hear the sniffs of mucus loosened by tears. I hear the whine.

My eyes open, real eyes, and see the real waking room. Darker than the one of dream. Messier. Pants strewn on the floor, discarded comic books, sentinels of empty Diet Dr Pepper cans. My arms can move, and I gather the covers to me, giving myself another layer of fabric to protect against the universe. The loudest thing is my breathing, and I settle it down. Force it to slow, allow one heavy sigh before normalcy. The next sound is not from me. It's from the side of my bed. I still hear the sobbing.

I will scream. I've decided. If she's in this house again, I will make a sound like no man has ever been proud to utter. It will be loud. It will be the entirety of my defense against the world. It will be all of me converted into vibration.

She's in the corner, the hair is over her face. It's dark, full, hangs all the way past her neck. But it is curly, too. It ripples and bounces as she cries. It's my daughter.

"Tal? What's wrong?" I ask, but specifics don't yet matter so I swing my legs over and go to her, kneel and wrap her in both arms. Tal's in the chair, my knees are on the floor. She's been acting like everything is fine in the time since she got back from Irv's, since his news, and yet here she is, in the dark, undone. I hug her like she's broken and I can squeeze her tight enough to mend.

"I can't breathe, Pops," is the only thing that gets me to loosen.

I try again, the whole list: what's wrong, whatever it is we can talk about it, nothing can be that bad. Tal says nothing more. I'm still holding her. I try a little rocking motion, but she resists. After two minutes, it gets awkward.

"Everyone I ever love will leave," Tal says finally.

"But new people come. Sometimes. Sometimes, when we make room for them." I think this sounds deep. I was just thinking of her, in my life, but it sounds like something someone would put in nice font over a pretty stock photo, so I'm proud of it. Tal is less impressed, though.

"Irv's going to die. I couldn't sleep. I was lying there, and I realized everyone I love disappears. They either die, or they leave. It's that's simple. I'm stupid, I only just figured it out."

"That's not stupid. That's the single hardest thing to accept in the world. That everything changes. Sometimes it changes for the better, though." I try again, and again I'm thinking about her, the fact that she came into my life, and now it is better. No question. And after this moment in time, she'll also go.

"That's the best advice you've ever given me," Tal says with so little enthusiasm that it tells me competition was nominal.

"That wasn't advice."

"Whatever." Tal pulls out of my arms. Standing, she snorts all the liquid she can with her nose, wipes the rest off with her forearm. "Disgusting," she says to no one, then walks out of my room.

I stay sitting on the floor long after she leaves. I will not go back to sleep. In the gloom, I can see the bed. I can see the foot of it. There's an indentation in the fabric of the fitted sheet I want to believe I'm just imagining is in the shape of a boney ass.

"Mouths shut, pencils sharp, let's get ready to scribble," I say, because that's what I've been saying to start for a while now and, perhaps because of its slogan-like nature, they tend to obey. Then I walk around and offer guidance and criticism one on one, which helps them to learn and me to avoid panicking that I don't actually know how to be a teacher. This works, on average, for about thirty minutes. I stroll through the room, check on the status of their projects. After the first few days resulted only in pictures of superheroes punching each other, Spider made sure they had visual references for their tri-racial isolate projects.

"But when are we going to do our presentations?" the little fat one says today. It is not right to call "the little fat one" "the little fat one," so out loud I call him Marcus, which works since it's his name.

"Well, Marcus," I say, largely to display my knowledge of his identity. This is important, because it compensates for the fact that for a few seconds I have no idea what he's talking about. When I see his poster board and the memory kicks in, it doesn't help me much, because it was Spider's assignment, and Spider isn't here. Today is a Non-Spider-Appearance Moment, which usually occurs about once a week without prior warning or later comment. "You get an extra point for diligence. I was going to wait until the end of class, but we can start now. Would you like to go first, then?" I ask, because I really have nothing planned for the class today anyway, and time is for killing.

Marcus doesn't bother to answer. He gathers his things and comes to the front of the room. His only request is for a plug, to connect his smart phone. And then, pushing PLAY, he stands before us, papers in hand, head down.

The beat comes on. It's bossa nova.

"Brasil," Marcus says, lifting his head up. Holding up his poster board, which says the same. Then he drops his head again. Behind him, a recorded woman's voice sings in Portuguese, and Marcus is respectfully silent until her verse is done, then he lifts his notes, takes a deep breath, and begins.

"O Brasil é uma sociedade mestiça. Foi invadido pelos europeus em 1500, e originalmente . . ."

It's clearly not fluent, there's a hint of phrase-book mimicry in his voice, but he seems to know what he's saying; there's rhythm in his sentences. I recognize enough cognates from Spanish to nod along.

I'm not surprised the class politely listens. They're good kids, for the most part. What catches me off guard is when Marcus ends with *"Não acredito que os professores"* and they all laugh, comprehending, at his last line.

"They take Portuguese, two hours a day, plus lab. Most of the kids. Brazil's the largest mixed-race population in the Americas. Dude, how did you not know this?" Spider tells me, when he finally shows up, after class has been dismissed. This time, he offers the excuse that a tattoo went long, which could either refer to the time it took to do or the literal length of the image.

"My daughter takes French."

"No, your daughter takes French Creole, Louisiana style."

"Papa! Tu ne comprends pas?" says Tai, whose hair is in cornrows today. I refuse to acknowledge this change in appearance, and we're playing a game to see how long I can keep that up. Tal's sitting on my desk, bored already, in just the seconds she's been in the trailer. I don't know the specifics of what she's said but I get enough of the gist to tell her to stop being a smart-ass and go meet me at the car.

"Why Portuguese? Nobody in America speaks Portuguese. Spanish is everywhere."

"Come on, you know how mixies are. Every one of us has some place they heard about, where people look like us, where we could totally fit in. Morocco. Cape Verde. Trinidad. Man, I pretended to be Puerto Rican all through high school. It's that dream: home. To finally go fit in somewhere. Isn't that what everyone here wants? To feel what it's like to be in the majority? To be home?"

I think of that word, *home,* when I stick my own key in the door of my father's decrepit mansion. It opens, but I don't belong here. We walk in and Tal immediately drops her bag right on the floor. I tell her to pick it up and lock the door behind us, but I don't want us to be locked in here forever. The word *home,* it sticks with me through lunch, as I watch Tal separate the peas and chicken and carrot squares from her fried rice until it almost looks like a healthy, balanced meal instead of bulletproof takeout. She doesn't even eat the peas; she gives them to the hamster. I know this because he doesn't like them, and doesn't eat them either.

"You could learn French, too," she tells me, after a while. "Creole zydeco is kinda crunk."

"You say 'crunk' now?"

"I *am* crunk now, Pops," Tal insists, but the white-girl shrug that follows is the same as it ever was.

Home. I go to my desk, try to draw it without predetermining what the image will be. I find myself starting with a street, and then that street becomes Germantown Avenue. I know its cobblestones better than any surface on earth. I know the story, that they were carried from England as ballast on the first ships, and then used to pave the road that stretches from here to downtown. Yet it offers no comfort in connection. Halfway into the sketch, the basic pencil lines already etched, I realize this image is about leaving this place, not loving it. That road for me is about getting the hell out, which has always been the central dynamic in my relationship to Germantown. So I scrap it, and think of Swansea. *You make me feel like I have a home in this world. That if a great hand shook the planet, I wouldn't fall off.* I wrote this at the bottom of an illustration I did of Becks, around the time I asked her to marry me. She hated the picture, but didn't tell me for years, then did it silently by leaving it behind when she moved out. And then I thought, I can fall off now. I can finally disappear into nothing.

But Tal is here, and now I can't anymore. And she makes me not want to either. She makes me want to build something, for her.

At car. Got the new issue of The Walking Dead. *Bring water.* The text comes and I look out the window and Sunita Habersham's station wagon is on the street. I know she's not in her car. She's in mine. Waiting for me. This is how she does it. No forewarning, no arrangement. Just a text, like this one. *Bring water* is actually a major step forward in our electronic foreplay.

I bring a glass of water, with ice, and think, Tal won't notice if I don't rush. I walk from the kitchen to the front door trying not to spill and Tal sees me and says, "You're not kidding anyone," and looks back at her homework.

At the Bug, Sun's sitting in the driver's seat. She's got the seat pulled all the way back, and stares up at the tattered ceiling. I don't get in. I stand next to her door.

"Look, why don't you come inside? At this point, it's just weird. We could order some more food, maybe? I had a big lunch but we could just get a coffee or something."

"Nah, I'm totally stressed out. Just get in here," Sun tells me. There's a wink offered, but I don't want it.

After a few seconds, acknowledging that I am not going to move farther, Sunita deigns to look up at me. Her eyes are passive and bored.

Then she looks away again. It's not until I tap on the window that she sits up and rolls it down, the seat still supine behind her.

"The night is young," I tell her. I want to get in and read comic books, enjoy the physical aspects of our friendship. But if I get in and we do this she'll just leave. I need to build a home. This automotive pied-à-terre, what is it constructing? This is no longer new sex. Now it's just sex. Just sex is good as well, but without the novelty it must meet more stringent requirements. I need more. Tal deserves more, a woman in the house who is actually willing to come inside the house.

"It'll get cold soon. We could forget the comics and just get to the finale." There's Sunita's smile popping. It doesn't erupt; she puts on her face like a pair of sunglasses.

"Let's just go inside. I was about to make dessert. Got a muffin mix. Let's break bread this time. Tal said there's supposed to be an amazing new series on Netflix. We could watch it together, when she's done her homework. Or something by ourselves, something date-like, that would be nice. We could even just go upstairs. But not in the car this time."

"Upstairs? With Tal home?"

I say, "She knows you're here already. This isn't about her," then sigh. It comes as a completely physical reaction to holding my breath a bit in the moment, yet it works perfectly as an emotional statement. I open the door, hand her the glass of water. Sunita Habersham takes it, sips.

"I need something more," I tell her. I almost say *we need,* which might have scared her even if she realized my "we" is Tal and I. "I don't know what this is, but I need something more if you and I are going to continue."

"Want me to dress up like Catwoman?" she asks. She isn't kidding. From her handbag, she pulls out a black whiskered mask and shakes it at me.

I turn and walk away. I'm at the steps when Sun honks the horn. When I turn around, she's gotten out.

"Fine. We'll go on a date then. A proper one."

"Okay. When? Now?"

"Tomorrow night. There's an acoustic concert, downtown. At Acousticism. It's every first Thursday, a lot of us go, from Mélange. Mostly the so-called Oreos, but some of the sunflowers too. Even One Drop's crew. We'll get something to eat first. Ethiopian."

"Yeah. Sure. Fine. Good," I say, my humorless, declarative tone matching her own. I don't say, *I was just going inside to get condoms*. I have no defenses against Catwoman-related seduction. "The restaurant is called Almaz. Elijah will be there too; it's his favorite place. Then we can see what this is. We all can."

"You know that crazy bitch invited me out on a date with her boyfriend?" I ask Spider. We're in the back of the faculty meeting the next day. I still can't believe it. I can't. I start thinking it's a test, that I'll show up and it will just be Sunita, that if I go I prove that I don't care and I still want to be with her. Or, it's a test to see if I'm a big enough eunuch to put up with something like this. Then I think of Sun's face when she said it, the utter lack of humor.

"Don't use that word. The *b*-word. *Bitch*. It's misogynistic and too easy and loses your argument before you even start. Also, 'crazy.' Mental illness is a serious thing. It's an *illness*. And it's also misogynistic: guys are always saying women are crazy. Why not try describing her as a 'deluded asshole' instead?"

"Thank you, Spider. Thank you so much. Can you believe what that deluded asshole asked me to do?"

"Yes, I can. It's foul, but yes. She has a boyfriend, man. She told you that. That means: mess. And this is messy." Spider sticks his tongue out, twinkles his fingers like everything's falling to the floor.

"But I thought she would get some of my good stuff and then she'd like it so much that eventually she'd leave him and Tal would have a new mommy and we would all live happily ever after." I say it, and I start laughing, at myself, because that's exactly what I believed.

"So Warren, I hear you're going to join us tonight at Acousticism?

That's wonderful. You're really engaging in our little community, aren't you? What about you, Spider? Are you coming this time?" Roslyn is standing there, behind us. Her posture implies no movement, as sturdy as a tree in spring. She may have been standing there the whole time.

"Oh no. This one I might have to sit out." He looks over at me, his eyes smiling so big the lids should be curved.

My mind slides down a run-on sentence: Roslyn couldn't have overheard that I was going to this music thing, because I didn't say the name of the place I was going, because I just said "a date" and that's all, which means Sun told her about us all going out, which means Sun probably tells her everything, which is why Roslyn smiles at me now like she not only knows everything I've been up to but has the pictures to prove it.

"You should come with me! We should go, as a date, together," I say to Roslyn, to see what will happen. I long to see Roslyn unnerved. And if she comes undone, maybe Sunita Habersham will be off balance because of it. That's what I want. I want to see someone else uncomfortable. It works. The tree sways a bit. I follow with, "Sun said there's a great Ethiopian place, we're going to meet up there first."

"Almaz," Roslyn shoots back. And there is no sway there. There is only rigidity. "You know what? I think that's a fantastic idea."

As Roslyn walks away, we both stare after her.

"You know what, man? You're a wild boy," Spider says when she's out of range.

"Don't use that word. That *b*-word," I tell him, at which he frowns with a total lack of amusement.

15

ELIJAH. I say his name for hours. I say it and I spit. Literally. Even when I'm indoors. Eel. Lie. Junk. I fucking hate him. I hate him when Roslyn picks me up in the center's school bus. I hate him enough to fill every empty seat gaping behind us as we drive downtown. I fucking hate him. And I'm sure he's a nice guy. I'm sure he's a great guy. I'm sure he had the strongest of college recommendations, that there are old ladies who just think of his horrible name and start to cry because humanity has a hope after all. I forgive Sun for being his captive. For being seduced by his lies. Because they must be lies, because he must actually be a horrible person, because how else could I hate him?

Roslyn knows where the restaurant is, and insists on guiding me from the school bus by my hand. They're sitting on the floor, on pillows. Elijah's white. This is fine, I prepared a special hatred program in case he was a white guy, and it's ready to roll out. I'll have to delete the black Elijah, Asian Elijah, and mulatto Elijah mental files, but this just gives me more room to focus. He's probably one of those white guys who think they're enlightened just because they've realized the obvious fact that black women are beautiful. He's probably one of those white guys who think poking their pink members in black women will somehow cure racism. I don't trust interracial couples. I don't even trust the one that made me: I think of who my father was, who my mother was, and I have no idea why they first hooked up, let alone fell in love. I don't know if I'm the by-product of a racialized eroticism or a romantic rebellion of societal norms. I'm fine with mixed-race unions that *just happen,* are formed when two people randomly connect. But there are other kinds of interracial couplings with suspect motivation, with connections based on fetishizing of black sexuality, or internalized white supremacy—those kinds exist too. Yes, I was in an interracial relationship myself, but I distrust my own initial motivation.

I can dislike interracial couples while acknowledging I'm the product of one. Every misogynist came out of a woman.

Elijah's got a ponytail. It's braided. This is a bonus, because I can hate this more and do. It's red and he says his last name and I refuse to register it but it's Scottish so I feel relieved in hating him without too much Celtic overlap. He's skinny, and he wears two gold chains that shine through his open collar, and this is fantastic for hatred. It's so good that I look over at Sun and find that my disdain is becoming so voluminous that some of my hatred for Eel-Lie-Jah is spilling over to her. I look at Sun, who looks at the menu as if bored. But I don't think she can be bored because we've been having sex several times a week for months and now we're having dinner with her boyfriend.

"Do you know what you want?" she asks me. Then she winks. Only I can see it. For the length of the time it takes for her lids to shutter down and up again, we are in the Beetle, and she is naked, on me, facing me, kissing me like she wants my tongue at the bottom of her stomach. And I blush and look down at my menu and say, "I'm just here for the pancakes."

"Their injera is pure love. A lot of places, they use an electric oven, but they use a traditional clay oven here. You can taste the authenticity."

Elijah says all this, and he's very warm about it too, his eyebrows pop up excitedly with the word *love,* and I look back at him and smile and wonder for the first time, Does he know me and his girlfriend are fucking?

"For Elijah, everything has to be authentic," Roslyn says. So she knows him well, clearly. Well enough for there to be a slight disapproval in her statement.

"What is something worth if it's not real? I just prefer truth. Some people choose otherwise," Elijah says back.

Roslyn does that laugh, as though a child has said something inappropriate, and drinks, and I don't know what the hell they're really talking about. I hold the menu. I hold it up to my face, releasing my facial muscles from the strain of hiding disdain. I don't read the words. I want to hold it like this all night. I could do that here, and at the concert next. Who's that? Oh, that's Warren. He's very serious about what he's going to order tonight.

"They let the dough ferment for days, then hand pound it," Elijah says. "You really can taste the difference. If you're like me, you're going to love it too. And it looks like we have the same tastes, right?" and I look up, and he's smiling at Sun. Whose response is, "You know what, I think I need to powder my nose." Because Elijah totally knows we're fucking.

Roslyn makes a motion with her arm like she's going to get up and go with Sunita and I reach over and grab her hand and say, "Will you help me pick some appetizers?" with my mouth and *Please don't leave me alone with this white boy* with every other part of my body. Roslyn gets up anyway, pulls her hand free. Before she leaves, though, I get a kiss, on my forehead, that lasts long enough that I have to be still to not hit her in the nose. And then it's just me and the white guy who's smiling at me.

"Let's get out the weirdness. Let's just get it out, set it free, send it on the road." This is his toast, two glasses *tink.* He brought his own bottle of red wine. The label is boring and not at all hip and I'm sure that that means secretly it is.

"Hit me," Elijah says. I look up from my glass. "Just hit me." I put the glass down. "Not, like, in the face, bro. I mean, the ladies are only going to be gone for a minute. Let's have mano to mano time."

Mano means hand. I kind of want to punch him with mine. Not really. Just a little, but not really. I'm suddenly tired. I want to go home. I have a daughter. Tal doesn't need this. Tal needs me to date a woman who can add something to both our lives. I don't need this. I don't even really need a penis anymore. It can go. I could use a tube to pee or something. It'd be awkward, but I could get over that.

"Sun said you used to be married?" Elijah asks when my silence becomes too much for him.

"Married. Divorced. The whole cycle."

"That's why you get it, then." Elijah goes to clink my glass again. It's already empty. He fills it up for me once more.

"Marriage for men, it makes sense in a world where the average life expectancy is thirty-seven. If you're a guy in a village of like sixty, eighty people, with just a few women of childbearing age. But in our world? Never catch me getting married." He twirls his ponytail as he talks. He twirls it faster and faster. I look at the hair; I can't look at him. I hear the words, I even think about them, but I can't look at Sun's white boy as he deems to *whitesplain* the world.

"Maybe we should just kill ourselves at thirty-seven. Have you considered that?" I shoot back.

"I think her ex was, like, thirty-four? When he killed himself?" he says and it takes me a minute to even realize he's talking about Sunita's, and I blush at my error.

"Listen, no faux pas, really. It's just, she's still really sensitive about it. You should know. But like in marriage, you have to kill yourself a little, right? Inside. To make it work. A long-term relationship is sexually fulfilling for, what? Maybe three years? It's great as it is—Sun and I have been together two—you got to get creative to make it last. So you have to make a choice."

"You can break up." I'm not being theoretical. I mean Sunita Habersham, and him. They can break up. The earth would continue to rotate. It would be lovely, even.

"Or you can get her to realize that our societal expectations just aren't realistic. When you have something deep, a quickie in the shallow end never hurts anyone. We're just apes, right?"

"Oh. Another bonobo fan."

"That's Sun talking. She reads all that pop geek bullshit." Elijah points at my mouth with his long, ringed finger, poking. "Those aren't the only apes. Did she tell you about the gorillas? What they do?"

"We didn't get that far." I don't want to get any further, either. I just want the women to come back. I look in the direction of the bathroom, sure they will reappear to rescue me, but they don't.

"In gorilla society, there's just one guy: the silverback. And he takes all the women, and kicks the other males out. The females, they stray every once in a while, but it's permitted because the alpha male gets what he wants."

"Sun and I are fucking." I say it. With little outward malice.

"I know! And thanks for your contribution to our union."

When the women get back, we're talking about football. The real kind that involves feet. He takes the subject there the second they enter into my peripheral vision, and I let him out of exhaustion. Elijah has some "fascinating theories" on the rise of "American futbol" and its statement on the post-isolationist attitudes in the age of the Internet. I have a theory too: that he's an asshole.

Sun sits right next to me. Close, next to me. I think this means something. I think, we are not just splashing in the shallow. We are swimming in the deep sea of love! The language of that is so horrid it sends me into a depression that lasts through the main course and into a third bottle of Cabernet.

"They have horrible wine here, unfortunately," Elijah says, comparing the last two house wines to his contribution and I don't know, maybe he's finally right about something, but it's still the kind of drink that makes things not hurt so much.

"Just amazing body. I love Madagascan grapes. We were in Madagascar—when was it, last year? Eighteen months?"

"Maybe," Sun says. She leans over, brushes against my shoulder.

"Or a long time ago, or whenever." Sun says the last part to me. It's almost a whisper. It's almost just for me. It's almost intimate, except for the fact that it's addressed to everyone and so it isn't.

"It was a buddhavistic moment of clarity."

"It was okay. I guess." Sun sniffs, then she shoots back another glass of the cheap stuff.

"It was . . . one of those rare moments of connection that you get. The rhythm of the drums. The surf. The rustle of the wind through the leaves. And my little Sunny."

The Sun of this moment goes, "Okay, does anyone have a cigarette?" She gets up and walks out the door. I can see her through the window, looking left, looking right, and then nothing. She's gone.

"Isn't Madagascar where you encountered Chlamydia?" Roslyn asks, and I want to go home now. There is a flutter on Elijah's brow, the reaction to a faint breeze of an ill wind, but nothing more. I reach for my wineglass and it's just a pool of drips at the bottom, the last bottle offering slightly more of the same.

"Charuprabha. Her name was Charuprabha. But yes. That was there. She was working with Tossing a Starfish." To me Elijah says, "They do work with the poor in the Vohipeno region. Very powerful stuff."

"Oh, she was wonderful. I remember her visit. So well. Also, who was the Swedish friend you made? Katnis. That was it. Katnis Lumner, the young thing with the long blond hair on her legs. You make so many friends in the world, Elijah! So many connections!" Roslyn finishes her glass as well.

There are still words coming out of Elijah's mouth, but I have reached my limit of Elijah sentences, so feel absolved of having to listen.

"Go outside," Roslyn says into my ear, while he's still talking. And then Roslyn pats me on the head.

I feel myself trying to get up, and I feel drunk. Tal would be mad. For her, I refuse to stumble. I refuse to recognize the uncertainty of my horizontal stability.

Sun found cigarettes. She smokes one. I walk over, and Sun keeps staring straight off to the street, one arm around her stomach. She's wearing the white outfit again, the one she wore when I first saw her at the comic convention. There's a jacket now, a Russian hat with flapping fake-fur ears, and the draping of a hand-knit scarf to accommodate the cold, but it's the same.

"You wore that the first time I saw you," is what I say to her, but it sounds like "I love you" and I don't even know if that's true. I usually don't know till much later, and then from the intensity of the loss after everything goes wrong. I said I loved Becks, and I can think of Becks now, place her in a day like this one. See Becks wrapped in the red wool scarf she used to wear, those worker boots she thought made her look more working class, the ones that went into the closet forever when she became a professional. I can see Becks stumbling ahead of me, giggling drunk, as we walked through the dark from the bars of Mumbles, ocean to the right, hoping for an available minicab somewhere in the buildings to our left. I remember seeing that sight, and knowing I loved her, that I loved a mousy-haired Welsh girl named Becky, and I remember that and feel nothing close to that now. I can live in the moment, but I can't trust the moment. This moment, where Sun exhales and I see all the smoke and I, too, want to spiral around inside her, it could be lying as well.

When Sunita turns, it's sudden and as deliberate and forced as the smile. The earflaps jump. The rest of the smoke inside her comes out of the forced corner of her grin, and the cigarette is flicked to the street beyond.

"Don't worry, Warren, they can't give you cancer if you sacrifice them to the sewer god."

"We can just go now. We don't have to go to this concert, you know? I'm tired. This was enough. Come with me. You could spend the night."

"Oh, come on. Nobody likes a quitter. Didn't you like your meal? I thought the food was fantastic!" Sun's still smiling. She wants me to be smiling. If we're both smiling, our lips will be too tight to verbally unpack what the hell happened in there.

"That's Elijah? That's the boyfriend?"

"He's okay. He can be fun. Really."

"Wow, so that wasn't a joke. That's the person you've chosen to be your real boyfriend. Okay."

"Hey, I don't have to justify him to you. My relationship with Elijah shouldn't be threatening to you, Warren. It's a separate relationship. It has nothing to do with ours." It comes out quick. It was already prepared, loaded in her head, and waiting to be delivered.

"So you admit it. We have a relationship."

"Sure. Fine. But I have one with him, too."

"But he's a self-centered asshole!" That I say this, more than the fact that the world is kind of fuzzy and unmoored, makes me suspect I might be drunk. When I follow with, "You don't love him," that confirms it.

"You don't know me. We fuck, Warren. We fuck, and we talk comic books. That's it. You barely know me."

"But I want to know more," I say, with far too much vulnerability. And it doesn't matter because I've already pushed things too far into ruin.

Elijah laughs. Not at this, but at something Roslyn's said to him as they walk out the door. Something he doesn't like, something he has to mimic joviality about and add "You know, I don't know if you know how funny you are" to complete his response. He walks right up to Sun and hugs her. Hugs, rocks back and forth, hugs. And then looking at me, Elijah smiles even bigger and goes to hug me. The man is hugging me. Really hard. His beard brushes against my neck. His ginger goatee. It reminds me of Becks's pubic hair, wet from sweat, shaved into damn near the same oval. Oh look, Sun and I have similar tastes in white people.

They walk right in front of us, the two of them, the official couple. The couple licensed and approved by time. Roslyn takes my hand again, pulls me on. I grasp it, keep staring ahead. She puts a hand on my chin, and aims my face at hers.

"You are a beautiful mixed man," Roslyn tells me. This is not true, but it is truly a lovely mantra. For I am a beautiful mixed man. "You are a strong multiracial warrior," she continues. "Thank you" doesn't seem enough so I give her a kiss on her cheek. The side of her face offers much-needed warmth as I watch Sun and Elijah entwined a few feet beyond.

There's a small, hand-painted, black-and-white sign with a white angel playing guitar on it. Under it is a door, and through that door, steps that lead to the second-story loft above an empty Greek restaurant. All the Oreos are up there. There are so many Oreos, it makes me want to eat one. "It really is a delicious cookie," I whisper in Roslyn's ear, and she nods and smiles because it's loud and she can't hear me. It is a delicious cookie, really, it is clear to me now. The chocolate crust, the creamy white cloud on the inside. "How could it be an insult?" I ask Roslyn, and she says, "I don't know. I believe it's guitars and banjo. Or perhaps ukuleles."

The space is a shotgun,with a stage at the back, a few couches already filled with people sitting on every available surface. Roslyn walks toward one of them, and I look at the people crowded around it and I know them. They are the faces of people I sometimes nod to as I walk the grounds of Mélange, and sometimes they nod back. And sometimes they don't, because I have an angry face or they heard the gesture is called a nigganod and want nothing to do with it. But they are fully invested in her, Roslyn, the great matriarch of the new people.

"How's that date going?" is screamed into my ear. I turn to see Spider smiling.

"It's gone to shit. I thought you weren't going to be here?" I yell.

"Came to see the aftermath," he yells back, then wags his head right and left as he laughs. He takes me by the arm, pulls me farther away from the speakers, sits right on the floor, and leans against the wall. I kneel down knowing how hard it's going to be to get back up again, deciding not to do so till the alcohol in me is ready to find its final resting place in the toilet.

"It turns out, I don't understand Sunita," I tell him. "I don't know if it's a gender thing, but I don't get her."

"Don't feel bad. I don't understand some women either, and I was born one." Spider shrugs, offers me a swig of the flask he struggles to yank out his hip pocket. I'm looking at the bottle, a lovely steel job, shiny, curved like the edge of his leg. But I'm thinking, He's serious.

"You really were a woman?" I lean harder against the wall. I push into it. I want the outline of my body to mold into the plaster so something in my life feels firm.

"Yeah man, I told you. Biologically. Never quite fit in any other way, though. So I did what I had to do. This is, like, what, fourteen years ago?" He sees the way I'm looking at him. Because I'm not looking, I'm inspecting. I'm checking the leathered folds giving parentheses around his smile, clocking the receding stubble of his hairline, looking for the bulge of an Adam's apple under the ink that crawls over his neck from out of his shirt. "Testosterone. It's a helluva drug," Spider adds. Nothing is what it is or what it was.

"That's the problem right there," he responds as if he heard my thought. "You gotta change. With life. Life changes, you got to go with it. Or you get pulled apart." I don't know if he's talking about me, or Sunita.

I close my eyes. I close out everything but the sound of a dulcimer. My dad used to make his own dulcimers. Cardboard ones mostly, but wooden ones too. It was a part of some hippie forecast of an apocalypse where knowledge of dulcimer construction would be essential. It's the first time in decades I've heard one and its music is light and tinny and the sound of a tipsy Craig Duffy, pipe of Cavendish hanging from the corner of his mouth and bathing in a tub of good mood. I open my eyes to see the player actually does remind me of my father as well, except he's younger and, of course, brown.

"Hey look, the civil rights movement had a baby!" I say it loud, but none of the people around me respond beyond a glance my way then quickly back to each other again. They're all young couples, in their twenties. Some wearing wedding bands, some about to put them on. They're so beautiful. They have that skin, that youth skin, like Play-Doh when you first pop the lid. Even staring blank-faced, the ends of their mouths tilt toward a smile. Nothing has happened to them yet that doesn't seem conquerable given their massive expanse of unused time. I look at each couple, examine them as they are now, add in any other moments from my memory when I've seen them huddled at Mélange, for my supporting data. I decide which ones will end in divorce when this moment is years behind them. Which ones will look at their partner and feel so little that the memory of any strong opinion seems a mirage? The ones that will say, I never truly loved you. Later, they'll realize that there was love, and it was real, and that the fact that real love can dissipate so completely is even more devastating. That love is the greatest thing we have, the best thing we get, the only thing worth waking for, and even it turns into a putrefying mess just like the bodies we're stuck in.

"A rocking night, right?!" one leans over to say to me. Skinny with a fat brown beard. The mop top girl with whom his legs are intertwined kisses him on the lips the second he turns back to her, as if he's been gone a million years and miles. They both laugh, because they are young love and young love is as arrogant and self-involved as youth in all other forms. I hate that I was them. I hate that Becks isn't here anymore. My Becks. Becks the abstract. The version of Becks I cared the world for. Not the actual person, who still exists now, out in the world. The real person—I don't miss being with her, in that actual relationship we created. The constant bickering. The long and loaded silences. The moments weighed down by years of piling resentments that gave even the smallest interactions the potential to bring it all crashing down. What I miss is what came before, what always comes before. The euphoria of love. With her, I remember it with her. I could cry right here at the abstract idea of it. I miss being able to believe in it, so completely. That's why I hate them, these couples around me. Not for their happiness, or for their love, or even for their self-delusion, but because they don't know. They don't know that the rot always comes. I don't just want to love again. I want to regain the privilege to love like a fool.

•••

They play "God Bless the U.S.A." by Lee Greenwood to make us leave. I've always found its corny country-infused paleo-patriotism to be comforting in a post-9/11 way, but few in the crowd agree with me. They sing along in groans. When it gets to the line, "And I gladly stand up," everyone sitting actually does, and soon there is a torrent heading for the door. At the exit, the crowd orbits around Roslyn, and she gives each their own personalized parting message.

On the sidewalk, I can hear the phone ringing in my breast pocket. I think, Sunita, but when I look at it it's Tosha's name and face staring back at me. I try to shut it off and I'm poking at it and then she's talking to me.

"Warren? Warren? Warren?"

"Natasha, I'm here."

In response, Tosha blurts forth with, "You're going to get a call from George asking if we're engaged so just say yes."

"Are you serious? Tosha, it's two in the morning."

"When he asks, just say, 'Yes!' Okay?" and then she's silent. I look at the phone's screen, and see she's disconnected. It goes dark. Then it lights up again, and I see George's name and number there.

"Hey," George says.

"Hey," I respond as if him calling me right now, at this time of night, is totally normal.

"So . . ." George continues. I don't know what to fill in here. Our past phone conversations were less stilted, but usually consisted of "How you doing?" followed by "Cool, man. I'll go get her."

"Warren, I don't want to hear any bullshit right now. I'm gonna ask you something, and I expect a straight answer. This involves me, but it also involves my children, and I don't play when it comes to my children, understand?"

"I understand," I say, because it's late and I'm out on this street and I want this over.

"So let me just ask you something: Are you fucking my wife? Or is she once again fucking with me?"

I think about it. I think about what to say. I think of nothing. So I hang up the phone.

I walk. I don't feel good. The text that follows from George, *You are dead,* doesn't make me feel better. Nor even does the one after: *Metaphorically. The previous text should not be misconstrued as a literal threat of grievous bodily harm. Shit head.*

I sit in the middle of the school bus, in the center of all the empty rows, as Roslyn drives me back home again. I don't say anything. I don't look at anything; my head stays in my hands, holding the weight of my skull. When the bus stops at my father's house, I don't even notice at first, think it's just another red light until the engine dies.

I look up. There's an outline in the dark. Roslyn stands before the exit steps.

"Rise up, fallen fighter. Rise and take your stance again," she says, not joking. I do get up, so I don't have to hear any more of that crap. "Don't fall to despair. You'll never win her heart like that."

"I don't know. I don't know women," I say this time to Roslyn, for the more feminine perspective.

"Women are just people, honey. You don't know people. That's worse."

I walk toward the bus's front door. Roslyn doesn't move out of my way.

"Come here. Come." One. Two. Three steps closer. I'm too close to her now. And she's still standing there, blocking me. I stop with one foot almost between hers. Roslyn grabs my hand, pulls me closer.

"Ask yourself, what do you want?" She squeezes my palm in hers, then takes my other hand as well. If she pulls, I will fall forward, into her. She does. I do.

She doesn't hug me, she envelops me.

"I've got you," Roslyn tells me. She has me. It's absurd; I'm pulled so far into her my chin is on her shoulder blade. Her body is warm and soft and her poncho feels woolly to my touch.

"I have you, baby. Let go. Same thing I tell Sunita: you can let go. Let me carry the load."

I feel her lift me. Just for a second. Just enough that I marvel at this woman's strength, will. Just long enough that I can feel my ankles lose their burden, lifting slightly from the ground.

"You just need a little mothering, that's all," Roslyn says. And then I really do let it go.

I cry. Without filter this time. First the damn tears and all their blurring and then I'm barking ragged sobs. I don't even know why. I just want to go home. I just want to be alone, even though that's the last thing I need now and it feels good not to be solitary in this moment. I miss my real mother. I miss her so much. These are her tears, not mine. Just that they've been stored in me, and now that I'm drunk they're escaping.

After Roslyn gets me in and upstairs, after I get my pants off, Roslyn tucks me into bed. She throws my blanket over my fetal pose. My dignity is gone. It's okay, life feels light without it. It feels even better when she tucks the blanket under my body, then kisses me on my forehead. And with the lightest "Sleep tight," leaves the room.

Nothing has changed but my mood. Roslyn is a good person. I get her now. And I am not a bad person either. I have my innocence, my vulnerability; that needs to be protected. I was wrong about Sunita Habersham, but I was wrong about Roslyn too. I haven't been tucked into bed since puberty. It's beautiful. It's a good, simple thing. I find it literally sobering.

I keep waiting to hear Roslyn walk down the steps afterward—my digestive system is out of its element with the Ethiopian food, and it's about to get loud under my duvet—but she goes into the bathroom. It's horrid in there, tiles ripped up on the floor, calcium stains in the cracked tub; Roslyn deserves better. She must have decided she does too, because I hear her leave it without flushing.

From the creaking doors and floorboards, my ears follow Roslyn going into the next room. There's nothing in there, just building materials, ladders, my father's debris. But I hear her. Pausing at the entry. Then walking in steady, deliberate footsteps into the room. Then walking back out. I hear her in the hall again, and just when I think she's finally going to leave, I hear her do the same thing at the next bedroom. Walk inside in even, rhythmic footsteps. Then walk out again. Then the next room. *She's measuring,* I realize. With her steps. Like my father used to do when he forgot his tape ruler. I don't know why. I don't know what she wants or what she's after. But I hear as she stands still, in the last doorway, taking it in. Pausing long enough to really inspect the space, then closing that last door lightly behind her and heading back to the stairs finally.

16

OFF THE COAST of Maine, about an hour north of Portland, on an island resting on the mouth of the New Meadows River, among those last spatters of New England where North America blends into the Atlantic, there lived a community of mulattoes. For real. There were about forty of them, and most shared a common black ancestor, a sailor who settled in the area a century earlier. The island, Malaga, as well as the town of Phippsburg just across the narrow strip of water from it, once had a stable economy, when shipbuilding and the commerce of the sea made the area a prime location. But the movement toward steam-powered boats at the end of the nineteenth century left these communities poor and isolated, like many coastal Maine towns. Still, impoverished as Malaga was, it did have some wealthy benefactors, and by 1910 a new school was built and the island showed signs of long-term improvement. The community might still be there today, the sole black neighborhood of rural Maine. But at the same time some were seeking to help this group, a plan was hatched to save the local economy by turning that part of the river into a tourist destination for wealthy urban vacationers. This plan lacked room for a bunch of poor Negroes sitting in the middle of the scenic landscape. Newspapers soon raged with headlines like STRANGE COMMUNITY ON MALAGO [sic] ISLAND and told stories of the "peculiar people" and their "romantic tales." Twisted by yellow journalism, the community became cast as a miscegenated Gomorrah. The public was presented with a living representation of the hybrid splicing H. G. Wells had just written a novel about, only this time, it was *The Isle of Doctor Mulatto*. This distorted and warped story provided cover for the state to seize control of Malaga and evict its residents, destroying the entire community. Eight of the Malagans, people too old or young to take care of themselves, were sent to The Maine School for the Feeble-Minded, where all but two would die. The state even dug up Malaga's cemetery, dumping the bodies in the sanitarium's potter's field, lest their blackness taint the island soil like lime.

It is a powerful, heartbreaking tale, even interpreted in comic-book form by an eleven-year-old. An eleven-year-old whose multiple stick figures look like a caveman's interpretation of a spider orgy. Cory Kurtz has no talent. Sure, he's eleven, but I have more faith in his absence of talent than Constantine had faith in God. Every time I look at his attempts at art I think, He's going to make a great accountant someday, the kind who never tries any funny stuff because he has no imagination. That last judgment I may have to reassess because the illustrations he has mounted on poster board before the class show an abandoning of realism so bold that if I didn't know the source I'd assume it was intentional. In an effort to negotiate his lack of skill, I've allowed him to create his images using collage instead, and little Cory Kurtz has seized the opportunity to populate the entire island of Malaga with images of mixie action superstar Dwayne "The Rock" Johnson. Lots of Dwayne "The Rock" Johnsons. Many different images of his head, from many different photos, all cut and pasted and put on coat hanger bodies. Some with long penciled hair and circle breasts, as Dwayne "The Rock" Johnson transgenders for the role. In this dystopian vision, our hero has been cloned and trapped on the nineteenth-century New England island, where he roams among mansions which, due to lack of perspective, seem smaller than him.

"I wanted to make sure that you could see they were all related," Cory responds on inquiry.

"Okay. So, the houses—" I begin, and really what I want to talk about is the word *perspective* and remind him what I've been trying to tell him for months, but Spider takes over.

"The houses, they're a bit grand. I'm pretty sure this one here is Thomas Jefferson's Monticello. On Malaga, there were more traditional, solid homes, but many of the people lived in poorly insulated shacks. Because they were broke."

"I wanted them to be living large. That was important to me," Cory shoots back.

"Well, that's understandable. But it misses the point. If they could afford grand mansions like this, they would have never been wiped off the face of the map."

"Come on, anything can be wiped off the map," I have to jump in. "There are tsunamis, tornadoes, hurricanes, wars. And that's just the physical; the emotional is worse. You can be in love with someone—or at least have deep, heavily weighted feelings for them—then, poof, it's all gone. Nothing left. Everything can be erased in an instant and you will never even see it coming."

The class just stares at me. A bunch of kids, they don't understand me, my ennui. They're still at the beginning, they don't know it all ends in excrement. The teens, you'd think, would at least suspect this outcome, but they're silent as well. Kimet doesn't say a word. I would think he'd be able to relate given his parents' divorce, but restraint keeps me from saying this out loud. They all want to leave, I see. They're even packing their bags—have we pushed through another hour of class? But I was just getting started.

In my hand is an envelope, in that a card, and on that a bunch of writing. It was delivered to me by my daughter, just before class, with enough time to open it if I could have brought myself to do so in front of everyone. The writing on it is not my daughter's, but Sunita Habersham's. Sunita Habersham, who has not talked to me in five days, since the night of our group date. Sunita Habersham, who responded to a text two days after the event with, *Sorry, been busy,* and nothing more. Just those three words. It's not that I haven't seen her—I do nearly every school day, when she walks by me nodding hello like I am just another virtual stranger on a world covered with them. Not that I don't hear how she's doing nearly every day from Tal, because she's doing wonderfully. She's a wonderful mentor. She's Tal's favorite dance teacher ever, favorite adult, favorite human being in every way. Sun is in Tal's school-day life, completely. She has left mine, equally so.

"Look at the Malagans!" I implore the room, yelling it. Some of them, they startle. I don't care. "Look at them! Can you see them? No, you can't. Because they're gone. That's life, kids. It's all destined for nothingness, eventually."

Spider waits till everyone's left the classroom to talk to me. "You're off your game, man. Your head's in your heart. You either go work this out with Sun, or you got to shut up. Like, forever, and never say another word. I don't know, we'll tell the kids you've gone mute or something. You're too horrible like this," is pretty much the gist of it and it's not particularly helpful or insightful given how little Spider knows. That I cried like a pathetic wreck on the suspect shoulders of Director of Services Roslyn Kornbluth, for instance. He doesn't know that. Possibly, Sunita Habersham does. I don't care at this point, or I'm willing to believe I don't. Tal is sitting on the steps when I open the art trailer's door. Her dance gear is still on, not the clothes she was wearing when I drove her to school.

"Did you read the note?" my daughter asks me. I didn't. I just saw the handwriting on the front of it.

"Why are you serving as UPS on this thing?"

"But did you read it?" I didn't, so I finally open it up. There's no detailed explanation of Sun's behavior. But also, no formalized rejection either. Just a few lines in the middle of an otherwise blank card, and boxes to check off.

I'm sorry I've been distant, but I needed to think. And I would really like it if we could talk. When is good?

- ☐ *Tonight*
- ☐ *Saturday*
- ☐ *Sunday*
- ☐ *In Hell*

"So what are you going to say, Pops?" Tal asks.

"This was private. Why did you read it?"

"Because you're miserable at home, and she's miserable at school. So now I'm getting two kinds of miserable. And I like her. I told you." Her eagerness, at bringing Sunita closer into our lives, is both annoying and a strong motivation to continue trying. I make a point of dramatically removing a pen from my back pocket and showing it to my daughter. Then I mark off the appropriate box and, with increasing flourish, place the note back in its envelope before I hand it to Tal.

"She's not your new mother, you know?" I say this mostly to myself, but it sounds like a dig at Tal. "She's just your teacher, and a friend of your father's," I add, softening my tone to the point, I fear, of being patronizing.

"This is why you're alone," Tal tells me. Then adds, "Besides me."

I get some pasta, use a lot of olive oil, throw in some grated parmesan, chives, all so that when you stick the entrée next to a decent bourbon, it looks like I've spent the appropriate amount of time for someone who only kinda gives a shit. I am serving my ambivalence. It's absent my libido, which has retreated from frustration. I am cured. Or if not cured, in remission, overcome by the other demons that plague me. I have digested this, the idea that Sun is connected to another man, and I find myself at ease with the concept. Racially even—I push my finger into my lizard brain and say, *What about a white guy?* and to my surprise find little extra resistance. After the idea of sexual ownership is stripped from my expectations, after the begrudging agreement that I truly don't want to own her, I'm left with a new, theoretic openness. But *this* man, Elijah. This horrid, coveting, appropriating, ball of self-love shaped like a man. How could she love such a man? How could she even be who I think she is, and have chosen such a despicable partner?

"It's over." Sunita Habersham stands outside my open front door, and this is the first thing she says to me. Tal is upstairs, showering in expectation of the arrival of her favorite adult.

"It's over?" I ask, and I can't believe she set this up, made a formality of it, involving Tal, just to dispose of me.

"Elijah, not you. We're officially done. That segment of my life is over. Two years. Two years of going nowhere, on purpose, over."

"Over," I tell myself. I don't seem to believe it yet.

"But I don't want to talk about it. After I come in this door, I don't want to talk about it. Not tonight. Not ever. I'm not carrying the past with me. So you want to ask anything, do it now."

"Did you love him?" I want to know. Not to torture either one of us. But if she did love him, and she just dumped him like that after two years, that scares me even more.

"No. I don't think so. That was kind of the point," Sunita Habersham says, and before I can ask her about the man who came before Elijah she pushes past me and walks in the door.

"The first boy I kissed was Lawrence Levy. You don't understand; he was so hot," Tal insists. We don't challenge her. "It was on a school trip to the Smithsonian."

"I don't want to hear this," I tell her.

"It was on the way back to Philly, back of the bus, in the dark. I sat by the window. He was pretty popular and the whole time I was kissing him I was totally flattered, you know? That he even chose to sit next to me? That he waited the whole school year for this moment? And then, when he acted like a jerk afterward, I remembered, 'Oh yeah, it was assigned seating.'"

"He told everyone about it, didn't he? Spread rumors, told everyone it was more, didn't he? That little bastard Larry Levy." I'm furious with this kid. The meal's evaporated, but the bourbon has sustained a position on the table for an hour. I take a sip and I want to hear more about this faceless Lawrence Levy. It's only been a few years, I'm sure. I could still call his parents.

"That happened to, like, two other girls that trip. But not me. This was worse: he told no one. Not a soul."

"No!" Sun gasps. Her bare feet are on my lap, and she leans over now all the way so that she can hug Tal's shoulders, tickling her in the process. We are one squirming, warm snake on kitchen chairs.

"It's serious! He told no one. Not one person. I couldn't either, because people would have thought I made it up. He never spoke to me again, and didn't brag on me at all. Not one dirty rumor. I was totally scandal-worthy! I am total brag material."

"Kimet brags about you." Sun releases her with a pat and a wink for me. "He's always, 'My girlfriend Tal says,' and 'My girlfriend Tal was.' "

"No he isn't." This is what my daughter looks like blushing. I love that. I love *love*. I don't even get scared that Tal's found it. I don't even say, *Don't get pregnant*. Instead, I offer, "Well, he's a talented kid. And I certainly enjoy his company more than his dad's."

"Oh, his dad's a bastard," Sunita Habersham announces. I try to give her a look to tone down the language, but Tal chimes in with "Total bastard" before I can.

"How do you know?" I can't imagine Sunita Habersham perusing the halls of the Umoja School on her own.

"That jerk formed a group that's been trying to get the Mélange Center shut down for months. He's called parents, congressmen, municipal offices. The city might have stopped trying to evict us if he hadn't been pushing on them."

"Spider says we're not getting evicted," I tell Tal. She has four months of high school left now. We should be getting acceptance letters soon; the possibilities will unfold. Just a little time, and then she's gone. Long term, Roslyn can take her tribe to the promised land, if need be. I just need a few months of stability, because that's what Tal needs.

"No, we're definitely being evicted." Sun says it so casually the statement is clearly beyond debate.

"She doesn't mean this year," I assure Tal, based on no other information than an imaginary document found in my brain in a folder marked ESSENTIALS.

"Oh no, I mean right now. The cops are at the compound with a dispersal order. I don't think they're going to leave this time. All my stuff's packed in the car, it's horrible."

I forget Tal is a teenager. Sometimes, I think of her as a child, look at her and see all the younger ages I missed. Often, because of her wit and feigned worldly manner, I also see Tal the young adult she is moments away from being. But when she lets out a scream at the top of her lungs, only breathing in to yell "No," in one elongated syllable, I see a teenager. "This cannot happen, are you kidding? Are you messing with me? Pops!"

"You're not kidding?" And when Sun's head shakes, the last of my composure dissolves. "How could you not say this as soon as you got here?"

"I didn't want to ruin the meal," Sunita offers quietly. Before I can respond, Tal continues screaming, louder.

"Pops! You have to do something!"

"Just stop! There's nothing I can do!" My volume, as unexpected as it is for both of us, calms Tal. Or at least the shock shuts her up for a bit.

"Actually, you can." Sun looks at me. Tal looks at Sun. Sun keeps talking. I start bracing. "The community needs someplace to go. Temporarily."

"Come here! They can all come here! This house is so big! And the land! Everyone could fit here!"

"Enough!" I try to match Tal's volume again, but can't.

"There's more than enough space on the lawn for all the trailers!" Tal continues, giving away everything before Sun can even bring herself to ask.

"It's not that simple," I tell her.

"Yes it fucking is."

"Go to your room!" I fall back on.

"My room is a tent, in the dining room," Tal points out. Literally pointing out, over to it.

"Then go upstairs and take a shower before bed."

"I already got a shower," Tal says, but she gets up and heads for the steps before I get the chance to tell her to take another one.

I make Sun come with me into the kitchen. I don't even do it with words. I just walk to the sink, turn and lean against it, and wait there silently until she gets up from the table and joins me.

"You knew." I want to whisper, I want to scream, I manage to do both. "That's why you're here tonight. Not for us. Not for me. Roslyn sent you here, didn't she? It's about the land. That's what this is all about, isn't it? How long? That's all I want to know. How long has she been planning this?"

"Warren? Listen to yourself. You're upset, I understand. So I'm going to choose to not get offended. But you're having a paranoid episode right now."

"I saw her—or heard her, at least. Roslyn. Here, in this house, scoping out the property. Creeping around in the dark, going into the rooms upstairs, oh yeah I heard her and I get it now. She wants this place, doesn't she?"

"Wait, why the hell was Roslyn in your house at night, upstairs?"

"Don't change the subject," I tell her. "Listen, I'm not planning on keeping this property, okay? They can't come here. I have other plans." I don't tell her, *Because it's burning down*. Because I can make more on the insurance than any sane person would ever pay me. Because I have the know-how to burn this wreck down, having done the research at the library, by looking it up on YouTube.

"I never said anything about them coming here. Tal is the one—"

Tal screams. From upstairs. Sun doesn't hear it. Sun is still talking. But I hear Tal. And though I haven't been there for her most of her life, I've been here these months, so I know my girl's screams. And this one might mean something, if I heard it right. So I wait. Look up. Like I can see through the exposed and rotting drywall on the ceiling. Sun's still making mouth noises, but my ears are aimed up. A second later Tal screams again and I start running. And at the steps I know Sun has heard it too because she runs with me.

We hit the second floor so fast I slide into the wall. The bathroom. There is nothing being screamed now, but I know. The crisp echo off the porcelain: the bathroom. I have nothing in my hand, my spear is lost, Taser in the car, baseball bats downstairs. I don't care. My weapon is my body. I swing open its door. White subway tile predating subways. White claw-foot tub. White sink. Not-white girl.

Tal's standing there, hands over her mouth. I look on her for blood, then in the sink, then on the floor. A gust blows in through the half-open window, cold, still winter. I go to the tub. I reach for the shower curtain, thinking someone might be on the far side behind it. Nothing.

"What?" I ask my daughter. "What is it?"

"Outside," Tal whispers. So light I don't understand. Not till she's pointing again. Then I look. It's dark. It's the night, the frozen night. I can't see. But then I do.

There's two people fucking outside my window.

That's not right. That can't be right. So, specifics: there's a naked black man. Fucking a naked white woman. From behind. Outside my bathroom window.

Both upright. In the dark.

I squint. Yes. It's dark, but that is what I'm seeing.

"Get the hell out of here!" I yell. All the anger there. All.

Sun shoots her hand to my mouth. Very slow, low, as if not to interrupt them, she says, "We're on the second floor."

We are on the second floor.

Those fuckers out there are floating twenty feet off the ground.

Another scream. I think it's Tal again, but when I turn around, no, it's Sun. Tal's hand is up, holding her phone at them as if it were an exorcist's bible.

I turn around. There's nothing outside the window but night again. I lift the window up higher, put my head out, look around. Nothing.

No one on the lawn. No one on the street beyond. I grab the window frame, slam it down and lock it.

Reflection. I think, Reflection, it must've been a reflection. There is a mirror over the sink and one by the door. There are no ghosts.

I start to run for the hall but Sun grips my arm, yanks me back.

Tal puts the phone down, says, "We can't spend another night in this place alone, Pops. Not just us. Not without more people here."

I need to search the lawn. But Sun won't let go of me. And Tal hugs me too. Their arms are woven. Sun's head is up. It keeps staring at the window.

My daughter's face is lit by her phone. She starts poking at it, trying to replay what just happened.

"Who were they?" Sun whispers aloud.

"The first interracial couple," Tal says. I look at her. She's smiling at the screen. "The first couple," she repeats, like this is an historical moment she's captured.

17

THE VIDEO IS in color. But barely. Faint pale tones only margins from gray. It takes a second—even having been there, it takes a second—to know that you're looking down a narrow bathroom. Mostly because the camera is aimed up at the window. It's only in a brief jostle of the lens, presumably as Tal balanced herself, that we get a flash of the sink, dislocated a good inch from the exposed plaster of the wall, or the permanently stained toilet that takes two pulls of its hanging chain to flush. The focus quickly resets on the window. First it's framed by the crumbling wood of the windowsill, then as it zooms outside the image is engulfed by the darkness of that night. But not all dark. There is something. I will grant my daughter that. I am not beyond reason. I am not so divorced from the facts before me that I can't say, "Yes, there is an image of vibrating figures." I saw it the first time. In fact, I am so intricately connected to reason that I must both acknowledge that I, too, did see something, something reminiscent of two figures fornicating, but also that I would have to be delusional to think it was a ghost. Or two ghosts. Or that they were the ghosts of the first black and white couple in America. Fucking.

The crackheads were in the house. Again. I know I am right, I have faith in my original estimation. The outdoor cams caught nothing. The vision was a reflection, no doubt. They were behind us. They were down the hall, their image refracted off the broken glass on the bathroom door. I can show you how they did it. I can draw diagrams. The eerie lighting that still sparks from that fuse box probably helped, I'm sure. I don't know how they keep getting in and the fact that I haven't found them doesn't mean that some other mad explanation must be true. We're talking angles and reflection here, simple physics.

"Ghosts of the First Interracial Couple" Tal titles it when she puts the clip online, because she's sticking to her faith. She creates an account called "Mélanged." It gets ninety-four hits in two weeks. The only other video uploaded to the account is one of Spider awkwardly yanking on one of his Creole accordions, which garners only thirty-seven views, presumably from the man himself. When pressed how she made the leap toward this context for the title, Tal says, "I can feel it. I just have this sense. They are it. They are, like, our Adam and Eve." I laugh every time she says it. Tal never does.

"Great ancestors of dark and light, through time and the veil of life, we beseech you! Your children of Africa and Europe! Show us your love!" Tal exclaims. She's in the dining room. She's broken down her tent for this, packed all her things neatly in the hall, out of the way of the stairs because that would be a fire hazard. "Reveal to us once more your glory, give us a sign to guide us toward your truth."

I've got fifteen teenage mulattoes all up in my living room. Tal, Kimet, their little mixie-pixie friends. Crammed in there, all sitting on the floor. All those zits and such. Lot of bumpy beige flesh. Sitting in the damn near dark. Nobody else saying a word. One Drop is the only one over twenty-one in the group, sitting on crossed legs, massive thighs protruding into the space of the crowded room. The kids I recognize as sunflowers, they hang around him, like always. He's got his eyes closed, along with a few of the others as they start to chant "Om."

I keep looking at him. I wait for him to open his eyes, because I'm fairly sure he's just here because he still wants to screw my girlfriend. I catch him, every once in a while, checking out Sunita Habersham. *I'm watching you, big boy,* my eyes say, but his are closed so it's an optical monologue.

"Your primal pain has blossomed generations of love. Let us praise you for your sacrifice." Tal's got the incense going, which I thought was a bit much at first but I appreciate later when several of the older ones show up smelling like weed. The rest of the community must be sane, because although Tal hung fliers all over my lawn, they're not here. "This is your home. This is your land. We are your people. Blended by love, in your image!"

"I got potato skins with cheddar and bacon!" I answer. "Who wants some?" It's hard to step through them, all sitting on the floor like this. Especially holding a tray in my hand. "It's very dark in here," I point out. "But I guess you need that for a standard séance. I haven't been to one before, but it'd be odd with all the lights on, probably. Not really the same mood-builder."

"Reveal yourselves once more! Let us praise you with our belief, bathe in your miracle!" my daughter begs the universe.

"These're T.G.I. Friday's. Not the take-out, but the frozen kind. I swear to God though, you can't tell the difference. They're delicious."

"Pops, shut up!" The crowded room, already hushed, becomes quieter. I leave the hors d'oeuvres on a sawhorse and walk back to the kitchen again.

"Get it out of your system! You can't have séances at Whitman!" I say back to her, because I'm so happy.

Whitman College. It's got a lovely theater and dance program, a cute little town, and sure the whole area was founded on the massacre of the Indians but where in America wasn't? It's in Washington State. Not in Seattle either—out in the boonies, far, far from Germantown. They've even offered Tal a little scholarship money; the insurance payment from the house fire should cover the rest. Good things come to those who wait, to burn down their homes.

They all leave, eventually. Even One Drop, who hovers, surely waiting for Sun to appear. "It's all cool, brother. Just being a supportive community and all. You should come out, hang with us sometimes. We got a domino game going every Thursday," he offers.

"Yeah, sure. Maybe, sometime," I brush him off. "Sorry there were no ghosts!" I yell at the last of them, as I see them off at the door, anxious to have it closed once more. A few laugh it off, wave goodnight. They're not bad kids, they're just all up in my house.

I walk out with the last of them, onto my porch. "Goodbye," I tell them, which is fancy talk for *It's midnight Friday, school is out, go the hell home*. The accordion, it goes now in the distance, having politely waited until Tal was finished. I go back in, grab my coat and hat. Go out to find Spider.

Mélange is on my goddamn lawn. With their RVs, their single-wide trailers, their rows of those little house-looking things. It turns out the latter are called "park models," which makes sense because they are parking their asses on my lawn. They've put them in rows, and grass alleys already show the wear of foot travel. It's dark, but the windows light my path. I've heard the Mulattopians living here call this stretch Biracial Boulevard. They call the residential area they've formed on the east lawn hosting the RVs class A through C, Mixed Mews, although I'm partial to the name Halfie Heights and use this moniker exclusively when mentioning it. Some of the biggest Oreos have parked there, possibly because it's the end of the property closest to the whiteness of Chestnut Hill. The sunflowers made the southern, North Philly end of the lawn their homestead, in a place they call *Little Halfrica*. Nobody uses the word *segregation,* though.

They've all been here for months. Swarming in the day after the "sighting" and acting like someone died and left them the place, instead of me. Roslyn offered to pay rent, most likely on Sun's urgings, though we don't talk about it. And it's acceptable, the little sum that Roslyn pays me for the circus she brought to my Germantown. I'd have had a better bargaining position if I wasn't leveraged by my concern for my daughter and Sunita Habersham, but it's okay for now. Not a fortune but enough to erase the last of my hesitation.

The grounds of Loudin Mansion have become a village to vagabonds. The long trailers resting behind the garage, used as classrooms during the daytime, comprise the commercial district. Over a hundred people during school hours, reducing to around forty-five at night. People who pee and shit. I pass the porta-potties, hold my breath till I'm on the other side. People who leave piles of trash every day. We have one dumpster by the gate. It's nearly full. I know from being woken up by the process that it was just cleared at five this morning. People who listen to music and even play music of their own and who sit around and laugh and get drunk sometimes and sing out loud.

"Big dubs!" One of the sunflowers yells to me. One of the fine young mixed men of the new generation. His homeboys, they all wave, go back to shooting craps before the heat of a drum of burning scrap wood. From the paint on the planks, I recognize them as loose pieces that were resting by the garage. They're burning my father's house, incrementally. The wood's moist; it smokes and smells of the chemicals it's covered in, but it's old and porous and breathes life into the flames. I notice the propane tanks, just ten feet past the barrel, and all the other ones for many yards in all directions.

In order for a propane tank to explode, it has to be surrounded by fire, and then have its container punctured with a big enough hole that the fuel and oxygen can circulate and properly ignite. If the hole isn't big enough, the gas will ignite, but only in a sustained blow of flames. If you want a boom, if you want to see the full tank burst in an inferno about the size of an elephant—not too big, not too small—you need at least a two-inch hole for complete exposure. A shotgun blast seems to work pretty well, according to the latest videos I've searched. Not on my phone, lest the record incriminate, but on Spider's.

He sits in front of his Airstream, on the porch he's made out of cinder blocks, fingerless gloves on to play his button accordion in the late spring chill. Spider keeps getting into his song, going a few notes, then getting lost, starting over again. Either his hands are stiff or he lacks the skill, or some combination.

"It's the rhythm. I can hit the notes; that's not the issue. It's the beat. It's polyrhythmic, tricky. But that's the African. Here, this is what it sounds like it without." Spider tries again. This time he's slow, full of clarity, and boredom. It's every uninspired elementary school recital.

"It's polka. Without that beat, it's polka. It's just European. But you bring in the African rhythm, and you get zydeco. Check it." Spider concentrates. He stares forward, up. His jaw slack. His ink-stained arms clench, and the music comes, and I hear it. The riffs, the excited, flourishing moments. Spider still messes up, but he gets further this time. Enough that I can hear what he's going for.

"'Eunice Two-Step.' Total mulatto music. You know, if we, like, called ourselves 'bi-ethnic' instead of biracial, that would clarify a lot of this. I tried to get Roslyn to go for that but she wasn't hearing it. But that's what it's about: culture, ethnicity. It's not about race. Race doesn't exist. Race is a false paradigm created by Kant to—"

"Your phone," I stop him, because he's high. It has a zebra-print case, and zonkey as the lock screen image. "Listen—can I ask you, if I started taking in all the used propane tanks and got them refilled for a fee, do think anyone would buy them?"

"Yeah, whatever," he says, opening up his phone's gallery, browsing through the photos. "You didn't take any pictures, man! How'd the séance go? No shaky tables? No lights going out or strange voices?"

"Only thing strange is that anyone actually believes that shit."

"Don't be a spoilsport. Communities need a shared mythology. It brings them closer."

"Yeah, but come on. 'The First Couple'?"

"Everyone here's already haunted by one interracial couple: their own parents. Real ghosts aren't that big a jump."

The trailer next to his is a streamlined fiberglass teardrop, street-traffic orange. So tiny that you can only stand up in the small section you walk into through the door, an upright crawl space shared with a stove, oven, and bathroom shower. On the other side is a small table with space for a person to sit on each side, except when a cushion is laid on top to make a bed. It is a bed now. Sunita Habersham lies on it. It's cold, but she's still nude, on her back on top of the comforter, seemingly unable to endure the weight of anything holding her down.

"So did Tal get any vibrations? Any ghosts take a bite?"

"One of the kids had a Ouija board. He came up with the phrase '*mon oil me damang*.' That almost spells, 'My eye itches,' in French. But Kimet got it to say, 'First!' So maybe he got trolled on a ghost message board. Whatever. It's all silly."

"You can joke, but we saw something." Sun rolls over to her side, grabs me by my jeans pocket, pulls me closer.

I take off my socks. I believe firmly that sex should involve the removal of socks. "I saw something too. I never said I didn't," I tell her, but don't go into the obvious junkie reality because I already know she's not trying to hear that once more. "I don't think if I was dead I'd be like, 'Hey this afterlife thing is great, but let's go over there and play with the cardboard square with the letters on it.' It's just my slant, but I think if there actually is an afterlife, it doesn't involve games from Parker Brothers."

My pants are down and out, and I'm beside her. Lifting off my shirt, I hit the ceiling. There's just enough room for both of us. For love. For sleeping though, Sun comes back up to the house. Sleeping doesn't cause noise. Sleeping doesn't lead to another incident where Tal yells, "You're shaking the house" at the top of her voice directly from the floor below.

"It was actually nice tonight, I guess. All those kids coming together. She's really connecting. But it's creepy."

"What if they were 'the first'?" Sun puts to me. "This is an historic area, you never know."

"Then my daughter shot the mulatto equivalent of the Zapruder film."

Sunita pulls me to her. "I know. Exciting, right?"

Sunita Habersham's flesh, her hair covering my face, that excites me. Besides Tal, it's all I live for. Even with this RV rocking, it's still way bigger than the cab of the Beetle. There's an added intimacy that comes from it not having a motor. But the best part is after, in the quieting of bodies after so much movement when, before either of us can drift off from consciousness, Sun rises, pulls her hair back into a bun, and pulls out the comic books. And we read. Together. The bliss of sharing a previously solitary act. We've upped our pull list to about thirty comics a month, and still go through everything new by the weekend. We've progressed in our relationship to reading graphic novels from our childhood, the ones that made us love the form in the first place. Books from the era when comics were for children. We don't care. Or I don't care and I'm amazed that she doesn't seem to mind. My inner child has found a friend.

After an hour of reading digital bootlegs of *The Micronauts: They Came From Inner Space* on her laptop, Sun grabs her shirt, and I look at her ass, at panties that say TUESDAY even though it's Friday night. She puts jeans over them, and I watch as she tries to discover where her socks are hiding. All this because her bed's too small for both of us, and because I don't want Tal sleeping in the house alone. And because Sun wants to literally sleep with me. Because Sunita Habersham says she's my lady now—although she still insists there's no ownership involved, so I don't really know if this means we're exclusive. Or more specifically, if she is. But I know she chooses to lie down for the night with me. For that honor, I can motivate myself to rise from postcoital bliss, dress, and walk out of her camper and into the cold to my father's house each night. Because she's my lady now.

"I'm not coming up," Sun says. I'm standing with my hand on the door handle, now frozen. "I've got to make a social call tonight."

I say, "You're going to love this: there's a black comic-book exhibit at the African American Museum, they've got Jack Kirby's first illustrations for *Black Panther.* I'm taking Tal tomorrow morning. Tosha is bringing her kids. You want to come? I was hoping you guys could meet." I shoot this out quick, to stop myself from asking who her social call is, if it's a man or a woman, if it's friendship or some other kind of unbearable intimacy.

"I can't, sorry. What time are you coming back from the museum? You want to meet after?"

I look at the time on my phone. I don't want to, I don't mean to, but I get so far into the gesture that aborting it would be even more awkward. It's 11:42 P.M. She's going to see someone she doesn't bother to name at 11:42 P.M.

"Are you leaving the grounds? Because if so, you really want to be careful," I tell her, as if she specifically suggested walking the streets of Germantown at midnight and specifically intends to not be careful about it.

"Don't worry, I'm just staying in Mixed Mews. But it's sweet of you to be concerned." There's a kiss there. There's a kiss in it for me, for my diligence in not being possessive.

"Who are you going to . . . ?" I try to do it casually. Again, I am solely concerned with her safety, and protection is different from possession.

"Text me tomorrow, when you're done, okay?" Sunita tells me, and nothing more. Because I already told her I didn't want to know about anything but us. I'm trying to be free of history too. And I don't want to know. But I have to know. I have to and I've waited this long and that alone should stand as a testament to my enlightenment. I have to know so I give another quick peck then hurry out.

My laptop's on in the dining room, the screen is dimmed until I resuscitate it. I look over to the tent, wait to hear Tal stirring in response, but notice only the unchanged rhythm of her slow and unconscious exhalation. Even so, I tilt the monitor away from her side of the house. And then I pull up the feeds from the security cameras.

I switch through the camera feeds until I find the one focused in the direction of Sun's trailer, then I zoom in. But not so far as to try to peer straight into Sun's windows. Because that would be wrong. That would be beyond security measures. I am not a stalker, I am just a cautious man sitting in the dark watching my lover through a spy cam as she leaves her trailer in the dead of night to possibly go to another person.

Sun walks out. She stops. She looks up. She looks up at the camera. No, just at the night. She goes back inside again, comes back with a scarf this time, wraps it around her neck and then pulls a hat onto her head as if to cap the entire outfit. She has something with her. A bag. No, a box.

I shouldn't care where she goes. I'm not worried about breeding, about protecting her womb from alien sperm. I don't believe she can use up any love that she could give me. So I must be doing this to protect her. That must be this horrid feeling, a will to ensure against harm. That's believable.

Sun walks toward the camera, up the hill, in the direction of my father's house. She is coming to the house. It has all been a test. She's coming to the house. I realize that I have to shut the equipment down and run upstairs before Sun actually gets to the house, but on the screen she turns in to a line of trailers and she's gone.

"I'm not ready for college," Tal says, all the materials her fat packet offers spread out on the table before us, my laptop open to a Walla Walla realtor's page. "This is crazy. I've never left the east coast. I've never even been to California. And I just got here. I want to stay in this house. This house feels right. I mean, doesn't this feel right? Like, this is where we're supposed to be?"

"Hell no. Feels like it's time to go. And I'm not going to leave you here with the ghouls."

"They're not ghoulish. They just want to be known," Tal tells me. And she's not kidding.

"That's some crazy *ish* you're talking, honey. Get your shoes on. We were supposed to leave for the museum ten minutes ago."

"Not yet. I want you to look at something."

"Honey, get your bag, get your phone, let's go. If you want to get clothes from Irv's first, we got to go."

"You're rushing me and that makes me feel like you don't respect me," Tal recites, and makes no move except to fold her arms.

"Fine. What?"

"Before we go gawk at other people's art, I want to show you something. My own art project. I've been working on it all week. I want you to see it. And I don't want you to just say nice things. I want you to be frank, Pops. Like the kind of critiques you give Kimet."

I grab my coat but follow her to her tent, wait outside as she goes poking around behind the canvas. "I thought you were all about dance. You're a painter now?"

"Sculptor," Tal says, and pushes it out in front me, resting it on the top of a stool. "I'm starting to believe that, like, 'found object sculpture' is my secondary medium, you know? I'm thinking, maybe not college? Maybe art school would be better for me? In Philly. Eventually."

It's my Frederick Douglass action figure. I use it in class as a body model. I know where she found it: in my cabinet drawer. Since Mélange's relocation, I've kept all my art materials in the house. She's stripped the doll down to a naked body. And it's truly a naked body, because Tal's compensated for the natural neutering of male dolls by adding a prosthetic penis to his groin. Oh great. It's not erect or anything, but she's been fairly generous.

Amazingly, Frederick Douglass's cock is not the most startling aspect of Tal's work. She's painted him white. No, she's painted half of him, right down the middle, pink. Pink and tan and white, the skin of a Viking in the dark winter months. The redness hints at those parts of his body where the blood runs closest to the epidermis. Oh, and his hair. It pains me to see it. Frederick Douglass is the Samson of African American history; his Afro basically freed the slaves. Here though, on what used to be my doll, half of that hair has been shaved off. Replaced with a flat blond mane just as voluminous.

"I got it off an old Barbie doll," Tal says when I go to touch it.

"Yeah. Okay." There's my trepidation; Tal hears it. I'm holding the doll, looking all around it as if the answer for how I feel about this could be found there. Tal goes to take the sculpture out of my hands, then stops herself.

"It's suppose to offend, you know that, right? I mean, you're supposed to look at it, and go, 'What the hell is that?' Then, after you do that, hopefully you ask yourself, 'Why does this piss me off?' Is it because black history types are considered, like, saints? Or is it the fact that this points out that he was half-white. Because he was, you know?"

"Genetically. Half-European. Whiteness—that's not really something you can be half of. That's more of an all or nothing privilege, perspective thing."

"You know what I'm saying, Pops." Tal yanks it out of my hand. I think the penis is going to fall off, but no, it's really stuck on there. She lays it on the table, on a fleece blanket. Tenderly wrapping it up, it looks like she's swaddling a baby. "You still haven't said anything. And saying nothing is actually even more shitty than saying something you'll regret later."

"I'm offended by it," I tell Tal, calm. "And then I wonder why I'm offended by it. And it makes me think on that. And I know, I mean I am pretty damn sure, that my reasoning is probably a lot different from what you're thinking about it, but it is making me think. So it's working."

Tal stops packing it away, but when I finish talking, she starts up again. "Cool," is all Tal says.

I hug my daughter from behind, kiss her on her head. "Ice cold," I say.

She repeats what I say right after me. "Ice cold." This makes me feel like I'm starting to do damn good as a daddy.

"I mean, I know you're a failed comic-book artist, but since you're my parental unit I value your opinion," Tal tells me.

And this pisses me off the whole ride to Irv's apartment. I already know I'm a failure. That doesn't mean I want to be called a failure by any voice not in my head. Certainly not by my own daughter. The fact that, again, I know I'm a failure, just infuriates me further. I grip the wheel. I get to the turn for the highway but I take the long, beautiful way instead, and it's a damn nice day and I should enjoy it. But I'm still pissed off. Winding down the Wissahickon's stream, out onto the Schuylkill River. It gives me time to take in the green space and the water and reflect on just how pissed off I am.

"It's so funny. Last August you were basically a white girl. It was all, 'the blacks' then, remember? Not even a year later and you're another Mulatta Militant," is the first thing I say, after a while.

"Jews aren't really 'white,' in the racial sense," Tal informs me, looking out the window so she doesn't see the self-restraint it takes for me not to immediately respond.

"I still can't believe you never went to the African American Museum. The whole time you were growing up in Philly. I guess white people just don't go to black museums." I thought I was changing the subject. Even when I stop talking, I think, thank God I changed the goddamn subject.

"Well, who's fucking fault is it I grew up around only white people?"

"Mine," I say. Then, "Don't say 'fuck.' To your father."

I don't say any more till we hit the Parkway. Past the art museum, past Logan Circle. I was going to tell her a story, about how my dad's family came to this part of the city from Ireland almost two hundred years ago, how they lived around this neighborhood until the 1950s, when the GI Bill allowed them to slip into the middle class. Driving past the natural history museum, I was going to tell the story of how my dad would take me to see the dinosaur bones, because I liked the idea of a world without humans and because he liked that it was free on Saturdays. I don't say anything, though. As we're stopped at a red light, our eyes meet for a second when Tal realizes I'm looking at her, then I have a green so I turn and sigh.

"You hated my sculpture," Tal tells me. The damn two-toned cock monster is still sitting on her lap.

"I didn't hate your piece, honey. It's just, when you create art about race, about blackness, you have to deal with the historical weight of the images that came before. You have to understand the ways art was used to diminish us, to dehumanize us. To negotiate all that, you have be informed, not just artistically, but also culturally. You can't just bludgeon the concept with heavy-handed imagery."

"Sun loved it. Sun said it was, 'as brutal as it was insightful.'" Tal pauses for effect, nods her head a few seconds after she finishes to make sure it's sunk into my head. "I hate to say this, Father, but I think you're responding this way because of me saying that you're an ex-comic-book artist—"

"You said, 'failed.'"

"I meant ex—"

"Daughter, I'm not an 'ex-' anything. I'm an artist. An illustrator. And I do comics. I don't know if you noticed, but I've been kind of busy of late. Mostly with you."

"Which I only said because I haven't really seen you do any work the whole time I've known you."

"You've only known me for a few months." I say it. Instantly, I hate that I say it. The guy that says that, he's a huge asshole. Three more blocks. Then I park the car. Illegally, in the tow-away zone. We're at Irv's corner anyway. Once the Bug is shut off, I turn to apologize to her, but Tal's already got the door open. "Tal! I told Tosha we'd be there now. Hurry!"

Tal slams the door as hard as an angry teenager can. I feel a flash of rage with the sound because I'm in annoyed-dad mode. I yell after her, "That's inappropriate behavior," and I can't help myself.

I sit in the car, waiting. I sit there, disliking myself, wanting to apologize to Tal, to restart, go back to the moment I was coming down the steps and she was brushing her teeth yet still managed a sudsy "Yo, Pops." Spitting the paste out in her cup then giving me a sloppy, green-foamed smiled. Yes, let's go back to that moment. I could win it from there if given a second chance.

Tal takes way too long. I stick the key back in the ignition, turn it just enough to give power to the clock I installed in the dash. 9:48 A.M. I know it's been at least twenty minutes, probably twenty-five, probably thirty. The anger is there within me, but I refuse to recognize it. I say to it, Go sit down. Wait for ten o'clock. Because that's when I can get mad and be fully justified.

At ten A.M. exactly, I leave the car and don't even slam the door.

I know where the elevators are and I'm halfway toward them when a brown hand reaches out from behind the desk and pushes on my chest. He must've said something first. I didn't hear him. What I hear are the words in my head—I put them there—that I'm preparing to say to my daughter without losing my temper: I thought we agreed that you would come in and out.

"I said, 'I'm going to need you to sign in.'" They got this brother dressed up like a general in the Protect White People Army. He's got the trimmed police hat, he's got the matching military formal wear, top and bottom. It's dark blue with a flippant sky-blue trim, a nice silly color to remind you that while the bearer of these clothes has authority, he is also subservient and nonthreatening.

I go to the desk, ask for a pen.

"You ain't got one?" he asks. It's then that I realize we're enemies. I'm not sure why, maybe it's just that he thought I was ignoring him initially. I look at his face. It's more than that. The suit says, *Welcome to Disney World,* but the face and eyes shoved in it? They hate me. Does he think I'm white? No, a black man his age, and his position, would instinctively know not to show such disdain for a Caucasian. So he knows I'm black. When I remove a pen from my pocket and sign my name in, he says, "I knew you was holding out." No way he would talk to a white boy like that. When I'm done filling out the time, he even says, "You going to let me see some ID or what?" I want to argue. But what I don't want to know is what it must be like to be a black man working up in here in this monkey suit for decades for these wealthy white folks. I never want to know that, and this man has intimate knowledge of all that must entail. So I show my ID. He looks at it, intently, then says, "So you the one that turned out to be Ms. Karp's father, huh?" When I don't say anything, he adds, "I remember her mom. Sweet girl. It's a damn shame what happened to her."

I take my ID back, but I can't look at him. I'm feeling a little dizzy when I hit the elevator button to go up.

The door to Irv's apartment is open. Not just unlocked, open. My emotions are alive and shoved together, my heart is a crowded bus.

"Irv? Tal?" I say from the building's hallway. Nobody says anything back to me, so I walk inside, through the kitchen, to the entrance of the living room. It's not quiet. There's a television on. Sports, or someone yapping about sports. And there's Tal, talking. She's watching TV. She's up here, watching TV, laughing, having a good time, laughing at me. Even if she's laughing at something else, knowing that I'm sitting in the damn car waiting for her, Tal's laughing at me.

I walk in. Yeah, the TV's on. On one of the sports channels, one of the ones where loud people talk about what's happening on the other sports channels. Irv's in his easy chair, feet sprawled out before him. His head's back—he's not even awake. The place reeks like dive-bar carpet.

"What the hell is going on?" I don't know. I don't yell because I don't want to yell, but also because of Irving Karp over there. Tal's still laughing. Hands to her face, presumably one holding a phone.

"When you say you can just be a minute, I don't actually assume it's only going to be a minute. I mean, I already give you leeway. As far as I'm concerned 'a minute' can be up to ten minutes. Maybe. Maybe fifteen. You got me down there waiting in the car for more than a half an hour for you."

Tal doesn't say anything.

"All this time, and where's the clothes? Where's your coat?"

"You're yelling at me and my grandfather just died!"

Really, only the first six or seven of those words even make any sense. The word I really don't get, even though she makes it out before the sentence transitions into a wail, is the *died* part. I look over at Irv.

Irv's head is tilted all the way back in the lounger, but his eyes are open and frozen and staring straight up above him. I actually look up there too, like there will be instructions on what to do next stapled to the ceiling.

Into the landline phone, I'm saying, "I'd like to report a death," but I don't like to. Not at all.

I look at my daughter. I want to tell her that I'm here for her, and I do, but it doesn't improve things because she can already see that I'm here, and the only reason I'm here in this apartment is for her.

"This is it, Pops," Tal says after I've hung up.

"What is 'it,' honey?" and I put my arms around her.

"This is what the ghosts were trying to tell me."

18

OUR FATHERS ARE dead. Tal's and mine. We are alone, together. Now we are completely in the present, the past having dissolved.

Tal tells everyone in Mulattopia she can that she knew. That Irv was going to die. Not because he told her—she now claims he didn't, she claims the words never actually came out of his mouth—that he was going to die. That the ghosts told her. Whether they believe her or not, the Mulattopians come to the house. In groups, mostly. Of at least three—one time, nine—and offer their condolences. But they also listen to her story. Not just politely, not just consolingly. They listen without moving their bodies. They listen for detail. Tal tells them, "I, like, knew." She knew as soon as she entered Irv's building. That she decoded the sign of the bathroom visitation en route. "I'm in the elevator, rising, right? And I'm thinking, This must be what dying is like, you know? And it totally hits me. What I saw upstairs, that night. What you have all seen, in my video. There's life, and death, and all that, and they're both happening at, like, the exact same moment."

"Yeah," some say and they nod and nod and some may actually

mean it. They finish by looking together at the clip on her laptop once more. They point out new evidence and theories from that night, and this seems to console Tal. I walk through the room after the first of these encounters, giving my daughter a casual sniff. She doesn't smell like weed or booze. She could be high on something else, of course, but I doubt that's it.

The attention is fine, the concern is fine, but when I try to talk to Tal alone about the loss, about enduring it, I just get the same platitudes. The only ones Tal really talks to are the ones who believe in the ghosts of her imagination, and Sunita Habersham. The latter insists on cooking for my daughter, even if she only knows how to make coffee and tea and instant oatmeal and other recipes that primarily involve the boiling of water.

"The First Couple told me," Tal says to the others who come visiting, condolences in mouth. Parked in my living room, nibbling at the donuts they just brought as an offering. Nodding their heads solemnly. *She means that as a joke,* I want to say. But it isn't funny. Nobody sees the humor in it.

I am trying not to feel any sense of relief about the passing of Irving Karp—but there will be the inheritance, that condo alone should be enough to pay for Whitman College and all the books and fees that entails, and any life insurance settlement on top of that will be an extra blessing to Tal's economic future. She will be left with more than a large, decaying house to depend on. I feel the relief of that like someone who has taken sharp stones out of their shoes. This feels so good, so buoyant even, that I have to force myself to think of Irv's face before I become giddy. Of the way he swung his long neck to look at you, or that laugh that sounded like years of smoking had added to his morbid sense of humor. Of what Tal lost, and what he lost in Tal's mother. And what the world has lost now that he's no longer walking in it.

We go to the funeral together. Sunita, Tal, me, all wearing matching outfits: black. We're in the Bug. And I'm driving. And in the echo of my head, we are finally a family. As real as any family I've had the opportunity to be a part of since my own short-lived childhood unit. I even start humming as I drive the Beetle to the funeral home. A tune I realize is far too pleasant for the occasion when Sunita pinches my knee wordlessly.

The service is depressing, but quick and efficient. The rules were set millennia ago. Soon we're back in the car, on the highway, off to the cemetery. Only family are at the grave site, and there's not even a headstone, which won't come till a year later at its unveiling.

"Everybody does burial differently. My dad didn't even want a funeral. No memorial, nothing," I say as I wait with Sun, down by the cars, for the family to say goodbye.

"I'm going to die in New Orleans," Sunita Habersham tells me.

"No one knows where they're going to die."

"I do. I'm going to go there, eventually. Definitely when I get older. Bask in the music, get fat on the food. But mostly, so I can die there. So I can get that jazz funeral, that's what I want. A second line band, marching down the street. Just make it a celebration, right? All life ends in death—you can't let it be framed in tragedy. That's how I'm going out. Also, I want to be dressed as The Dark Phoenix. Just in case the zombie apocalypse kicks in."

"Do we do the pebble on the tombstone thing?" I say, looking over at them.

"I think that's next year. Every year after till there's no one to remember. That's beautiful too. Look at them."

I do. They're over there. There's Dot, and Art, and Dot's daughter, Elissa, and others woven together with unseen bonds. Tal's got her cousins. They stand together, watch. One lanky kid stands a few feet off, texting.

"In the end, we just have our people, our tribe," Sun says, and she grabs my hand, squeezes it. "Even when you're gone, when your biological family's gone, your tribe's still there. Keeping your memory alive."

Dot is not very observant as a Jew. I know this because Dot says "I'm not very observant, as a Jew" to me when she gives me directions, and again when she answers the door at her house. Still, all the mirrors are covered, and she's sitting shivah, although she's not sure she's sitting it properly, which she also confesses. Dot's an excellent host, though, and a damn good cook. Or her friends are. And many trays and delights are offered for consumption. I stand with Sun. Tal, she flutters by every few minutes so that I know that despite the fact that I recognize almost no one here, I'm in the right home. I poke her shoulder at one passing, ask how's she's doing, and she snaps, "Fine!" annoyed at the suggestion that she would be anything else. As if this whole occasion were merely a house party with old people.

"She's drifting apart. From me. Already. And we just met, really."

Tal has her phone out. It's way too big for her. It's nearly a tablet. The others, the teens, the twenty-somethings, they gather around Tal to look at what's in her hands.

"Oh God, she's showing them her damn ghost movie."

I put down my little plastic plate on a breakfront and take a step toward Tal, when Sun's hand falls on my arm and stops me.

"It's morbid," I whisper to her.

"It's helping her cope," she says back. "She needs to feel special. It helps with the loss. Like Peter Parker becoming Spider-Man after he lost Uncle Ben. When I lost Zeke, for me it was helping to start Mélange."

Zeke. There, for the first time, is the name. The word that defines the wound of her heart. I reach out for Sun's hand. It goes into mine, but absently. She doesn't seem to realize that this is the first time she's told me even that much about him.

Others are starting to leave. Others are, so we should. Before I can start the process though, Art comes over. He gives me a hug like I'm the one who's lost a brother.

"Tal has you. This was a gift. You are here to be a father. There are no coincidences."

"God willing," I say.

"God is dead, but we still have Jung. Forgive me, I get very philosophical at events like these. The next, it'll be mine—at least I hope so.

You start, you're the youngest one in the family. At the end, you're the oldest. Then you go. But Tal has you, and I think that's wonderful."

He gets a hug from Sun for this. Takes it, squeezes too hard, winks over her shoulder at me. Letting go, he starts to leave, then turns around again.

"And you know there's no money, right?" I assumed there would be no hat passed, so say yes. He sighs heavily, smiles, walks back to hug me again. Says in my ear, "Irv played the market like it was horses. Nobody wins at horses. Also, greyhounds: he lost on those too. Between that and the medical bills, nothing. But thank Jung, a young girl going to college soon has her real father to take care of her."

And then he lets me go.

"What was that about?" Sunita Habersham asks me when Art has rejoined his sister in her hosting duties.

"He's drunk. And Irv was fucking broke," I say, a little too loud for the room.

"It's got, like, a thousand page views on YouTube," Tal tells me. "Pops! Look," she says, leaning over from the backseat and trying to push her phone into my face while I'm driving. I want to point this hazard out but see the image in a flash.

"But it only says 907 hits, honey." Sun's hand on my knee starts pinching again, but I don't bother looking over for the reproach I know is waiting in her eyes.

"That's *like* a thousand," Tal corrects. "And it will be over that when my cousin Nate puts it on Channel Six News."

"It's going on TV?" Sun turns to ask. She actually sounds happy about this.

"No. On their YouTube channel. That's bigger—way bigger. Because I don't think anyone watches, you know, live TV anymore? Except for HBO?"

"You're up-speaking." She's up-speaking. Lifting the end of her sentences an octave higher. It's a white-girl affectation, one Tal'd largely dropped over the last few months. A habit, most likely, reacquired in the hours with family before. Her other family.

"Well you're up your own ass," Tal responds, then the headphones are on before she has to endure my admonishment. She gets out and slams the door as soon as we pull up back in our driveway.

"You're worried about money," Sun states after the silence. "You were thinking Irv's estate might have helped, and now you're dealing with the disappointment of that. And that has you angry. The fear, it has you angry."

"And I'm angry that I'm angry. And I'm broke."

"You're not broke. You're cash poor. But you're land rich."

"I really don't feel like a member of the landed gentry at the moment. I'm thinking, maybe I should burn down the house, make it look like it was an accident or crackheads or something, and whatever's left from the insurance payout after I cover Tal's education we, you and me, and her eventually, should take it somewhere it can last. Like Belize," I say out loud. I actually say it out loud. It's made sense in my head for months, but when it hits the air there's an oxidizing reaction and it sounds a like a joke. Sun just looks at me. Because she knows I'm not kidding.

"You know that's crazy talk, right? If you did that, you'd go to jail. And where would we go?" she asks and I know she means an entirely different *we* than *us*. "Roslyn's got lots of leads for permanent settlements, but one of them is here. You need to go to her."

"I'm not going to her. She's been sniffing around this place for months, even before I moved y'all in. Why was she here that day she Tased me?"

"You Tased her first."

"Yeah, but still? Or when I caught her checking out my rooms? I know she wants it, but that old lady is sneaky. She'll try and rob me, watch. I know you hate me saying it, but I don't trust her. She's got her own agenda."

"If she wants to buy the place, her agenda is the same as yours. Talk to Roslyn," Sun says, as always ignoring my bias on the subject.

• • •

It's later that afternoon when I wake from a nap to hear Tal's voice talking to someone downstairs. I don't give it further thought till I hear voices coming up the stairs. I hear Tal say, "It was up here," and then multiple footfalls banging down my hallway.

"What the hell are you doing?" There's a guy with her. When he turns around, I see he's one of the kids from the funeral, the one that was texting at the cemetery. Tal's crouching at the bathroom door, like we were that night. She stands to yell at me.

"Pops, put some pants on!"

"He doesn't need pants. We can just film him from the chest up." And then there is a video camera in my face. It's reaching up, and suddenly a light is shining in my eyes.

"What the fuck are you doing," is the appropriate response.

"Pops, this is Nate? Did you guys meet? Nate Karp? My cousin?"

I look down at my groin. I'm wearing boxer shorts. My reproductive organs are not showing. So I reach out to shake his hand. Tal says something about pants again, but to punish her for her tone I make no motion to go put mine on. These underwear could have passed as basketball shorts in the seventies. Doctor J went out on the court like this all the time.

"So, some quick questions. Did you see the ghosts?"

I can just make out Tal next to him through the glow. She wants me to say "Yes." She's nodding "Yes" in slow deliberate motions, like that will influence me, and it does. I don't want to hurt her.

"I saw something. Definitely," I tell him. The last word I say with added gravitas to make up for the vagueness of the answer.

"Okay, so you say you saw something, too. Do you think it was ghosts?"

I look at Tal. She's not moving her head anymore. She's just staring at me, intently.

"No," and in response to her eye-rolling I add, "look, I'm not going to sit here and lie. Come on. You can't expect me to do that." Her cousin peers at me, lifting his gaze from the viewfinder, then turns to Tal for cues.

"But you said you saw something. What do you think it was?"

"Crackheads. I'm pretty sure I saw crackheads. But I don't know." I throw in the last bit to be generous, but Tal gives up on me anyway and walks down the hall.

"Well, could they have been ghosts, do you think?" he asks. Tal stops walking. Turns. Looks at me. I look at her. Then I turn to her cousin.

"Sure, they were ghosts. Ghosts of who they once were. You could say that about half of the city of Philadelphia."

19

I TRY FORMALITY, send an email. The header is *Loudin Mansion Is for Sale*. This is as straightforward with Roslyn as I can possibly be. The body of the message has bullet points and text in bold. The most important of these says the house has been appraised at $1.8 million if fully restored; another bullet offers the house for the generously discounted rate of $1.3 million, which is a steal based on the $310,000 in estimated repairs the property would need. My father bought the place for $800,000, but that was at auction, at risk, and he paid much more personally for the purchase later. I don't reveal to her that the mortgage payments will drain the money from his cash accounts in months, a fact no one but Sirleaf and I know. Another sub-bullet point, under a category I term "Advantages of Buying Loudin," it says, "$0 Moving Costs." At the end of the email, back in sentence form, I state that I would like to discuss this further at her earliest convenience. I even provide a link to my calendar. I sign it with *Sincerely,* for I am nothing if I am not sincere in my urge to be rid of this place.

The writing, the proofreading, the balancing of directness over noncommittal pleasantry, it all takes an unexpectedly long time. I send it and head to the kitchen to find food scraps to sustain me for the next few hours, when my phone pings and Roslyn's text comes through.

Come see me, honey.

There's no way she could have read a word. I check the time stamp on the phone with the one on the laptop still in my hand. Two minutes. So maybe she could have read the whole thing, but there is no way in my understanding of reality that this happened.

Are you free in one hour? I text back to her.

Come to me now, my warrior child, she texts back to me so fast I think at first it's an automated reply.

I put on a blazer before I go over there, because I am not a child, I am a man, a grown-ass one. A crisp shirt with a tag inside that says, DRY CLEAN ONLY. I take an extra ten minutes to iron my jeans as well, until their starched legs become my armor, for I *am* a warrior. I look at myself in the mirror. Then I take the whole thing off and put on a suit. And a tie.

"Look at you, all cleaned up and some such."

"You look lovely as well." She does. Roslyn looks more formal than I do, a full suit with pants, a silk shirt, hair pulled back in an aerodynamic slick perfect for lunging.

"You look like you mean business, Warren. So let's do business. Come in."

Her cottage-looking trailer is set off at the farthest end of the Halfie Heights, the Victorian country house of RVs. The roof has wooden octagon shingles, stained so you can still see the grain. The cedar siding of the little box is vertical, in the New England fashion. Past the intricate white latticework of the porch railings, I see she's painted its ceiling haint blue. I move through her open door. The whole living room is a card table with two seats.

One, a Shaker chair, sits by a ladder leading up to a cubby loft of a bed. The other seat doubles as a windowsill, and when I crawl into it I have to be careful not to lean back and burst through the glass.

"Let us have coffee. Something about the aroma, it reminds me of professional efficiency. Don't you agree?"

I don't, but do. I can already smell it, and I don't feel particularly efficient at the moment. I feel a bit confused. I've been largely avoiding this woman since she moved her people here. I've seen her, but rarely alone, and now we're crowded into a room so tightly we're like twins in a wooden womb.

When she finally sits down Roslyn has, in addition to coffee, two binders in her hands.

"Well, I read your email, and I reviewed your initial asking price. And I found it interesting." She picks up her coffee with both hands, takes a sip from it, and holds it there. Smiling. I wait for her to say something more. She doesn't. She just grins at me. I unpack her words for her, because they're the only ones I have. *Initial.* She leaned on it too, just enough to get it noticed. And she's still staring. Still smiling.

"I mean, it could be adjusted. If you're interested—and I think things have been going very well and people are getting settled in and making a home here. So I'm sure we can come up with something fair for the whole family."

My emphasized word is *family*. Because that includes me too.

"I know, and poor Tal—so sorry for her loss. I understand she might be going to a private college in Washington next school year? That's so soon. I understand what a burden that will be for you."

She has so much concern that it compels her to take her hand off her coffee mug and grab my fingers, which had been tapping loosely on the table. Roslyn holds my thumb up to the light. "You need to cut your nails," she says, before I can release myself.

"The thing is," she tells me, "I've been thinking about other options. Not only in this area, but nationally. We can only afford to buy one property. Just one. So we have to ensure it's absolutely the right one, do you understand? For the betterment of our community."

The other hand puts down the coffee, pulls over one of her folders, and hands it to me. It's full of maps. I turn a few of the pages, find Wikipedia articles in there too. Places. Towns, counties. Yellow highlights over "Population Density" and "Racial Makeup." I know these articles. Because I've read them. Because I've given them to my students. They're tri-racial isolate locations.

"I don't think—I mean, Natchitoches Parish, Louisiana?" I say pointing one out.

"Such a beautiful natural landscape. Right on the Cane River, Creole country. So rich in history. And we'd fit in well there. Visually, at least. We could have an amazing Loving Day celebration, out in the fields. Spider's leaving to scout it as we speak."

"Yeah, but it's also in the middle of nowhere. Look: '230 miles to New Orleans.' You're trying to build something. You want to be in the middle of a vibrant territory. Conveniently located in a major metropolitan area, easily commutable to New York City, Baltimore, and Washington, D.C. And for the price I'm talking about—"

"A million dollars to live in a ghetto?"

"I find that term offensive," I tell her. "A million two for a mansion and seventy acres in the fifth largest city in the country." I pause. I have dropped $100,000 off the asking price to win an argument. I am amazed and infuriated by my own magnanimity. The sigh, I let it go. Mixed with the CO_2 are my dreams. And then I suck it back in, because it's all a tell, and I must show her nothing.

"I *love* your passion. Look at you, the fire! I'm so proud that you've moved past your, you know, sorrow." I blush. The reddening of my cheeks is a breach in my defenses, but I'm helpless. "If you ever need a good cry again just know that I'm here for you."

"Germantown is an up-and-coming neighborhood!" actually comes out of my mouth.

"I agree. For eight hundred thousand, I could make the argument that it's worth the risk of seeing to the truth of that. It's not the safest of places, is it, though? The pathology of poverty, of all that's been done to our fellow black people. The effects of institutional racism. It's all just past the fence."

"Not one person has been mugged, robbed, attacked, or otherwise harmed in the months that you guys—that *we*—*we* all moved here."

This is actually a true statement. Not once, not one reported assault of any kind. It's a miracle, really. God protects fools, horses, and mulattoes.

"You're right. Nothing's happened. And we are all so thankful for that, and for you giving our clan the opportunity to be here—"

"And I'm happy you're here, and I want you to stay and thrive forever," I say with all the earnestness I feel about this statement. I don't want to be here with them, or for Tal to be—or Sun, I want her with me—but I would love to see them stay here. Except Spider; it'd be cool if he came with us, if he wants.

"But to make it truly fit, it would mean making substantial changes. Significant investment. Turn to the end of the book."

I do, and I can feel her watching me. I struggle getting the thick sheets over their little rails, curse in the process, but in all that time Roslyn is unmoving, focused on the pages.

"This is here," I say when I see it. A map. A map of Loudin Estate. I recognize it from the shape of the property, the names of streets to the north and east. But the house placement is all wrong. And there are other structures as well, ones that don't exist outside this ink. "Why is the mansion over here, in the back?"

"Because that's where we'd have to move it. It's the only way we could maximize the site for further construction. That house is hogging all the space, don't you agree? It's a simple process, really. Workers cut the building into smaller pieces, then snap them together like LEGOs, apparently."

"It's got historical restrictions, you can't just—"

"If they can move Alexander Hamilton's house, twice, we can move a house once owned by somebody nobody remembers. That's not just my opinion either, that's my lawyers'. My lawyers are *amazing*. But expensive. So you see why I couldn't possibly offer you a penny over nine hundred thousand dollars."

"No. No, that's not, that's not the range we're talking about here. A million one, maybe. But I can't just give this away."

"It'd be a shame if we had to go away, I agree. But you must see,

Mélange could thrive in any of the places in that binder. There's even an island in there. Sometimes, I think our own island would be the best place for us to be."

"The First Couple says different." I thought, in the moment "The First Couple" passed my lips, that it would sound silly. Overly momentous. But it doesn't. It sounds like scripture. It sounds like canon. Still, Roslyn smiles wide, wraps one hand around her waist, the other to her chin, pulls back to take in the whole of me. "And they are in that house, nowhere else. I saw them," I continue. In this moment, I don't know which of us is infidel, which is believer.

"Your daughter sees and believes in them. Others are listening, I'll give you that."

"They are. And Tal's going to college next year, and I have to take care of her. And if it means selling this whole place to someone else, ghosts and all, for one point two million, I'll have to do it. You see the bind I'm in here. I want this for you." I reach out my hand toward her and hold it there, wait for her to take it. Roslyn looks at it like it's an appendage she's never seen before, then relaxes and finally grips it before I can prove myself a fool. "For all of you. For all of us. Our clan."

"Tal is us too, now," Roslyn says, and I smile because who cares what she means by this. It's positive, so we're going in the right direction.

"Look. A million one. Say one word, one syllable, and we can make this happen," I tell her.

"One million," she says, and my relief is so great I don't care that she smiles like she's won.

When I call Sirleaf to go over the details, I remember to ask him if Tosha has been in contact about her divorce, which of course she hasn't. A few texts later, Tosha agrees to let us all meet at her house, a compromise only reached after she first tries to decline based on needing a sitter. So, two hours later, when I arrive at Tosha's door, bottle of the best champagne that can be bought on Chelten Avenue in hand, I expect to see them both, and do. What I don't expect to see is the image of Sirleaf Day, on Tosha's couch, getting his foot massaged. By Tosha. Right there in her living room.

"Do you really want to do that?" I ask her, putting the bottle on the coffee table.

"What's wrong with my feet? This is a legitimate exchange for my expert legal advice," Sirleaf protests.

"Did you actually get any divorce advice?" I ask Tosha.

"Not now. I'm taking a five-day training course in Kansa Vatki. I have to practice."

"That's right, she has to practice!" Sirleaf insists. Tosha looks over at me only to roll her eyes, then gets back to rubbing like the last hope for the universe can be found in this old man's corns. Sirleaf moans, lifts the couch pillow he's holding off his face just long enough to look at me, moans again, and drops it to the floor.

"We carry our stress in our feet," Tosha tells me. "Or our feet carry it, or something, shit, I don't know—I'm only two days in," she adds, when my look of confusion doesn't dissipate. Both sentences come with a frown, because she knows me well enough to anticipate my response without me having to say it.

"Sirleaf? We got to talk about the finances," I say. This at least gets Sirleaf to stop moaning and open his eyes again.

"Everything's fucked, son—excuse me Natasha, forgive me. I should say 'FUBAR,' to use the polite acronym. Because, I'm not going to lie to you Warren, it is definitely 'fucked up beyond all repair.'"

"What the hell are you talking about?"

"She's gonna leave me, man! Can you believe this shit?"

"What? Look, can we just handle my business first?"

"My woman wants us to move to fucking Brazil!" He stops himself again, looks to Tosha. She ignores his cursing, puts his foot down, shoots more oil into her hand. "First, she starts talking about us going on a couples counseling trip to Bahia. Afrocentric couples counseling! Can you believe that shit? I give in there; next thing you know, she's talking about moving there. We haven't even gone yet. Brazil! To find herself! Woman's sitting right there!" Sirleaf screams, as if stabbed.

"You gonna work it out," I tell him. I don't believe it. I believe she's going to leave him, because I believe that is the way of the world. But I believe he will love again, because he's Sirleaf Day. And I feel optimistic in this moment too, because I thought the FUBAR had to do with my personal finance. "Well, we got an offer on the house, so at least things are working well on the business side. It's low, but after we pay the bank, there will still be enough for Tal." I can't help the cheer in my voice, because it's so simple now. Not as much money as an insurance payoff, but so much less risk. No literal flames, just metaphorical ones.

"That's fantastic! Because it turns out your ex-wife really is suing you."

He means it. "Becks?" I ask.

"How many ex-wives you got?" He's not kidding. He's just curious.

"But you said she couldn't since she's not an American citizen."

"She will be soon. She married an American. Name's Albert Jackson, got a law office in Manhattan and everything. But it's cool—"

"It's not cool. It's the opposite of cool. It's specifically a hot mess. I don't have the money I owe her yet. It's—"

"Calm down—we just sign the property over to your daughter. No problem. That will protect you."

Tosha looks at me, to gauge my reaction. I don't have one yet to give to her. The fact that Becks is remarried stirs no part of me that hasn't died already. The idea of my daughter, my future, getting my future, seems a minor adjustment of formality.

"Your father's will already states it belongs to you or your descendants. We give it to her in a trust till she turns eighteen. When's Tal's birthday?"

"In May sometime. A couple of weeks."

"Perfect, so we got no problem. Trust me, I'm not about to let someone steal Craig Duffy's legacy. Ain't gonna happen. Paperwork's already done."

"And this will limit my liability?"

Sirleaf cannot be bothered to answer such silly questions. Instead, he motions to the coffee table. I get up, go to get the paperwork. Tosha gives Sirleaf the tap on his feet to say her work is done, and rises up next to me.

"My hands." Tosha frowns when Sirleaf leaves, hustling to the sink and letting it run hot. After five minutes, she's still standing there, rubbing them down, reapplying soap.

"If it's that nasty for you, why?"

"Jesus washed feet. It's got a strong tradition," Tosha says, repeatedly rubbing down her hands with a full-sized towel. She won't look up at me. "I have to grow. I need to be more nurturing. I need to be more giving, as a person."

"Do you actually believe that? Because that seems like some bullshit. That seems like some George bullshit, specifically."

"Don't say anything about him. Don't."

"Why?"

"Because. George came over, last weekend. He spent the night."

"Okay. So is he leaving the other woman?"

"Thanks for the whole faux boyfriend thing. It worked. Men are so possessive."

"Right, but is he leaving the white woman?"

"I can rescue this," Tosha answers by not addressing my questions at all. "I just have to give him what he wants. It's that simple. He wants nurturing: I give him nurturing. That's what a wife is supposed to do. No biggie. That's the only thing I can do. I can't just leave. I want to. I'm so sick of his shit. But the kids," Tosha says, and lets the sentence fragment explain itself.

"He already left. If he leaves her and comes back to you just out of duty, do you really want him?" I ask her, and she avoids me by going to the fridge, pulling out a bottle of wine, and pouring it all the way up to her glass's edge. "You can end something that's hurting you," I answer for her. "You can. You're allowed."

"Well, you are the expert on divorcing," Tosha tells me, but there's no malice in it.

"I am."

"Divorce isn't the answer for everyone. Every problem looks like a nail when you're a hammer."

"Yo, some problems are fucking nails."

Tosha pours me a glass too, a shallower one. I pull out my phone, go to YouTube and Tal's video, and in explaining it give us both a chance to talk about something else.

"Crackheads," is what Tosha says when it's done.

"That's what I said!" Tosha gets me. We know. We know Germantown. And we know there is nothing exotic here. We know Philly.

"They must have had a ladder or something. Who knows? They're crackheads. Or meth heads—one of them's white, you never know, she could have hooked that brother. Probably trying to break in through the second-floor window."

"You can't see in the tape too well, but they did look like they were fucking. It was crazy."

"Crackheads are crazy. You definitely got a crackhead problem." Tosha walks me back out to the couch, lies down on it. I follow, force her to stay in the moment.

"No, I don't have a problem, the Mélange Center for Multiracial Life has a problem. Once we do this deal, we're gone. Tal's off to Washington, and I'm free to follow." It's this that gets Tosha to turn around.

"That's who you're selling to? Are you serious? They're going to be here forever?"

"Okay, they're a little kooky, granted, but they're harmless. Nobody cares about their little Mulattopia. Nobody is even going to notice them."

"Did you see how many views it got?"

I didn't. I pull my phone back out, scroll down the page. It now says *2,771* over a long green line.

"Warren. Come on. You're really going to let those Uncle Toms stay here permanently, in our neighborhood, pumping their Oreo bullshit?"

"That's not how they are—actually some are sunflowers. They just believe—" It's a wasted effort, only managing to bulge Tosha's eyes wider in annoyance the more I talk. She just doesn't want to hear it. Even more, she can't hear it: she's made her decisions on race, on what it is and what it most certainly is not, and all other discussions on the topic she registers as an attack on her reality. "Look, I know it's hard to be open-minded about this, be there's no choice: the moment is changing. Black people aren't used to not having the final say on race in America; it's uncomfortable."

"What the fuck did you just say to me?"

"I'm just saying, you are used to having the moral high ground on black and white issues, so it's understandably upsetting when another group comes in and redefines who we are. I know it doesn't just affect mixed people, it affects the whole black dynamic. I get it."

"What is this 'you' bullshit?"

"I'm just saying they're kooky, but they're not crazy. They have some valid goals. They're just trying to change things so they're better for mixed people."

"What mixed people? They're black. If these Oreos are trying to change things so that they're not really black, how does that help anyone besides themselves? We've got black boys being used for target practice by white cops out there, we've got a prison system overflowing with victims of white judgment. We have a crisis. Right now. Not in the eighteenth century, not in the civil rights era, but right now. How does them quitting blackness help the Trayvon Martins out there? How does it help the Michael Browns? The Renisha McBrides, and all the black women out there struggling to hold it down? How does running away from blackness not make that worse?"

"That's a false equivalence. Having people acknowledge all of their ethnic heritage doesn't mean they're abandoning social justice."

"But they're not just 'acknowledging.' They're trying to challenge the basic fiber of the African American identity. These people, these sellouts you have living up in your house, they're forming their own exclusive community. That's not 'acknowledging,' that's a cult. Somebody needs to call out this nonsense. It's bad enough that you're messing with that foolishness, but you got your own daughter in that mess."

"It's been good for her," I try, but Tosha isn't trying to hear me.

"Warren. I love you like a brother, in every sense of the word. But you are lost right now. You got your own daughter worshipping crackheads like they're miscegenation angels. What kind of crazy Oreo shit is that?"

I'm so worked up on the walk through the dark back to Loudin that I'm not even worried about getting jumped. There are things I think of now to say to Tosha—mainly, I am not an Oreo! I am a sunflower! I think this and an older part of me goes, No Negro, you're a black man. A very pale black man, a very pale, very confused black man, and maybe this has gone too far. Maybe I am lost. I got divorced, and then my dad died, and then Tal came, and crackheads, and then Sunita Habersham, and maybe I got a little lost. The Mulattopians, yes, they are a little cultish. Yes, I can admit that to Tosha. Readily. I don't like that bit, no, and I am not going to let my daughter be sucked into that part, I would have assured Tosha. The ghost thing too: it's utter madness and I am not going to stand for it anymore. That video, it's coming down. Enough. But having conceded those points, I don't feel I'm "lost" in what is, despite even my own resistance, a minor identity alteration. And it is a little thing, saying "I'm mixed" instead of "I'm black," yet it's like the difference between the comfort of wearing shoes that fit as opposed to bearing the blisters of shoes just one size too small. I might have said. It does feel like a relief, an actual relief of pain, just acknowledging—yes I use the word *acknowledging*—all of who I am, to myself. I would have said to her.

I come in the front pedestrian gate, still mentally reciting my rebuttal, and there's no one there. There should be someone at the gate at all times, it's locked but only six feet tall. Anyone can climb it; I climb it, because I can't see which key to use in the dark. Also, where are the lights? This, this is a representation of the Mulattopians', specifically the Oreos', basic detachment from reality. There should be fog lights here, or something. Usually, all the lights from the caravans are enough to keep the place lit up, populated. But now it's dark. There are no lights on inside the property. Not from the trailers, not from the string of bulbs they placed up between their makeshift alleys. It's completely engulfed in shadow, aside from patches from the streetlights off Germantown Avenue. No one is here. I head toward the house. I know something is wrong when I see all the people crowding out of my father's house onto the porch. There're about thirty of them. It's a whole damn party. I did not invite them here. I did not give Tal permission to invite them all here. It's nearly midnight, but here they are pouring out onto the steps. Looking in the windows. Listening at the open door. They don't pay me mind until I stomp right through them. Until I yell, "Tal!"

They start parting then. They start giving me room to reach her. The house is even more full of them. The whole camp. It's here. All of them. Faces I recognize but don't care because my daughter is in so much trouble right now.

"Tal!"

The crumbling mansion is packed. In the hallway, on the stairs, into the dining room, all facing the living room. Chop it up, chop it up now.

"Tal!" A few people point into the living room. They seem scared. They are scared. They are scared of me.

Tal sits on the couch. To her side, sitting up on the couch's back, rests Roslyn, who has a hand on my daughter's shoulder. On the other side is Sun, who looks more concerned than anyone in here, but not scared. Concerned for me.

"What the hell is going on?" I ask my daughter. Nobody else here matters more. Nobody else in the world.

"Stop embarrassing me."

"Why is everyone in my house?" It comes out lighter, slightly deflated. But only slightly.

"I saw them," Roslyn says. She's smiling. She's excited. Everyone is excited, smiling too. Everyone but Sun. Sun stares at me, monitoring.

Looking across the room at my eyes, Sunita Habersham mouths *Stop*. But nothing here is ending. Roslyn says louder, "I saw them too. I finally saw them."

"She saw them," a few other voices reiterate.

"In the front top window of the house. I had my doubts. I admit it," Roslyn says to me and the rest of the room, with an emphasis on the latter. "But I saw them. The First Couple. It's all true," Roslyn continues. Heads nod around me. Quick words say the affirmative.

"I had a séance and they actually showed up. How cool is that, Pops?" Tal asks, holds out a hand to the air for a high five. When I don't step forward and smack it, Kimet gets off the floor and does it for me.

A cult. Tosha is right about this part. About them. This has officially passed into madness. Later, I'm sure, I will tell this story at dinner parties, and to new friends. And when they ask, "Were they really that bad?" I will tell them this story. I will leave no detail out, either. How they all sat on the floor Indian-style, around Roslyn, who sat on the couch above them. How they lit Pottery Barn candles trying to pretend at mysticism. How sage burned in the air, misting around behind the older woman. How Afro Celt Sound System played in the background, and I'm sure a whole bunch of other ethnic hybrid hot hits were cued behind it. And I'll add this part: what One Drop, standing behind the couch, says to me with two hands on Sunita Habersham's shoulders, massaging them absently the whole time he's talking.

"Hey man, your daughter, she's a spiritual seer, Holmes. You don't know this, but she's a powerful woman."

There are several responses to this statement that would be appropriate, and I go through them in my head, I do. I take a good three seconds to consider each one, carefully, and Sunita Habersham, bless her, she sees me do it. Her face goes from annoyed to cautious to seriously worried about how I'll react to the stimuli given. I know this because she removes One Drop's hands off her shoulders and starts to come for me. Our eyes lock, and that actually helps—she won't realize it, but it does, in some quiet part of me, the part not about to start roaring.

"Get your hippie half-breed asses the fuck out my father's house and away from my daughter before I kick the Uncle Tom out the lot of you!"

Roslyn doesn't bother to frown. Everyone else is still as well. They just stare at me. Even Sun freezes, for a moment. But only a moment. When the air stops vibrating, when the biggest sound is the weight of my breathing, then she gets up and walks by.

"Don't," she says. No extra verb. Don't talk to me. Don't look at me. Don't screw me. Don't kiss me. Don't bother explaining yourself. It's all in there. And then Sun's past me. Into the hall. Out the door. Down the steps. We all hear her feet go, boom, da boom, boom. Still, it's motionless inside. Tal looks like she is about to cry, but other than that, frozen. Roslyn has dropped most of her smile, but the sides of her lips still tilt the edges of her mouth.

"Get out of here!" I follow with. Still that doesn't work. Nobody moves. I close my eyes, to listen for it. To listen for movement.

What I finally hear is, "It's okay. My father needs alone time."

I stand there. I don't open my eyes again. I don't want to see them. I don't open my eyes till the last footfall moving past me has grown silent.

I can breathe normally now. I am myself once more. The rage has escaped me. I have returned to normal. The house has returned to normal. Almost normal. When I do open my eyes, the overhead lights are back on. The candles are blown out. The music has been silenced.

Tal is gone.

Roslyn is not. She sits right where she did before. Staring at me. Smiling.

"You didn't see anything," I tell her. I know this. I know this even though I've seen things.

Roslyn keeps smiling, but doesn't bother looking at me. Slowly she rises.

"They might believe you, but I can see what you're doing, that's what I see," I say into her silence. Roslyn reaches for her purse at the couch's end, brushes something off of it, then puts it on her shoulder. When she doesn't respond I say, "You're turning this into a cult."

"It's not a cult. It's a karass. A people linked by a higher purpose," she says lightly as she walks by me to the door.

"That's the kind of shit people in a cult say," I get out, but Roslyn doesn't look back, my sound just another creak in the room.

20

SUNITA HABERSHAM IS NOT taking my calls. Her line rings, I see her face on my phone, and then the only voice I get is the one recorded for the entire world. Tosha won't talk to me either, but this I barely notice, because Sunita Habersham is not taking my calls or responding to my texts and I feel the loss like one leg is gone and I have to struggle every moment not to fall over. I don't leave my father's house. I don't go out. I don't go to see her. I know she's there. I know Tal is with her. Tal contacts me, after The Explosion, with a text that says, *I'm staying with Sun now.* Followed immediately with another text that says, *Cuz UR an asshole*. Tal, I miss, but she's my teenage daughter and teenagers are supposed go through a period where they hate their parents and so basically this puts us right on schedule. As long as the cult doesn't steal her, that door will reopen. The door to the life of Tosha Evans, that will reopen as well, we've been friends too long to not be now just because of mulattoes. There's another door I keep thinking about. The one to Sun's trailer. It's a little aluminum door, with white metal siding on the outside. If I don't get that door open again, eventually it will rust shut on me forever.

Everyone else in Mulattopia, they're cordial. Very tolerant. Polite. The guy who still owns the land to this place? He should be tolerated. No one stands before the house and denounces me. I am never cursed back out. No one will look directly at me as I walk around my own property either, but they don't make faces or other visible displays of disapproval.

I'm not mad at them, for this genteel shunning. I can feel my own shame, at the way I chose to express myself. My anger, having been given full vent, is largely exhausted. This primal emotion has been replaced with another: loneliness. The major cause of this is Tal and Sun not speaking to me, but I'm surprised to find that this is not the entire cause.

Yes, I believe this has become a cult. But it was a cult in which I was a member. Part of the allure of all of this, even as I've struggled against it, has been the seductive feeling of my own group inclusion. I still move through these people, but I feel disconnected from them now. I feel the absence of a kinship I took for granted. The only thing worse than a cult is a cult that won't have you as a member.

It does get better, slowly. A week later, I do garner a few uncommitted head nods when I make direct eye contact. One of One Drop's crew even follows with, "You feeling better since The Explosion?" I don't go out as much, but when I do, when I leave for the store or interact with the parents and others as I teach the remainder of my class, several others make a point to discuss the night with me as well. They use the term *The Explosion* in a way that conveys that the events have been discussed in detail and a title for this historical moment has been formally approved. *The Explosion*. Very dramatic. According to them, The Explosion was perfectly normal. Something many at the camp have gone through. A part of the process. A necessary phase in the creation of a new worldview.

My favorite of these discussions comes at the gate. As I struggle to keep the bike upright in first gear, freshly bought groceries filling my saddlebags, One Drop steps right out in front of me.

"Yo man, I just want to say, it ain't nothing to be ashamed of. We all been through it, it's part of the awakening, you know?"

"Thanks, One Drop." I like saying his name to him. It's so goddamn ridiculous and the joke seems to hover a yard in front of his face, just out of his reach. He hangs that way before my face now, my front wheel between his legs. The bike stalls; he doesn't notice. I flip up the visor on my helmet to add to the message that I want to get by him, but he doesn't read social cues. It's another language in which he's illiterate.

"For real, Holmes. It's a struggle, this mixed identity thing. I fought it too. Just like you, yo. Even more, bro, even more. Because my blackness, right, it's my essence? It's in me. You know what I'm saying?" One Drop tells me as he bangs his chest. So that's where it is. Because it certainly isn't outside him. "I didn't mean nothing, the other night. It's just, I saw the First Couple, and my mind was kinda blown. I'm just glad you're down with the cause, bro. You ever want to talk about it, sunflower to sunflower, I'm here, yo."

Into all this, Spider's truck returns from its extended scouting mission around two in the afternoon, but I don't go outside in daylight. I stay here, in the damned house. I go out at dark. I go out when I can walk fast and be largely unseen. I want to go immediately, so I can talk to him before the rest turn me into the villain, and I actually get as far as the door, but I don't. They'll all know what I'm up to. It will just make it worse.

It takes Spider ten hours to respond to my text, my simple, *Hey, when you get settled, come up to the house and hang.* And when he does, Spider's message is just *Come down, man.*

Spider sits on his trailer's steps, playing his accordion again, managing to keep the song going as he talks.

"What happened while I was gone? Everybody looks like they saw a ghost!"

He's been waiting all day to say this line, and from the way he laughs it met expectations. He's gotten better. On the accordion, in just a few weeks' time. The notes don't come between labored pauses.

"How was Creole country? Must have been nice to have a paid vacation." I'm not sure that Roslyn funded his trip until he says, "I know, right? It was sweet! I guess things are going well here, but even so, I'm definitely headed back. Already got a gig, too. No matter what, we should take a road trip. Just you and me. Dude out. You need a break."

"I think I already broke."

"Shut up. You lost your shit. I've lost my shit, found it, and lost it again a dozen times. And this whole mixed thing, it's like racial sacrilege. Especially for the sunflowers." He leans forward, lowers his voice. "For the Oreos, I think it's a little easier, because they got a bit of that white entitlement in them, and they think they're allowed to do whatever they want." Leaning back, he returns to full voice. "Or that just might be my vestigial prejudice talking."

I take a seat next to him, and a beer when he hands one over. We drink. Then I drink, and he plays the accordion some more. A sad song. "O, bonsoir Moreau," he sings to me, and some other lyrics I don't have the language to understand. I shoot the beer down before he finishes, grab another from his cooler. I am going to get drunk now. Since Tal's gone.

"You want to find your shit?" Spider asks me, a six-pack in.

We are at Sunita Habersham's trailer. It's not that late, it's only just after midnight, but the shades are drawn. Still, you can see the lights are on. It even comes through the doorjamb. Spider decides to go in on his own, have me wait outside, which is fine considering the delicacy of the situation.

He's in there long enough for me to doubt he's coming back out. I think, They've won him over, he's gone to the other side, back to the feminine, away from me. But the door opens.

"What?" Tal asks me. Not even *Hello*. Not even, *I missed you*. "Spider says you have an eighteenth birthday present for me. I don't believe him. I don't believe you anymore." Her last sentence, I don't believe. She can barely say it. I grab Tal into a hug, and she's not expecting it, almost falls over. I hold her steady and whisper, "I love you and will always love you and you can always trust that," and don't let go till she nods. And then I step back, and continue the previously scheduled performance.

"I have a present for you!"

"I don't see any presents, Pops."

"This!" My arms go out, up. I motion, circle, get a little dizzy, stop. "You see all around you. All this is yours! I am signing over Loudin to you. I'm signing the inheritance over to you! To do as you like! As long as that's selling it and taking the money and going to Whitman College! And giving me the rest to live on!"

Tal looks around, caught for a moment, then says, "Wait, you were going to pay for the college anyway. That's not really a gift."

"But now you're going to pay for it!"

Tal starts to walk away. I look up, at Spider, leaving Sun's trailer, alone. The door shuts behind him. Spider shrugs. At least I got one of them, his gesture tells me.

"What do you want from me?" I yell after my daughter and it sounds annoyed and I don't mean that so I try again with "Whatever you want, I'll give you whatever you want," which I immediately realize is something that should never be said to a teenager but, there, I've already done it. And this gets Tal to stop.

When she looks at me, I know she doesn't know what she wants. Or she does, but they are not things a mortal can do. She waits it out though, thinks on it. I'm proud of her for that. The genie has granted the wish. She is trying to think of an answer better than "Three more wishes."

"I want my Sesa tattoo. I've earned it."

"You're not eighteen yet. I said when you're eighteen."

"Dad. My birthday was two days ago."

Tal's arm is swabbed and prepped and Spider seems very professional about it, and I don't want to be here. I want to end the day, admit defeat, call it a night. I want to end the month. I want to end the life. I can't end my life because Tal needs me and that hurts, the lack of chance at the alleviation of pain, but she needs me. And I need to be a good father. I will never be a good father, though, so I just want to be a better father. The kind of father who buys a calendar and puts important dates on it. At least that kind of father.

"I'm so sorry," I say one more time, then again with another "so" in it. I'm building a mountain of apologies. Tal isn't answering me, she's not talking to me at all, but I'm going to climb the mountain of regret and reach her someday, so it has to be tall.

Spider lays a stencil on her skin, presses it down, and I know that soon he will take a needle and pour ink into her bleeding flesh. There's giggling from Tal as she's branded with the preliminary etching. I don't find it funny, because soon it will be permanent. To Spider she talks, even smiles, when he holds up her temporary design, the swirl outline with the Star of David on the inside.

"I was hoping you'd at least throw a little Gaelic twist in there, for your old man." I try to play along.

"Do you want that, sweetie?" Spider asks Tal directly.

"No," Tal says, so I know she can hear me.

After the design is pressed on wet paper to her skin, Tal looks at it in the mirror like it's a good thing it will soon be made to last the rest of her life. Spider has the needles. Spider has the true ink. Permanence comes with pain, as always.

"Okay, now here's the big question," Spider says to her. He's holding up what looks like an airbrush gun in one hand, and a ruler-sized wooden rod in the other. "Do you want to do this modern style, or do you want me to go the traditional hand-tattoo route?"

"Spider, you are not needling my daughter with a stick."

"It looks primitive but actually hurts a little less. A little."

"Honey, listen to me. This thing, it's forever. Are you sure you really want this on your body forever? Are these people that important to you? This Mélange thing, I know you love it, but it's only going to be a couple months in a long life. You're off to college, then you have your whole—"

"Poke me with the stain stick," Tal tells Spider.

"Is that okay, dad?" Spider asks me, and takes my shrug.

Tal flinches at the initial piercing. I go to her before I even think of doing it. Kneeling on the floor, I pat Tal's head, transitioning from my hand to a towel when I feel the sweat beading on her brow.

"Pops? You have no idea how bad this stings," Tal says finally. I don't know. I am the last untattooed man on earth. I am He Who Has No Ink. Everyone else has made their decision, has chosen their totems. The lack of paint on my skin at this age—where it seems like even babies are written upon in the maternity ward—has made me the last of my own clan. We, the undecided.

"You could go next, dude. It's been a long year. Join us! It's not a Mélange thing; it's a mixed thing. You've earned it."

"Yeah, no thanks. My plan is to finish this life unscarred."

I can't actually see what's happening. Or I can't actually bring myself to see. I look at Tal's face. I force myself to stop flinching when she does. There's her pain. And here I am, finally. I missed her flu shots, her first fall from a bicycle, even her ear piercings, but for this I am present. Tal's first tattoo. The moment she is forever marked. The moment even her body loses its pretense to being a blank state. We have stories. Now you can just see one of her chapters.

It's taking too long. "Can I do something for you, honey?" I ask Tal. "What can I do for you right now. For the pain?"

"Bring me vodka."

"No."

"Then bring me Sun," Tal tells me, adding a yelp when I seem reluctant to carry out the order.

I knock so lightly on Sun's door. I'm so polite. Just cute little taps, evenly spread out, I'm very controlled and considerate.

"Sunita? Please. Open up. I need to talk to you."

When that doesn't work, I hit a little harder, and a little more so every few beats. "Sun. Please. It's not for me. It's for Tal." My voice is low, but it doesn't need to be. There's no one else outside to hear me.

I have no idea where everyone is, but they aren't walking the grass alleys of Halfie Heights. There must be a party. A party to which I wasn't invited. Two parties, most likely, one for the Oreos, one for the sunflowers. You would think the sunflowers' party would be rocking more bass, but Little Halfrica is silent.

When I sit down on the stoop, I say it again. "It's for Tal." Because it all is for Tal. These steps, they're metal and narrow and hurt my ass but I don't care because it's for Tal. Also, it's pathetic. I want Sun to see me being pathetic. I want her to see my regret. I want—

The light goes on beside the trailer. Just appears, no sound. Bright light. I look to Sun's windows. Curtains still drawn. Space behind them now dark inside. It was the outdoor motion detector. I haven't moved.

I go upright silently. I don't move any more than that. I don't breathe. I hold my breath and listen. I hear nothing. Not cars. Not radios. Not humans. Not crickets. And then I'm scared, because I don't hear crickets. There is always the sound of crickets, at night, in Germantown, in May. There are no crickets. There is nothing.

There is the white woman.

There is the sound of footfalls, running.

She is there and then she isn't there and she's running away. Goddamn half-naked white woman running through Germantown. That's all it takes to ruin everything.

I run after her.

I run before I realize I can barely walk. I bang into the trailer next to Sun's, hear some Oreo scream in the shaky inside, keep running. I'm going to catch her. I'm going to end the hoodoo nonsense. I am going to rid the land of all crackheads forever. She glides beyond me. I will push her to the ground, hold her there and scream, sit on her till the police come and Tal too, with half a tattoo but who cares because now she'll know the lie of this place.

Bare pale white feet, black on the bottom. Ghosts don't have dirty feet.

"Ghosts don't have dirty feet!" I yell when she cuts through another line of trailers.

"What the fuck?" comes back, but not from her, from another trailer I slide into because the dewy grass is slippery and my balance even more unreliable.

A white shirt. Long. Like a gown. A dirty white gown. Maybe a hospital gown. But it's her. The woman from the house. The burglar. I know her. I have seen her. Not like the others claim, not in some mystical revelation. I have seen this crackhead asshole and I know her and I don't even know where from besides my dreams but I know her. It's her. I am running. Stopping. Spying her through the maze of mobile homes. Running again.

"This is private property!" I yell like I own the place. I own the place. Or now Tal owns the place, but I would know if there were any white people living here. There are no white people here. There are tons of half-Europeans, but no whole ones.

Darting to the end of the trailers, she heads toward the last one, turns out of sight at its corner. I chase after the shadowed blur of her pale body. She runs from me like she's guilty and she is and I will capture her and reveal her to the world.

"I see you!" I yell at her. "Everybody wake up! I see her! Come see her!"

It will be like *Scooby-Doo!* I do it for my Velma. Everyone will surround us while I whip off the ghoul's mask.

I turn the corner and she's gone.

She hasn't gone farther. The grass is empty beyond. No one is that fast. She did not vanish into thin air. Only ghosts vanish into thin air. Ducking down, I look under the Victorian trailer, see nothing. I look up at the door. It's Roslyn's door.

It's Roslyn's door.

It's Roslyn. It's always been Roslyn. I am drunk and I am tired and I am breathing really heavy now too, but I know, it's Roslyn. Behind it all.

Roslyn, who answers the door after only two knocks, because she's awake. Of course she is.

"Where is she!"

"Warren? It's very late. What's wrong? Why are you doing this?" The expression; she plays it perfectly.

"I know she's in there."

Roslyn, who just stares at me. Standing in her doorway. Nothing but a long T-shirt on and a sleeping bonnet. Standing there like a door herself, a closed one. In a backward, inside-out T-shirt with the tag showing. Who won't say a damn thing more. And I win. I win. Because she lifts up a finger and points down to the far end of the property, wags her head in defeat, and goes back inside.

I walk in the direction noted. As far into the dark as the compound allows. Along the line of the most rusted of the property's fence, below where the slope of the hill hits its sharpest downturn, where the angle hides it from the rest of the property. I am coming for her. I am coming for him too, if he's here. I'm coming.

I see a light. Not the steady drone of the streetlight. A spark. A flicker. Candlelight. Against the farthest corner of the yard. I see her, on the ground, before it. I start running, trying to get all the way before she can escape, am at full momentum again when I can already tell it's not the white woman.

"What the hell is your problem?" comes from Sunita Habersham when I reach her. She's on her knees. There's not one light before her, but three. Bodega candles. Leaning up against the middle iron rods of the border. Their light flickers off her face, and the intimacy of her posture makes me feel the embarrassment as it takes over.

"Did you see a white lady?" I ask, because I can't bring myself to ask what she's doing, what this is, what is going on with her. Or why she's frantically gathering up the pictures that I now see are lying on the ground before her, pulling them into a loose pile and sticking them in a cardboard box. I don't look at them, don't even want to guess what they are. I want to run past her, continue crackhead-hunting, pretend this is normal behavior on both our parts.

"I'm not crazy," Sun insists.

"I didn't say you were crazy. I wasn't even thinking that." And I wasn't, because I hadn't even gotten that far.

"It's a ritual. For closure." I look down at my ankle, which I realize is hot. Because it's burning. I hop from the pain, see something fall off my pant leg. I lift it up, hold the remains of a photo, the image of a man's flannel shirt obscured by a destructive line of ember that glows in the darkness.

"Wait—What the hell? Are you burning these?"

"They're just prints! It's a releasing ceremony, okay?"

"So this is where you've been going? All those times at night when you disappear?" There is actually relief in my voice, and that leads to a little levity, which I understand immediately Sun takes as mocking.

"Not every night. Just some anniversaries."

"You're out here, making an alter?" I hand her the singed image. Sun takes it, blows on it gently, like suddenly it is something to take great care of.

"Roslyn says my problem, with getting over Zeke, isn't that I never got a note. My problem's all the other reminders he left behind. I mean, that's the idea. I don't know. Roslyn suggested it."

"Oh, okay. Roslyn suggested it." I don't intend for there to be any sarcasm in my voice. I don't even think there is; Sun just borrows my cynicism from earlier conversations and applies it here. It's enough to break the spell of her defensiveness, put her into an opposite mode.

"What the hell are you doing out here?"

"Tal would like your support as she gets her Sesa tattooed," I say. It just comes out of my mouth, overriding the more problematic subject of fake-ghost-hunting. I wasn't even thinking about my original motivation; the sentence was just sitting there, waiting to escape, waiting for the moment when my brain shut down. "I let her get it. Since I forgot her birthday," I add, when the first explanation clearly doesn't seem good enough.

"Tal's birthday isn't until next week," Sunita Habersham tells me, fastening up her box with rubber bands. "Next Thursday," she says before blowing out the candles. Sun saves "She played you" for when we're walking back.

21

IN FOUR PIECES, it will go, the house that Loudin built. The structural mover assures me that they can do the job, that the initial deconstruction shouldn't take more than a week at most, that the restorative work to hide the surgical cuts shouldn't take more than a few months. While he talks, mistaking me for someone who cares, his men measure and take notes and hold little detectors to the walls to see where the beams are, spraying orange paint in response to their finds. They can do the cuts right down the line of the wood. When it's reassembled, you won't be able to tell the difference, the project manager tells me. You could take this halfway around the world and it would hold. Houses like this aren't built anymore.

The call from Tosha interrupts this, and I'm still not ready to take it, but I don't want to talk about my father's house anymore.

I answer with, "I'm sorry."

"It's too late for sorry, Warren. I'm just calling to tell you, I will be there. I watched it, and I'm not letting this get any further. And not just me, I'm not the only one who thinks this has gone too far. We will be there. The community. With our own press, our own cameras. We're not just going to let this divisive bullshit happen. I still care about you, but I can't believe you had the nerve to go on TV talking about jungle-fever ghosts. And in that dirty ass T-shirt."

I'm asking her what she's talking about. I'm saying "Wait, talk to me," before I realize she's hung up.

The anchors' lead-in is "Spirits of Philadelphia," and a bunch of prattle and toothy grins, and even though it's just a clip you can tell it's the last segment of a slow news night.

"Why didn't you tell me this came on?"

"I didn't have time," Tal says, which is a lie. She must have known it would be broadcast last night, which is why she has the show's site bookmarked already, and why she didn't say a word through breakfast. So I brace myself.

The first shot is Loudin, in the daylight. It's taken from the street. Then the camera takes a stroll through Halfie Heights, and the voice-over describes it as "a new commune exclusively for black people who are half-white." Spider's Airstream: "They live in makeshift motor homes for now, but they insist they're here to stay, and that they are the future." Roslyn comes on. She's sitting on the front porch of my father's house like she already owns it. "We offer a sanctuary for people of both African and European ancestry to move beyond the cold war of black and white in America, and come to peace with themselves."

Tal, who hangs over my shoulder, straightens and steps back now. So I know it's coming.

"But not all is peaceful at Loudin Mansion," the voice says in a campy fifties horror-movie style. Same shot of the house, but now a filter flips the image to a black and silver negative. "Sightings of two ghosts, one female, white, and one a purportedly black male, have been reported throughout the camp." When Tal comes on, her name appears at the bottom over the title "Property Owner/Ghost Witness."

"They were here. I believe it was a sign. I believe it was the first interracial couple, welcoming us. Telling us the house is ours."

The light of the camera simultaneously flattens Tal's makeup-less face and makes the poof of her hair appear wild and expansive. My daughter looks as crazy as this sounds. They show the clip of her bathroom video; a link to the YouTube page where it's hosted even pops up. It's even grainier, filtered through the lens of television. After describing the footage, the voice says, "Not everyone agrees about who's doing the haunting."

"They were the ghosts of crackheads," it edits me as saying.

"Tal!" I yell in real life but I no longer feel her behind me. I'm described in a screen tag as "Witness's Father." The voice-over says I am a longtime Germantown resident so it can interrupt me until I blurt out my next comment out of context.

"I saw something. Definitely," my image tells the world.

The anchors are laughing. One says, "That's some story!" Then the other says, "Skeptics can come see for themselves. Loudin Mansion will be open for tours this Friday, June twelfth, for the Loving Day Festival. Loving Day celebrates the anniversary of the *Loving* v. *Virginia* verdict that allowed interracial marriage nationally." It then goes black. *Replay,* the screen dares.

I look over at the tent. The flap is down, the zipper is tight. She's in there.

"We are not having tours of the house tomorrow," I say to it.

"It's my house. I can do what I want," comes back to me.

I scroll down the page, look at the comments. Some Mulattopian, surely, has posted an event listing for Loving Day, under the name CrispusAttacks. Besides that, though, lies the subconscious of ugly America. PatriotGoEagles writes, *Ghosts come from trauma. That woman was probably raped by that black guy.*

"Haters gonna hate," Tal says after I read it to her. The sub-comment discussion for this entry reads like watercooler dialogue at a Klan meeting. One of these replies links to an article already written in reference to the clip, billed as a *Must Read Response*. I click on it. The article is called, "Mongrel Separatists? Obama's America Invades Philly." The first line is: *Remember when we warned of Reverse Racism, and the Libertards all laughed—now we know why they were really laughing.*

What comes after that, my daughter doesn't need to hear, so I stop reading it aloud. Into my pause, Tal says, "That's so stupid. How can you be racist against ghosts?"

"Listen, honey. Here's a news flash from outside the Mélange bubble: Americans know how to be racist against anything. People look at interracial couples through their own, distorting racial lens. It doesn't matter what form they take."

"That's just one nutjob," she tells me.

"That article has eighty-four likes. On Facebook. So those are just the people willing to link their names to it."

Tal doesn't say anything in there for a bit, but I can hear her on her own laptop.

"Well the First Couple video now has 22,786 page views," Tal says back triumphantly.

I only know about Tal's membership in the Loving Day Planning Committee because Tal, in her insistence on leaving the house for the final meeting before doing the dishes, chooses to reveal this to me. A teenager's every move is their opportunity for the clandestine and the only way I get in on this is to demand that I come. I have to be there. I have concerns. I have concerns that need to be raised. I have to be there also because Roslyn is not answering my texts or calls directly. Tal gets a response, though, and I'm allowed. "As my guest," my daughter makes the point of telling me.

It's a late-spring day, but we're inside the administration trailer, encased by its depressed low ceiling and wood-veneer paneling. The room has more than a dozen people shoved into it, the hum of an air conditioner forcing everyone to speak a little too loud for grace. My attempt to grab Roslyn before the meeting begins is foiled by a delegation of half-breeds from other mixed-race organizations and locales. Apparently not just black and white people are sleeping together. "Everyone is loving everyone, always, everywhere, and this room is proof of that," jokes the hapa dude after his introduction. He flew in all the way from Oakland. For this. It's going to be huge.

I sit through forty-five minutes of prattle and minutiae. Also, I sit through the way Roslyn stares at me. Like she's won, and like she's happy about it. Staring over at the Amerasian issues therapists, and the multiracial marketing coordinator, all the other lords of their own online and community mixed-race support groups, the Great Mulatto Queen addresses her court of subjects. The regality of her chandelier earrings, the rich draping of scarves over head and breast—none is as majestic as the look of joy in Roslyn's eyes. Or maybe she's actually happy. Maybe this is all her dream. Maybe it's all come true, everything she imagined in her darkest hour would bring her bliss and fulfillment.

"It's going to be protested," I say the second Roslyn asks if there are any questions. "I talked to a friend. She made it clear. There are going to be protests, the whole damn day I'm sure." Roslyn looks at me as if I'm not even speaking. As if the only reason she's even facing my way is to read me like a clock on a wall. So I turn, physically, to the rest of the room.

"This is an existing neighborhood. There is an existing order. Racially, locally, all that. Blowback is going to happen. And with that video circulating online, who knows how many other wackos are going to be drawn out. You need to seriously consider canceling this. This whole place will be on the news for something a lot less silly than ghosts. This could be bad."

"Protests mean press. All press is good press, generally." Roslyn, always pleasant, always smiling just enough to promise not only happiness but the opportunity for more. "We want the world to know we exist. Nobody cares about marches or rallies anymore. They want spectacle. They want ninety-second clips they can peruse on their choice of mobile device. Our guest speakers are already here, the bands and equipment are booked."

"My house is a mess. And not ready for a tour," I point out.

"Fine. But people are already in cars, trains, planes, coming here. For this. For us. For all of us. This event is happening. Protesters are just the final ingredient to make the day monumental. How many agree?"

"Agreed!" comes from across the room. Even Tal, she says it. I hear her voice distinctly because she's the one I love here and also she's right by my side.

"Sarah, make sure you resend the press release immediately. Add the part about the expected protesters. Make it a headline. Use the word 'controversial' in it too. Also, 'outrage.' They'll see 'outrage,' and think page views."

I get one voice on my side. One fellow champion of sanity in the whole lot of mutts. I have no idea what ethnic groups she's mixed with, either. Laotian and Ecuadorian? Pakistani and Italian? Who knows, she's just another member of the international legion of tan. But the woman is wearing a business suit, and is by far presenting the most professional air in the room, so I take special pleasure in cloaking my agenda in her gravitas.

"Does this dovetail with the image that you hope to promote, though? If the intent is to create an atmosphere of acceptance to interest the marginalized?"

Standing to speak to us all, opening her arms high like a bear staking its territory, Roslyn says, "This year, it's about making our presence known. About thrusting ourselves into the dialogue. Not just locally. As far as we can. Nationally. Internationally, if possible. Next year, our second Loving Day event will be at our new rural location, and then we can focus on message refinement. This year, this year we announce to the world that we are here, this is our time to be heard, our time to be whole. If this is big enough, next year, they will come from all over to find us."

"What 'new rural location'?" And I know Roslyn hears me, because she responds to everyone else.

"Tomorrow night, we have a major announcement. The Mélange Center for Multiracial Life will be unveiling a new satellite retreat in a setting that combines natural beauty with major historic resonance."

"What 'new rural location'?" I ask again, and keep asking, but no one can hear me over the applause.

...

Tal follows me out because she can tell I'm mad and it's not with her. "We don't have to do the ghost tour, Pops. I mean, it would be so awesome, but I was thinking, you're right we would have to clean, which is a pain in the ass. And now there's all the orange spray paint. And honestly I don't know if the ghosts would like it, you know?"

"This isn't about ghosts."

"It's about Roslyn, isn't it? You know she's awesome, right? Look at all she's done here. It's going to work out. You have to trust her," Tal finishes with, which is what gets me to slam the front door behind us.

"No I don't, and you don't. Or you shouldn't. I am your family. They are not your family. She's a liar, Tal. Did you hear that crap about the second location? She told me she only had money to buy one. Just to get the price on the house down. She lied to me. She lied to *us*. Do you know how much that probably cost us? Thousands. Hundreds of thousands, probably."

"She didn't lie," Tal tells me.

"Roslyn lied," I say. Calmer now. It's just true. It's simple. The words don't need emphasis. I walk up the stairs. I want a shower. I want a drink. I can do both up there.

"She didn't lie," Tal calls after me before I can reach the top. "I'm not selling her the place. Not yet. I'm going to keep renting to Mélange for a little while, so they can buy the other place first. It's an opportunity we can't miss, and we can't afford to do both."

I fight the urge to yell by walking down the steps, slowly. I take my time. Because I want to be calm when I get there. When I get to her. There's an air of menace coming off me, I realize, in the slow and deliberate fall of my feet before I get to Tal. But it works too, because by the time I'm there before her I'm speaking in almost a whisper.

"Honey? You can't. Do that. *We* need that money. You and me, the real 'we.' For college. I need that money. To live."

"I don't want to go all the way to Washington State. I want to be here, with them."

"You have to go."

"I want to be with you, Pops. This is my home."

"Trust me," I tell her. Let the words sit there. "It's time to grow up. It's time to get out of this house."

Tal turns around, heads to leave out the front door. Then, confused by the metaphor of her actions, turns and goes into her dining room. For a while, the only sound in response is her zipping up the entrance to the Coleman. But I still stand there. Because it's not over.

"I'm not selling. It's my house. Legally, it's my house! You can't make me leave here."

But I can. I can.

22

WHEN THE PROPANE TANKS are stacked cheerleader-pyramid-style behind my father's house, it only takes the top one, unscrewed, to release enough gas to be ignited by the broken fuse box just two feet above. The fire bursts forth like Satan popping a zit. Within minutes, it engulfs the back of the house. And no one notices, because the festival is going with enough chaos of its own to have all senses engaged. The open window allows the destruction into the kitchen, welcoming it into the house beyond. There it rages, hidden from the party on the lawn, engulfing the staircase and climbing higher, and no one even notices. Not until the windows in front of the house burst from the heat that only minutes before was just cold kinetic potential. Someone runs for the door, but they're stopped. Because it's too late. Far too late. And all those other propane tanks? They go boom. Taking with them any evidence. As the explosion goes off, I walk away without looking back, like in muscleman movies. No, better: I turn with everyone else and look surprised. Even more so, because I'm losing my father's house. Maybe I wail a bit, scream, get near One Drop so he can hold me back from rushing in there and rescuing the hamster. I can see it. I don't get out of the shower until the entire scene is fully visualized.

"Anyone need a propane refill?" I ask, and so many say yes that soon the shopping cart I push around the grass is so full I can barely get it back to the Bug. The white metal containers fill up the backseat in a pile three tanks high and I manage to fit four more in the passenger seat as well. In Kabul or Baghdad or any other place we left fighting, the sight of me driving around with so much explosive power would probably result in my arrest or shooting, but in America no ones cares. I'm just someone who really loves barbecue.

The only resistance I find is from the cashier at the Stop-N-Go, who only seems annoyed when I hand them all in for exchange simultaneously, forcing him to lock up the store so he can open up their little gated cage outside and allow me to clear out his entire stock.

I am a man who hasn't slept. I am a man who instead made a list, first on paper and then—having ripped up the paper and set the pieces on fire in a dirty cereal bowl lest evidence remain—in my head. A list of the positive and negative reasons to burn a house down.

The positives are clear: gain a significant amount of income from the evil corporate underwriting industry, to free myself from Philly's trap, to free my daughter from Mélange's trap as well. There are other less tangible, yet still compelling, reasons. To be free of the past in a blaze of glory. To just be done with it all, all of this period, now.

The negatives are tangible and real, and I understand that fully and they cause me fear and make it so I can't sleep and yet am so tired. I could be arrested. Arrested, and not given the insurance money. Tal could start to hate me. Sunita Habersham might hate me, permanently. All of these substantial fears, though, hinge on one major one: being caught. This is the primary fear. But I know how not to be caught. And if I'm not caught, all of the other negatives will float away like ghostly ash.

I stop by the liquor store, purchase a flask of bourbon so flat and curved as to be almost invisible in my pocket. I drive by Tosha's house on the way back. They're all there, on her lawn. On the porch. The black folks who aren't going to take it anymore. Making signs. There have to be at least thirty of them. Kamau's testing his bullhorn. Someone's had T-shirts made, nationalist ones, black with green and red lettering. I sit in my car, parked across the street, and it takes a minute to see that the shirts read *A people united will never be defeated*. I want one. I don't want to be defeated either. I could go for feeling united as well. I want to open up the door, go in there, see what happens. See if a Negro who looks like a Lithuanian rugby player is allowed to put on the red, black, and green, too. Surely today. Today, I would be welcomed even.

I pull my door open, see George come out his front door, then close it again. Their youngest daughter is in his arms, sitting on his hip. She's too big to carry. That same shirt, too big to wear, but a red belt transforming it into a dress on her. That little girl, she's so happy. She's seven and she has her father. And she'll remember this day forever. I pull off after the two of them are around the side of the porch.

In front of Loudin, on the far side of the street, another crowd is already forming. A bus behind them, parked, with even more people coming out. I haven't seen a large group of white people in Germantown for so long I think they must be a clan of sunflowers, come to celebrate the cause of biracial love. But they're real white folks. Old ones. I see an oversized placard of the Constitution leaning on a brick wall, and I know we're in trouble. I don't know what the hell the Constitution has to do with any of this, but when old white folks start waving the Constitution like landlords with a lease, it's trouble. I see this before I see the sign that says REVERSE RACISM IS THE TRUE RACISM. Paused at the light, I look at the guy holding that gem too long, and he comes up to my window.

"Hey buddy, take some of these, and be careful parking around here, if you know what I mean." He winks, because he must think I'm white. He hands me a stack of fliers. Not printed, mimeographed—I can still smell the ink. *Rest For The Raped,* it says, with a crude illustration of a crying white woman, with wings. I get as far as the sentence, *In 1954, in the Germantown section of Philadelphia, Agnes Goines was raped and murdered by black man Charles Jefferson, yet her spirit may* . . . and then I throw it on the floor of the passenger seat, where hopefully it can later get stepped on.

When I ride up to my father's driveway in the Bug, I know this will be the last time. I see that damned house up there on the hill, watching the circus on its lawn. If it had a memory, it would think back to the time Washington's Continental Army did the same, and how far it had come, just by staying in the same place. It must be tired. It must be ready to go. It has reached the completion of its circle.

The Bug is barely through the gate when I'm stopped by Spider. He comes up to the side of my window and asks, "You got my tank?" and I say yes and start driving till he *whoa, whoa, whoas* me down again.

"Yo, let me get it out, right? You're bugging, dude," he says, then starts laughing, pointing at my father's car. "You're bugging, get it?"

"You see those crazy white folks across the street?" I ask him. "I mean, you know today's going to be insane, right?"

"Ah, man, that's nothing. Let me tell you what's crazy: they gots a zonkey, man!" I look across the street. No zonkeys. Just honkies.

"No, at the petting zoo! There's going to be zonkey rides! I saw it—I think it might just be a pony they painted but the kids are going to love it." Spider opens the back of my car before I can, goes to pull a canister out, then looks at me watching him through the back window.

"You all right?" he asks.

"Oh I'm fine."

"You don't look fine. Hey, three o'clock, main stage. Don't miss it," he tells me, which gets me to turn over in my seat and look back at him. "You don't remember? The Miss Cegenation Pageant, man. I think Tal could totally win," Spider says, and starts walking away without closing the back door behind him. I drive off fast enough to close it with the certainty that I really do have to do this thing.

I try parking the Bug in the garage and carrying the tanks over, but after straining to lug one, adjust my strategy. Slowly down the grass, about ten feet from the house, I park and start rolling them out. Straight to the fuse box. Lining up some bricks as a wedge, I lay four on the bottom, and start building up from there. I can hear the music echoing from the other side, and start dropping the tanks down in beat to cover the sound. But it doesn't matter. No one can see into my heart, no one knows what I want or what I don't or what I'm intending. I include myself in that ignorance. My body has its orders. My mind doesn't even have to do anything beyond continue willing.

A small group of Mulattopians drifts back behind the house as I'm finishing, and it doesn't even matter. When they light a joint, I point to the containers and say, "You really don't want to be smoking around here."

I watch most of the day from the front window, drinking. I am drinking to access the courage. Or I am drinking to get drunk enough to not be able to do anything at all. It changes between swigs. Once the whiskey loosens my mind, I start imagining the scene again, but can only see it darkly. I see an explosion, all the tanks lighting at once in a blaze of glory, but with me accidentally in the middle of it. If I die, I realize, Sunita Habersham will think I committed suicide, and will be destroyed by it. Maybe not destroyed, but it wouldn't help her general spiritual growth to have another boyfriend croak, I'm sure. So I write her a note on some copy paper. It says, *If something happened to me, it's because I'm an idiot, but not because of any self-destructive impulse. I would never do that to you, because I still love you.* Which has the balance of focused and vague I was going for. I sign it and with that productive task out of the way, I go on to check and recheck the security cameras, make sure the back one is aimed high enough to miss the show. I take the box of pictures and Tal's things to the garage where they'll be safe.

Then after that, I'm ready.

There's a cake in the fridge. It's homemade. It's either a yin yang symbol, or patterned after a New York black-and-white cookie, I can't tell, but it looks delicious, and in a fire it would be destroyed anyway. So I eat it. I eat the whole cake over two hours. When more than half of it's gone, it just seems like a shame to waste the rest of it, which is the same logic I apply to the flask.

They're out there. Everyone on the lawn, swirling in their mass. Black and white balloons are pulled by children, tied to trailers, and line the property like they're trying to lift us all to the half-breed promised land. And everyone past the gate, they're just as festive. The white folks stay across the street, angry, wanting something back: their country, their dominance, their youth. Petrified of a world where they don't make all the rules. They chant for a bit, something about this being America. I think everyone here knows that, though. I don't think this could be happening anywhere else. Across the street from them, on our side—of the sidewalk at least—the red, black, and green balloons wave in the wind, strong. I'm pretty sure those balloons weren't here this morning. Somebody must have been sent to get them. Someone must have thought the Loving Day balloons demanded a helium response. I can't see the kids out there, the stone base of the fence is too high, but I see Kamau. It's hard not to, he's got his horn going. "Umoja!" is his favorite call. None of the white folks across the street speak Swahili, I would wager. They probably think it's Zulu for "Sharia Law." I see Natasha and George as well. They march together, south on Germantown Avenue, reach the end of the property, then they march north again. Repeating in an endless loop with all of the rest of the protesters, chanting whatever they can to stop the spell being cast by the larger Loving Day crowd on the grounds.

Cast with live bands. Cast with a bouncy house. Cast with lemonade and funnel cakes and white-looking people dressed in Ashanti throws and black-looking people dressed like Sally Hemings's in-laws. There's even a couple dressed as zombie colonists. No, they're dressed like ghosts. Like *the* ghosts, I imagine, or they do. A white woman and a black man. The costumed couple even comes to the door of my father's house, shaking the doorknob in shock when it doesn't open for them. They find a more receptive audience in the news crew that shows up hours later; I watch the duo venture outside and to the front of the queue for an interview. Everyone is eager to share their thoughts about how other people should categorize themselves. The cake is long gone and in my stomach it discovers the liquor and the horror of being inside me, but I don't leave the building till the news van does, heading to the main stage when I see Tal standing with all the other would-be Miss Cegenation queens.

It's not a beauty contest. It's not a talent contest. I don't know what the hell it is, but a large crowd has formed around the stage so I slip in and discover more as everyone else does. Tal is wearing a dress that I didn't buy for her, presumably given to her by Sunita, from the slightly baggy way it's fitting. The bustier top is wired to carry the weight of significant mammary heft, and on Tal it just catches air and the idea of breasts as an intellectual concept. I don't catch the question asked of her, but the answer Tal gives is "I believe that we are the living embodiment of our ancestors, and to deny them, any of them, is, like, to deny ourselves, and disconnect ourselves from the very essence of Gaia."

Oh so she's referencing Gaia now, wonderful. Tal doesn't even have any Greek in her, but the crowd loves it. They applaud. The zombie couple, they're there, they applaud. I assumed I would recognize them from the camp on closer inspection, but even under the white face paint I can tell I've never seen them before. Yet they still have Sesas. On his arm, and then, when she turns, I see one on her shoulder. Looking around, new faces are the majority. It's spreading. And all clapping for my daughter like they know her better than I do.

There's a white lady up there in the competitors' row—at least she looks like a Caucasian, and female—wearing a traditional Nordic bunad dress and a bone through her nose. It's definitely a bone. I keep looking at her, waiting to discover if I should be either offended, or—what? I have no idea. I'm mystified. This petrifies me too; perhaps I should go stand across the street with the terrified ofay crew.

George looks through the bars, smoking. He looks at my daughter. The nicotine mist pours out of his jaw-dropped mouth. And then he looks at me. It's far, but I know he's looking at me. I know before he shakes his head, and joins the circling rage once more.

"Biracialism buys into racism!" I can hear the black side chanting now. "Segregation is wrong!" is yelled from the white side, without any hint of irony.

"She did great!" One Drop says, walking over to me. "Of course, she's got home-court advantage, man. She's one of *us* now," he says, and then goes and joins in with all the other *us*-es in drowning out the world beyond the gate with cheers of their own.

"A donkey, without stripes, is not a horse!" the Mulattopians chant. "A donkey, without stripes, is not a horse!"

Tal is not one of them. Tal is not even one of me. Tal is whoever the hell she finds out she is eventually and even that must change with time. So I go to Sunita's empty trailer and push the non-suicide note under the door where she can see it and no one else can. Then I go to burn the house down.

There's an invisible line in the grass. If I cross it, this thing is going to happen. I want to step over it casually, but instead I just push into it. Invisible, but I can see it in my head, yellow and rubbery and I pull it when I go past, all the way around to the back of the house. I lean against my father's car and the line is wrapped around me, waiting to pull me back to sanity, insisting I haven't crossed it yet.

I pause for a second. Because I can't do this. I can't *really* do this. I will turn back. Give this up. This is crazy. This is not the proper course. Then, from beyond, I hear the saccharine stylings of Paul McCartney and Stevie Wonder's "Ebony and Ivory" echoing across Germantown via loudspeaker. I get the lighter out of my pocket and the invisible yellow line snaps in two retreating strips when I test the flame.

The tank on top is the only one I need. I lift it up, so it's sitting upright on the pile. I breathe. I don't think. I unscrew it. I smell . . . nothing, but I can hear the gas spilling. There is still time to turn back. This is still my window of sanity. I think again. There are other ways of doing this. Less literal. Less dangerous. Requiring more bravery. More patience. More time. So much more time, and I have it but I don't know if Tal does. I look at the back wall of my father's house. It's not a bad house. It's just a house. It is history given form. It is Europeans trying to build a dynasty. But where are they? Their descendants? They're across the street, red-faced, yelling like babies for a bottle. Here, it's just me. The Afro-Celt. Not even half of the right kind of honky. But it's mine now. My inheritance. Tal's too. And then, while I'm looking, I see a whole new foundation crack in the façade. Unknown of before because I never bothered standing here, looking at it, for so long. I reach my finger out, poke my pinky's tip right inside it. This is the house they think they can just cut up, and move twenty yards? While I still own it. While Tal actually still owns it. I put two fingers into the crack, concrete crumbling down around them as they wiggle. It's a trap. It's always been a trap, since first construction.

I light the fire.

I actually see it. The air becoming flame. It doesn't come to me in a moving image, but instead in three comic-book panels. The first is of a line of orange fire, one as long and seemingly solid as my own arm. It shoots out past my lighter like a ray of sun late to get somewhere. The second image is of a cloud, one that must have always been there invisibly, but now blares into light, connecting each billowing segment, taking over the space all around me I thought was reserved for oxygen. The third image is the simplest. Just flame. The last thing I see before I close my eyes. Before sound is the only sense I can handle. Before even the pain which, as I lie now on the ground, I know will come, because my face has been bathed in the fury. Unless I die, in which case I'll be spared.

That sound, it doesn't make a bang. It's a pop. The sucking of air inward, into whatever portal in the universe I've opened. My hand starts to hurt, and I realize I'm gripping the grass. I am blind. No, I just haven't opened my eyes. I do, and they even work, somewhat. The tears make it hard to see, but I do. And I look to the house. There is a black scorch above the space where the tank once rested. It looks like it hurts. My face hurts so much, surely the house must too. But there is no inferno. I can hear the flames, smell the burning now, but looking at the house, I see no fire before me. Not even inside the window. And I see no top tank. I have exploded the tank. I look at my body. For the pieces of it. For the unfelt shrapnel. The evidence that I am actually going to die now. I see none of it. But I hear the fire. I think to turn to look to the sound of the fire.

There's an inferno coming out of my father's Bug.

Such a big flame, such a tiny car.

When they find me, I'm still trying to pull the propane out from where it's lodged under the rear bumper. The heat is so strong, I try to kick the tank, but only manage to stick it farther in there. My hands are already burnt, and even though the flames are reaching up to twice my height over the back engine I am certain I can just reach in there, on the bottom, and pull the metal cylinder loose. I feel someone pulling at my feet so I just kick back and keep crawling. As I get closer to the car I am entering a reality where every molecule of my body wants to dance fast enough to become a gas. There is pain but life is pain so I reach out for the tank and get just enough that I send it rolling out and away as my hands fuse to the metal. But they don't because I'm pulled back again before the torch shooting from the tank's now whirling spout can bless me. At my legs, there is still normal feeling, and I know from uneven grips that a different person is pulling on each leg. I feel the grass under my chest, and the roughness of the soil as I scrape along it. And then there is air again, and the relative coolness of a late spring day, and the clouds are so thick and beautiful. I just look at them. Like when my dad was driving the Bug and I would lie down on the backseat and stare up through the window. In the blissful era before mandatory seat belts.

My eyes still blur, but I can see who saved me. I knew it would be One Drop, from the strength of the grip. The monstrous One Drop, who is reaching out to my face, and then seeing the shape I'm in, he pulls back like this might do more damage. I get the sense from this that I don't look too good. And the other ankle puller. It's Sun. It's Sunita Habersham.

Sunita Habersham. She squats down. She puts a hand to my face, where it stings. She has the sense to ask, "Baby, are you okay?" and I lack the sense to say anything but, "Oh yeah. I'm fine. I'm chilling." To prove this, I go to get up, which turns out is a hard thing to do after your hands have been barbecued. But I rise, still. And Sun hugs me, and I realize she called me baby, which was very nice, yes. I'm in a lot of pain. And there are all the other people. They are all around us, the whole camp, everyone. Tal is there, Spider is there, almost everyone I know now and all the faces I know who have names attached I've never bothered to remember. But look at them. They look so concerned. And not about the blessed car, because that's gone now, I can accept that. And not the house, because the house has not altered its trajectory in the slightest. They look at me. They care about me. My unintentional community. They stand at a distance, sure, crowding together and leaving us in the epicenter of their circle, but I think this is a gesture of respect for the emotions of the moment. And also, yeah, because of the car being on fire.

Still embracing Sunita Habersham, I turn her gently, so I can look back at the ruining of my father's car. This accidentally aims her gaze toward the mansion. Sun just saw the house, I realize, when she pushes me away. She saw the house, and what I did to it.

"Baby," I start to try back at her, but the slap she hits me with, it really hurts. Emotionally. But largely, physically. It's very sobering.

"How could you do this to us!" is screamed at me. Sun is pointing. I follow her finger, to the damned house façade. The fuse box, it pops. Too late. The sparks not even remotely close to the blackened mark of the first flames climbing up the wall. Jumping to the conclusion of arson would makes no sense, out of context. But Sun has context.

"Which *us*?" I ask, and my general confusion at the moment, my blurry vision, the growing distraction of the intense biting pain emitting from large portions of my epidermis, would seem to add to my clueless innocence. But not to Sunita Habersham, who slaps me again. Who then takes me with two hands by the front of my shirt.

"I can't believe you could actually be so stupid," she whispers, her nose almost touching my own. *But you burn pictures,* I want to say, but don't.

"I didn't do anything." I didn't. The house is still there. The house will always be there. They can try to move it a couple feet; it doesn't matter. The house will always be here. It's not my inheritance, or Tal's, or my father's. It's history itself. It is its own legacy.

"I know what you did. What you tried to do. You did this to *us,*" she says, before letting go of me and walking away.

"This was *my* releasing ceremony," I yell. I start to stomp after her until George makes my momentum halt.

"What the hell is going on?" he wants to know. I don't know why he's here, on the other side of the wall. I turn to look at him and see the massive black smoke cloud still coming out of my father's dying car, so yeah I kind of know. The sirens, I can hear them coming too, getting closer, and that makes more sense, so I push George's hand off my shoulder. And I start running toward Sun before she can get to the crowd and this is all over.

"I asked you a question. Don't just walk away," he demands in full cop voice.

"No. I'm running," and I take off full speed for Sunita Habersham.

George is running too. He tackles me from behind, and I go down. I'm on the grass once more. On my face first, and then on my back when he flips me over.

"You need to calm your ass down." George's hands hold my wrists, his body's weight seals my pelvis to the earth. I try to lift them, to get him off me, but his move is practiced, time-tested, without counter.

"Sun!" I yell. I lean my head back, try to see her. I do see her, the back of her once more, walking beyond where the crowd has spread for her. "Sunita Habersham!" again, but nothing.

Then, into the gap in the crowd, strolls a vision. A vision as exotic and out of place as all of us. An animal. A *zonkey*. A real life zonkey.

Stripes in the front and the back all white ass. It strolls up, into the gap in the crowd. And it looks at me. Confused. Then gives up, bends over, and starts chewing the grass in front of Roslyn's feet. The older woman stares past the beast to the house, looking genuinely pained when she looks back in my direction. She pulls on the zonkey's rope and walks him off as if she's protecting his innocence.

"You reek. You're drunk, aren't you? Is there nothing you don't screw up?" George leans in, seemingly waiting for me to give thoughtful answers. "I know about you and Natasha," he whispers. "After all that time waiting for your chance, you even fucked that up."

"That's my father." The voice is so calm, measured, that both George and I turn in surprise. Tal stands there, high above both of us. I can't see her features because of the glare of the sun above. I can make out enough, though, to see that she reaches out and puts a hand on George's arm. I feel a warm drop hit my face. It's George's sweat, and it's disgusting, but for a second it creates the only place on my face not burning.

"Miss, you need to take your hands off me and step back."

"You need to get the fuck off my pops," my daughter says to him.

George takes his left hand off me to remove Tal's grip from his arm.

That's when I punch him in the mouth.

23

THE 14TH DISTRICT Police Department holding cell is actually not so bad compared to the City of Philadelphia Detention Center, which is where they take me when the alcohol wears off and the pain can occupy the vacated neurons and I really start feeling the fullness of my situation. I spend the first night handcuffed to a bed. There is metal on my wrists. Bonds. But I'm actually fine with this, because in exchange they handcuff the other eighty-seven guys in the room to their beds as well, and these men worry me more than slavery metaphors.

During my booking, I am unable to provide adequate fingerprints, due to the fact that my tips have blisters on them. After much discussion about this, I am given a pen and paper to provide a handwriting sample in the meantime. My mug shot, however, goes over like gangbusters, and is viewed by not just George, who is clearly already enjoying himself immensely, but by several of his colleagues, whom he calls in to check out my portrait on the screen so that their day may be brightened. On being returned to my prison hospital bed, George, his jaw clearly swollen from where I popped him, takes me aside so that I can view the masterpiece myself.

Looking at the photo, I don't recognize this man. He has no eyebrows. His skin is red and shining from the ointment applied by the nurse that afternoon. His eyes are dulled by painkillers. He is trying to smile his cracked lips, but his cheeks hurt so much that his grin comes off as a grimace. Gone too is the hair on my head, and I reach one gauze-covered hand to feel that my hairline has been burnt back past my ears.

"You look like the Red Skull," George tells me.

"Come on, man. I'm sorry. You gotta let me go."

"Actions have consequences," George tells me, smiling, pausing enough for me to take in the message privately even though there are two others in the room. Then, "This is how it works. You assaulted an officer."

I didn't assault an officer, intentionally. I assaulted a George. I explain this to Sirleaf Day, via his answering machine, which tells me in response that he is "out of the country pursuing investments, leave a message and I'll be sure to get back to you." After three days, I'm not so sure, so I then explain this to the public defender before my arraignment and urge her to bring up this backstory to the judge, but she is not really interested in hashing it out at this time. My assigned attorney is more focused in setting bail, aiming for a reasonable $20,000. I question her strategy when the bail comes in at $100,000 instead, due to the seriousness of my crime and the fact that I'm a flight risk. I also get a trial date. In a month.

The last time I see George is when he stops by my table after the judgment to say, "I'm taking Tosha to Sandals Jamaica tomorrow, so don't expect any visits. You enjoy your vacation too."

Sunita Habersham is not going to rescue me. I know this. And I know why. And I understand, too, although I desperately want her to, although I fantasize about it, although once a nurse comes by in flip-flops and I think it's Sun for enough seconds to be crushed by the truth. When Tal doesn't appear, I know why as well. Because she knows what Sun knows now. That I tried to burn her beloved house down. And Tal might even know why I tried to do it, that it was for her as much as anything, but I know she doesn't forgive me. Forgiveness comes later in life, after you've created enough disasters of your own. The biggest revelation, I'm surprised, is how many other Mulattopians join in the silence. No Roslyn with her army of lawyers, not even to gloat. No Spider. Because they all know. That much is clear by the third day, when they release me to the general prison population and no one comes to bail me out. They all know. About my intentions. About the house. I know that they all know.

But I know more than this. Because when the charges are listed—Assaulting an Officer, Resisting Arrest, Burning without a Permit—that not one of them told my story. Because for days I wait for the real charges to hit: First Degree Arson, Attempted Arson, Destruction of Historically Protected Property, and so on. But they never come. The mulattoes never snitch on me. They protect their own.

My cellmate, Héctor, doesn't seem to be a bad guy. He doesn't talk too much, which is a good thing, because the cell is too small to navigate through awkward conversation. His is the top bunk, and there he cries every night, which really frees me up to start doing the same if I'm so moved. Besides the one morning he says *"La vida es triste,"* and shrugs, we don't talk about it. I like it in the cell better than in the lounge, which is much too communal for my tastes. The scary black dudes, the scary white dudes, and the scary Latino dudes all hang in their own sections of the hall, surrounding a loose collection of just plain scared unaffiliated dudes who sit in the middle waiting to see which tribe is going to victimize them. I try to hang over by the black dudes, but get the look that tells me I'm a racial suspect, so go sit on the edge of the Latino section a noncommittal distance from Héctor. In the great American mulatto tradition, I pass myself off as a Puerto Rican. By the end of the first day, this proves to be a wise decision, and the only cost is the sacrilege of lying about both my dead parents' entire ancestral lines. Which is not a small cost, and hurts every time I repeat it in my pathetic high school Spanish. It hurts more than later, when one of the guys calls me the "Crimson Coconut," a name which sticks in the ward across cultural lines, even though the burning redness on my face is already starting to fade away. But it's worth the humiliation to be allowed into even the outskirts of a tribe.

My first visitor comes two days later. It feels like much longer, so much so that when I get called up, I tell them my name again, because I think they have the wrong guy.

"Someone, they love you," Héctor says from the bulge of the top bunk. He sounds slightly surprised.

Sunita Habersham sits in a crowded cafeteria-style room at a round table, and doesn't look up at me even when I sit down across from her. In front of her, a stack of comic books sits in a perfectly organized pile, but even still she adjusts the corners of it with her hands, identifying some invisible lack of symmetry. When I say hi, she says, "I got you this week's pull list, and last week's; I don't think you read them. I could have brought in more but Spider chickened out. He's scared of prisons. He's waiting in the car." Sun's voice trails off at the end, and then she finally looks up. And then she stares straight at me. And we're not talking.

"I'm sorry," I say, and in doing so realize while I truly need to express these words, and am completely and eagerly willing to say them, they are also utterly inadequate.

"What the hell were you thinking?" Sunita asks me too loud, but nobody else in the place turns around, because that is not just an appropriate question in this room, it is the whole theme. It should be painted in ornate gilded letters on the wall. But Sun knows what I was thinking. And the only addition I could add would be offensive: that I thought I could pull it off.

"Tal wants to come, to see you. I told her not to—I don't want her to see you like this, Warren."

"Me either. But please tell her I love her. Tell her I'll talk to her when I get out."

"We can try to get the cash for the bond, but that amount . . . Jesus. I know Roslyn has it, but she's been bugging since Loving Day. The protesters are still there, you know that right? The white protesters—the black ones left, I think they had to go to work. Somebody got the city to serve eviction papers this morning, now they're saying all the propane tanks constitute a fire hazard. Roslyn's told everyone to kill their cell phone service, instituted a 'media blackout.' She's even telling people you tried to destroy the 'sacred house.' "

"To be fair, I did try to destroy it." I have to admit.

"Yeah, but she's acting like that shit hole is the Temple Mount. All this while the construction crew has started chopping it up." Sunita starts laughing, covers her mouth when she can't stop. I smile but am silent. I want to laugh too but am in jail and that isn't funny. "I can't deal with all this. Your court date isn't for weeks, but I think I have to get out of there. Tal's fine, has everyone around her. But I need a break. Spider's going down to work a zydeco festival in Louisiana next week. I'm thinking of going, but I don't want you—"

"Go."

"I went on your computer, emailed your friend Tosha. She said she thinks she can get her husband to drop the charges but I don't know how soon—"

"Go on the trip, get a breather," I tell her. "I'll wait here till you get back." And Sunita Habersham starts to smile a bit at that too, as I intended, but looks at me again and stops.

"Wow. You really fucked up."

"Yeah. I do that sometimes."

"Yeah, me too," Sunita Habersham tells me, then pushes the comics across the table.

It won't be for another hour, when I'm be back in my cell on my mattress, that I'll open the first comic on the pile, *The Manhattan Projects* 12. It will take until then for me to see the note that I'd forgotten I'd even written to Sun, as it falls out onto my coarse blanket.

Thanks for leaving this. Love you too, it now says at the bottom in Sunita Habersham's handwriting.

• • •

I finally manage a successful career in comics, both as a merchant and an artist. The comic books I read to the point of memorization, I sell. Their market value in cigarettes and stick deodorant proves to be so high that I use that boon to trade for pencil and paper to start drawing daily comics of my own to cash in on the boom. The result is really some of my best work; it's like printing money. Thursday's full-page spread of our local representatives from the Latin Kings portrayed as superpowered mutants goes to the highest bidder for three breakfast muffins and a mini-tube of Aquafresh. Some of the black crew are so impressed by it that they're even talking of claiming me now.

Ten days later, the guard comes to my cell and gives me three minutes to gather my things and get out.

"Holy shit, the mutts bailed me," I say when he leaves. Héctor hears me.

"'Mutts.' This gang you say you hang with, what's up with that?" Héctor hits me with this as I'm rushing around, gathering my remaining illustrations in a pile.

"They're just a bunch of mixed people. Half-black and -white folks. African and European. A little Indian. They got a kinda club."

"So, they like Dominicans or Puerto Ricans or something?" Héctor rolls to a sitting position on his mattress, and from my bed I get a good view of his hairy beige feet.

"No. They're American. Just black and white. And Indian, sometimes."

"But yo, how is that different?" Héctor bends over, so I see the tips of his little dreads and his eyes staring at me, confused.

"I don't know. They speak English," is all I can think to offer.

"I speak English too, bro," Héctor says, lying back on his bunk, finished with the discussion.

The mutts didn't bail me out. There is no bail. There is no bail because there are no more charges. There is no one waiting for me but a clerk from my public defender's office, who delivers this news and no more. As I walk back on the street, though, I decide to read my release as a silent gift. From Tosha. And I silently thank her as I rush toward Suburban Station and the way toward home.

24

THERE ARE THREE TRAINS that are supposed to stop at Wayne Junction, which is just two blocks below the mansion. Hardly anyone gets off there, though, because the train costs $1.50 more than the bus and is mostly for middle-class people and there aren't a lot of those living on the border between North Philadelphia and Germantown. The conductor seems surprised when I ask him to make the stop, which I have to do or they'll just crawl right by the platform as if the driver is covering his eyes the whole time.

I trudge up the hill of Germantown Avenue bringing flowers. For Tal. Roses. White for my little big girl. It's trite and feeble and they're a little brown around the edges because I got them at a kiosk in the station, but I don't know what else to do. I don't know, but know I have to do something, start somewhere. And if anyone else sees me—and everyone will, everyone will see me coming in—I want them to know that no matter what they think of me, this is what I think of her.

But no one in Mulattopia will see the gesture. Because when I get to the gate, I see that no one is there.

I stop walking. Look to the other side of the street. Try to figure out how I could get lost. In my own hood. I'm next to a park now. The fence looks the same, but nothing else. I look across the street, and the row houses look the same. But nothing else.

The trailers are gone. All the trailers are gone. Halfie Heights is barren. Mixed Mews is no more. I can see the earthen marks of worn ground, the dead brown patches in the grass, but all the other trailers are gone.

I look up the hill. I look up the hill, and at all the grass, and at the walkway. I keep looking because I can't believe it. I walk closer, looking for someone to explain this. For something that will make sense to me. I don't see that thing. Everyone's gone. Everything's gone. The garage is there. I keep walking along the fence, in the gate left unlocked and open. I keep walking. I walk up the hill. Don't see her. Tal is gone. I keep walking.

The house is gone.

I stand on the top of the hill, by where the mansion's front steps are supposed to be, and circle around, looking around. Looking and looking. There's nothing to see. An exposed and barren basement squints at the daylight, its cover having run away. A brick-lined hole in the ground. Inside an old water heater. Pipes connecting to nothing. Spools of wiring like dead vines. Scraps of wood and snow of sawdust.

I sit down because I can't stand for this. I sit on the lip of the hole and look inside, then again around.

Tal is gone. The house has gone. The house has absconded.

I've lost Tal.

The house is gone.

The door to the garage opens, and Tal comes out. My daughter. The garage door slams shut behind her before she realizes that it's me, that I've come for her. Before I realize, it's her, that she's stayed for me.

My daughter starts to run my way, so fast at first, then slows, then stops halfway. Her arms drop, hang still, and she takes a slow step back even. Staring as if I am the unnatural aberration.

"You didn't break out, did you? Because that would be really stupid, Pops," Tal asks.

"No, honey. The charges were dropped," I tell her. And I don't get up. And I don't mind that it takes her a moment to come closer, because as she's standing still like that I can just look at her, see her again. When Tal reaches me, she reaches down. She hugs me while she's still standing up, and doesn't let go as she bends her knees and sits on the cellar edge beside me.

"Honey?" I ask over her shoulder. "Where's the house?"

"Roslyn bought it."

"Okay. But where is it?"

"I had to sell it. I thought I had to get you out," Tal tells me, then grows quiet after I audibly thank the Lord a few times and adds, "Not the land, though. They just bought the house. They just took the house part."

I pull back from Tal, hold her arms in my hands, look at her face. Wait for her to crack a smile, to tell me she's joking. Instead she says, "They wanted to keep it safe," and I have no response to that.

My daughter says Sun and Spider are supposed to be arriving back today as well, but I don't want to go into the garage, where Tal has moved the rest of our things, and wait for them. I don't want to go inside at all. I've been inside for sixteen straight days. I don't want anything in between me and the sky until it's necessary.

When it gets dark, it's not cold, but the mosquitoes come, so we gather the scraps of wood the house shed in its departure, make a pyre on the packed dirt floor of the hole, close enough to the wall that we can keep sitting on it. Tal wants to use the art projects my students left behind as a fire starter, but I gather some newspaper from the recycling instead.

"Where did they go?" I ask when Tal's finally gotten the bigger pieces of wood siding ignited. She pulls herself up to the wall, sits down next to me.

"Malaga."

"Malaga," I say, and I lose it. I can't help myself.

"They bought the island. It was the big surprise. Roslyn told everyone at the last minute then three days later, they were off. What's so funny?"

"Maine. One Drop's in Maine. He finally found a place he can feel black enough."

Tal's quiet for a bit, staring at the fire with me. Waving the smoke out of the way in the moments when the wind blows it back. After a while, after the wood cracks and sparks and the structure we built falls in on itself, Tal says, "Pops?"

"Yeah, honey?"

"You know part of why you hate that guy is because you're projecting your own racial insecurities onto him, right?"

"I do, honey," I say, but I didn't before.

Tal falls asleep on my shoulder before the embers die. There's a light mist of rain, but not enough that it matters. Leaning my head on hers, I almost fall asleep as well, but then I worry she'll fall forward into the basement, so I scoot back and lay her head and shoulders in my arms. She's heavy, I'm tired, but it's no burden. Because even though she just turned eighteen, asleep like this I can still see the last moment of childhood on her. The last fleeting sparkle. Tal's eyes are closed, her mouth is open, her chest rises and falls, and in the firelight I catch a glimmer of the baby she was. I see it there and I rock her lightly in my arms, I rock her, and I can feel it right on her when I lift up one hand and wipe the dew off her forehead.

It's just a Wednesday in Germantown, but the streets are quiet and the lawn is empty and I look around at what is left after the house is gone. And I see a savannah.

I also see them.

Off at the far end. Only two, but they come up from the slopping bank at the back of the property.

I watch them as they walk up the hill. Disappear behind three oak trees, reemerge on the other side.

They stop there. Looking at me.

They're so far away. They can come closer. The drizzle, it starts hitting a little harder. I don't care, we're not running. I want them to come closer. There's plenty of room around the fire. But still, they've stopped there.

I see, even from here. One is a man. One is a woman. He, black. She, white.

Standing together. Staring, across the tall ghetto grass. But I'm not scared. I hold on to Tal, who breathes in more life and future. I have everything but nothing that can be taken from me.

I'm not scared. I see them. I see what they are, or what they were. Just lovers. Just people.

ACKNOWLEDGMENTS

It's my extreme good fortune to be able to work with my editor, Christopher Jackson. His assistance with this novel, as well as with my last novel, *Pym,* has been invaluable and essential in bringing these stories to life in their final form. Heartfelt thanks to novelist Emily Raboteau, who read the novel I hoped to write before I actually wrote it. My gratitude as well to my wife, Meera, whose partnership has allowed me to have a full life away from the page.

PHOTO: © MEERA BOWMAN JOHNSON

MAT JOHNSON is the author of the novels *Pym, Drop,* and *Hunting in Harlem,* the nonfiction novella *The Great Negro Plot,* and the comic books *Incognegro* and *Dark Rain*. He is a recipient of the United States Artist James Baldwin Fellowship, the Hurston/Wright Legacy Award, and the John Dos Passos Prize for Literature. He is a professor at the University of Houston Creative Writing Program.

matjohnson.info
Facebook.com/matjohnsonpage
@mat_johnson